Child of Night

Book One
of the
Sentinel Wars

Caelin Paul

authorHOUSE™

1663 LIBERTY DRIVE, SUITE 200
BLOOMINGTON, INDIANA 47403
(800) 839-8640
WWW.AUTHORHOUSE.COM

© 2005 Caelin Paul. All Rights Reserved.

No part of this book may be reproduced, stored in a retrieval system, or transmitted by any means without the written permission of the author.

First published by AuthorHouse 11/02/05

ISBN: 1-4259-9999-9 (sc)
ISBN: 1-4259-9998-0 (dj)

Printed in the United States of America
Bloomington, Indiana

This book is printed on acid-free paper.

Cover Design by Ryan White

Acknowledgments

This book is dedicated to my sweet wife Layna (Anyal) and the two dancing girls that call her mother. May Brianna and Misha always live in the light and never lose their love for music, dance, and one another.

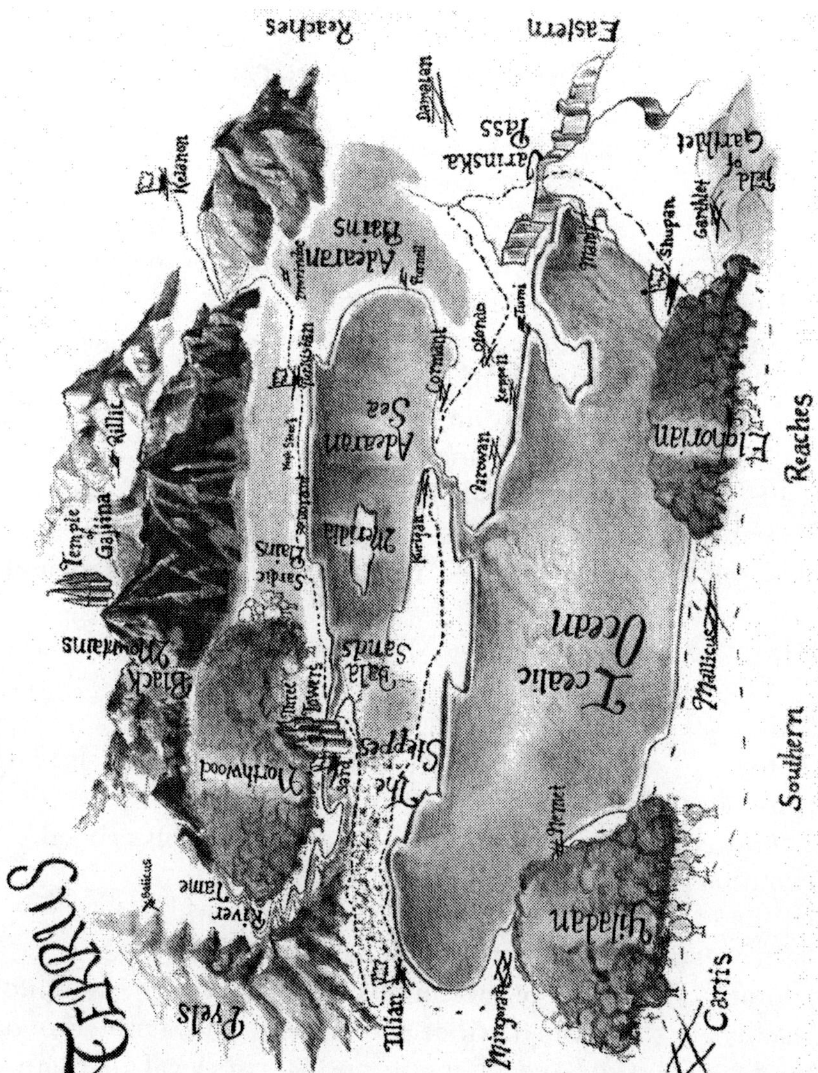
Northern
Reaches
Southern
Reaches
Eastern
Reaches
Western
Reaches
Black Mountains
Temple of Gajiina
Northwood
Three Towers
River Tame
The Steppes
Bala Sands
Saric Plains
Aderan Sea
Aderan Plains
Tecalic Ocean
Elgnorian
Mallicus
Cartis
Jarinska Pass
Shupan
Garthlet

Characters

Acrina	Only daughter of King Koradin and heir to the elven throne
Anyal	Student at the Academy
Bartrand	Member of the mage council and master of fire
Basq	Eunuch from Damalan
Beran	Soldier in the Meridian military
Brack	Sentinel of dark and oldest bastard son of Prince Jesobi
Brina	Infant twin to Misha and daughter of Milaw
Celebus	Long dead first king of Terms
Chaniya	High Priestess of the Sisterhood and Superior at Temple of
Corrin	Chief librarian at the Academy and member of the mage council
Crill	Captain and Leading Officer at Illian Garrison
Damal	Sentinel of dark and youngest son of Prince Jesobi
Darkwitch	Evil sorcereress and banished sister of Elam and Jesobi
Dax	Admiral of the Meridian Navy, 1st Officer of the Catlina
Duikin	High order mage from the Academy
Elam	Vanished prince and father of the Sentinels of light
Fameran	First born son of King Koradin
Gajiina	Oracle credited with starting the "Sisterhood."
Horatius	Queen Sara's First Counselor
Jakes	Squadlead within the Meridian militia
Jalin	Second born son of King Koradin
Jaloran	Leader of the Guildsmen, Ruler of the Underlife
Jesobi	Vanished prince and father of the Sentinels of dark
John	Gate-keeper, monk, and Storm's legal guardian
Kalon	Arch-mage and principal of the Academy
Kell	Weather Mage and crew member of the Catlina
Koradin	King of the Elven race
Leskel	Member of the mage council and master of air
Ludi	Mythical God of impossible odds

Mirren	Member of the mage council and mistress of water
Misha	Infant twin to Brina and daughter of Milaw
Nicholas	Abbot at Three Towers, Sentinel of light, and youngest child of
Nishu	Mythical God of fortune and good luck
Nolina	Member of the mage council and instructor of the healing arts
Reesa	Orphan child raised by Terel
Remog	Mythical God of retribution
Rune	Sentinel of dark and oldest legitimate son of Prince Jesobi
Ryad	Swordmaster, Sentinel of light and third child of Prince Elam
Sajan	Mythical God of warriors
Saltorini	High order mage from the academy

Chapter One

Traveler

Rain burst forth from the heaven in torrents. Dark skies ablaze with jagged lightning trembled at the firmament's roar. Never before had the Sardik Plains seen a night so hostile and foreboding. The swollen River Tame rolled and its rising waters tore viciously into the eroding bank. Still the rain continued to beat unmercifully down upon the submissive earth. Throughout the elemental onslaught the little town of Sard slept on, oblivious to the suffocating vehemence raging outside bolted doors. Coursing wind screamed through the narrow valley as the town's dogs bayed their terrified greeting to the storm. No man, woman, or child braved the power of the tempest. Even the most loyal of shepherds had surrendered his flock to the mercy of the elements and the voracious appetite of the wild wolves.

Suddenly, the air hung heavy with pulsing beads of electric energy. Unbidden, a scythe of light plunged its vicious forked tongue into the mountainside. The iron-rich granite repulsed the blow and sent a wave of fire careening down the valley. Its fateful path was finally impeded by a hardy oak tree whose destined life ended this night. As the ancient oak burned, flames leapt skyward and charcoaled wood hissed. The once placid waters of the Tame crept ominously over high-walled banks, yet still the storm refused to relent. At the height of this passionate exhibition, a dark figure stepped from beneath the refuge of the trees.

From the shadowy forest emerged a body, hunched and hooded. On his back he bore a heavy pack and a gnarled right hand gripped a sturdy rosentimber staff. To outward appearances he seemed garbed in the dress of a traveling cleric. The habit he wore was black as coal, the hood revealed no face, and heavy leather sandals bled profusely from battles with the inhospitable terrain. The storm grew ever more violent as the mysterious traveler strode out onto the plain. Finally, the banks of the river could contain the surging flood no longer. Water spewed into the air, springing determinedly toward the village and the unsuspecting journeyman. As the river prepared to engulf him, he paused, raised his staff high into the air and voiced words unheard. A flash of blue erupted from his hand and immediately the waters fell back, bowing in humble reverence throughout their ignoble retreat. The traveler continued up the gentle slopes till he reached the town's main gate. With a simple gesture, the gates swung open noiselessly. Still the hurricane-like gales beat down, shadowing his every footfall. The townspeople slept restlessly. Only the sleepless dogs acknowledged the passing of the hooded stranger, but their complaint succumbed to the screaming of the wind.

Soon the brave itinerant arrived at the footstep of the dark mountain. For the first time since leaving the safe harbor of the tree-line, he paused in stride to catch his breath. From a pocket deep within his robe he produced a tasteless biscuit. After swallowing the last meager morsel he struggled to his feet. With one last fleeting look at the daunting journey that still lay before him, he leant into the wind and forced tired footsteps onward. High above, there rose the narrow winding mountain path that led to a building with three towers. Treacherously steep, even the hardiest of villagers would take an hour to make the climb. On this night an hour saw the traveler but a fourth of a way to his goal. Despite the continuous buffeting, he remained resolute in his quest as one agonizing step after another he progressed slowly up the craggy trail. The winds reached out sinuous arms resisting every motion, yet still the lonely pilgrim refused to suffer defeat.

After a seeming eternity of struggle, the traveler rounded the final switchback. There in front of him loomed the ominous watchtower and the welcome realization of his impossible pilgrimage. Inestimable miles had faded into irrelevant history; now the culmination of his painstaking trek was at hand. On reaching the gates, he unhitched his heavy pack and placed it down carefully beside the watchtower wall. From around his neck he unclasped an odd looking amulet and cast it to the ground. Silently, wind-torn lips moved, the utterance of alien words lost in the unforgiving gale. The heavy staff descended with a mighty blow upon the amulet. A powerful blue light pierced the stony earth. A moment later, darkness returned and there on the ground, where once the amulet had lain, remained two metallic crescent pieces. The mysterious nomad clasped one half to a chain around his neck, then, tucked the other inside the now discarded pack. With one last look at the tall towers, he turned and set off boldly down the trail. The winds having admitted defeat began to fade and dissipate. In their wake the strange hooded traveler melded into the emptiness of the moonless shadows.

Chapter Two

Arrival

The old rooster sang out proudly heralding the arrival of dawn. The fearful storm of the previous night was now a mere memory. Throughout the town and surrounding area, trees lay on their sides uprooted and lifeless. Many a woodsman bid prayers of thanks to Nishu, God of Fortune. No axe blade would be dulled by a tree's lifeblood this week. The streets of Sard bustled with energy and activity. Today was market day and farmers from many leagues distant converged upon the sleepy town to sell their wares. One such farmer was a mountain of a man by the name of Aron Barley. Few knew this friendly giant by his birth name. On the contrary, even his very own family had come to call him by the more widespread pseudonym, Wolfy. Several years previous Wolfy had slain a pack of wolves single-handedly, armed with nothing more than a fence post. They had been after his sheep and the farmer was not one to give anyone a free meal. Since that day, he never more experienced trouble from the hill wolves who made a concerted effort to skirt his land.

Despite his formidable strength, Wolfy was a good man and possessed a warm and loving heart. Today he was on his way up the mountain trail following in the steps of the mysterious nighttime visitor. Every week Wolfy would make the exhausting journey up to the place called Three Towers. Behind him, he pulled a wagon laden full of meats, vegetables, fruits, and other market fare. This contract always fell to Wolfy, for only he had the requisite strength to haul the load up the mountain. Though he complained the loudest of any farmer, he truly did not mind this trek. He really liked these customers and more honest folk could not to be found west of the Adearan Sea. Not only that, but he had come to expect a sumptuous breakfast feast as partial payment for his toils.

As Wolfy drew up to the wrought iron gates, a voice from the watchtower called down to him. "Wolfy you big oaf, you are twenty minutes late."

"I'll give you twenty minutes late," bellowed back the smiling farmer.

"What would you say if I told you we didn't need anything today and your exertions were for naught?" enquired a smiling Brother John.

Wolfy was just preparing an insulting retort when his attention was captured by a noise that seemed to rise from the foot of the tower wall. Crouching down beside the crumbling brickwork, he reached behind a small bush that sprouted directly from the masonry. Withdrawing his hand he found he held a small traveling pack. Again, a strange gurgling sound entertained further his curiosity. The farmer pulled back the straps and opened the top flap. There smiling up at him lay a beautiful baby boy not more than two moons in birthtime.

"Hey John you had better get down here right away. There seems to be a little lad here who wants to join your club."

"Be down in a moment," answered the curious monk.

In no time at all the gates opened and there stood Brother John, a huge grin splayed upon his face. "What have you got there my friend?"

"A package for you I believe," answered the burly farmer thrusting the baby into the befuddled monk's arms.

"He's not mine," exclaimed John, attempting to push the baby back toward him.

"Well, he's definitely not mine," retorted Wolfy. "I have a wife and an army of younguns at home. Bess would put me out on the street if I dared bring home another mouth to feed."

"What do I do with him?" asked John.

"No idea. But, I suggest feeding the little mite would be a good place to start." With the mention of food, the baby started to wail.

By now the quadrangle had filled with many of the brethren who had come to explore the commotion and to find out how much longer they were going to have to wait for breakfast. Soon there was quite a crowd gathered around John and the baby. Seeing his opportunity, Wolfy crept silently out the front gate forsaking the morning meal. He had no intention of being lumbered with the child.

It wasn't long before the Abbot also entered the quad. As he approached, a path opened as the brothers fell back in reverent acquiescence to their spiritual leader. Every brother within the monastery held Abbot Nicholas in the highest esteem. As he approached the gate, more monks drew back leaving the perplexed John standing alone holding the baby.

The Abbot walked smoothly with authority across the courtyard. A tall man with a balding pate, his very manner commanded respect. The little hair that still clung tenuously to his crown grew silvery white, mirroring the heavy growth of hooded eyebrows that converged above a hawk-like profile. Furrowed lines etched themselves deeply into a face wizened yet kindly. The Abbot's eyes were soft and grey, constantly moving as if to appreciate every detail of the world that regarded him. A long habit of brown coarse cloth flowed down around his slender frame, cinched tightly with a sash of white braid. The hem of his robes caressed the ground, sliding haltingly over hardy leather sandals that protected well-worn soles.

"Follow me," ordered the Abbot. John followed Nicholas through the maze of passageways to the Abbot's study.

"Please shut the door John," asked Nicholas gently. "Now where has this child come from?"

"I really do not know sir," started John. "Wolfy, um-uh, I mean Farmer Barley found him outside under shelter of the watch tower. The sack in which we found him was still wet so I assume someone left him there during last eve's storm."

"Well aren't you at least going to take him out of the pack?" asked the Abbot.

"Of course sir," answered John sheepishly. As he tenderly lifted the child from the knapsack, something bright and shiny fell to the floor. Nicholas stooped down and picked it up. He studied the trinket for a few moments. All of a sudden, his face drained of color and he fell heavily back in his chair.

"Are you alright sir?" asked a worried John. Never before had he seen his mentor look so haggard and fearful.

Nicholas quickly regained his composure and ushered for John to come closer. "Listen, John! I am placing you in charge of this child. You are to be his guardian. You must watch over him at all times and in all places. You must be his mentor, teacher, and friend. It will be a difficult and trying task I am sure. Can I trust you to do this for me?"

John was a little frightened at the tone of the voice and the seriousness of the request. However, he loved the Abbot dearly and would do anything that he was asked. "Sir you can rely on me."

"I know I can John," the Abbot answered. "Well he is your responsibility now. Tell me, what are you going to name him?"

"Well sir, I really don't know. Last night sure was tempestuous. Perhaps it would be fitting to name the child Storm."

The old Abbot let the name pass over his lips a number of times then smiled at Brother John. "You know I have a feeling such a name will suit the boy more than we may both know." Nicholas took the infant into his arms and studied the tiny boy. "Yes John, Storm most certainly is an apt name for such a child."

Chapter Three

Mischief

Storm grew quickly into childhood. His hair was black as obsidian and his skin dark and tanned. But the trait that set him apart from those of the local community, were his haunting green eyes. Deep-set orbs of jade regarded a people that treated him with something akin to fear. The years since the "great" storm passed quickly and the brothers had come to love and accept the green-eyed boy. However, no member of the order loved him more than his guardian and constant companion, John. Storm was what the Abbot termed a "catcher." He learned things quickly and from an early age displayed a multitude of special gifts. The boy learned to run before he could walk, was able to play many instruments by ear, and launched directly into conversation before being able to speak a single word. Before the age of five, he had surpassed many of the lowlier members of the order in word power and was able to read every sentence of the holy books by the age of six. Now eight summers in age, he appeared, in his mannerisms, very much older. He reciprocated love to his friends in the monastery but was forever getting into trouble. As the only child at Three Towers, his mischievous pranks often occurred as a consequence of boredom.

One such instance occurred while the monks convened in the chapel for morning prayers. Not yet old enough to join the monastic brethren for the canonical hour of matins, Storm passed the time playing in the quad. His favorite game, when no one was around, was throwing stones at the big black crows that circled overhead. The crows were considered beasts of the dark and not to be trusted. Thus Storm didn't think much about trying to scare them off with a few well-aimed throws. An incredible marksman, he would often send pebbles crashing into the wings of unsuspecting crows. Time after time an unlucky bird would plummet to the ground or flap off nursing angry contusions. Always one to challenge himself, he let fly a rock with his eyes closed. His aim was true and he smiled when he heard the thud of the stone and the disconcerted squawk of the target. However, his smile evaporated with the unmistakable sound of breaking glass. Opening his eyes, he was just in time to see crow and rock disappearing through the ancient stained glass window of the chapel. Bird and stone plummeted to a disconcerting standstill right in front of Abbot Nicholas.

"John!" shouted the Abbot, "get Storm to report to my study right-a-way." With that the seething Abbot hurried out of the chapel door only to be bowled over by Storm barreling down the corridor at a frenetic speed from the other direction. Both collapsed into a sizeable heap of arms, legs and robes.

"I'm so sorry!" blurted out Storm as he attempted to disentangle himself.

"Come with me," growled the Abbot, hauling the boy to his feet with a hard tug on his disheveled shirt collar. Nicholas led him to the kitchens where a stack of pots and pans reached skyward towards the vaulted ceiling. "Get to work then! And don't even think about leaving the kitchen until every single pot, pan, spoon, and fork, is spotless and put away in its rightful place." As the Abbot left, he sneaked a peak over his shoulder and grinned. He loved Storm as much as anyone else, but someone had to contain the boy's unbridled fervor for mischief. Meanwhile, Storm regarded the metal mountain with despondency. With a sigh he rolled up his shirt's sleeves, filled the wooden basin with hot water from the pump and set to work. He knew it would be dark before this task was finished.

A few days later, Storm's penchant for pranks caused the Abbot much greater concern. The boy was forever playing jokes on the brothers and townspeople. However, undoubtedly, his most favorite victim was Wolfy, the giant farmer, who eight years previously had discovered the young boy outside the monastery gate. On market day, Wolfy had arrived in the courtyard with his heavy wagon. The mischievous Storm stood patiently waiting for him as always.

"Hi Wolfy, the Abbot wants to see you right away. It sounds like you are in big trouble," stated Storm.

The farmer looked down at the innocent face, and after setting down his harness strode inside to find the Abbot. No sooner had the farmer vanished than Storm, grunting and groaning, lifted up the wagon, steered it to the front gate and then proceeded to transport it down the mountain trail. When he had reached the bottom, he let it down gently and ran back up the path as fast as his little legs could carry him. He was just in time to see Wolfy, red faced and a little annoyed crossing the quad. Storm hid behind the buttress wall trying desperately not to laugh as Wolfy searched fruitlessly for the cart.

"Oi John," shouted the big farmer. John's head popped up in the tower.

"Hello Wolfy my friend." Seeing his friend's dark expression he asked, "what ever is the matter? Your face is a little crimsoned today!"

"My wagon has just disappeared," replied Wolfy, "and I'd wager half my autumn harvest that that little prankster of yours has something to do with it. He sent me in to see the Abbot, and would you believe the dear man was in the bath tub and had no idea what I was talking about."

With this last revelation, Storm could contain himself no longer and burst into fits of giggles. Wolfy, hearing him, leapt behind the wall dragging the boy out by his ear.

"Alright green-eyes," bellowed Wolfy, "where have you stuck my wagon this time?"

Storm's ear was beginning to go numb so he graciously conceded. "Down there," he whimpered. By now, John had descended the stairs and joined the two of them in the courtyard. John looked at Wolfy, Wolfy looked at John, the two of them looked at Storm, then all three burst into laughter.

"John, can I borrow this little trouble-maker for a wee while?"

"Be my guest," replied the monk.

"Uh-oh," grunted Storm as he backed away and prepared to flee the scene. But before he could take off, Wolfy caught him by the collar and threw him effortlessly over his shoulder and strode purposefully out of the gate. He didn't put the struggling boy down until they reached the foot of the mountain. There waiting for them under the shelter of an old elm tree was Wolfy's wagon.

Wolfy turned to Storm with a mischievous twinkle in his eye. "Well, my young mischief-maker, you think you are quite funny don't you? Let's see if you can drag this here cart back up the mountain."

Storm let out a groan, but determined not to give up on a worthy challenge, he picked up the harness and draped it over his tiny shoulders. The shoulder straps were wider than his arm and the heavy leather yoke dwarfed his head. With a grunt and several hundred groans he got the wagon moving. The flat stretch wasn't too difficult but as soon as he reached the first incline, the wheels ground to a rumbling halt. Storm pulled with all of his might. Muscle flexed against bone and every tendon strained against his miniature frame. To no avail, he could not shift the wheels another turn.

"Give up?" enquired the jovial farmer.

"No way," came back a breathless response. Just as Storm, for the first time in his life, was about to admit defeat, a strange event occurred. As the boy became more and more angry at himself, a wind began to swirl around him. In hushed tones it seemed to whisper "fight Aruk, fight Aruk, fight Aruk, fight Aruk." The wind disappeared as quickly as it came. Storm stole a look at Wolfy, who was nervously searching the heavens.

The farmer rubbed his palms upon his overalls and walked toward the cart. "It looks like the weather is about to turn, you had better let me carry the load the rest of the way."

Storm didn't hear a word his friend said. Through his head charged the words "fight Aruk." He felt a strange energy infuse his body with strength. Suddenly, unbidden from his mouth rang a barrage of strange words foreign and alien. Strength surged through his muscles and the wagon began to move. Storm broke into a run. The wagon, creaking reluctantly, followed the boy's path up the mountain trail. Soon, a stunned Wolfy was left far behind. By the time Wolfy had reached the top, Storm had fully unpacked all that was on the wagon.

Wolfy stayed for dinner that night and told all those gathered at the table about what had transpired during the afternoon's event. Wolfy was a wonderful storyteller and had many of the monks falling off their chairs with laughter. Everyone enjoyed Wolfy's embellished story, except Abbot Nicholas, John and Storm. Despite his many pranks, Storm was actually quite shy and did not enjoy undue attention. Nicholas listened quietly but intently taking in every detail, stealing glances at Storm every so often. John watched the exchange and noted the seriousness of his mentor's disposition. After dinner Nicholas called John to his study.

"Ah John, well met. Thank you for coming to see me. Please close the door and sit down. I have something I have been meaning to discuss with you, and it seems with recent events the time indeed has come for us to talk." The Abbot's tone frightened the faithful monk but he took the proffered seat and waited for Nicholas to continue.

"John," began the Abbot, "when Storm first arrived, all those years ago, I think we both knew there was something special about the boy. The happenings of today only confirm my suspicions."

The Abbot reached down into his robe and pulled out the amulet that had fallen from the travel sack the night of Storm's arrival. Nicholas passed it across the table to the puzzled monk. "Study it if you will and tell me what you make of it," asked the Abbot.

John turned it over in trembling fingers. "Well sir, it looks as if this is only a half piece of a larger whole. I can see where the inner edges have been cut unevenly. On one side there appears to be a family herald and on the other a man's face. The inscriptions are in a foreign tongue of which I have never before seen the like."

"Everything you have said is quite accurate," stated the Abbot. He stood up and reached for an old book that was tucked away in a dark corner of a very dusty shelf. Nicholas blew a cobweb from the cover. "This afternoon, Farmer Barley said that the very wind had seemed to whisper the words "fight Aruk," well look here." Nicholas opened the dusty tome. The language was old Sardish, and John had some difficulty in translating the words contained therein. But at length and with some prompting from his teacher John read:

> "There is a power in the world which holds the balance of light and dark intact. This power is the Aruk. In all four corners of the world there are Sentinels; protectors and defenders of all that is alive. Four belong to the dark, four to the light. The balance of power can survive only till such day as the ninth son is born and the Darkwitch is dead. Then at Cartis in the land of Bal, the one called Fleet of Foot will hold the fate of the world in hand."

"I have heard of this Aruk," said John, "but I thought it only a legend and an old wives tale. How does this affect Storm and I?"

Suddenly, the Abbot looked very old. "John, the Aruk is no old wives tale, and I now have reason to believe that we have among us the ninth son."

John visibly started, "you cannot mean Storm. I mean he is only a simple child. How can you be so sure?"

The Abbot took a deep breath. After a moment of silence he spoke once more, this time in hushed tones. "The boy is anything but simple my friend. The reason I know, John, is because I am one of those sentinels that belong to the light. This monastery is one of the Holy Places of the Aruk. The inscription on this amulet is written in a language that no longer exists in modern day times. It is a language used only by the sentinels.

"Why are you telling me all this?" asked the perturbed monk.

"I am telling you, so that you might know a little more of your responsibilities. I trust you emphatically John. Our little boy Storm will not be a child forever. One day he will be a man, and I fear that day will come sooner rather than later. At such time he will hold in the palm of his hand the balance of the Aruk and the very fate of the world we know. I want you to watch over him and be at his side always. On his eleventh birthday I will begin to prepare him for what he is to face."

Chapter Four

Darkwitch

In the years that followed, Storm waxed strong and grew ever more in the affection of his monastic brethren. He enjoyed his time at Three Towers but he only knew true happiness when running barefoot with the deer of the Sardik Plains or when swinging through the trees of the Northwood. Although the boy ranged widely from his home, his friend and shadow, John, was never far behind. The boy embraced every facet of life and the natural wonders of the world around him. Storm could not imagine any greater joy than that experienced in the confines of the surrounding wilderness.

***

Unfortunately, not everyone in the world shared the boy's content. In the farthest reaches of the kingdom, far beyond the Sardik Plains, beyond the Adearan Sea, even as far north as the Black Mountains, there had gathered four very unhappy people. The moon was full and the eagle owls were out in force waging their predatory battle amongst the sparsely wooded slopes. A cave, hewn into one of the craggy peaks of the Black Mountains, was the chosen meeting place of these four mysterious figures. A fiercely burning fire, in the center of the cave afforded illumination for the dark gathering. Yellow flames swirled upwards racing and dancing toward an onerous night that looked in on the proceedings with quiet indifference through a small hole in the roof. Shadows whirled in a passionate frenzy throughout the place, their orchestra the disharmonic crackling of burning rotted wood. No one said a word. Four bodies, faceless, hunched, cloaked, with heads bowed, and flesh unexposed, sat huddled around the fire.

From a corner of the cave emerged a horrible wart ridden visage. Its hair hung in greasy hanks. Crooked teeth of putrid yellow jutted from a chinless orifice. Eyes blind with the blood of hate regarded the guests with disdain. Oozing pus sacs supported what was left of the hag's face, and as she approached the circle, her tongue darted to and fro between decaying teeth. She was attired in dirty rags and the threadbare skin of a long dead mountain cat. Around a leathery clavicle swung a necklace adorned with twenty shrunken rodent skulls.

To those who lived aware of this wandering monstrosity, she was known simply as darkwitch. Story held that once upon a time she had been born into a royal household, but because of her disfiguring ugliness had been cast out into the wilds. The dark were always in need of servants and she had joined them willingly.

She had now shuffled to the circle and taken her place with her back to the cave entrance. Her four silent companions this night were none other than the four lords of darkness. From the south Lord Brack, the east Damal, the west Vilus, and finally, the most powerful, from the north, Lord Rune. It was the latter that spoke first. His voice was metallic and harsh, yet seductively powerful.

"We have all traveled a very long way. It has been many long years since last the Lords of Dark have had the need to meet. For eons each one of us has enjoyed the notion of immortality, but now our very lives are threatened. The ninth son has been born. Where, we do not know. Moreover, his current location is well guarded and beyond our arts to discover. While he lives we are mortal and the balance is held in sway. We must find him and strike him down before he reaches his day of age. Darkwitch, work your evil arts and show us where we might begin the search for this bane." With the echoes of Rune's voice still reverberating around the walls, the Darkwitch reached down to her feet and scooped up a cracked clay bowl.

A deathly pallor enveloped the room. The bat, the owl, the coyote, even the wind, held still its collective breath. The world, for a moment, stopped turning and past, present, and future seemed to merge and confuse. The air bristled in anticipation of the evil incantation set into process by the mumblings of the old hag. Darkwitch filled the bowl with blood that spilled from a deep slash she inflicted upon her own right wrist. Slowly, she moved the bowl in a circular action all the time rocking backwards and forwards while murmuring a strange and unintelligible song. Unbidden, the putrid liquid began to bubble and froth. With a piercing scream, the witch thrust the bowl into the fire. Once more the conflagration seemed to spring into life. The flames cracked louder and ever more provocatively.

Faces began to materialize within the body of the fire. An image of two monks talking in a spacious courtyard coalesced in the flames. From a small building to the right bounded a small boy. He paused briefly and looked up into the sky as if searching for something. At the sight of the eerie green eyes the Darkwitch keeled forward on to her knees and, with one final anguished scream, fell dead into the flames. The picture vanished swiftly. In the center of the cave the hag's spirit disappeared into the ground. Within seconds no evidence of her existence remained other than twenty faceless skulls shriveling in the dying embers of the suffocated fire.

"Is that it?" blurted the scratchy voice of Lord Vilus.

"Have we learned anything from such a vision?" resonated the booming voice of Damal.

"Patience brothers," returned the voice of Lord Rune. "We have indeed learned much from our aunt's dying efforts. Moreover, we have all seen the face of the ninth son. Remember it well, for when he reaches manhood in some five winters time he will learn the cruel curse of his own mortality. Now we must leave this place before our joining is discovered. Vilus, you have work to do. The boy whom we seek I believe will be discovered in the west. Farewell."

With those last words, the dark-lord of the north disappeared into the night. Damal and Vilus followed quickly after, leaving Brack alone beside the fire. This was a man of little words, but those who knew him feared him above all other fears. His reputation for cruelty, unkindness, persecution, and conquest was well established in the southern-most reaches of the kingdom. This lord had ambitions beyond those of his peers. Slowly, he rose to his feet and followed his family into the night leaving the word "Fools," to reverberate around the now lonesome cave.

Chapter Five

Legend

Only a week earlier, John had been complaining to Wolfy about how hard it was getting to keep up with his over-active charge. Today the burly farmer had a surprise for both monk and boy. As always, Storm waited beside the front gate for the arrival of his favorite giant.

"Hi Wolfy did you miss me?" grinned Storm.

The farmer hauled his load to a shuddering halt upon the polished cobbles of the courtyard. "Not half as much as I am sure you missed me little fella," laughed Wolfy.

"I did not," retorted Storm, attempting to put on a convincing expression of disinterest.

Wolfy stifled a laugh and stretched out his arms and shoulders. "Oh well, I guess you won't be wanting the surprise I brought along for you then?" Picking up a box of cabbages, Wolfy barged past the boy on his way to the kitchens.

Storm followed in hot pursuit. "Surprise! What surprise? I promise I won't play any tricks on you for a whole month if you give it to me."

Wolfy grinned knowingly. There was no way the green-eyed boy could keep such a promise. He tried hard to suppress his merriment but finally relented and turned to the persistent child.

"I hear you have been giving poor old John the run around, so I have brought along someone to keep an eye on you. He's in the back of the wagon if you want to go meet him."

Storm stood in the quad with a befuddled expression on his face then took off at a mad dash. He sprinted over to the wagon and threw back the cover. There in front of him was the most beautiful animal he had ever laid eyes upon. It was a beast of many legends, a snow wolf. In the old language the animal was called a Latsu and was extremely rare. The Latsu had wandered the northern reaches for many centuries. When the hunters arrived, they hounded the wolf almost to extinction because of the inestimable value of their silver pelts. Storm had never seen one before, but he had read countless stories about them. They were incredibly fast and mighty hunters. The nomadic wanderers of the Adearan Plains claimed that the Latsu was sentient and had magical abilities beyond the understanding of mortal man. Most scoffed at such a notion, particularly the hunters who could easily retire if they were fortunate enough to trap and kill even one of the mythical creatures. This wolf was still only a cub and swung his paw playfully at Storm's hand. Storm let him out of the makeshift cage and immediately the Latsu clambered on top of him licking the boy to laughter. Wolfy watched from the kitchen window grinning from ear to ear. The farmer had found the cub chained to an iron post in a neighboring market. The owner had no idea that the animal was a Latsu otherwise Wolfy would never have been able to pick up the cub for the proffered sheaf of wheat. The animal, then, had been grubby and caked in red dust. Once Wolfy bathed him in the river his coat had positively sparkled.

The Abbot Nicholas was not an advocate of animals, particularly ones that would grow into mighty carnivores. At first he was not prepared to let Storm keep the cub in the monastery. The moment tears welled up in the boy's eyes the Abbot knew he could not prevent the two from living together. He was even happier to accommodate the situation on hearing what an asset such a companion might be in helping protect Storm on his daily sojourns into the woods and valleys surrounding Sard. Storm named his new best friend Zira, a name meaning prophetically, 'protector of light.' From the day they were first introduced, boy and wolf were inseparable. They were never to be found more than a few feet apart. Storm even smuggled him into the dining room at evening meal-time. The Abbot soon put a stop to such an escapade after Zira attempted to steal leftovers from the Abbot's own plate rather than Storm's clandestine drops beneath the tablecloth. Zira slept in the watchtower with Storm and Brother John. The cub would nestle up close to his master with a wet nose under the covers and a giant paw across the pillow. At first John had attempted to dissuade Storm of keeping such sleep habits but eventually was forced to concede. Keeping the two of them apart was akin to trying to prevent the sun from rising. John really didn't mind all that much. Zira was certainly making his life far more manageable, a Latsu was far better protection for the wayfaring child than an aging monk.

***

At length, Storm reached his eleventh birthday and now only two summers away from his coming of age ceremony. As was his custom, he awoke bright and early and leapt out of bed. No one truly knew the exact date of his birthday but Nicholas had attempted a pretty good approximation. After dressing quickly he dashed out of the room with Zira playfully nipping at his heels. On reaching the foot of the tower steps he found the Abbot waiting. An uneasy feeling seized him. The old Abbot had never sought him out this early in the morning. He reasoned that he must have done something especially bad to warrant such a visitation. Approaching Nicholas warily, he searched his memory for what he might be in trouble for and how to wriggle out of the ensuing punishment. Before Nicholas could even say a word, confessions flooded out of Storm's mouth.

"I'm sorry for putting frogs in Brother Paul's bed, and I really did not mean to drop all of those eggs on Wolfy the other day, and I was truly meaning to come see you about the crack in the back kitchen window, you see my shoe fell off and just took off toward the window before I could stop it and it cracked the window pane, and then the…"

"Quiet," spluttered the bemused Abbot, "it's far too early in the morning for confession."

"You mean to say that you are not here to tell me off?" asked the surprised boy.

"No of course not you daft lad, I only wanted to be the first to wish you a happy birthday, and ask if you might like to take a walk with me."

The boy breathed a visible sigh of relief as he finished tucking in the tail of his wayward shirt. "I would love to," answered Storm. "Can Zira come with us?"

The Abbot frowned, then, smiled, "of course he can."

"You know sir, I was only joking about all those things I said I did," exclaimed Storm.

"We'll see about Brother Paul's bed frogs later," said Nicholas with a grin on his face, "but for now I'd like to tell you a story." As the three of them set off down the mountain trail, the old Abbot began to tell his tale...

"Many, many years ago there lived two brothers. Their names were Elam and Jesobi, and closer brothers could not be found on the face of Terrus. One day Elam fell in love with a beautiful peasant girl named Kerrell. Now Elam was a wealthy prince and Kerrell a very poor shepherd's daughter. Every day the two of them met secretly at nightfall in a secluded forest grove. They loved each other with all that a heart can possess. Alas they both knew that the match would never be accepted by the royal family. In fact the king had already arranged a marriage for him to a neighboring princess.

Well, one day Elam told his brother Jesobi about Kerrell, and how he loved her dearly. Elam told his brother that he was considered running away with her. For the first time in their lives, the brothers began to argue. Jesobi could not understand how his brother could possibly love or marry a woman not of royal lineage.

One dark and wintry night, Jesobi, with a handful of his cutthroat friends stole into the village and kidnapped Kerrell from her home. He took her to his castle and imprisoned her in a very tall tower overlooking the sea. Elam was distraught and would neither eat nor drink for many weeks. He promised rich rewards to anyone who might be able to bring him news of his lost love. Alas, Kerrell was never again to see the freedom of her home.

Caelin Paul

The whole time she was prisoner, the evil Jesobi attempted to persuade her to come to his bed, but she refused him time and time again. Finally, Jesobi went to a local witch who concocted him a spell. This enchanted potion would cause any that drank it to fall into a deep sleep. The witch required in payment that the first child of Kerrell be given unto her. Jesobi drugged Kerrell's food then forced himself upon her. The drug had made her so sleepy that she could not resist though tears streamed down her cheeks and turned to stone as they touched the floor. Nine moons later a baby was born.

During the agonizing childbirth, Kerrell died suddenly. Jesobi willingly gave the child up to the witch and she took him and named him Brack. The houses of Jesobi and Elam went to war after someone close to Jesobi, in a drunken fit of boasting, told one of Elam's men the true story of Kerrell's disappearance.

In the meantime, Jesobi had fathered three more children, Rune, Vilus, and Damal. Elam too had married and fathered four children, Sara, Tyrel, Ryad, and one other. The houses of Elam and Jesobi fought the bloodiest battle ever recorded. Hundreds of thousands of innocent people lost their lives. The outcome of the battle remains a mystery as both of its opposing generals mysteriously vanished from the field of battle at its most bloody peak. The old witch it turns out was the brother's sister. Cast out from the royal household on account of her unspeakable ugliness, she had never forgotten her family's unkindness and cast an evil enchantment upon all eight of her sibling's children. The enchantment is as powerful a curse that has ever been cast and is called the Aruk. This spell makes each offspring of Elam and Jesobi immortal. Jesobi's children became the defenders of the dark, and Elam's children became sentinels of the light. All these years the balance has remained intact. The power of the Aruk remains as potent today as the day it was first brought into being. Well that is my story. Do you have any questions my boy?"

Storm chewed thoughtfully on his lower lip and pulled distractedly at a loose strand of hair. "Only one sir, if you don't mind me asking, who was the fourth child of Elam?"

The Abbot looked down at the boy with twinkling eyes and in hushed tones whispered, "ah yes, the fourth born child, my lad, was named Nicholas." With that the Abbot turned and strode back up the trail towards the monastery, leaving Storm gaping open-mouthed after him.

Chapter Six

Prophecy

From that day onwards, Storm met with the Abbot every day for most of the afternoon. Storm had experienced lessons before, but the prior responsibility of his education had fallen to a handful of the monks. Brother John had instructed him in letters, numbers and the basics of account keeping. Brother Felix, the head gardener, tutored him regarding all the different trees, plants, herbs, and animals indigenous to the region. Brother Orm, the chief cook, taught him how to make delicious pastries and pies. Storm enjoyed these latter lessons the most, especially as he always got to sample their culinary creations. There were also the more tedious lessons led by Brother Robard and Brother Tomas. These sessions involved studying and translating the old texts. Though Storm loathed them, Robard and Tomas loved to teach them. The boy had a perfect memory and the uncanny ability to remember everything he was taught. However, the vast majority of his learning took place beyond the stifling monastery walls. In the river he learned to swim, and how to catch the cavorting yellow salmon. From the townspeople he learned a little about village trades. He was a quick learner and before too long was an accomplished apprentice weaver, blacksmith, baker, carpenter, and builder. The farmers taught him much about animal husbandry; how to milk the cows, shoe the horses, fleece the sheep, and bale the hay.

However, of all his teachers, he loved the woodland animals the most. Whenever time permitted he would leave Three Towers far behind and venture into the forest with Zira at his side. John had now taken to wandering only a little way into the trees before settling himself down to wait patiently for the boy's return. Storm had a unique rapport with the woodland creatures. Squirrels would often sweep down from the trees to steal away bread crumbs from his hand. Birds whispered on his shoulder while the feral foxes curled languidly around the boy's legs. The wild ponies allowed him to ride upon their backs, and spirited deer ran along beside him as he raced between the towering trunks of giant trees. As the years passed by, Storm became stronger and faster. Soon, even the gazelle had to work hard to keep up with this swift-footed child.

With the advent of his eleventh birthday, lessons had taken on a more serious tone. The youngster would often go hours at a time separated from his beloved Zira who sat obediently outside the Abbot's study door. Inside, Nicholas would watch patiently over the snow wolf's master as he read from ancient texts. Every once in a while, the Abbot would ask a question to which the answer would always be correct.

One late evening, after Storm had been studying the theology of some forever dead religious sect, he got up the courage to ask the Abbot more about the Aruk. It had been a number of months since Nicholas had first shared with Storm his story.

Clearing his throat, Storm fumbled to articulate a question. "Sir, can anything impact the power of the Aruk? I mean is it possible to break the curse?"

Nicholas paused in mid-sentence, put down the book he was reading and removed the fragile spectacles that framed his fatherly countenance. The Abbot smiled as he regarded the enthusiasm that exuded from the face of his young student. "Curiosity is indeed a wonderful thing in youth. I wondered how long it would be before you would ask that very question. Come sit down and let me show you something."

The Abbot pulled a book off a shelf, and opened it to the selfsame page he had once shown Brother John. "Now we shall see how well your studies of the old Sardish language are progressing. See if you can read what it says here on this page." He handed the book to the boy who studied the dusty characters. At first Storm's brow furrowed with deep concentration, then slowly he began to read the archaic words:

> *"There is a power in the world which holds the balance of light and dark intact. This power is the Aruk. In all four corners of the world there are Sentinels; protectors and defenders of all that is alive. Four belong to the dark, four to the light. The balance of power can survive only till such day as the ninth son is born and the Darkwitch is dead. Then at Cartis in the land of Bal, the one called Fleet of Foot will hold the fate of the world in hand."*

Storm paused and looked up from the pages. "What does all this mean? Who is the ninth son? Who is the darkwitch? Where is Cartis? Who is this fleet of foot? Are you one of the sentinels?"

"Questions, questions," laughed Nicholas. "Let us just say little Storm, your homework assignment is to determine answers to all those questions by yourself. Now, no more procrastination back to work."

Storm sighed as he returned to the boring text that lay open before him. He looked up to ask another question but thought better of it when he saw the stern expression on the Abbot's face.

That night in bed, his dreams were full of witches, mountains, and hooded strangers. No matter how much he tossed and turned the images would not remove themselves from out of his head. Flushed skin beaded with perspiration. Sensing his consternation, faithful Zira, reached up and licked the boy's cheek offering a settling peace and reassurance. The emotion had a soothing effect, as images of hooded faces were replaced by dreams of a black haired youth hurtling along woodland trails with a silver-coated canine streaking behind in hot pursuit.

Chapter Seven

Vilus

While Storm knew the plague of dark-night dreams, one of the creatures of his restless nightmare-ridden sleep busily plotted his demise. The dark-lord Vilus, within the refuge of his castle, sat impatiently awaiting the return of his scaly winged messengers. Baticus Castle was unoriginally but appropriately named. From every rafter and every window ledge there hung row after row of giant bats. Vilus adored these, his pets, and like the blind creatures that decorated his home he loved the dark.

From without the walls, there approached a loud rumbling. The sound of beating wings grew to a resonant crescendo and the walls of Baticus shuddered at their approach. In, through the window, flew the most malevolent creatures that had ever deigned to walk the world of Terrus. Faces bore a transient semblance of humanity. Obscene bodies wore a suffocating shade of night, and bloodless eyes gleamed with aqueous opacity. Forked tongues lashed purposefully from spiteful jaws. Each demon stood over ten feet tall and several man-lengths wide. Monstrous pinions hung limply along armored underbellies. From two-toed feet sprang razor-sharp talons, an adaptation of natural selection best suited for ripping mortal flesh to pieces.

The tallest of the brood stepped forward. He nodded his head in reluctant reverence. As he began to speak, the putrid stench which leapt from his mouth caused even Vilus to cover his mouth. The night demon reeked of evil. Hatred and death was the only means to satiate this beast. "Master, we have located the one you look for. He dwells in the town of Sard."

"Where exactly in Sard does the boy reside?" spat Vilus. The demon shifted his scaly feet nervously before answering.

"Sire, he resides under the roof of one of the Holy Temples of Aruk, the monastery of the Three Towers. On hearing the boy's whereabouts, Vilus stood up and, enraged, hurled his throne toward the scaly servants. Accepting this as an act of dismissal, the monstrous demons quickly retreated through the throne room door.

Vilus fought to regain a semblance of composure. "So the little runt has found sanctuary with cousin, Nicholas. Well, well, well, we will just have to see how long it remains that way." Vilus tossed back his head and shouted aloud a spell of transposition.

*　*　*

A mere instant later, Vilus found himself standing in the royal chambers of Lord Rune, the oldest legitimate son of Jesobi. Vilus's eyes burned as he stepped into the brightly lit throne room. Rune sat nonchalantly at the head of a long dining table. Seemingly, the older brother had expected company, for laid out upon the dark wooden board were two crystal goblets and a decanter of blood wine.

"Ah brother Vilus, I trust this intrusion can only mean that you have discovered the whereabouts of the ninth son?"

Vilus strode confidently to the table and tossed back his hood. The disrobement revealed a face that once had been handsome, but now etched skeletal as a consequence of long hours spent in the dark. Bloodshot eyes were sunken and moved furtively from side to side. "Did you doubt my ability to complete such a task brother?" grunted Vilus.

Rune sneered with unfeigned sarcasm, "of course not, brother. Well what have you found out?"

Vilus poured himself a large goblet of the crimson colored wine and drank noisily. After pouring another dram, he downed it in one gulp. "Yes, I have found the brat, but he is holed up with our favorite cousin at Three Towers."

Rune suppressed the involuntary flinch that rose within him

"It seems as if very soon we will have to pay Nicholas a little family visit. In the meantime, I will let you inform Damal and Brack of your splendid discovery. Now if you'll excuse me I have much work to do."

Vilus disappeared without as much as a wave goodbye. As he left, unsaid curses rested upon his tongue. How he hated the condescension of his self-righteous older sibling. Even as he returned to Baticus, Vilus renewed his crude oath. Soon he would take all of Rune's power and ensure that the sentinels of light were all destroyed. If that meant committing a little fratricide then so be it.

Chapter Eight

Test

A grand contagion of excitement pulsed throughout the little town of Sard. In just two days time, the humble hamlet was to entertain a royal visitor. No one of the royal blood-line had ever visited the plains before, at least not in living memory. The streets were a bustle of activity as streamers, banners, and silken ribbons adorned the tree-lined avenues and narrow side streets. Womenfolk were to be seen everywhere busily scrubbing window panes, front doors, and the pitted cobble-stones. Townsmen scurried abroad like worker beetles carrying tables, chairs, and colorful tents. The Mayor of Sard, a rather plump, rosy-cheeked man, had declared a two-day celebration. With the holiday decree, the townspeople had set to work preparing the largest culinary extravaganza the town had ever seen. From every window the delicious smell of apple crumble, shepherds pie, meat rolls, and sweet-spiced pastries flooded the morning streets. Preparations were something of a rushed affair as news of the impending royal visit had only reached Sard the previous day. A young boy had ridden directly to the Mayor's house to deliver a letter bearing the regal insignia of Queen Sara of Meridia. The purpose of the queen's visit was a mystery but little could assuage the people's enthusiasm at the prospect of entertaining a royal guest.

The queen's home, Meridia, was a tiny island kingdom situated in the very heart of the Adearan Sea. Queen Sara was the last known descendent of the House of Celebus. It was Celebus who, many centuries before, united the out-world kingdoms in a mighty conflict versus the Terror Wraiths. Celebus had unlocked the key to the wraith's power, single-handedly saving the lives of all those who lived upon Terrus. An immediate legend, Celebus was rewarded with a kingship and the unequivocal love of a grateful people. Hundreds of years had passed since the long reign of King Celebus. Many children seeded a ruling progeny and the Meridian kingdom grew to cover most of the known land within the reaches.

Several generations later, Prince Elam and Jesobi had been born into the royal line. With their mysterious disappearance the royal family began to die and lose favor with the people. Queen Sara of Meridia was the last vestige of royalty still recognized upon Terrus. It was said that she had siblings but no one knew if they still lived. For many years Queen Sara had ruled from the sanctuary of her island kingdom being seen in public only on rare occasions or at times of dire peril. The island kingdom of Meridia was itself a place shrouded in legend. Hidden within the confines of a deep grey fog, the local fishermen gave it a wide berth. The queen, however, was accepted as a wise and generous monarch in spite of her reclusion.

Some of the older townspeople in Sard remembered a time when the town had faced a winter of famine and a spring of drought. At their darkest hour, Queen Sara of Meridia had sent a royal barge with enough food and water to see them safely through the dry season. On another occasion, barbarians from the Black Mountains had attacked Sard with great violence, raping and pillaging everything that stood in their path. The more fortunate members of the community had fled their homes and taken refuge at Three Towers. Just when the barbarians were about to breach the monastery walls the Meridian Cavalry had arrived and obliterated the invaders relieving the siege with unparalleled military precision. This event had occurred nearly one hundred years past. Shortly afterwards, the Abbot Nicholas had arrived at Three Towers.

The townspeople respected the Abbot but viewed him with emotion akin to fear. They could not understand the Abbot's longevity. So many generations of Sardinians were born, lived, and passed into dust, yet the Abbot continued to survive the ravages of time.

The residents of Three Towers were almost as excited as their secular brethren regarding the prospect of entertaining royalty. Brother Orm had locked himself in the kitchens, preparing his endless blue-ribbon specialties. The rest of the brothers chaotically scrubbed, polished, and washed every tile and stone. The monastery had never enjoyed such a showering of attention. Storm, too, was caught up in the festive atmosphere. Wolfy had asked the boy to help him stake out flagpoles down in the village. Only one person in Sard did not share the joyful anticipation of the impending royal visit. Nicholas stood brooding at the study window. His face was a picture of consternation and his eyes were bloody from nights of sleeplessness. If the queen was journeying to Three Towers, it could only portend of present or future calamity. It had been near on a century since he had seen his dear sister, and almost as long since he had last sat with his closest friend Kalon. Kalon, older than even the Abbot was the world's last Archmage. He had been Nicholas's tutor, friend and confidant for many years. Now, in his twilight years, he served as chief advisor to the throne of Meridia.

Storm arrived back at Three Towers shortly before nightfall. Zira trotted faithfully at his heels. John waited patiently for him at the front gate. "Hello my young ward. I trust you are not too exhausted from your work down in the village, for I fear your work is not yet done tonight. The Abbot is looking for you and requested that I send you directly to him. It seems as if a holiday in the village is not a reason to neglect your studies." John winked at his young charge.

Storm groaned. "Alright, I'm on my way." As Storm reluctantly shuffled off in the direction of the library, John couldn't help but smile. He had watched Storm grow from a feeble excuse for a child into a strong young boy. Now in little more than a year, a thirteenth summer would make him a man. John shook his head in disbelief, where had the last eleven years gone.

Nicholas impatiently awaited the arrival of his impetuous young student. Storm bounded through the door and promptly ran headlong into a chair, collapsing in a heap at the Abbot's feet.

For the first time in several days a smile rose unbidden upon the aged Abbot's lips as he watched the raven-haired youth attempt to disentangle flailing limbs from the guilty chair.

"You really are a klutz dear boy. When you have finished battling the chair I would like for you to take a little test."

Storm finally regained a vertical position. Sheepishly he looked up at his mentor. "Great, I love tests," said Storm. "What subject is it today? Math, Geography, History, Law?"

"None of those," replied Nicholas with a twinkle in his eye. "Every test I have issued, you have completed with unfathomable success. I thought it time to really challenge you. Sometimes it is better to fail and learn humility than pass and earn glory. This test might just push your limits."

Storm's eyes flickered with interest. If there was one thing he enjoyed more than anything else, it was a challenge. "I'm ready, what would you have me do?"

The Abbot smiled and then continued. "There are two parts to the test so listen carefully. By the way neither part requires you having to write."

Storm put down the quill he had picked up, "just the sort of test I like."

Nicholas grinned. "The first part of your test is to place in alphabetical order every one of the books you see before you. I have endeavored to make it a little more challenging by mixing them all up a little."

Storm looked around and viewed row upon endless row, aisle upon endless aisle, shelf upon endless shelf, with books arrayed in complete and utter disorder.

The Abbot continued; "the second part of the test is to locate an old book entitled, *The Archmage Path*. You have just one hour to complete the task."

"One hour" came back Storm's disbelieving voice. "It will take me weeks to complete such a task."

The Abbot turned to the boy and quietly whispered, "a task which for mere mortals would take a day, for immortals with the power of Aruk, the same task might take just moments." With that Nicholas turned and strode stiffly out of the library. As he departed, the heavy oaken doors slammed shut behind him.

Storm flounced down into a chair and stared hopelessly at the task that lay before him. "What kind of test is this anyway?" Storm grunted at the unaccommodating silence. Slowly he dragged himself to his feet and wandered over to where the A's began. The first two books he yanked off the shelf were entitled *Zand's Anthology* and *Maps of the Southern Passage*. The shelves really were in a mess, not a single semblance of alphabetical order remained. The time allowed for the test evaporated swiftly. The hourglass already spilled half empty and Storm had made little headway in the impossible task. Despairing, he threw himself down on the window ledge and placed his head upon his knees.

"I'm going to fail he groaned." Exhausted, he succumbed to a fitful sleep. As he slept he began to dream. A beautiful woman's face slowly materialized into conscious thought. She smiled at him and softly whispered the same words he had first heard a few years before on the nearby mountain trail; *"fight Aruk, fight Aruk!"* The gentle whispers filled his head and were joined with other words from a language he did not recognize. Though he slept soundly, Storm grew conscious that his lips began to move. Without warning, all around him books began to fly. For several minutes the fluttering of pages sang throughout the library. Brother Tomas heard the commotion when passing the door. Trying the handle he found it locked fast. Quickly, he scurried off to find the Abbot. Without knocking, Tomas burst into the Abbot's study. "Sir, there are many strange sounds coming from the library and when I tried the door handle I found it locked."

The Abbot grinned then turned to the frightened brother. In a calming voice, he said, "do not fear it is only young Storm doing a little bit of spring cleaning." All of a sudden, the window sprang open. The wind blew inwardly through the casement. Tomas and Nicholas watched dumbfounded as a wispy hand took shape and reached for a book on the uppermost shelf of the Abbot's bookcase. Having gripped the book, the phantasmic hand withdrew to the window and back into the night.

Without waiting to be questioned by the shaking Tomas, Nicholas headed for the library as fast as his aged legs could carry him. He fumbled within his robe for the key, turned the lock, then threw open the doors. Storm was just beginning to stir from his nap. Cat-like he stretched and yawned. His spirits fell when he looked up to see the Abbot watching him. Hanging his head in shame, a beaten voice spluttered, "I have failed your test. It was just too difficult."

Just then, the catchment at the window shattered. Through the window floated a heavy book that landed in a cloud of dust particles and an almighty thud on the table in front of Storm. The startled boy read the title out aloud, "*The Archmage Path*!" In moments, he was on his feet running from bookcase to bookcase. Every book was in its rightful place. Turning to Nicholas, he excitedly exclaimed, "I did it, I did it, I, really did it." Then his face dropped. "But how could I have done this, I fell asleep at the window?"

Nicholas walked over to the boy and in a rare exhibition of emotion wrapped an arm around the confused adolescent. "The how question, is one we will answer very soon." Nicholas then picked up the heavy book that had landed so emphatically upon the library table.

"No wonder I couldn't find this book in the library, it was hidden in my study the whole time. Storm, this book was written by the greatest teacher that has ever lived on Terrus. The day after next you shall meet this teacher. His name is Kalon, and he is the chief advisor to Queen Sara of Meridia. As he once was my teacher, perhaps one day he might be yours. In the meantime, I need for you to keep all that has happened here our little secret. I also want you to take this book along with you and read it. In light of the royal visitation, I shall extend you a brief hiatus from your studies till after the royal party has left. At that time we shall meet and talk again."

The Abbot then left the boy alone surrounded by avenues of knowledge and a mind swathed in confusion. Dreams that night were untroubled and filled with the adoring face of the mysterious woman who had helped him pass the impossible test.

Chapter Nine

Damal

    The townspeople and the residents of Three Towers were not the only ones preparing for the royal visit. News of the Meridian monarch's impending departure from home had reached Lord Vilus. For days he had sat within the dank confines of a musty throne room hatching his own evil welcome for his royal cousin. It had been over a hundred years since two Sentinels of the light had last met together. Moreover, the ninth child would be in attendance at the reunion.
    "What power would be mine if I could break up this little party and kill the boy in the process?" Vilus spoke aloud his question to the darkening shadows that flitted chaotically throughout the chamber. "My dear brothers would have no choice but to bow to me if I was to have the ninth son's power to wield as mine own." The dark-lord's shrill laughter echoed within the walls. Turning to a curtain beside his throne, he pulled hard upon a fraying cord. Moments later, the echo of evil laughter was joined by the reverberations of heavy bells. Before the fading of the last chime, Vilus was joined by his servant, Maula.
    "Come join your master, Maula," grated the high-pitched voice of Lord Vilus. The demon, somewhat unnerved at his master's apparent jovial demeanor approached the throne cautiously. "Listen carefully dragon spawn. Two twilights from now, I desire for you and your brood to pay a social call on our friends in Sard. When everyone is gathered in the village, away from the safety of their

accursed tower, I want you to conjure all the pain, anguish, and death possible upon the hateful little mortals. The boy you need to bring back to me breathing but not necessarily intact." The darklord's eyes glinted evilly as he licked his lips at the thought of the pain he would afflict upon the child in his own time. "I can assure you Maula, success in this endeavor will bring you great rewards. Needless to say, failure will have consequences too. Now go and do not let me down." The demon bowed low as he retreated from the room.

***

Vilus was not the only dark-lord to have heard of the planned royal visit. While it had escaped the notice of Lord Rune and Brack, Damal, Lord of the East had been keeping a close watch on his Meridian adversary. Damal and Sara both called the East home and little occurred that the other was unaware of. Damal was the youngest of the dark-lords and hated that fact. The jealousy that blossomed in his evil heart consumed him. For many years he had been plotting damnable schemes aimed at unseating his brother Rune. He, like Vilus, was determined to make the ninth son's legacy his. For years, he had walked in the shadow of his older siblings. As the youngest he had no memory of his parents and hated them for cursing him with immortality. Although he wasn't necessarily against living forever, he hated the fact that he had no free agency in the matter. As a child he had tempted the Gods again and again by throwing himself off of cliff tops and raging waterfalls. Each time he had woken the next morning sore but very much alive. Damal lived the most flamboyant lifestyle of all the dark brothers. His palace was the most ostentatious of any residence on the face of the planet. It had been built upon the backs of many generations of slave labor. The walls were rose marble interwoven with panels of black obsidian. More than a thousand rooms were connected by an endless maze of corridors and hallways. From every wall hung elaborate tapestries comprised of the richest silks and most expensive velvet. At every turn there arose an even more flashing manifestation of the dark-lord's wealth. Rare stones and gems adorned the balustrades and heavy mahogany doors and window frames were intricately carved by the most skilled of artisans. The rooms themselves were cavernous and purposeless. Despite this apparent lack of use, each room sparkled with the perspiration and attention of the dark-lord's servants. Hundreds of eunuchs lived within the city palace for no other reason than to clean the empty rooms and cater to the pretentious whims of their master. Exotic plants grew in the grounds and every manner of wild beast roamed freely among the trees. Waterfalls and fountains flowed unabatedly, and small ponds of rare fish littered the verdant garden pathways that were lined with marble statues of nameless unclothed figures.

Unlike his solitary brothers, who entertained very few guests, Damal hated being alone. He often threw wild parties, inviting all those that would come, and those that would not come he forced to attend. The latter, included hundreds of women to whom he would extend every fashionable courtesy, that is until he had them alone in the bedroom. His conquest assured, he would then submit noblewoman, princess, servant girl or peasant to the self-same hideous tortures. His dungeons were littered with the soiled bodies of those unfortunate enough to attract his lustful attention. Yet still his reign of fear in the east continued uncensored despite the disproving opinions of Lord Rune and the constant conflict with the saintly Sara of Meridia.

Damal was arrogant and feared no one. Unfortunately, the lowly farmers who reluctantly called him neighbor were not immune to the emotion of fear. The winged servants of Lord Damal were a plague and menace to the flocks of sheep and cattle that represented their very livelihood. Damal, on arriving in the east had forged a dark alliance with the dragirds of the eastern isles. Half bird, half dragon, these frightening creatures, wreaked havoc on the fishermen and villagers of the eastern reaches. Damal gave them his blessing to hunt throughout his lands in return for their allegiance to any dark cause he chose to pursue.

Their skin was an olivaceous shade of green. A thicker armored skin was not known on Terrus, for no weapon of man could pierce their adamantine hide. From head to tail they stretched some four man-lengths. Legs swelled thick as barrels making their movements on land clumsy and awkward. In flight they relied on heavily feathered wings that could carry them untiringly for many thousands of miles. The bird-like visage was fearsome to regard with a hooked beak that protruded from beneath hooded eyes. However, the fiercest and most tenacious characteristics of the dragird, were the jagged teeth housed within grotesque mandibles. Few men lived to tell the tale of just how powerful such jaws were. Now, Damal called upon his willing allies to run the self-same errand, unbeknownst to him, asked of the night demons of Lord Vilus.

Chapter Ten

Anticipation

The day of the royal visit had at last arrived. Hundreds of people converged upon Sard to enjoy the festivities and to catch a glimpse of their queen. Storm was over-awed. Never in his short life had he seen the townspeople of Sard so excited. Smiles sang on children's faces and even the crotchety elders were dancing in the streets. Storm stood off to the side, wishing earnestly that one of the children would ask him to play. Storm had no friends his own age. Most of the town's youth feared the green-eyed boy who, reputedly, talked to the animals. Not many had forgotten the day Storm had calmly walked up to a wild bear that had wandered into the village. The boy had taken the giant mountain dweller by the paw and guided him back into the forest. He had only been eight summers of age at the time, but such events had made the other children wary of the strange child. These days Storm didn't mind as much, preferring the company of his faithful Zira to that of the town's children.

The Meridian monarch was due to arrive by royal barge around mid-day. The welcoming party was to include the mayor, the blacksmith, the Abbot, and Caron the elder. Caron was the oldest resident of Sard, and the only member of the community who had ever met Queen Sara. Across the street, Storm spied his friend Wolfy seated at the forge. He wandered over to say hello and found his friend sat on an anvil, smoking a pipe, and listening to a blacksmith story. Tom was known for miles around as an eloquent storyteller. Storm and Zira slipped unnoticed into the forge. Quite a crowd had gathered and as usual the brawny smith was enjoying the attention. The topic of his tales this morning was the mysterious legends of Meridia.

"You know there is meant to be an old weather mage living on Meridia. He controls our rains and sunlight so that we continue to enjoy good harvests." Storm perked up his ears. He had been reading the *Archmage Path* and had read that one of the talents of an Archmage was control of the elements. He wondered whether the blacksmith was talking about the Abbot's teacher Kalon. Abruptly he was brought out of his reverie by a roar of laughter. Clearly, he had missed a very funny joke. No sooner had the guffaws and giggles ceased than Tom launched into another story.

"You know people say that this Queen Sara is over five hundred years old. Others say that she is related to old Abbot Nicholas," whispered the Smithy, gesticulating upward toward Three Towers as he spoke. "They say Queen Sara is indescribably beautiful and on account of her youthful charm received a courtship from the elf-king's very own son. Why if I had had the good fortune to meet her in my younger years I would have willingly traded her in for old Mary." Little did Tom know that 'Old Mary' had come to stand right behind him. With a look of disgust upon her face she promptly deposited the contents of a nearby slop bucket over the unsuspecting Smithy's head. The crowd roared with laughter. Even Storm found it difficult to suppress a giggle. Poor Tom really looked a sight, red-faced and bedraggled with water dripping from head to toe.

"Perhaps it is safer if I tell the next story," said Wolfy. Wolfy took a deep draft from his clay pipe and gathered his thoughts. Effective, the dramatic pause caused all the men and women to lean forward in anxious anticipation of what the farmer would tell them. "Many of you have probably heard that no one is seen coming or going from Meridia. You have probably been told that people mysteriously disappear after setting foot on the island. Others believe that the island is a barren rock covered in barnacles. To all these I say – poppycock! A very good friend of mine was, for a time, the royal boatman. Everyday, he would make the voyage from Bala Sands to Meridia and back again. I have it on good authority that beyond the white blanket of fog is a land so beautiful you could only view it in your wildest dreams. Every color created or imagined is to be found on Meridia. Lake and river waters are a vibrant blue and the salmon play happily without fear of the angler's rusty hook. Bountiful trees are laden with fruit so large that the sinewy boughs can barely support their weight. The island kingdom of Meridia is the most alive expanse of land the God's have ever created. Most beautiful of all is the crystal castle that stands majestically in the heart of the island, its towers spiraling graciously toward the heavens. The reason you see no one enter or leave Meridia, is simply because few are invited to visit and fewer still choose to leave. Not every man or woman is able to make the journey to the island. It is a sacred place whose soil may only be touched by a person pure in heart. Sadly, today the dark claims more souls than ever before."

A voice from the crowd interrupted with a question. "What ever happened to the boatman?"

Wolfy tapped his clay pipe against the wooden sides of a barrel before answering. "Ah yes my friend from the sands. He stole an apple from one of the golden trees. When next he attempted a crossing, he found that his boat could not pierce the cloud. An old man floated out to meet him on a boat that moved without oars. He told my friend that his services would no longer be needed upon the island. Then, as quickly as he came, he dissolved back into the mist. That was the last my friend ever saw of the fair land of Meridia."

During the telling of the story a deafening hush had descended upon the forge. The silence was rudely and abruptly fractured by the miller's son who raced up the high street bellowing, "she's a comin, she's a comin." In seconds the crowd dispersed surging down towards the waterfront to vie for the best position for viewing the royal arrival. Soon Storm and Zira were left all alone in the dusty street. Abbot Nicholas noiselessly materialized beside him. "Well my boy don't you want to come see what all the excitement is about?" The Abbot didn't wait for an answer, but strode masterfully down the hill towards the riverfront with wolf and boy a scant step behind.

Chapter Eleven

Sara

By the time Storm reached the heavily peopled riverfront, a boat glided in toward the landing area. From the towering mast flew the golden insignia of Meridia. Directly within the center of the barge rose a white tent that offered the royal visitors protection from the blazing summer sun. Surrounding the canopy were ten giant soldiers. The queen's household cavalry were esteemed to be the finest fighting men in the whole kingdom. Upon weathered faces, each man wore a stoic expression suggesting an undying loyalty to their monarch. The noonday sun was unrelenting and the royal bodyguards had discarded their more formal armor in favor of thin white tunics emblazoned with the royal crest that depicted a magnificent red dragon. At the warriors' side hung heavy leather sword belts intricately decorated. Within jewel-encrusted scabbards the dangerous edges of their famed scimitars lay hidden. Patiently, the living statues stood upright and tall with arms set across muscular chests.

Without warning, the scene suffered a breath-taking transformation. Passivity was replaced by efficient activity. Each bodyguard sprang to life making precise preparation for securing the boat to the dock. Finely tuned athletes leapt from the barge to take their places along the jetty. The captain of the guard, distinguished only by a simple black band that he wore around his right arm, pulled back the canopy flap. An anticipatory lull descended across the gathered crowd. Men and women leaned forward on tiptoes and children craned their necks atop parent's shoulders. Some of the older youth wriggled through legs or scaled nearby tree limbs. Excitement fused the air. Every man, woman and child wanted to be the first to capture a glimpse of their queen. As the Abbot approached, the crowd reluctantly allowed him to pass. Spirited applause and raucous cheers followed his passage toward the dock. Discreetly, Storm, with Zira leaning heavily against his right leg, followed his mentor to the waterfront. Standing off to one side, he wondered at the excitement that seemed to radiate from the people surrounding him. Finally, a woman emerged from the shadowy confines of the royal marquee. The crowd erupted into a deafening cacophony of welcome. Sara paused, smiled and waved to those that saturated the landing area.

    Storm stared hard at the woman who now moved slowly along her avenue of bodyguards. She looked so young. Her white gown flowed behind her like a fast-moving glacier. Storm found the sight of Queen Sara confusing and baffling. Abbot Nicholas, himself, had told him that they were siblings, but how could this be? He looked first at Nicholas, and noted the convolutions of wrinkles and shimmering of grey hair. Then he regarded the thousand-year old queen. He noticed immediately the striking resemblance between her and the Abbot. The siblings had the self-same dark eyes, shallow cheekbones, and slightly pointed nose. They were both tall and held themselves with a subtle confidence and gentle disposition. Yet to his young eyes, Queen Sara of Meridia looked little more than a third the age of the Abbot. Never in his life had he seen a woman more beautiful. The crowd continued to cheer and sing as she reached the end of the dock.

    The welcoming party was waiting with apparent impatience and visible nervousness. The blustery mayor could not stop fidgeting as he silently rehearsed the speech he had prepared. Tom, the blacksmith, attired in his one and only dress tunic, stood open-mouthed mesmerized by the beauty of his queen. Caron, the elder, seemed bewildered and vigorously cleaned his spectacles with a handkerchief. Could his eyes be deceiving him? The queen looked as young and beautiful as he remembered her the day she had paid a visit to the fishing village of Dorant. He remembered the day still vividly despite the fact he had been a boy of only twelve summers. As for the Abbot, his face surrendered little emotion. Staring intently at his older sibling, a stern wrinkle deepened upon his forehead.

Meanwhile, the royal visitor and her colorful entourage had now reached the presentation area. The Mayor of Sard was the first to formally welcome Queen Sara to the town. Puffing out his chest, he launched into what was to be undoubtedly the most important and most memorable speech of his entire life. Fortunately, in all the excitement he had forgotten most every word of his carefully prepared oratory. The next in line for the royal handshake was the star-struck smithy. She was even more breathtaking up close so the poor Tom could only stammer an inaudible grunt while extending a weathered palm. The crowd was enjoying the occasion immensely. Cheers, whistles, and goodwill wishes flailed randomly in the afternoon sun. The last member of the welcome committee was Abbot Nicholas.

"Hello Sara," said Nicholas.

The queen flung her arms around the old man's neck and hugged him tightly. For a moment she clung tenderly to him before taking his hands and looking up into his eyes.

"Hello Nicholas, you look well. Have you missed your older sister? I have missed you and I cannot wait for the opportunity to catch up. Oh and of course I very much look forward to meeting a certain young boy. Is he here?"

Nicholas laughed, "if I know Storm, he is not very far away."

The two embraced again briefly. Distractedly, the Abbot's attention was drawn to a withered old man who stood patiently, hitherto unnoticed, directly behind the queen. This old man leaned heavily on a stout wooden staff carved along its length with many different runes and symbols.

The Abbot looked almost boyish as he stepped around Sara to greet the man that hid within the queen's shadow. "Kalon? Is that really you?"

The Archmage's face erupted into a volcanic grin. "My young pupil looks well in these dark and difficult times. The monastic life seems to suit you well. I am looking forward to visiting this famed Three Towers of yours."

Kalon was attired in a simple grey robe drawn to his thin body by a simple belt of white silk. The vestment was long and covered the old man's feet, hands, and neck. Few recognized the old man for what he was, the last vestige and only survivor of the Archmage race. In contrast to the youthful queen, Kalon had not resisted so well the ravages of old age. His face was a mass of wrinkles and folded skin. Across the left cheek there raked a jagged scar that crept evilly toward his left eye. Softly, Nicholas spoke a further tender greeting to his old friend. However, only one person in the crowd caught the strangeness of the conversation rendered in Old Sardish. The wild-haired Storm thought it a rather odd way to welcome an old friend. Roughly translated, the Abbot had said, "the days of balance draw to a close."

With formal pleasantries concluded the royal party, accompanied by forty gaily-dressed foot soldiers, was escorted toward the old town hall. The meetinghouse had been prepared festively to play host to the finest banquet ever experienced upon the Sardik Plains. Storm, determined to get a closer look at Sara, raced off up a shortcut across a hilly ridge. He reached the top of the river trail just as the royal party came into view. Leaving Zira pining at the foot of the tree, Storm shinned quickly up a scraggly alder that extended out across the roadway. Nicholas and his sister huddled in serious conversation as they proceeded up the hill. Despite, the heat, the queen had chosen to walk up the hill to the town, which only endeared her even more to the hard-working common folk. As they moved within a few strides of Storm's hiding place, the queen paused suddenly. She cast her eyes into the branches looking directly up at Storm. Royal pools of blue engaged emerald orbs of forest green. Storm held the gaze for a momentary eternity during which time, thousands of images exploded into his mind. The boy felt dizziness overcome him followed by a feeling of vertigo. This sensation continued long after he met the dusty road with a dramatic thud. The very last thing he remembered, before succumbing to peaceful oblivion, was the aura of Zira standing protectively over him, and the concerned face of a queen rushing to his side.

Chapter Twelve

Dragons

When Storm at last awoke he found himself lying on a mattress of soft straw with John sitting patiently beside him. "Oh so you decided to wake up then," chuckled the monk. Storm tried to sit up but felt a shooting pain rip through his left side.

"What happened to me?" asked Storm.

"You fell out of a tree you daft lad. Gave everyone quite the scare and stirred up quite the commotion. The whole royal party stopped in its tracks and the queen herself tended to you. On Queen Sara's orders you were placed in the royal litter and carried here to the blacksmith's house. Everyone was extremely concerned, that was no small fall that you took. It is well into the night now and you have been asleep for a good many hours. Did the beauty of her highness bedazzle you so that you had to fall out of a tree in order to get a closer look?"

Storm went to punch his friend, but thought better of it when pain surged through his shoulder. From the window floated the sounds and smells of a town in celebration. There was singing, dancing, storytelling, and Storm could only imagine the mouth-watering delights he was missing out on. "Where is the queen?" inquired Storm.

John wrung out a wet cloth in the bowl beside the bed and placed it upon the boy's forehead. "Queen Sara has gone up to Three Towers for a meeting with Abbot Nicholas and Archmage Kalon. She left strict orders that you were to be made comfortable and that you were absolutely not to be moved until morning. Now, would the little tree-climber like anything to eat?"

Storm felt his stomach grumble at the mention of food and realized that he hadn't eaten anything since before dawn that day.

"Yes please John, and could you bring some food for Zira too?" The wolf curled up at the foot of the bed, perked up his ears at the mention of his name. Rising to his feet, the adolescent cub carefully stepped across the bed-sheets and nuzzled his master's cheek.

John had only been gone a few moments when an almighty commotion erupted outside the forge. The music and dancing stopped. Sounds of laughter and merriment were swiftly replaced with fearful shouts and high-pitched screams. Ignoring the pain, Storm raised himself to the height of the window ledge. Outside, people ran chaotically with fear blistered upon terrified faces. With painstaking slowness, Storm pulled back the bedcovers and dragged himself to his feet. Little light penetrated the bedroom from the open window. Storm felt his way along the inner wall until he felt the door frame. Outside, the sounds of pandemonium swelled to a fearful crescendo. Eerily, the villager's screams were soon joined with the sound of powerfully beating wings. Little could prepare the boy for the sight that greeted his eyes when he at last pushed open the door. A night demon swooped down in front of him snatching up a helpless little boy who vanished kicking and screaming into the night sky, his cries lost in the chaos of the ground battle. The winged monsters were everywhere preying upon the townspeople like rabid locusts. Some of the men had bravely taken a stand against the barbaric onslaught. Armed with shovel, hoe, and broomstick they fought courageously to protect the women and children.

Nausea erupted in unbidden waves and he felt his stomach heave. Helplessly, Storm watched from the doorway as the demons continued to sweep unwitting villagers into the sky and on to certain death. The delicate flesh of human-kind was no match for the razor-like talons of the winged monsters. During the massacre, John emerged from the Great Hall. The monk broke into a run when he saw Storm exposed in the doorway. John was not the only one to have noticed the vulnerable boy. Maula, the demon's gargantuan leader also sighted his sought after prey.

With a guttural battle cry, Maula dove from the heavens in all his venomous glory. Storm stood mesmerized by the cruelty that played out around him, oblivious to the threat from above. Tears flooded vision as he swallowed back the bile that rose in his mouth. He did not see the shadow of the winged beast pursue him. John could only watch in paralyzed horror as Maula's fatal talons extended their death grip toward his unsuspecting ward. Storm smelled the putrid breath of the night demon before he saw him. Staggering against the doorframe, he instinctively threw up hands to protect his face. A flash of silver burst out of the black room. Zira lunged past Storm, sinking angry teeth deep into the night demon's scaly scapula. Maula screamed out in fury as he fought against his attacker. In that moment of distraction, John grabbed Storm by the collar and threw him roughly back into the house.

Zira, meanwhile, clung defiantly to the dragon's shoulder refusing to relinquish his grip. Maula rose into the air and, with his unshackled arm, reached across his body. Cruel nails bit into the snow wolf's neck as the demon took grip, flinging Zira violently against the side of the forge.

The villagers, inspired by the heroic courage of the young snow wolf, fought with the passion and determination of seasoned warriors. Yet still the evil ones wreaked injury and death upon the populace. Just as the arms that wielded pitchfork, stick, and hoe began to tire, a reprieve was ushered by the arrival of an unlikely winged savior.

Lord Damal had dispatched the dragirds for the self-same purpose as Lord Vilus. Unfortunately, neither dark-lord had considered the ramifications of their respective servants meeting. Dragirds and Night Demons both shared loyalty to the dark. However, their insatiable hatred for the other was unparalleled. When the dragirds came into sight of their most mortal enemies, all remembrance of Damal's orders faded into irrelevancy.

Chapter Thirteen

Extinction

    Long ago, long before true time dawned, mighty dragons had roamed the world. There were two orders of dragons, the higher and the lesser dragons. The higher order beasts ruled Terrus, whereas the lower orders were forced into servitude. The latter built the great dragon palaces and mined for treasures buried deep within the forming mountains. The higher order dragons lived easily on the fruits of their servant's labor. Ultimately, the lesser dragons rebelled and met their ruling masters in battle at the Field of Garthlet. The conflict raged for many moons and through history the event had come to be referred to as the Clash of Fires. The lesser dragons might have won the war had it not been for the treachery of Gargelon. Gargelon, was a descendent of the night demons and had persuaded his family to run from the field of battle, leaving the other families to fend for themselves. Gargelon, believed such a move would endear him to the higher order dragons. Every family of lesser order dragons were exterminated save a small group of dragirds. The higher order dragons banished all dragirds from the land of plenty and sent into exile with them the night demons. The treacherous withdrawal had never deserted the collective memory of the dragirds. Many battles had been fought through the millennia between the two last surviving lesser order families. There in Sard, as the villagers cowered beneath the devastation that once was a town, the bloodiest conflict the two dragon families had ever fought was joined.

The dragird brood crashed into Sard like an angry tidal wave. Night demons let fall their two-legged prey and turned to meet their hated cousins. Black scales clashed with green and sparks of energy filled the skies. The anguished howls of wounded lizards flooded the streets. Many citizens crept stealthily from hiding places to watch the deathly confrontation. Others took the opportunity to scoop up the remaining children and run for the refuge of underground cellars and salt rooms. The battle was joined in the air but dragirds and demons alike experienced many a death blow in the sardish dust. Evolution and natural selection had created some startling adaptations respectively. While the dragirds had lost the ability to breath fire they had evolved to almost twice their created size. Their demon counterparts were significantly smaller in size but no less violent or barbaric. Dragird jaws and talons fought night demon fire and claw. The nightmare unfolding before the townspeople's eyes was bloodied and horrific. High above the meeting hall a demon was locked in a fatal embrace with a giant dragird. Fire cascaded across the dragird's back and the pungent odor of burning flesh and feathered wing fused with the acrid smell of opaque body fluid that oozed from vicious wounds inflicted through lethal bite and scratch. Howls of rage and pain sprung intermittently between the two combatants. Suddenly, the dragird, wings afire, plummeted toward the ground. Determinedly, he refused to relinquish the hold upon his adversary, and the body weight of the defeated caused the demon to fall too. So it was that two dragons crashed through the thatched meeting hall roof. People scattered as the two dragons continued their convulsive battle to the death on the floor of the banquet room.

Similar bloody contests raged at every turn. Storm lay oblivious to the fearsome struggle. His injuries from the earlier fall combined with shock forced his body to succumb to a state of unconsciousness. John stood protectively over the comatose boy, praying in earnest to Nishu. The monk had not meant to be so rough in pulling Storm to safety, but what else could he have done?

Meanwhile, the events of the night had not gone unnoticed by the residents of Three Towers. Nicholas, Sara, and Kalon had been sequestered in deep discussion when news of the battle arrived.

Their conference had been interrupted by the panicked beating of a brother's fist upon the study door. The alarm bells of Three Towers clamored with disturbing dissonance. Before the bells had finished their sixth pull the Abbot and his two guests were hurrying into the courtyard. Nicholas stepped quickly to the gate tower and asked for an explanation. Brother Jentry pointed a shaking finger toward the town at the foot of the mountain. Even from this height and distance the torched houses could be clearly discerned. Not only was the chaos visible it was also disconcertingly audible. Terrified screams and shouts sang from the innocent Sardinians. Nicholas turned to Kalon, angry emotion ablaze in his eyes.

"The dark! They seek to capture Storm. We must protect the boy and my people."

Kalon took the two sentinels by the hand and held his staff above his head. The world shimmered and dissolved around them. A blinding light seared into their vision. When night returned and sight regained they found themselves standing in the meeting hall. An eerie distortion of sound echoed above their heads. Kalon, realizing the impending danger, uttered a spell of protection and immediately a shell of blue light enveloped them. Seconds later the ceiling exploded into splintered fragments. Two mighty beasts enjoined in a hateful embrace crashed through the thatch continuing their macabre dance of death upon the cratered floor. As the trio stepped towards the main hall door, Kalon dissolved the protective sphere from around them. The wizard gestured toward the heavy doors and they swung outward. The streets outside were a mosaic of carnage and blood. Bodies, human and otherwise, littered the ruined roadways. Houses burned and people ran confusedly amidst the rubble. Yet still dragird and night demon fought their vicious conflict. Few winged combatants had escaped injury and many lay dead or dying upon the blood-spattered earth.

The normally peaceful and even-tempered Abbot felt his pulse quicken and the beginnings of rage stir within his breast. Sensing his emotion, Sara reached out a hand of reassurance, or perhaps it was a hand of warning. Whatever the motive, it engendered little notice from the patriarch. Nicholas moved away from his sister and stood in the middle of what had once been the high street.

Casting his eyes to the skies, he regarded the beasts of evil with pitiless disdain. Without warning he raised his hands high above his head and began to utter words in the old speech. Seconds later his entire body began to glow with a phosphorescent hue.

"No!" The warning rose unheard from Sara. She lunged forward to reach her ghostly brother. Showing surprising strength for a frail old man, Kalon held her back. Helplessly, the two watched as Nicholas drew to him the very life power of the earth. Thin strands of light burst forth from the ground. Whites, yellows, blues, reds, greens, oranges, purples, and silver luminescence leapt towards the human conductor. The Abbot's form became enshrouded in a prism of dazzling light. Throughout the drawing, the holy man's eyes remained closed but now they splayed open wide. Crackling energy burst from his extended fingers leaping skyward like a cross-bolt, impaling the night demon nearest to him. Such was the power of the cast that no death scream was forthcoming. Indeed moments after impact no evidence of its existence remained. Time and again, the incensed Abbot cast forth projectiles of pure light and repeatedly, a dragon evaporated into space. This pyrotechnic assault was a fearsome power to behold. One by one, dragird and night demon experienced pure light, and one by one the lesser order dragons lost their lives. After several minutes of the Abbot's violent assault, the minions of the dark began to accept the seriousness of this new enemy. The skies were no longer saturated with beasts of evil. Dragird and night demon, fearing for their lives, began to attempt escape. The relentless sentinel allowed no reprieve. Those that tried to flee found an inescapable band of light pursuing them. Others among them turned their attention to the source of their destruction. The braver of the breed attacked with vehement fury only to be dispatched with powerful efficiency by the human conductor. Electricity fizzled as it leapt from hyper-extended extremities. As the last demon sucked in its final breath, Nicholas collapsed in a crumpled heap on the roadway. Sara was at his side immediately, cradling his silver head tenderly in her arms. Tears welled up in her eyes.

"Nicholas! My dear impetuous Nicholas, why oh why my dearest brother? We could have helped you. We could have shared the burden of such a task. What power have we now passed to the dark through your sacrifice?" Sara sobbed and continued to rock backwards and forwards.

The Abbot's eyes flickered open briefly. He smiled up at his sister. "I had no choice dear sister. These were my people. So much death, so much sorrow, I could not let such a crime go unpunished. Sara! Storm must go with you to Meridia. He is a catcher and he must pursue prophecy. If the light is to survive and if we are to protect the inhabitants of this world you cannot fail him. Let Kalon be his teacher. He must reach Cartis before the dark can touch his heart. Promise me sister. Promise me that you will help him."

Through tear-streaked vision Sara nodded her affirmation and whispered, "I swear upon our mother's grave, I will see him a man untainted by the dark. The balance will be preserved." Then, amid the silence of devastation Abbot Nicholas died.

Chapter Fourteen

Wakening

Lord Rune stood pouring over his maps in the inner-most chamber of his citadel when the wakening began. Ripples of energy coursed through the ground on which he stood. Without warning threads of light were sucked like a vortex toward the dark-lord. In death, Nicholas, once sentinel of light, could no longer control the power vested to him by the Aruk. As his soul lifted toward Tellus, the final resting place of mortals, his spirit fought desperately to follow. Alas such pursuit was never permitted. True death was only realized in the divine separation of body, soul, and spirit. To die meant the three could no longer co-exist. The children of Terrus grew up singing a nursery rhyme that told of such a struggle:

The old man died and now he's dead
Fast asleep upon his bed
The soul to Tellus travels
The spirit then unravels.
One goes up the other goes down
Soul is happy as a clown
Spirit cries and gnashes teeth
Body dead succumbs to grief.
Good soul to paradise, bad soul to hell
Where spirit goes no man tell
Good spirit dance and play
Bad spirit run away.

Even as he spoke his final words to Sara, Nicholas knew immediately the dire consequence of what he had done. So much life power had been surrendered in his attack against the lesser dragons. Not only that, but he had lashed out in such revengeful manner that his actions, although worthy in intent, fed the dark powers that sought to extinguish light. With the ninth son's birth, mortality for each sentinel was assured, at least until such time as the balance was restored, or one side vanquished the other. The harsh realization that his selfless sacrifice for the people he loved would ultimately lead to more power for the dark was agonizing. Even as the body of the Abbot lay in death, tears fell from gentle eyes. Now in passing, his spirit sought vainly for reunion with his now departing soul. The light of his spirit traveled with immeasurable speed across the surface of Terrus. This once, gentle, tender, loving, selfless, spirit even now came unknowingly to Lord Rune.

Lord Rune felt the life energy fizzle around him. Like the electro-magnetic fields of the North and South, the death of light was drawn inexorably to the life of dark. Rune felt himself lifted from the floor. The map held in his right hand instantly disintegrated as it fell to the ground dissolving to ashes before his very eyes. Rune's entire body became encapsulated in an eerie orange glow. Tentacles of air and bands of pulsing electrons plunged into his body. Rune's hair whipped backwards and he unleashed an agonizing scream. The body convulsed as light scorched skin, hair, and bone. In concert to his screams, more light jumped from the granite floor searing unprotected eyes and throat. By now Lord Rune hung spread-eagled some twenty spans from the floor. This forced levitation left every limb distended. Still the electrical force refused to relinquish its hold. Finally, the dark-lord felt his mind begin to return control to his limbs. Throwing back his head, he laughed wildly and slowly returned his body to the floor. Charcoaled robes hung limply to his musculature frame. He continued to laugh with ugly delight as he viewed his increased form within the looking glass. The dark-lord was still enjoying his newfound, and quite unexpected, gift of power when fearful servants arrived to attend his summons.

***

Lord Vilus also stood alone in his private quarters when the wakening arrived. He saw the creeping filaments of light before he felt them. Fearing an attack, he backed away from the ripples of radiance as they crept ominously towards him. Carefully, he retreated away from the throne and tripped clumsily down the steps toward the door. Still the light pursued him. Years of languishing in the dark made the uninvited guest a torturous housemate. Eyes burned raw in their hollow sockets. Covering his face in his hands he ran blindly through the hallways of Baticus. The unplanned path took him upwards toward the tower. Stepping out on to the starless battlement, he slammed shut the wooden door behind him. Vilus stooped over with hands on knees wheezing and forcing clean air through the respiratory sacs of unclean lungs. All was quiet for a brief moment, then the very ground and air around him became alive. Sensuous luminescence stole from cracks in the masonry, a ghost-like apparition of white energy contortedly extended through the tower door. The dark-lord bellowed a fearful rebuke long before the first light finger caught his leg and began to seductively entwine itself about his body. Vilus fell to the floor sobbing loudly, pleading for his life. Still the light swept towards him covering his entirety with its willful cloak. Tiny intangible claws raped his mind and body. The writhing evil within him embraced the capture of power. Within moments his terrified demeanor transformed into gibbering giggles. Then the pain arrived. Electricity careened into every orifice and pore. The darklord laughed hysterically as he lost all control of his body. Urine flowed neglectfully down his leg and spittle covered his lower lip. As quickly as the light arrived it departed, leaving Vilus a blubbering madman atop the tower of Baticus Castle.

*　*　*

Lord Damal had waited impatiently throughout the night for news from his Dragird raiding party. One thing he was not known for was patience. Indeed, three eunuch slaves had already been butchered that night as a vehicle to stem the tide of his frustration and impatience at the wait. Now he prowled the shadowy galleries looking for a new distraction. The first door he came to was one of the many harems he kept within the palace walls. Forcefully, he pushed open the oaken doors and thundered across the threshold. The room was vast. Twenty of the most beautiful women on Terrus looked up at their Lord. Scantily clad they lounged gracefully atop cushions of silk and goldweave. Not one of the women met directly his gaze. It was no secret amongst them that few of Damal's lovers ever returned to the harem suite after a night spent in his private chambers. Damal stood selectively inspecting each body. Never once did he look into a woman's eyes. Why should he? The dark-lord had no interest in facial features that served little purpose other than to remind him of the coldness and evil that resided within his own callous heart. Finally, he made his decision choosing a lithe ebony girl not more than fifteen winters in age, along with a buxom, sandy-haired woman. Both females were tall and shapely with large breasts and tapered hips. He pointed to them and immediately a eunuch ripped off their clothes for further inspection. Damal nodded and ordered them to follow him. He led them, nude, down the hallway and up a winding stairway with solid gold railings. A shaved man-servant quickly opened the door and led his Lord into an exquisitely furnished bed chamber. Damal lay down on the massive four-poster bed and beckoned for the women to join him. Fearing the displeasure of their dark liege they complied with all that their sex could offer.

    Damal had just started to become aroused by the concubine's generous attentions when the first tremors of the wakening began. Enraptured by the silky soft forms that sensuously caressed his loins and chest, he knew no warning. A scythe of raw energy thrust through the floor and manacled Damal to the bed. As he screamed, bands of light fettered him to the bedposts and beads of radiation pulsed through his body. Turgescent skin rippled with chaotic sensation. Hands both tangible and intangible rubbed his naked body. At first the caress was tender and gentle. Then suddenly it became violent and angry. Damal torn between pleasure and fury, attempted to rise and smite his concubines. Raising his head, he watched tongues of flame spring from the rich floor rugs. The girls looked up in horror as the bed burst into a raging inferno. Their screams echoed sinisterly with the passionate urging of the chained dark lord who let out wild convulsive shouts of euphoria. Blazing bolts of light surrounded his expanding form; shaking him violently to a mighty climax. Then the flames were gone. Exhausted Lord Damal staggered nakedly to his feet. The entire bed lay in ashes and two charred skeletons, still adorned in jeweled necklaces and bracelets, lay crumpled within the cinders.

∗ ∗ ∗

The last dark-lord to accept the wakening was Lord Brack. Situated far away within the southern reaches, the final vestiges of the passing Abbot's spirit met him last. As if expecting such an event, he sat patiently awaiting its arrival. Seated in the atrium of his fortress estate beside a black-carved fountain, he listened to the pattering of water upon the tile and gazed unseeingly out toward the Northern night. Across the horizon a distortion in the fabric of darkness heralded the coming of the wakening. A far distant shimmering argued for an early dawn. The precipitous light came at first unsurely then gaining in confident impetus it poured across the southern passage, diving and prancing in the depths of the Icealic Ocean. Ancient ice floes melted at the finest of touches. Steam rose venting from the ocean surface as the heat of light slept briefly upon the dormant cold of darkness. Brack entertained himself solicitously with a wry grin and dreams of future conquest. The fact an immortal had died surprised him little. All the fuss his brothers were making over the ninth son was a distraction he could live with. As the silent maelstrom neared, Brack relaxed and opened his mind in preparation for the onslaught. Sensing this mental preparation, the light seemed to pause briefly in flight to consider such a challenge. Yet still the light advanced and soon dazzling specters of energy and electricity attacked the waiting sentinel. Like an arrow to its target, Brack absorbed the energy willingly. Unlike his ill-prepared kindred, he suffered little physical pain and distress throughout the wakening. He merely captured each individual spark, pulse, and electrified light particle with a mental cognitive net. Light pulsed through him searching for a hold. Brack laughed as he felt the dying spirit of Nicholas become trapped in the intricate mental web he had engineered. Whereas his brothers had felt a surge and increase in their respective powers as Nicholas surged through their world, Brack not only experienced the surge, but was able to capture and confine much of the power before it considered escape. Lord Brack was under no illusions of grandeur. He would be the most powerful man on Terrus and there was nothing his foolish brothers could do about it.

Chapter Fifteen

Grief

"Mother, why do you weep?" The little girl, no more than eight summers in age, carried on her head a pitcher of water from the well. Crossing over to the hearth, she took her mother's hand in her tiny fingers. Terel sobbed loudly and hugged tightly the sweet young child.

"I am crying because this past night I lost a dear friend. I cry because he leaves this earth without a good-bye or a hug from the older sister who loves him so. I cry because the world I have come to love and treasure might now change before my very eyes. Sweet Reesa, I cry because my heart is heavy and I love my children very much."

From outside the farmhouse door floated the sound of singing voices. Terel smiled. The children had all awoken early to help her as usual with the household chores. Now joyful voices were raised in celebration for a new dawn. From the milking sheds wafted girl's voices joining with a treble accompaniment from the hay loft.

In the shadows of the farm kitchen, Terel sat quietly recuperating from her spiritual wounds. Several hours earlier she had been roused from her sleep by the wakening. Nicholas had cried out and called her by name as his soul departed Terrus. She had not been prepared for such a loss. An unseen force had stolen into her bedroom and over-powered her senses. From deep inside, she felt power wrenched forcefully away from her. No matter how hard she fought to recapture that which was drawn away, no enchantment, summoning, or earnest plea could prevent departure. Now she rocked alone beside the fireplace wondering what calamity had occurred to force a rupture in the Aruk.

Terel lived very humbly in the village of Marindoc. Marindoc was a gateway settlement, situated at the Goshan Pass which spanned the narrow canyon separating the Adearan Plains from the Black Mountains. Terel lived reclusively upon an expansive acreage of farmland. She kept to herself and entertained very few guests. Kerridge Farm had been the only home she had known since the accursed Aruk had been initiated. However, despite her solitariness, she was never alone. A few hundred years previous her first visitor had been a young orphan girl who had knocked upon her doorstep begging for food. Terel's heart had been overrun with compassion and she had invited the girl to stay. Now almost ten centuries later she found her door-step had become a temporary, or permanent, stage for many a child's journey. Currently, twelve children aged between four and fourteen called the farm home. Some were transient and stayed only but a few nights. Others, like Reesa, remained for five years or more. Terel turned no child away and so they continued to come. Now as she sat gently stroking her foster child's head, she wondered what evil was unleashed upon the world with the passing of her brother.

* * *

Of all of Elam's children, Ryad had been the closest to Nicholas. So it was that he came to feel the greatest pain and anguish in the early hours of morning. Like Terel, he had been sleeping, albeit many hundreds of miles distant in the Shupan garrison. When the siblings of light were forced to take up residence in the four points of the compass, they had each found themselves called to humble vocations. Nicholas had always been a member of the holy orders as monk, priest, cleric, or abbot. Terel, found her fate sealed in the tilling of the earth and the teaching of children. It had fallen to Sara, as the oldest, to carry forth the monarchy, albeit a quite reluctant acceptance. Ryad, on the other hand was a warrior. For a millennium he had lived as a sword-master. The lord of light had fought in every conflict since the Aruk's inception. He had died a hundred deaths upon the battlefield but no point of steel or shaft of wood had power over him. Every death was but a fleeting moment as fatal wounds healed themselves. Once he had been pronounced dead and suffered a burial with all the rituals of state. On that occasion he had remained trapped within a coffin for a week until Queen Sara had discovered the error. A thousand years had made Ryad an accomplished warrior and general. With the cross-bow and sword he knew no equal. Few in the known world could compete even with his mastery in hand-to-hand combat, or accuracy with knife and dagger. For the last fifty years he had been assigned as swordmaster to the Shupan Garrison. It was no secret that Lord Brack entertained thoughts of conquest and indeed had pursued such ambition throughout the far southern reaches. It was Ryad's responsibility to maintain a constant vigilance and surveillance upon his ambitious cousin.

Ryad and Nicholas had been born only a year apart. They grew up the closest of brothers and shared together all the discoveries and joys of childhood. Now his boyhood shadow cast a shadow no more. The wakening had been fierce in the south. It seemed that the spirit of Nicholas yearned to once more experience Ryad's companionship. The Abbot's subconscious flew upon an isolated thread of light yanked from the main flow that streamed toward Lord Brack's domain. The naked filament of light worried the sleeping soldier awake. Ryad extended his palm catching the spark in his hand. Instantly, the image of his childhood friend awoke in his mind's eye. Nicholas pointed to a green-eyed boy asleep upon a straw-lined cot. As the image faded, whispered words issued from the vision, "protect him, teach him, love him." Then the light died. A raging wind burst through the guardroom door picking up the Sentinel and hurling him against the back wall. Ryad felt his internal organs convulse and tear as an invisible thief reached inside his heart to extract what energy it could lay claim to. Never in his life had he experienced such excruciating pain. No battle scar or sword wound could prepare him for the rape of his power.

It was many hours before Ryad could bring himself to move. Every movement brought with it tidal waves of painful nausea. Finally, he sank to his knees and vomited the entire contents of his stomach. On bleeding knees he retched convulsively while salty tears flowed freely. There was no doubting the events of the night. Nicholas was dead, and the ninth son was in danger. No longer could he risk being careless in battle, he now lived as mortal as the soldiers he commanded. Life would never again be the same.

* * *

Sara barely noticed the stealthy burglary of her Aruk powers. So overcome with grief was she, that physical pain registered little recognition. For long hours she remained upon the roadway cradling her beloved brother's body in her dust-stained arms. Kalon had seen to the disposal of the dead and dying bodies of fallen dragird and night demon. The surviving townspeople wandered the ruined town in a daze. Of the hardy population, less than half remained to re-build their town.

John continued to conduct his vigil over Storm. The boy had remained unconscious throughout the entire conflict. The first inklings of daylight were prodding the veil of night and with the prompting of dawn Storm began to stir. He sat bolt upright and tears gushed from his eyes. "John!"

"I am here my son," replied the monk.

Tears poured fast and freely. Between waves, the boy sobbed inconsolably. "I felt Abbot Nicholas die, John. He appeared to me in my dream. He sat me on his knee and took me by the hand. He was so sweet to me. He told me that I was loved and that he was proud of me. Then I saw dragons and people dying. Then I felt him die. John, what are we to do? How can he be dead?"

John shifted uncomfortably and smoothed away hysterical strands of black hair. "It was just a dream Storm, I am sure he is safely tucked up in bed at Three Towers." Even as he spoke the words, John knew the import of the boy's words. He too had felt the awesome power that had been unleashed right outside the door. It was all too quiet outside now, but John had been awake for every scream, every howl, and for every lightning bolt, and thunder clap.

"Wait here while I ensure it is safe. And Storm, whatever you do, do not come outside."

John left quickly and Storm reluctantly lay back down. A moment later he sprang upright again. Zira! Where was his beloved Zira?

"Zira, Zira where are you?" The boy struggled to his feet and unlatched the door. Staggering into the street, his attention was immediately drawn to a circle of people less than a cart length from where he stood. Staving off faintness, he struggled over to the throng. Storm shouldered his way through the circle of people. There in front of him lay the ashen, lifeless body of the Abbot. Sensing the boy's pain, Sara looked up and beckoned the boy to her. Together they cried their tears of grief while all those around them wept for family members and friends recently buried.

Kalon returned to the side of his mistress and gently disentangled her hands from those of her dead brother. The queen rose, drawing Storm with her. Tenderly she brushed the wild hair away from his face. Kneeling down in the dust, she looked up into his eyes.

"Storm, my brother loved you as a son. He has entrusted your care to me. I ask that you and Brother John come with me to Meridia. I realize that this is your home but your life may be in great danger if you remain here. Will you come?"

Suddenly, Storm broke away from her embrace. "Zira, where is Zira? He fought off the dragon and saved my life. Has anyone seen the Latsu?"

"I have him my young friend." Wolfy strode into the open with the lifeless body of the snow wolf draped across his muscled arms. Had it not been for his unmistakable height and width he would have been difficult to recognize. No living citizen was caked in more blood, dirt, and angry wound than the farmer. He had fought all night long and spent the entire morning helping to bury the dead including, the bodies of his wife and five children. Now he stood before his queen devastated, exhausted, beaten, and grief stricken.

Not a whimper sounded from the cub's mouth. Storm rushed to Wolfy and with tears clouding his vision, took his most beloved companion into his youthful arms.

Child of Night

"Noooooooooooooooooo! I will not have every one I love die on me. Zira wake up." The boy shook the animal with all the strength his tiny frame possessed. Still the wolf remained motionless. In answer to the boy's emotion the wind picked up. Storm's eyes glazed over and he began to talk intelligibly in a language older than the world. The wind became a gale that centered upon the boy. Everyone was thrown backwards leaving the lonesome youth within the eye of the conjured tempest. Storm's legs buckled and he fell to his knees. A single scythe of lightning flared from the ground and into his fragile frame. An aura of white light enveloped boy and wolf. Within the maelstrom, Storm sent his conscious out into the darkness seeking for any strand of life that remained within his friend. He raced past slower life threads, all of which fought desperately to hold on to mortality. Accelerating his thoughts, he recognized the distinctive differences in light and energy. Every living entity emitted its own unique signature. There were trees, children, men, women, animals, mythical beasts, ocean creatures, and other components of creation. Swimming amongst the energy of those that recently died, he searched chaotically for any sign of Zira's life force. Storm felt the speed of passage increase disparately as the Tellus ceiling dove to meet him. Suddenly, he caught hold of a familiar signature, no not one but two. Just above him, just beyond reach, he viewed the frayed and tattered soul of the Abbot about to pierce the firmament veil. Beside him soared the mercurian light of Zira. Storm threw out a link in a futile attempt to capture the dying tendrils of Abbot and wolf light. All too late the Abbot pierced the veil with Zira right behind him. For the barest of instants the matrix of power slowed and rewound ever so slightly. Storm caught hold of the finest particle of silver light and pulled with every sinew of conscious desire and unconscious thought. Alone he was lost, but the Abbot in one last selfless act of love drove his tail of light sideways across the veil. Silver met the blue barrier. Light exploded as the Abbot was forever separated from earthly life. In the moment he left the plane, Storm felt one last sensation directed toward him from the dying blue. The most fleeting, most tender of kisses floated through light and dark to land directly upon the boy's ethereal forehead. Zira, experienced the violence of the catch. Silver fused with the green of Storm's life force. Human intelligence joined immutably with animal sentience. Boy and wolf became one as they suffered every pain and endured every trial. Each knew the other's happiness, and together they rode the purest emotion of all back towards the earthly plane – love.

When Storm next opened his eyes he found everyone staring at him, their faces a picture of fear and undeniable concern. The boy placed Zira on the ground and watched in awe as from every direction, the earth returned Zira's spirit. Moments later, the snow wolf flickered open soft yellow eyes that spoke only to his master. Storm heard the voice of Zira in his head.

Thank you dear friend, I thought I had passed and now we live again to hunt together. I will forever be at your side.

In like silence Storm responded, *I too am indebted to your bravery courageous one.*

Kalon looked on aghast as if not believing what he saw. The two somehow communicated, and only he understood that Storm had retrieved his companion from a place that not even an Archmage had powers to travel. Who was this boy and what purpose would he serve in the war that was surely to come to Terrus? What side would he ultimately fight for?

Chapter Sixteen

Retribution

During Storm's sojourn to the soul matrix, a creature of the dark stirred. Kalon had been efficient in his quest to eradicate the dead dragon bodies. Despite his painstaking thoroughness, he had neglected to check on the two dragons that had earlier crashed through the meeting hall roof. Had he done so, he would have found one body where once there had been two. The dragird had sustained fatal injuries and lay bloodied and cold amid the crumbling masonry. Meanwhile, the demon had invoked a spell of concealment and taken to the sky limply with the power of only one useable wing. The night demon felt his skin blister and wilt. Long hours spent in the dark, ill-prepared him for flight during the daylight hours. The people of Sard had not seen him rise from the old meeting hall. Even the Archmage had not sensed the demon's clandestine departure.

Maula reached Baticus by mid-day. His injuries, while not death-bound, caused him to rest on more than one occasion. Vilus awaited his servant in the ominous surroundings of the caverns that threaded throughout the rock on which the castle was situated. Since the wakening, Vilus had taken to wandering through the dark passageways talking to himself and his leathery pets. Maula approached his master warily. The dark lord was caressing the ears of a large bat that had alighted upon his shoulder. Without turning he spat a greeting.

Caelin Paul

"Well demon, I see that you return alone. Where is the boy child and where are those that traveled with you?"

Maula shifted uneasily from one foot to the other. "Master, we did all that you asked. We attacked Sard after nightfall but then from the east came Dragirds. We were forced to defend ourselves against our most hated enemies. Just as we were about to win the battle and take the ninth son, the old Abbot appeared and summoned magic from the ground. He destroyed every one of us. Dragird and night demon just disappeared."

"Yet, you seem to have escaped the monk's wrath?" remarked Vilus.

The night demon nervously continued, "I barely escaped with my life. After the Abbot died…"

Vilus cut him off in mid-sentence. "Did you say the Abbot died?"

"Yes sir he lay dead in the streets as I fled Sard. Some old magician was wandering around finishing up the Abbot's handiwork. I cloaked myself and he did not sense me depart."

"So Nicholas is gone," said Vilus. "That explains my new found zest for power, and that explains why now I have the power to do this." Vilus swung around casting his hand in an arcing motion before him. Energy rippled through his emaciated frame and leapt towards the retreating night demon. Maula let out a mighty shriek and erupted into a blue conflagration. Vilus laughed as his servant burned to death before his gleeful eyes. When at last the flames puttered out, having used up completely the dragon's body, Vilus went and stood over the ashes saying: "No one can say I am not a man of my word. I said there would be consequences if you failed me, and I think this most definitely constitutes a failure." With that the madman snapped back his head and burst into eerie laughter that echoed throughout the caverns and on into the Terrus afternoon sun.

Chapter Seventeen

Aftermath

The brethren at Three Towers had never before experienced such grief and sorrow. For five days now, they had prepared the ceremony of last passage to the Sardinian dead. It was a solemn and unpleasant duty that no one at the abbey relished. Their beloved Abbot had been the last to receive blessings before his body was committed to the monastery crypt beneath the south wall. Every brother had contributed to the burial ceremony and few were able to pay their last respects with composure. Now with last rites ended, the monks cloistered themselves in the chapel to meditate and seek divine inspiration toward the selection of a new Abbot.

Storm had recovered from his injuries and though he bore no physical scars the emotional damage was severe. The same was true for the townspeople. Not a single member of the community was without grief of their own. Every Sardinian had lost a spouse, child or other close relative in the recent conflict. No man had experienced more personal loss than Farmer Barley. Storm's erstwhile friend had watched helplessly as his children and wife were butchered in cold blood while he fought desperately to protect them. He had spoken little since that fateful night and now worked feverishly through every daylight and moonnight hour to help the survivors rebuild the town. Toward week's end, the devastated farmer was summoned by Queen Sara to Three Towers.

The queen, for her part, had slept little also. The kindly monarch spent long hours consoling widows and playing with the town's children. Her personal guard worked tirelessly beside the townspeople building and rebuilding homes, shops, stables, and the destroyed meeting hall. Miraculously, a royal barge had arrived the day after the battle laden full of food, lumber, and medical supplies. Archmage Kalon also walked amongst the population using his healing arts to alleviate the pain and distress of the great many injured.

It was a resilient people who set about repairing the physical structures of Sard. Unfortunately, the emotional and mental state of the builders was precariously fragile. Now, at week's end Sara called a meeting of community leaders. Storm had seen little of the queen, and even less of the townspeople. Since the most recent demonstration of his strange power, John had suggested to the boy that he remain within the abbey walls until things had settled down. Fortunately, Zira was still weak from his battle with the night demon and so Storm spent most of the time watching over his partner's convalescence. Although he had not been formally invited to Sara's town meeting, he stole along the back corridors and slipped through an infrequently used dining room door. The tables had been removed and chairs had been set throughout the hall. Storm cast his eyes around the room. Sixty people or more gathered into the tight space. Half the gathering comprised the monastic brethren of Three Towers. On the right-side of the room sat the mayor and city council. Incredulously, not one member of the eight-man council had lost their lives. Tom, the blacksmith, and Mary, his wife, were there along with some of the guildsmen and elders of the town. Wolfy sat alone towards the back of the room with his head cowed to the floor and shoulders slumped forward. Storm walked tentatively over to his friend. Hesitantly, he extended his hand and placed it on the farmer's shoulder. Storm's small hand was dwarfed by that of the bigger man. Wolfy looked up at the boy with tears flooding his vision. Pulling Storm to him, he enveloped the small boy in a strong bear-like embrace. Quietly, the kindly farmer surrendered to his sorrow. Warm tears fell upon Storm's collar as he felt himself crushed in the desperate emotions of a man who had lost everything precious in life. No one noticed this quiet moment of relinquished feelings save for Sara who had chosen that precise moment to enter the room.

"My dear friends and honest citizens of Sard, thank you for coming to meet with me today. The royal party will be returning to Meridia tomorrow morning and we wanted to take the opportunity to bid you farewell. Words cannot truly describe the feelings of sorrow and despair that I have felt in this last week. Like many of you, I, too lost a part of me the night the dragons came. As some of you are aware, Nicholas was my dear loving and kind brother. He died while trying to protect your town. The Abbot's love for the citizens of Sard was immeasurable. He was loyal and courageous to his last breath. Not only was my brother brave, but so too were the gentle people of Sard who died protecting those they loved. In light of recent events, I have decided to station a royal garrison here in Sard. My only regret is that I have failed to realize the importance of such a decision until now. As a demonstration of my intent I will be leaving behind all fifty of my household cavalry. They will station the formative years of the garrison. I will never again in my reign leave your town so vulnerable and unprotected." As she said these words, tears welled up in her eyes. She had experienced and seen enough pain to last a life-time, but her position allowed little time for personal grieving.

"Brother Tomas also has an announcement that he would share with those gathered here." The monk shyly shuffled forward to the center of the room.

Nervously, the monk took the floor. "Since the passing of our beloved Nicholas, the brothers at Three Towers have been united in spiritual meditation to ask Sulan, for guidance in the selection of a successor. It has fallen by unanimous and heartfelt trust to announce that Brother John will be instated as the next Abbot at Three Towers."

Storm, who had only been half listening to the proceedings, suddenly pricked up his ears at the mention of the name of his guardian John. He could barely suppress his surprise and accompanying fear. If John was to be Abbot, then he would not be going with Storm to Meridia. First, Nicholas, and now John was being stolen away from him. Storm pulled himself away from Wolfy and ran from the room. He was still running when he arrived in the watch-tower bedroom. Storm snuggled into bed beside the wolf and cried with all the release of a mountain stream. He could not help but feel that all the pain, loss, and despair was somehow his fault.

Wolfy had stood up to go after the boy but stopped when he felt a restraining hand upon his shoulder. Turning, he found Brother John standing before him. "A few minutes more Wolfy and the queen would like an audience with us." The farmer shrugged his shoulders and re-seated himself. The remaining meeting consisted of negotiated trade contracts, protection promises, and other gestures of goodwill upon the part of the crown. Finally, the conference was adjourned and Queen Sara bid her subjects a fond farewell. Soon the only people that remained in the room were Sara, Kalon, John, and Wolfy.

The queen turned a kindly eye to Wolfy. "I have heard a great many commendable things about a certain farmer."

Wolfy blushed, "you shouldn't believe everything you hear your highness. One does what he can with the skills the Gods afford him."

"Farmer Barley you are too humble by far. They say you have not slept since the night of battle. Your friends say you have worked every hour of the day to help those who have lost their homes. Many have told stories of how you fought bare-handedly against the dragon brood when they attacked Sard."

"With all due respect your highness, any stories of courage you have heard are but fallacies. I could not protect the only people who ever have meant anything to me. Every member of my family died that night and I could not prevent the scaly bastards from gutting them right in front of mine own eyes." Again tears of anger welled up in the farmer's vision as he mentally revisited the night a dragird ripped out the internal organs of his wife as she stood defiantly protecting their three-year old son.

The queen spoke gently to Wolfy touching him tenderly on the forearm. "You do yourself an injustice. Many of those rebuilding their homes owe their very life to you. Furthermore, there is one who needs you more than any child could need a parent. One who loves you more than you may even appreciate. I have a request of you Wolfy. If your answer is no, I will truly understand. John has been initiated as the new Abbot at Three Towers. Consequently, he needs to be absolved of his guardianship of Storm. The boy is still very much a child and is both lonely and vulnerable. He needs a friend, a guardian, a father. He needs someone who will watch over him and protect him. He needs someone to mentor him and to love him. Wolfy, I would like for that man to be you. Will you come to Meridia with us to help prepare Storm for the uncertain future he is destined to face?"

The farmer was taken aback. "You want me to leave the town of my birth and travel to an island kingdom to protect a boy that has more power in him than the damnable Gods? Why?"

"Remaining here will only feed harsh memories of all that you did not do or could not do. Journeying with us to Meridia may help you heal in time, and will allow you to focus on all that you can and still have left to do. Storm might be powerful, but he is much like the spirited horse that when untrained will race head-long over a precipice because he has never had the benefit of a loving master to care for and protect him. Storm has power it is true. What that power is and what the nature of that power we know not. He could represent the life, or death, for every man, beast, and creature that calls Terrus home. However, he is still only a child. With John's call to the seat of patriarch, and the death of Nicholas, he has lost the two most important friends he has ever had. Losing you would perpetuate fully his devastation."

Wolfy paused in deep thought. His queen was right about one thing. How could he remain in Sard without being tortured by the images and ghosts of his departed wife and children. He loved the wild-haired boy as if he was his own. Could he lose him also? He knew that the decision was not a hard one to make.

Wolfy looked up into his queen's expectant face and nodded. In hushed tones he whispered, "I will come to Meridia."

Chapter Eighteen

Departure

It was a strange party that threaded its way down the snaking mountain trail from Three Towers. The pre-dawn light only added to the somber mood that hung heavily over the company. Six bodies had emerged from the tall abbey gates. By the time they had reached the royal barge, moored on the banks of the Tame, another body had joined the group.

Zira trotted along beside Storm, *"I do not like leaving the home of the prayerful ones."* The words caught Storm by surprise. It had been a week now since the gift of telepathy had been bestowed. At first Zira's conversation had caused intense headaches as the rational mind attempted to control the unusual intrusions. Now the snow wolf's thoughts flowed freely through the boy's mind engendering only minimal levels of discomfort. If Zira experienced any of the self-same discomfort from Storm's mental communication he never volunteered it.

"I will miss my friends too Zira. We will be back to visit them soon I am sure." Even as he sent the words, Storm knew that it would be many a year before he could entertain the possibility of a return to Three Towers.

A solitary member of the royal household cavalry stood guard beside the boat. As they approached he stood erect and beat his right hand across his chest in reverent greeting. Queen Sara was the first to board the vessel, closely followed by Kalon. Wolfy threw his pack onto the deck then stepped across the gunwale.

Child of Night

The sun slyly poked its brow above the tree-line to watch Storm say goodbye to John. Determined to be brave he choked back the tears. The newly appointed Abbot was not so stoical; as he spoke, tears flowed openly.

"I still remember the day you came to us so many moons ago. I remember how little you were when I held you for the first time in my arms. I remember every birthday, every sickness, every mischievous prank, every joyful moment, and even every heart-ache. I have never loved another so completely. You are a remarkable young man. One day our paths again will cross and we together will ride once more in the Northwood. Before you leave there is something I would give you." From beneath his robes he drew out a little red box which he placed in the boy's hand. "It is not much but it is something that in time you might find useful."

Storm opened the box and pulled out a circular white ball composed of a strange metallic substance. The ball was flawless in its workmanship and smooth to the touch. As he rotated the sphere in his hand he felt the ball pulsate and become warm. Imperceptibly the color of the ball began to shift and change. In seconds a white orb had been transformed into a ball of deepest blue.

"It is a collusk," said John. "Nicholas gave it to me when you were very young. He told me to make sure you were given it when the time was right. I do not know if this is the right time but I do know he wanted you to have it. The very essence of the collusk is the energy that feeds life to the earth. When the collusk is white the world is in balance. When it glows blue, as it does now, it can only mean that it feels the power of the light. If red, the ball tells you that the powers of darkness are close at hand. The collusk might well color differently in the presence of other earthly powers, but the color we all must fear the most is black. If the ball should ever become black, then the whole of Terrus will have much to fear. Guard it well Storm. The Abbot believed that this simple sphere was engineered to play a great role in the balance of the Aruk. He never told me exactly what, and I am not even sure he knew. But this I know, keep it close to hand and you might at least have some warning of danger. The night the dragons came the ball burned the reddest shade of blood. It became so hot in my pocket that it burned right through the herringbone thread."

Storm replaced the ball in its box and stuffed it into his pack. "Thank you John, I shall treasure it always."

"I know you will my dear boy." John strode forward and took Storm in his arms in one final heartfelt embrace.

The barge drifted away from its moorings. Storm stood at the bow watching his home fade away. John, on the bank, waved furious farewells and whispered prayers of safe travel. Wolfy appeared beside him and put his massive arm around the boy's shoulders. Tree and sapling lay rooted to the deck, lost in reminiscence of more joyful days spent with friends and family; days forever now lost to them. The barge floated with the current and rounded a high-walled curve in the river. With Sard now out of sight, Kalon, the Queen, and the remaining houseguard stepped out into the middle of the boat. Sara in a soft, almost musical voice asked Storm and Wolfy to join them. Zira stepped down to the lower deck beside his master.

For the first time, Storm noticed that the barge was completely devoid of oars, sail, or any other mechanical vehicle of propulsion. He was also surprised to see that the reigning monarch of Terrus traveled without the protection of her royal guard. Sara seemed to sense the boy's disconcertion and interrupted his thoughts.

"We travel to Meridia today a little swifter than you are probably used to. Do not be afraid though, Kalon is very talented in the arts of transposition."

"Transposition?" enquired Storm.

"Ah yes," the old Archmage grinned. "Transposition is a form of teleportation. We simply see ourselves in an alternate place and transpose our life energies to that place. It is much quicker than relying on unreliable winds and uncooperative currents."

Storm suddenly grew very nervous. He had read a great deal on higher order magic and much of his reading included the stories of unsuccessful transpositions where people were transposed directly into a tree, or an unsuspecting animal. Spells of transposition could not be countered if a mistake occurred during passage or arrival.

"Please hold hands everyone, or in Zira's case a paw." Kalon chuckled to himself as Storm reached down and took Zira's right paw and Wolfy the left. When the circle was complete, the Archmage uttered several unintelligible rhyming verses and without warning, Storm experienced the sensation of falling. The world around him went completely black. He squeezed hard to his right, where once Sara had stood. A reassuring squeeze returned and with an explosion of light the sensation ceased.

"Where are we?" asked Storm as his eyes adjusted to the brightness.

Sara knelt down beside the boy and took his small hands in hers. "This is your new home, at least for as long as you choose to remain with us. Welcome to Meridia."

Chapter Nineteen

Brack

Lord Brack entered the royal box and looked out into the ring. Two mountain cats prowled restlessly within the narrow confines of the arena. Dark stains upon the boards and scatterings of skeletal remains were the only suggestions of the gruesome spectacles viewed here in past weeks. Human sacrifice and blood sports had long been outlawed in Terrus, but Queen Sara's rules had little influence on Brack. Few land barons in the south had the courage to oppose him, and many more swore fealty to the dark-lord in order to prevent from being killed and conquered. Every full moon, Lord Brack would host a spectacle in the appropriately named 'pit.' In all the centuries of bloody entertainment, not a single man or woman had survived their appearance in the arena. Brack was not a merciful man and the pit was his court, trial and jury. The only thing that was unchanging was the verdict, for no man, woman, or child brought before him in the arena was ever found innocent. The court was comprised of the spectators, a mindless mass of cutthroats, pirates, bandits, and thieves that called the southern continent home. The trial always played short and to the point, where the judge, namely Lord Brack, asked few questions and heard even fewer pleas before rendering judgment in the form of some creative fight to the death. Some judgments were effected swiftly, and the defendants knew little of pain. Other convicted souls were less fortunate and endured slow and agonizing deaths.

This night, Lord Brack sat in judgment over ten accused persons. Seven were soldiers from the Illian Garrison, who had been captured by Brack's pirates while defending a trade route to the southern passage. The pirate ship had boarded and burned the Meridian naval vessel killing everyone on board save the seven men that now stood defiantly in front of Brack. The remaining three prisoners consisted of two men in rags and a young peasant woman. The men stood accused of stealing apples from Brack's orchard and the woman of stealing bread from a market stall. The prisoners stood before the royal box atop a narrow platform. Their hands and feet were bound in chains. A mere few feet below them roamed two hungry mountain cats.

A trumpet heralded the opening of court and a tall stringy courtier strode forward to read the charges of the first two captives.

"You are accused of stealing from the royal orchard? How plead you?"

The men were not permitted to answer as a trapdoor slid open and they plunged into the arena below. Eight men in black helms and loin cloths hurried forward from a gate in the wall, holding in their hands angry looking swords. Before the accused understood what was happening, they were grabbed and hauled to a wooden block. While two of the black garbed men kept the cats at bay the remainder of the group forced the groveling prisoners to their knees. Their arms were spread out across blood-stained wooden blocks. The crowd buzzed expectantly. This show of brutality was nothing new but there was always a twist to the dark-lord's dispatch of justice. Brack rose to his feet and a hush descended across the pit.

"You have committed a crime and you must now pay the consequences of that crime. A man may find it difficult indeed to steal from me without the use of his arms." Brack nodded to one of his soldiers. The sun sparkled and danced off the sword blade that was extended high above the mercenary's head. The steel sang loudly as it cut through the air and down through flesh, muscle, and bone. The prisoners screamed out in pain. One slumped down against the block unconscious while the other fell back into the dirt writhing in agony. Quickly the guards departed leaving the maimed prisoners to the mercy of the mountain cats. Brack had seen to it that his pets had been starved for three days to ensure a voracious appetite. Armless, the two men stood no chance against the ferocious beasts. Few in the arena could bear to watch as jagged teeth tore into the helpless innocents. The unconscious man never knew the reality of his death for his soul and spirit departed the ground long before his compatriot. The latter was not as fortunate, his woeful lamentations continued long after internal organs were exposed to the sun.

The next prisoner to be roughly thrust forward was the woman. Again the trumpet blared and the brightly attired announcer stood.

"You stand accused of stealing food from the marketplace. How plead you?"

Throwing herself to her knees the woman begged desperately for compassion, her head pressed subserviently to the boards of the wooden platform. The announcer looked sneeringly down at her then kicked a lever beside his foot. With a high-pitched scream, the girl careened to the dusty floor below. Solitary and alone, the woman stood visibly shaking while all around her the crowd yelled and jeered. Brack once more stood to his feet.

"Woman you have broken the law and so you must be punished. Perhaps in the next life you might see fit to pay for your food instead of stealing it from others." With that he clicked his fingers and a gate at the far end of the arena opened. From the dark depths of the tunnel, there sounded a host of shrill cries. After an interminable wait, five creatures shuffled out into the glazing sunlight. Each wore animal skins and walked uprightly on two legs. They had pronounced hunchbacks and facial deformities that bespake an ugliness not of natural creation. Hair hung in greasy hanks from bulbous heads and emaciated limbs. Their language was a mix of unintelligible grunts and hisses. These creatures, known as Ferrals, were a cannibalistic cave people from beyond the known continent. Every now and again a wandering Ferral would appear in a Southern town stealing away women and children. Ferrals were meat-eaters and not particular as to whether the flesh eaten was fish, animal, bird or human. They stood three man-lengths in height and lived on the instincts of a wild animal. Nostrils flared as the five tried to organize the myriad of smells that flooded their olfactory senses. The woman backed into a shadowy corner sobbing loudly and rocked backwards and forwards on her knees. One of the ferrals disengaged from the group and crossed the pit towards her. Standing over her, saliva dripped from his jaws. In a flash of movement he grabbed the terrified woman by the hair and dragged her kicking and screaming back towards his clan. Nothing could prepare the crowd for what happened next. In a frenzy of fury and brutality, the ferrals began ripping the hysterical woman's limbs from their sockets. The crowd watched in stunned silence as one by one, arms and legs were wrenched from the woman's torso. Blood spurted in all directions as the carnivorous creatures ripped flesh from bone, oblivious to their victim's death cries. In a matter of minutes little evidence remained that a woman existed save for the grisly bone remnants that even now the ferrals continued to gnaw and chew.

The remaining prisoners furiously strained against their chains during the entire feasting session. Tears rolled from some eyes, anger and hate blazed from others. Not a man amongst them could look upon the shattered remains of the kingdom woman. While the arena was cleared below, the royal announcer once more stepped to the podium. His squeaky voice accused the royal navy men of piracy. All seven were dispatched with the self-same efficiency to the pit floor before they could even conjure a word in their own defense. With a cruel glint in his eye, Brack rose one final time to speak.

"You are accused of piracy and for that your crimes carry with them the penalty of death. However, in my leniency I will allow one of you to live. You will all fight for our entertainment, the last man standing will be granted his life."

A large broad-shouldered man stepped forward and spat on the ground. "We are the Queen's men and we will have no part in your sick pleasures. We demand that you release us by order of Queen Sara of Meridia."

Brack threw back his head and laughed hollowly. "Queen Sara of Meridia is of no interest to me and has no claim in my court. Now begin fighting or I shall be forced to kill you myself."

The prisoner's spokesman again spat on the ground and glared up at the dark-lord with all the contempt his spirit could muster. "We will not fight each other for your amusement, nor shall we shed innocent blood unless provoked."

"Then provoked you shall be, you foolish man, and I, will gain great pleasure in watching you die." Brack snapped his fingers and the door opened below the royal box. Twenty armor-clad warriors armed with lethal broadswords stepped over the threshold. The prisoners backed away as much as their chains would allow. Unarmed and manacled as they were, they faced the oncoming inevitability of death with stalwart hearts and great courage. Brack's swordsmen, with blood-curdling battle cries, ran straight towards the retreating sailors. The defiant soldier, Beran, met the first two attackers with angry force. Sending a powerful fist pummeling into one man's helm he then threw the other attacker into the legs of those that ran behind him. Four antagonists went down in the ensuing pile-up and Beran took no time in snatching up two weapons. Throwing a sword to one of his comrades, he then waded into the wave of black armor swinging the broadsword in deathly arcs. Beran was a berserker, known for their unparalleled strength and tenacity in battle. Often their eyes would glaze over as adrenalin pumped rapidly into engorged muscles. Strength increased a thousandfold and one man, while in a berzerker's rage, could fight with the power, speed, and force of five. So it was that Beran fought through the onslaught with blood-thirsty precision in his blows. The crowd was awestruck and warmed to the tall fair-haired warrior. Beran forged relentless in his battle rage. Inspired by their countryman's energy, the remaining three navy men had also armed themselves with swords from the dead.

Beran soon found himself beaten back and cornered by four black swordsmen. Warily they approached their prey. They had seen what damage this madman's sword could do and not one of them wanted to engage the sailor alone. Blood from a gash on his brow momentarily clouded Beran's vision. In the brief moment he wiped it away with the non-sword hand, the most impetuous of his would-be murderers took the chance to thrust a blade towards Beran's exposed flank. Beran whirled sideways as the steely blade found purchase in the wooden wall rather than his gullet. Moving quickly, he swung across his body cleaving the head cleanly from the man's shoulders. Beran gripped the hilt of the embedded sword and drew it swiftly from the wood. Twisting the swords in a circular motion in left and right hand, Beran pushed off from the wall. Without looking he caught the right man's blade, unarming him in one up and down motion, the left man's blade he parried then riposted straight into the neck. Without slowing he brought his foot up into the groin of the central attacker and then drove him off his feet with a powerful head butt. Stepping over the unconscious body, he buried the point of his blade in his adversary's exposed stomach.

Three of Beran's friends had also fought expertly enough to preserve their own lives. When the accounting had concluded, four bodies within the arena still stood, and much to Lord Brack's chagrin not a single one of them belonged to him. Beran stepped forward defiantly pointing his sword at the royal box.

"I, Beran of the House of Landoran, swear loyalty to the one true monarch of Terrus, Queen Sara of Meridia. Any one who swears otherwise is a traitor."

Cries of "Beran, Beran, Beran, Beran," erupted around the arena. Lord Brack was in a rage. How dare these upstart sailors come into his arena and win over his crowd. He jumped to his feet and stood forward on the platform.

"I am a man of my word. I said that all must be punished for their crimes and so it shall be." Brack threw out his arm and dazzling waves of incandescent blue energy congealed around his fingers. When he opened his hand a single beam of pure light leapt outwards toward the three sailors standing off to the side. Before any of them could move, they experienced the briefest sensation of searing heat as skin melted and bone collapsed into ash.

"No!" screamed Beran. To no avail the devastating show of power had left Beran alone in the arena. A deathly hush had descended over the pit. Brack had just begun to summon more en-

Caelin Paul

ergy into his hand when his attention was drawn away by a summoning. So suddenly did the summoning arrive that Brack had no time to counteract its calling.

Chapter Twenty

Beran

Brack arrived abruptly in the royal chambers of Lord Rune. Rune was waiting for him at the dinner table. Within his hand, Brack still held the remnants of blue energy. In his anger, he released this energy directly at Rune's feasting table. Blue light shot forth from his hand shearing the heavy oaken board in half and sending plates, fruit bowls, and crystal goblets scattering in every direction.

"How dare you summon me without warning," began the irate Lord Brack. "If you were not my brother I would make you regret such rudeness. I was dealing with a matter of business that is now left unresolved, and I do not like loose ends brother."

Rune, somewhat taken back at the wrath and power displayed by his older half-brother, stammered a semblance of an apology. "Perhaps I should have given you more warning but we have more pressing things to worry about than entertaining the masses in that archaic arena of yours."

Lord Rune quickly regained his composure and called for servants to clean up the mess Brack had made.

"I'll expect payment for my table at a later date, but for now, I must speak to you of this little matter of the ninth son. No doubt you have heard, or perhaps even have felt, that Nicholas is dead. Now that he is gone, it becomes imperative that we get rid of the troublesome child. I am talking to you for a number of reasons. I know of your ongoing feud with our cousin Sara, and I thought you might like to know that she now offers sanctuary to the little brat. That accursed Archmage will have the opportunity to recruit the child to their cause. We need to somehow draw them out. For years we have tried to pierce Meridia but we might as well try and capture starlight. In this matter I have chosen to speak with only you. Since the wakening, Vilus has become a blubbering mess and Damal is too wrapped up in his own personal beauty to be useful. They both attempted once to capture the boy, and they both ultimately paid the price for their respective greed. The idiots both chose to send their winged minions to Sard. Did they really think that capturing the boy would be so easy? Now the lesser dragons walk Terrus no more."

Brack withheld the curiosity and surprise that burned within him. The two youngest brothers had always been the most impetuous, but he found it hard to believe that even they were stupid enough to attempt such a subterfuge.

***

Meanwhile, all manner of confusion was in effect at the pit. Lord Brack's dramatic disappearance had caused something of a riot to occur. The commonfolk were not accustomed to, or enamored, with dark magic, and watching three men blasted to ashes and then the perpetrator disappear in thin air was a little too much for the average citizen to stomach. Beran took advantage of the chaos. Smashing the sword hilt down upon the locks that bound his feet, with nimbleness befitting an acrobat rather than a massive warrior, he scaled the inside wall of the arena. On reaching the terrace he followed the people running for the exits. Merging with the sea of humanity he found the open streets and melted in with the crowd. Night-time swiftly approached so he ducked into an alleyway and took refuge under the covers of a warehouse wagon. There he waited patiently until day surrendered to nightfall.

A cloud-basked sky greeted Beran's eyes as he emerged from beneath the oily canvas cover. Few people walked the streets, and fewer still had the courage to. Most of the cities of the southern reaches were saturated with every imaginable cutthroat, murderer or pirate. No formal city watch or law enforcement existed, only the fear of Lord Brack and the terrors of the pit kept people from being too visible in their law-breaking. Beran crept stealthily towards the outskirts of town, making sure to stay hidden amongst the deepening shadows. More than once he was forced to seek out a hiding place as small bands of mercenaries crossed his path. He had to walk several miles before he found an unguarded road leading out of town. Unbeknownst to Beran, Brack's royal advisor had placed a bounty of a thousand gold pieces on his head. Coquatan, did not want to be the man to tell Lord Brack that the prisoner had escaped.

Once out of the sight of city lights, Beran broke from the road and headed cross-country. Without moon or star to guide him, he could only hope that his feet took him in an easterly direction. Since his capture he had become so disorientated that he had no idea how far away he was from the legal kingdom border. After hours of hiking through ragged vine and prickling gorse, he found a mossy dell in a culvert cut into a rocky scree slope at the step of a lake. There he collapsed in fatigue and surrendered to dreamless sleep for the remainder of the far retired night.

Awaking in the harsh light of morning, he found his body stiff and wracked with pain. The ordeal in the pit had cost him a hundred or more cuts, some of which were already beginning to fester and become infected. Carefully, he removed his outer garments and slid into the freezing cold waters of the mountain lake. Beran washed out as much dirt and grime as he could, then dragged his clothes in for an impromptu wash. When he emerged from the water he felt refreshed and invigorated. Kneeling beside a spring that emerged from the rock face he drank thirstily. His stomach grumbled and he realized, to his discomfort, that he had not eaten in the three days since his capture. Getting to his feet he saw a ratnag tree with a few late fruit holding on perilously to thin stalks. Too tired to climb he shook the tree hard and was rewarded with a handful of the gelatinous fruit. Beran had three loves in life; fighting, women, and food and not necessarily in that order. Few men had the intestinal capacity of this warrior. Indeed he had been banned from open table at more than one inn in his home town.

Content, but far from satiated after his morning repast, he set out again on his journey eastward. The sun had risen early which helped him determine some semblance of direction. During his night run he had traveled directly north, so this morning he turned himself into the warming glow of sunlight and headed into the woods. Before long the wood became impregnable. So densely encroached were the trees, daylight visited the mossy floor quite infrequently. Beran found the going difficult and had to make numerous circuitous sidetracks in order to pass through the foliage. On one such detour he found himself standing atop a high-walled ditch. Ten feet below ran a shallow brook which seemed to meander in the direction he wanted to go. He slid on his backside down the muddy trench and waded out into the shallow current. Though wet, the going was far easier than the dense, murky forest. At length the brook became a stream, and a mile later the stream a turbulent river.

"I guess this river must be heading somewhere in the direction of the ocean." Beran mused aloud. The only answer came from the gurgling of the fast-flowing water.

Up ahead the trees thinned out and Beran came in sight of a road. He climbed out of the torrent and knelt down to study the road. A great many tracks permeated the dust but none appeared to be too fresh. Tired of wading, he decided to brave the road. It wasn't long before the decision proved to be an ill-begotten one. A steady rumbling behind him suggested the disconcerting pursuit of horses and riders. Calmly he picked up the speed of his walk. When he heard voices he started to run. The pursuers had spotted him and Beran did not have the patience to wait and find out if they were friends or enemies. Not once did he look behind him, but ran with long lengthy strides looking from left to right for a place to hide. The hoof beats grew louder and Beran could feel their vibration beneath his feet. The voices were excited and loud and it was obvious that these men were hunting the prisoner who had escaped Brack's lair. There was nowhere to flee so Beran reluctantly turned to face the horsemen. On the edge of the road he spied a stout tree branch and stooped to pick it up. There were twelve riders in all. By their garb he judged them to be mercenaries or bounty hunters. They slowed as they came up on Beran. One horse separated from the others as the leader of the group trotted forward and looked down on him from the saddle. The horse was a tall sleek thoroughbred and glistened with sweat. Its nostrils flared as it regarded the traveler with distrusting eyes.

The seated rider was the first to speak. "So where do you travel my friend?"

Shifting his weight to achieve the most optimal defensive fighting stance, Beran answered slowly. "Where ever the road leads me friend. It is a great time of year to explore the southern continent don't you think?"

The mercenary's eyes narrowed as he regarded the assumed posture of the traveler. "You know you bear a striking resemblance to a man who caused a stir way back in Mallicus. The man escaped from the judgment house and there is a sizeable reward for those who bring him in."

"Is that so," said Beran. "Well, I wish you luck in finding him."

The mercenary leader laughed unpleasantly. "It seems we have already had lady luck on our side today. Half the men in the Reaches are looking for this man, and would you believe we just happen to bump into him on this lonely road."

The rest of the riders had already drawn their swords. The lead mercenary grinned as he withdrew his own blade from its scabbard. The grin soon transformed into a pained frown as Beran drove the end of the branch he was holding into the man's solar plexus. The momentum of the blow unseated the rider and the horse reared into the air kicking wildly. During this interaction the wily mercenaries had spread out around the action. Beran soon found himself completely surrounded with the only weapon at hand, a well worn tree branch. Beran whispered a quick prayer to Ludi, the God of Impossible Odds, then prepared to fight. He felt the berserker rage start to well up inside him, but before it took hold a whistling sounded in his ear followed by a dull thud. Beran whirled around just in time to watch a mercenary rider topple from his saddle, an arrow protruding from his back. The whistling then began in earnest, and one by one the riders were unseated by deadly wooden shafts adorned with white fletched goose feathers. Throughout the entire exchange, Beran stood bewildered and rooted to the spot. To any persons passing by, the scene would have been extraordinary. A lonely man stood in the middle of the dusty road armed with only a tree limb, while all around him lay dead mercenaries spackled with arrow points. Beran barely dared move but his curiosity won him over and he turned to face the direction from which the arrows had rained.

Out of the woods materialized six forms. Clad in earthy green and brown they were barely distinguishable from the forest fauna. They stepped effortlessly and their movements seemed to coordinate gracefully with the motion of the trees from which they emerged. Beran was a young man in human years, just twenty summers in age, but these strange creatures seemed older than the earth, yet younger than he. In every physiology of form they resembled humans, yet their ears were pointed and their slender limbs longer.

A beautiful woman moved into view and Beran knew the emotion of true love and an appreciation for beauty. She was clothed in a close-fitted leather tunic of mottled green. Loose-fitting brown pants extended down long legs that ended in soft-skinned boots. Her skin was bronzed from hours spent under the warming glare of the sun. Around a finely-tapered waist she wore a thin belt that housed a sheathed dagger. Across her chest was slung a quiver full of arrows and in her left hand she still bore the deadly long bow that had contributed moments earlier in the saving of his life. The woman's features were perfection personified. Deep blue eyes regarded Beran with an expression akin to light-hearted amusement. The nose was slightly pointed and her dark hair glistened in the morning sun. Despite her travel clothes, Beran could not help but recognize the hard sensual curvature of an athletic body.

When she spoke her voice was musical and lilting. "Good morrow to you friend traveler, you are well met and welcome to our forest home. We have been sent to find you by one who would call you to his service." So lost was he in the beauty of this enchanting woman, Beran stood open-mouthed and speechless. Perceiving his sense of awe, the woman reached out and gently took his hand leading him deep into the woods.

They walked for several miles among trees that seemed to open willingly to their passing. The whole time the young woman held Beran's hand, she led him flawlessly through the undergrowth. They soon arrived in a narrow woodland glade. Directly in the center of the clearing lay a pool of water shimmering like a glass mirror upon the grassy floor. One by one, Beran's lithe companions jumped into the pool of water and, without as much as a ripple, disappeared beneath its surface. His beautiful guide was the last to leave him squeezing his hand saying, "there is nothing to fear, we travel swiftly." With that she sprung over the ledge and vanished. Without pausing to think what he was doing, he followed her into the pool.

As quickly as he left he returned. The glade was identical, and the pool from which he climbed seemed the same, yet the trees were somehow different and seemed to whisper welcome as he clambered up on to a grassy knoll. Shaking his head, he realized that his clothes were completely dry despite the passage through the mirrored pool. Looking around, he found that he was all alone. Desperately disappointed, he sank to his knees. No woman had ever stirred his heart the way the fair woodland archer had. His reverie was interrupted by a gentleman who strode out from the trees uniformed in the dress of Queen Sara's royal guard. On closer inspection, Beran realized that the man's shoulder bore the mark of two crossed swords reserved only for the rank of Meridian Swordmaster. To his knowledge there were but two swordmasters on Terrus and here, in front of him, stood one of them. Beran rubbed his eyes and began to convince himself that he was in a dream.

"Do not fear my friend, this is no dream and this is only the start of many adventures, not the end of one. My name is Ryad, and I am the Swordmaster and Commanding Officer of the Shupan Garrison. This is the very edge of the Elghorian Forest. Those that rescued you from the dark fate of returning to Mallicus were the kind spirited elves that call the trees their home. Oh, and the young woman who you seem to have become somewhat enamored by is Acrina, the daughter of Koradin, Lord of the elvenkind."

"Elves?" stammered Beran. "I thought elves were only creatures of myth and legend?"

"Indeed they are," said Ryad. "Few myths and legends exist that are devoid of connections to our life friends the elves. But enough of the past, let us eat together and talk about the future. Adventures, yes indeed adventures. I believe you and I shall share many ere this year is done."

Chapter Twenty-One

Meridia

It hadn't taken Storm long to settle in to his new island home. All the stories he had heard of Meridia paled in comparison to seeing it with his own eyes. The island was a veritable paradise filled with natural wonders. For the first few days of his stay, he and Zira had explored the surrounding countryside. Meridia was far vaster than he had imagined. To the North grew a verdant forest of towering trees. Storm had never seen such a place. Every species of tree indigenous to Terrus grew within its boundaries. It was not uncommon to find a weeping willow resting in the shade of a mighty oak, or a conifer surrounded by birch trees. Sycamore, ash, poplar, redwood, chestnut, spruce, and fruit tree all lived synergistically on the island. Off to the east of the island, Storm and Zira lost themselves in the panorama of wide canyons and river valleys. Majestic waterfalls cascaded over smooth-worn granite ledges plunging powerfully into crystal pools below. Boy and wolf played happily amid the sparkling waters, diving off rocky buttresses and flowing with the currents wherever they would lead. To the west stretched the ocean and miles of deserted sandy beaches. Storm had taken to walking the sandy shelves at dusk, enjoying the breath-taking sunsets in calming solitude. Finally, south of the palace there extended acre upon acre of green pasture and rich-soiled farmland. Storm ignored the fields and pastoral lands, preferring to spend his time adventuring in the woods and canyons.

Caelin Paul

Since their arrival, Storm and Wolfy had spent little time within the walls of the crystal palace. Wolfy continued to grieve for his family wandering the gardens alone with his sorrow. Sara was sensitive to the needs of her guests and demanded little of their attention in the weeks that followed their arrival on Meridia. Storm and Wolfy were at first given stately accommodations in the east wing tower, but neither one of them felt very comfortable lying in silk sheets and sleeping on feather down mattresses. One night Storm tossed and turned and finally fell out of bed. Wolfy, who was pacing in the next room, heard his friend's fall and ran to his aid. The sight of the tousle-haired boy fighting to free himself from richly embroidered sheets conjured a rare smile from the farmer. From that night on, the two conspired to find more comfortable quarters. The very next day, they converted the stable's hayloft into their own personal bedroom suite.

One oddity was the apparent lack of people on Meridia. Wherever Storm went he saw no one other than the occasional servant. Though he perceived no people around the palace, or outside in the grounds, he felt presences coming and going at all times. Sometimes he felt as if he caught glimpses of movement out of the corner of his eye, but when he turned there only remained empty space. Wolfy had similar experiences and was convinced the palace must be haunted. According to the visible eye, no living person farmed the expansive crop system, and no one else seemed to live in the castle despite the expansive corridors of bedrooms. Zira was especially uncomfortable within the walls of the royal house. On more than one occasion, the snow wolf had sent Storm visions of different people that he claimed to have seen. Storm laughed at the images, for the outfits they wore were of a fashion he had never before seen the like. The boy found it strange that Zira would make up such imaginations but there was never a soul to be seen when such an image blazed into his head.

The mystery solved itself through a bizarre occurrence late in the evening during one of Storm's preambles along a nearby sandy beach. Boy and wolf had just enjoyed a majestic sunset where the horizon had inspired a dramatic dioramic display. The sky underwent a chameleonic metamorphosis of blue to purple to red to yellow and finally to burnished gold. The concert of color was worthy of an audience of thousands, but this night it was enjoyed by only two, or so he thought. Heading back towards the stables, Zira stopped suddenly with hackles rising and falling. Storm was immediately assailed by an image of a beautiful young girl with jet black hair wandering the beach in front of him.

"What is this image you send me Zira? I see no one on this beach besides you and I."

Storm felt the undertone of disgust and frustration that flavored the wolf's communication. "*I smelled the human before my eyes found her. Can you not do the same?*" asked Zira.

"*I am sure my nose is no match for you my furry friend,*" laughed Storm. "If there is another ahead of us why can we not see footprints in the sand? Explain that to me wise one?"

Zira quieted for a moment and then sent an image showing a girl that floated on pockets of air six inches off the ground. Storm could not help but laugh at his four-legged friend. "Zira, now you are telling me that there is an invisible girl in front of us that is floating on air."

The wolf sent back a flash of red, an indication that he was beginning to get annoyed.

"*Master if you would but see with your nose; run with me towards the crystal cave.*" With that Zira set off at great speed toward the palace. Storm laughing, took off in hot pursuit. Zira slowed down just enough for Storm to catch up. Suddenly, the wolf veered off to the right. Storm kept straight and then found himself up-ended in the sand as he ran headlong into an invisible object. The object let loose an indignant yell as it was thrown sideways into a sand dune.

The moon was rising and offered some illumination to the startling collision. Storm sat up and shook the sand from his hair. To his amazement he found himself looking directly into the fierce eyes of a raven-haired girl no more than twelve summers in age. The girl stood up and approached him with angry fire burning in her eyes. The whole time, Zira was running in circles sending, "*I told you so, I told you so, you found her with your nose, you found her with your nose.*"

"I am so sorry for running into you," stammered Storm.

"I should think so too," retorted the girl. "What are you thinking charging around on the beaches without a moment of consideration for the welfare of others?"

"Others, what others?" Storm felt a wave of irritation rise within him. "I thought I was alone, and how can I be held responsible for running into something that I was unable to see?"

The girl frowned then burst into fits of giggles. "You are new to Meridia aren't you?"

Storm shook the excess sand from out of his shirt. "Yes, I arrived just a few days ago from Sard. I walk on the beach every evening and I have never once seen another person."

"Ah that explains everything," replied the girl. "My name is Anyal and I am from Bal. I am one of Kalon's students here at the academy."

"Academy? What is the academy? Who are these students? How many are there? Why can't I see any of them?"

Anyal giggled. "I see I have some questions to answer. Will you walk with me back to the palace and I will attempt to explain." As they began to walk, Storm noted that two sets of footprints appeared in the sand where once there had been only his. He shook his head and turned his attention back to the girl who walked beside him.

"Archmage Kalon is the prefect of the Meridian Academy," started Anyal. "He invites children from all across the kingdom to come study here. Some last only a few days, but others live and study here for many years. I came to Meridia just two years ago after my family was killed in a raid on my village. I was only ten summers when the evil men came. I was fearful for my life and hid in the woods with my eyes shut. The next thing I knew I had levitated myself into a tree. I remained in the tree while the mercenaries torched the village and stole everything they could carry. We were only a small village and fewer than ten of us survived. Kalon arrived soon afterwards and invited me here. They say that I am a catcher, but I do not know yet what that means. There are currently a hundred children and adults studying on Meridia. The rules allow for no more and no less. Catchers are meant to be important students because Kalon says we have been blessed with special gifts. Most of the lessons are boring but sometimes we have fun."

By now the two had reached the edge of the gardens. "So why is it that I cannot see any of these students wandering around?" asked Storm.

Anyal smiled, "that is the beauty of Meridian magic. Everyone lives their lives in the manner they see fit or to the vocation that they are called. You probably do not know this but the fields over there are filled everyday with farmers working the land. You cannot see them because they choose not to be seen. The people you see are only those who choose to reveal themselves to you."

"Then how am I now seeing you?" asked Storm.

Anyal fluffed her hair and grinned conspiratorily. "You see me because I chose to make myself seen in order to give you a piece of my mind. Oh, and everyone is very real. Though not always seen, we are all tangible and can be touched. Are you here to join the academy? It would be nice to have a friendly face around. Life can sometimes be very lonely, and as an orphan I have no family like the others."

Storm felt Anyal's pain like a barb in his heart. He reached out and touched her hand. "I would be honored to be your friend. I am not sure if I will be asked to join this Academy of yours, but you can be assured that I will forever call you friend."

Anyal found her cheeks blush the shade of a rose and she pulled her hand away. Dropping to her knees she distracted herself in petting Zira. Zira enjoyed the attention and rubbed his head against the young girl's shoulder.

"Your dog sure is cute," said Anyal.

Zira perked up his ears at the insult and sent a flood of red images to Storm. Storm chuckled, "yes, I have to agree my dog is very cute." Zira indignantly strutted away, leaving the two young people to birth a friendship.

Chapter Twenty-Two

Breakfast

The morning after Storm's adventure on the beach, a page arrived at the stable with an invitation to breakfast with Queen Sara. Wolfy roused Storm with a well aimed bucket of water soliciting a swift wake-up. Zira saw the bucket coming and escaped quickly out the door. Storm, on the other hand, was soaked from head to toe. Wolfy laughed as the bedraggled boy jumped up coughing and spluttering.

"Time to go visit your friend the queen," said Wolfy. "By the way, what time did you come in last evening? I thought I heard you talking to a female voice. Is my little half-pint in love?"

Storm threw a boot at his friend and then grinned broadly. "I am too young to be in love, although, I have to concede Anyal is the most beautiful girl I have ever laid eyes on."

"The queen will be jealous," said Wolfy. "I think she thought that you believed her to be the most beautiful girl in the world."

Storm laughed, "Queen Sara is the most beautiful woman, Anyal, is the most beautiful girl."

"Ah, now I understand. The logic of youth wins every time," laughed Wolfy. "Well my young whippet, we should not keep the most beautiful 'woman' in the world waiting, we are due in the banquet room in ten minutes."

Storm was still dressing himself when they arrived at the doors to the dining hall. They were met at the threshold by a bespectacled older gentleman who introduced himself as Horatius, the Queen's first counselor.

"Her royal highness is delighted that you have chosen to accept her invitation to break your fast. Please come with me. Oh, and young sir, your shirt would benefit from being tucked into your pants."

Wolfy winked at Storm and promptly experienced a swift rabbit punch to the bicep. Horatius led them through two plain brown doors that opened into the largest room the boy had ever seen. Clearly, by Wolfy's open-mouthed reaction, Storm was not the only one to appreciate the immensity of the dining hall. At the distant north end of the room waited four persons. Seeing them enter, a woman broke away from the group and hurried towards them. Queen Sara was resplendent in a long flowing green dress with gold and silver embroidered flowers curling around her middle and down to her knees. Encircling her neck, a string of ocean pearls seemed to change color as she moved. Velvet shoes passed noiselessly across the floor, and on her head perched a simple silver circlet, the only evidence of her regal station. Sara greeted them enthusiastically. Dropping to her knees, she took Storm into her arms in a tender mothering embrace. Releasing the bashful boy she stood and smiled at Wolfy.

"Mr. Barley, I trust your young charge is not being too great a handful? I also pray that your wounds heal swiftly during your stay with us." A knowing look passed between the two of them. Sara and Wolfy had come upon one another's sorrow on more than one occasion in the palace gardens. "Please come eat with us, there are some people I would have you meet." Sara took the two of them by the hand and led them across the expansive floor to the head of the table where six place servings had been set.

The Queen took the seat at the head of the board with Storm on her right and Wolfy on the left. Kalon took the seat next to Storm, and from the face of wrinkles, Storm accepted a mischievous wink. Across from Kalon was a bearded man who Sara introduced as Mage Dulkin, one of the teachers at the academy. The Mage was a short man with ferret eyes and a hooked nose. Since the moment Storm sat down Dulkin had stared intently at the boy, almost as if trying to read his thoughts. Storm immediately threw up a cognitive defense. He had learned this little trick from Zira, who found it exhausting having to experience every thought, sensation, and emotion that hormones and adolescence conspired to bring. Dulkin gave Storm the creeps and he knew instantly that he was not going to like this man. Unconsciously, he reached for the collusk that had become a constant in his pant's pocket. Dulkin continued to stare at Storm and the collusk grew warm to the touch. Quickly he withdrew his hand and attempted to ignore the Mage's piercing scrutiny. The final guest at the table sat next to Dulkin. Also an instructor at the academy, he was introduced as Mage Saltorini. Saltorini was the antithesis of Dulkin, and Storm felt positive energy exude from him. Tall and dark-skinned, the man had eyes the size of plums. Similarly to his colleagues, he wore the grey robes of the mage rank but he looked many years younger than Kalon and Dulkin. He also turned out to be the most talkative of the table guests as he pursued wonderfully funny stories of strange adventures from his youth, or magic experiments that had gone terribly awry.

Servants brought to the table platters filled with meats, fruits, and cheeses. Warm spiced rolls with thick curls of butter came in unending baskets and juices from the vineyards flowed from bottomless pitchers. Storm could not remember the last time he had eaten so well. Sara had asked the three men to attend the breakfast to educate Storm about the academy. It was Kalon who did most of the speaking concerning the school, in between bites, chews and swallows.

"The academy is an institution of higher learning and a vehicle of inquiry into the truth of concepts beyond the understanding of the mind's sense of reality."

Saltorini interrupted by saying, "what the master means is we study magic." Kalon frowned but Saltorini just grinned back.

Kalon continued. "The study of magic is a part of the academy, it is true, but our institution exists for far more than teaching simple parlor tricks. Those fortunate enough to be invited here to Meridia possess aptitudes or intellectual skills that set them apart from their peers. Some that study here are of advanced years, while others number fewer than ten summers in life-length. Only one hundred men and women are permitted to study at the academy at any given time. We are very selective about who we invite for this reason. Our libraries are the oldest and best stocked of any on Terrus. There is no book written that has not found a place within the archives of the academy. The most acclaimed scholars, teachers, and spell weavers from around the known world have connections with Meridia. The reason we tell you these things is because we would like to offer you a bench in the academy."

"A bench, what is that?" asked Storm.

"That is just a figurative way of saying that your skills have earned you the right for admission invitation. If you say yes we will begin your education directly after breakfast. If you say no, you will be free to live your life on Meridia in any manner you choose."

Sara, who had been listening intently to the exchange, spoke softly to Storm.

"My brother had great faith and respect in your abilities. He believed, as I do, that you have many gifts that, in time, may contribute to enriching the lives of all those around you. With such gifts comes responsibility. An old saying on Terrus states, 'to he who the Gods bless with talents, let him sacrifice all to the greater good.' I realize you have made many sacrifices already by leaving your home to come to Meridia. Truly, the academy can teach you to better understand your abilities and in time to aid you in contributing to this greater good."

Storm sat quietly listening to everything that was shared. Throughout the conversation he opened a mental conduit to Zira who waited patiently outside the hall doors. Periodically, Zira returned emotions and images. Some images were of the woods and rivers where the two of them played. Zira informed his master how much he would miss their daily sojourns if he had to study all day. Still other images were of flashbacks to Storm's startling displays of uncontrolled power, advocating to him that he should join the academy in order to learn how to harness such powerful energy. In this way Zira played the role of conscience, desire,

Caelin Paul

and devil's advocate. By the end of Sara's monologue, Storm knew there could be no doubt to his choice. He would join the academy and learn more about the Aruk.

Chapter Twenty-Three

Academy

Breakfast concluded and servants arrived to efficiently clear the table. Sara rose to take her leave asking Wolfy to walk with her. As they departed from the hall, Kalon turned to Storm with a grin on his face.

"I have been meaning to ask you, did you ever finish reading that old book Nicholas gave you?"

"Indeed I did sir," replied Storm. "I especially enjoyed the section on natural energies in chapter seventeen."

"Pray tell me young lad what did I have to say about polaric plate fusion?"

Storm knitted his brow in concentration then answered, "on page three hundred and eight you state 'polaric plate fusion is a conductive process through which iron ore conjunctions may produce intricate atomic emissions whose purpose it is to transport nucleic composites throughout the earth which ultimately conjoins magnetic polarity.'"

Mage Saltorini, bellowed with laughter and slapped the boy on the back. "He not only read your book but it sounds like he memorized every word. By the way, to be honest young Storm, I have not the smallest inkling of what any of that meant. Nucleic composites and magnetic polarity was not one of my strengths in school."

Storm grinned back, "I haven't got the foggiest idea what any of it means either." The only table companion that didn't seem to find comedy in the exchange was Mage Dulkin who sat emotionless beside Kalon.

The Archmage spoke next, "it seems as if the suspicions of Nicholas were well founded. Indeed, we might have found ourselves another catcher."

"Catcher? I met a girl yesterday evening that claimed to be a catcher. Will I be studying with her at the academy?" asked Storm.

"Anyal? Yes she is indeed a gifted student and I daresay the two of you may find plenty of time to study with one another. Now let us introduce you to your fellow academics."

The Archmage clicked his fingers and the next moment the party found themselves in a large auditorium. The ceiling vaulted beyond the scope of vision and the floor shimmered with starlight. Row upon endless row of windows spanned the entire length of the hall. Beside each window, many stories off the ground, there floated a bench and an accompanying desk. Storm looked down at his feet and to his horror regarded nothing beneath him but empty space. Suddenly, he began to fall. Saltorini caught his arm and hauled him up beside him.

The good natured Mage chuckled. "The Hall of Windows is a mere illusion that all who enter have the ability to control. If you perceive emptiness beneath your feet you will fall forever, that is of course, until you choose to land. In order to travel the Hall you must control your own sense of reality and establish your own path of travel."

Kalon nodded approvingly and then continued. "All men and women have an energy and life force. Unfortunately, few have the ability to manipulate these personal energies. Within this hallowed hall you can take your first steps to reconnecting with that which naturally resides inside of you. Your bench is the one up there to the left of the blue tapestry."

Storm looked up and saw a bench floating thirty feet above his head. "How do I get up there?" he stammered.

"Each must choose their own means of travel within the Hall of Windows," answered Kalon. "However, I might suggest steps an appropriate vehicle by which you might achieve your goal."

Saltorini still held a strong grip on Storm's sleeve. "So are you ready to take your first steps alone?"

"I think I understand," countered Storm. Closing his eyes he detached himself from the mage's hold and stepped upwards. His foot alighted on solid ground and slowly he climbed the imagined staircase. A few steps later, he opened his eyes and saw to his surprise that he had arrived at the bench beside the blue tapestry. The tapestry felt as intangible as the hall. He gazed intently at the figures scattered throughout the wall hanging. They seemed somehow alive and, allowing curiosity to lead him, he let his imagination seep into the velvet cloth. Suddenly, the tapestry began to pursue a children's story that he had grown up fond of hearing. A behemoth of a dragon battled a knight clad in silver armor. The knight was about to deliver a killing blow when a fair maiden ran from the forest and staid his arm. As the mighty dragon prepared to give up his last breath, she threw her arms around his neck and whispered words of love. The red dragon raised his head and bellowed a mighty roar. In dreadful concert to the unleashed cry, flames leapt from the dragon's mouth. The fire consumed the beautiful woman, burning the fair maiden where she stood. Imperceptibly her body started the transformation into a beautiful golden dragon. Rising like a phoenix from the fire, the intensity of inferno grew greater in its power. People from miles distant shaded their eyes at her passing. One dragon bequeathed a vibrant spirit in breathing life to another. Storm stood enthralled by the story that played avidly before his eyes. At the conclusion of the telling, Storm felt breathless and sweat saturated his tunic. Looking down along his arms, he started visibly when he viewed the finely scorched arm hair.

Far below him, surprised expressions etched silent upon the faces of his new teachers. Clearly, the tapestry production had not escaped their notice. Storm sat upon the hard wooden bench in front of an even more nondescript paneled desk. On the seat of the bench he saw his name decoratively inscribed. To his right was a window with four panes of beveled glass. Through the window, he gazed out upon acres of wheat, rice and potato fields. Concentrating hard, he began to distinguish shapes, forms and faces. Suddenly, his vision altered and his sight captured endless rows of farmers working in the fields. Women laughed and sang while they worked, and children played amongst the tall wheat sheaves. Storm returned his attention to the room and almost fell off his chair. In front of him, behind him, to his left, above and below were the floating benches he had seen on entering the hall. However, now they were filled with students, all perusing various books and papers. Many were writing or copying old letters, but most had heads buried in aging books and disintegrating manuscripts. Somewhere in front of him he thought he saw a girl that resembled Anyal. His accurate eyesight was acknowledged as she turned suddenly and waved a cheery hello.

When Storm looked down upon his desk he found a book lying there. It was old and dusty and the leather spine was tenuously hanging to the musty pages. He blew the dust from the cover and read aloud the title – "The History of the House of Celebus." Storm thought this a strange first book to read, but before long he was lost in the pages of political intrigue, historical events, and strange adventures of the long-dead descendents of Queen Sara. He was interrupted from his study, some hours later, when a loud bell rang. On the twelfth peel the room underwent a startling metamorphosis. Without warning, Storm found himself standing upon a tiled floor surrounded by other students. They were all moving towards an archway at the end of the hall. In the press of bodies, Storm found a familiar face. Pushing through the throng he sidled up alongside Anyal. "Where is everyone going?"

"It is time for classes silly," replied the dark-haired girl.

Storm's voice failed to contain his confusion. "But didn't we just have class?"

"Oh no, that was morning independent study. The mages choose reading material appropriate to our skills to start the day. I was just reading Chronicles of Dragon Lore, interesting stuff but the language is archaic and hard to understand. What were you given to read?"

"I had some old book about the royal family," answered Storm. The two of them had reached the archway together and passed through. On the other side, Storm emerged into sunlight and a small courtyard where ten other students gathered. Looking around for Anyal, he was disappointed to not find her in the group. The Archmage appeared nonchalantly in their midst with his customary cheerful smile.

"Welcome new students. Most of you are visiting Meridia for the first time so I thought I would take this opportunity to give you the grand tour of the gardens. My name is Kalon, and I am the Archmage and architect of the Academy. You have all been invited here because you have displayed a myriad of special talents. Some of you have much to learn, others have much to teach. Think of this meeting as your orientation to our school and do not be afraid to ask questions." Kalon leant heavily upon his wooden staff as he talked. "The arch you passed under moments ago is the arch of choosing. It is perhaps the most ancient and most powerful of the structures here on Meridia. Each day it will permit you to join classes it judges most appropriate. Its choices are sometimes surprising, occasionally unpredictable, but always with good reason. Often myself, or one of the other teachers, may seek you out for special lessons, but till such time, you must respect the election of the arch. There are eight mages at the academy, all of whom you will meet in due course. Many of you will spend your time here under the tutelage of Mage Corrin. He is the chief librarian and is responsible for the archives, books, and ancient manuscripts. Those of you with an interest and talent in the healing arts will be assigned to Maegess Nolina. A select few of you have demonstrated latent abilities with one or more of the elements. Thus, you might find yourselves tutored by Mage Yurl, master of earth, Mage Bartrand, master of fire, Mage Leskel, master of air, or Maegess Mirren, mistress of water. Finally, the instruction in higher order magic will always be conducted by Mages' Dulkin and Saltorini. Are there any questions?" Kalon looked into the eyes of each person, his gaze lingering a few seconds longer on Storm. When no questions were forthcoming he moved on down the courtyard path.

The Archmage moved at surprising speed for a man of his advanced years. Some of the older students were breathing heavily as they hustled to keep pace. Without pause, Kalon continued to talk about Meridia.

"Many of you know that our fair island is protected by a powerful circle of enchantment. Only those pure in heart and purpose are permitted to enter Meridia. If you are found partaking in illegal activity or are pursuing activity contrary to the spirit of light that pervades this place, you will be removed from the island immediately and your return will be forever prohibited." The Archmage's stern voice left no doubt in the minds of the students that such a claim was no idle threat. Kalon continued; "as some of you have discovered on your own," he winked at Storm, "the island is an alive and vibrant community. However, its residents are a shy and unassuming people, choosing to be observed only at times of their own discretion. The surrounding countryside is unparalleled in its beauty. You are welcome, and indeed encouraged, to take advantage of the peace and solitude it affords. Every morning, by the bell's ninth chime, you must be at your bench in the Hall of Windows. Any student failing to make their independent study appointment will automatically forfeit their opportunity to take classes for the day." Kalon had now reached the royal gardens, and spent the next hour wandering its paths pointing out flowers, shrubs, trees, and herbs, calling them by both their known and founding names. Storm was amazed at how much the old man knew about Meridia's flora. Then again, Storm was beginning to appreciate there was not much the Archmage did not know. The impromptu horticulture lecture ended abruptly as Kalon excused himself from the group and disappeared into thin air. Storm took that to mean class had ended and sprinted off down the garden path to find Zira.

Chapter Tweny-Four

Shupan

Perspiration riddled Beran's clothes and sweat beaded his brow. His opponent lunged forward impetuously, aiming a sword point at his throat. Deftly, Beran brought his sword up to parry the blow and simultaneously drove his elbow into the other soldier's nose. The latter instantly crumpled to the floor howling in pain.

"Alright, that's enough Captain Beran. I cannot have you injuring every single soldier in my command, even if it is in the spirit of training them." Ryad strode over to join his newly recruited captain. "It sure is good to have a younger man here to help me train this motley crew of militia. I am getting too old to wield a sword day in and day out."

Beran grinned. From what he had seen of the swordmaster's skill and stamina in the training ring, he doubted very much such a claim. Almost a month had passed since the soldier had first met Ryad in the Elghorian Forest. Now Beran found himself promoted to First Captain of the Shupan Garrison. While at the Illian Garrison, he had served two years as an enlisted soldier and part-time sailor. He would never have dreamed that within the first two years of service he would find himself serving as a captain, responsible for over five thousand men. The Meridian military had a simplistic hierarchical structure of leadership. There were five garrisons stationed throughout Terrus. Each swore fealty and loyalty to the true Meridian crown. The garrisons had a commanding officer, and under him four captains all ranked by seniority. The ranking officer beneath captain was squadlead. Each squadlead had a responsibility for squads of one hundred men. The Shupan Garrison, like its sister barracks, housed four thousand soldiers, forty squadleads, four captains, and one commanding officer. With the timely arrival of Beran, Ryad had promptly retired all four of his aging captains and promoted a more youthful cadre to leadership positions.

Ryad arrived just as Beran finished up a training session with his ten squadleads. Despite their strength and experience, most lacked competency in their sword-work. Needless to say, Beran was making it his personal responsibility to solve that oversight. Ryad was the only man within Shupan that could best Beran with a blade. The newly appointed Captain still bore a bruised pride when he recollected how the swordmaster had unarmed him twice in the training ring on his very first day at the garrison. However, despite the humbling first day on the job, he had established a quiet notoriety for himself since arriving at Shupan. Beran's escape from Mallicus had become something of legend throughout the Southern Reaches. Moreover, Lord Brack had increased the bounty on his head to five thousand gold pieces.

Beran also came to understand the extent to which he owed his life to the swordmaster. Ryad had learned of the kidnapping of Illian Garrison soldiers from a tip within his elaborate spy network. On hearing that a kingdom man had escaped from the pit, Ryad had immediately called upon his friends, the elves, to keep watch upon the Elghorian for any sign of the escapee. So it was that a group of elves just happened to be watching the south-east road from Mallicus.

In the time that followed their first meeting, the two men had spent a great deal of time together and had become fast friends.

"Well Captain Beran, do you have time to grab a bite to eat?" Stomach answered the question before voice as the brawny soldier acknowledged his hunger.

The two of them left the garrison and walked into the nearby town. Few knew whether it was the garrison or the town that had come first. Shupan had grown to be one of the largest centers of commerce in the south. Located on the south-east corner of the

Icealic Ocean, the town played host to a number of the kingdom's oldest trading houses. The population was large and generally well behaved. With the garrison's close proximity, a plethora of inns and whore houses had sprung up to cater to the needs of the soldiers. Beran and Ryad strolled towards the docks. It was early evening and a great many traders were still enthusiastically plying their wares. Delicious smells wafted from bakeries, grocers, and various eating establishments. Ryad turned in at the door of an inn on the main thoroughfare. From rusting brackets hung a grey tabard illustrated with the faded picture of a prancing unicorn. The Unicorn was a favorite haunt of the garrison men. The inn-keeper, a jovial happy man, was one of the more reputable and honest businessmen in the borough. The plates of food were large and the beer mugs grew tall.

Despite the early hour, the main floor was already filling swiftly. Buxom barmaids hustled around the room serving up piping hot bowls of soup and icy cold ale. The two soldiers took a table in the corner. Years of experience had trained Ryad to be always cautious. A seat that commanded a full view of the room, its occupants, and the door was a necessity for any soldier who valued his life. Shupan lay at the southernmost kingdom boundary with only the Elghorian Forest separating the world of order from Lord Brack's territory of chaos. Needless to say, Shupan was a port of call for many mercenaries within Brack's pay.

Dinner passed uneventfully, save for the occasional flirtations of a particularly well-proportioned barmaid. Ryad was immune to such temptation and Beran was still infatuated with the face of a certain elven princess. However, this apparent lack of interest contributed little to dampening the woman's ardor. The two warriors conferred on matters of training regiments and defense strategies. Soon they lapsed into a discussion of politics and the need to curb Lord Brack's aggressive sorties into the east. Ryad looked up when the door of the inn opened. The warm evening breeze sent a billow of air to ruffle the long tresses of a hostess serving drinks in the front foyer. Through the door slunk five undesirable looking personages. Each wore leather jerkins and heavy traveling boots. From hips swung sword belts that housed mercenary blades. Their leader wore a black patch over his left eye. The remaining good eye searched flittingly the room taking in the details of every face. That beady macular froze when it perceived Ryad and Beran seated at the corner table. Without staring directly at them, Ryad studied every movement the five men made. He noted where on each body weapons were worn, the height and weight of the men, and the safest route of passage out of the inn.

The sword-master recognized Brack's men immediately. Beran, however, ate, unaware of what transpired at the door. Ryad kicked him hard under the table to issue a nonverbal warning. Beran didn't have to turn around to know that trouble loomed only a few tables away. Ryad thrummed all five fingers on the table to let Beran know the odds against them.

The mercenaries, after consulting with their leader, fanned out around the room. Two remained beside the door while the other three slowly approached the table. Several of the patrons, sensing trouble, rushed to leave. The inn-keeper, hoping to stay the inevitable, intercepted the one-eyed man as he crossed the room.

"Kind sir, perhaps I could interest you in a meal or a pitcher of our finest ale?" With one hand the mercenary brushed him off and continued his ominous advance toward the corner.

Ryad imperceptibly nodded his head to signal that one man had come within sword reach of their table. Beran exploded from his seat kicking the bench back into his startled attacker. The mercenary went down to the floor and Beran leapt forward driving his sword hilt into the man's head. Bone splintered where the man's skull experienced the crushing death blow. The dead man's friends ran quickly to join the fray, only to find Ryad's sword eagerly awaiting them. While Ryad engaged the two door-men, Beran drew himself up to his full height and prepared to meet the remaining swords. Ryad jumped sprightly up onto a table and with lightning speed dove under one blade and parried the other. The mercenary that had over-committed his attack was dead before he completed his less than graceful swoon to the floor. In the same swing of his sword arm, Ryad cleaved off the head of the second attacker. With a wry grin, he then sat on the fireplace and waited for his captain to finish his duel. By now the inn had emptied completely save for the inn-keeper who hid quaking behind the ale caskets. Beran, not accustomed to fighting in such close quarters, was having a difficult time with his two antagonists. One had discarded his sword in favor of a long knife and jabbed dangerously at Beran every time the captain parried his partner's sword blade. On each lunge, Beran left his entire right flank exposed. Tired of the game, the captain picked up a pitcher of ale and threw it into the face of the swordsman. In that brief moment of disorientation, Beran focused an attack on the knife wielder who backed quickly towards the door. The captain reacted with the speed of a mountain cat and in just two strides was upon him. In a last act of self defense the knife man hurled his lethal blade directly at Beran's chest. Beran deflected the dagger expertly off his broadsword, and sent his next stroke downwards through the man's wrist and into his lower abdomen. By now the last standing mercenary had recovered from his brief loss of sight and approached menacingly from behind. Beran sensed the heavy breathing man and cupped the hilt of his sword in both hands. Powerfully, he drove the point swiftly underneath his own armpit. A gurgling and the sudden heaviness of his blade gave him the satisfaction that his blind thrust had cut true.

"Thanks for the help master swordsman," grunted Beran.

"You had everything under control. I especially liked that lightning reflex bouncing the dagger off your blade. We'll make a master out of you yet," laughed Ryad.

The inn-keeper emerged from his hiding place all of a bluster. Walking toward the front door, Ryad threw him two gold coins to help pay the cost of the damage.

"I think it is time for us to return to the barracks my friend." Ryad took one last draught from a pitcher of ale that had somehow remained intact throughout the fight. Exiting the Unicorn, they heard the inevitable whistles that blared to alert the night watch. Ryad loathed dealing with the bureaucracy of the local policing force. The chief watchman loved nothing more than jamming thorns in the proverbial backside of Shupan Garrison's commanding officer.

"Come Beran, I will wait and file a report in the morning. I am far too tired to deal with the pompous watch chief tonight.

Caelin Paul

Oh, and until our friend, Lord Brack, chooses to forget about you, we had better take to eating our meals in the garrison mess hall. We get enough sword practice during the daylight hours without having to dull our blades on vermin of the dark during our downtime.

Chapter Twenty-Five

Conspiracy

Lord Brack was not in the best of moods. He had returned from the North only to find that a prisoner had escaped. Not accustomed to being denied or surprised, the dark-lord had demonstrated more than his usual vengeful anger. His advisor, Coquatan had met a grisly demise at the paws of his beloved mountain cats, and many more of his expendable servants experienced similar fates. Lord Brack swiftly ensured that every mercenary from Cartis to Shupan, and every bounty hunter from Mallicus to Kelanon, was made aware of the handsome price he had placed on Beran's head. Greed was an accomplice of the dark, and he knew five thousand gold pieces was more than ample incentive for his avaricious followers. It would only be a matter of time until Beran appeared again before him in the pit. When he did, no expense would be spared to make sure that justice was rendered slowly and very painfully.

The meeting with Rune had been a pointless waste of his energy and time. He knew better than most how impossible it was to attack Meridia. Rune had grandiose plans of building an army and marching through the Southern Passage, sailing the Adearan Sea, and knocking on the queen's door. Brack thought his brother a fool in not considering the defensive power of the Archmage and his council. He, on the other hand, had already started in motion a more subtle means of undermining his cousin's stronghold. Already, he had found a man to infiltrate the Meridian community.

Now all Brack had to do was bide his time and determine how best to use the mortal before the subterfuge was discovered. Needless to say he had not shared this success with Rune. He had his own agenda, and ultimately it did not include collaborating with Damal, Vilus, or Rune.

＊＊

Meanwhile, Rune was frustrated. For years he had attempted to discover the secrets of Meridia. In recent years he had enlisted the aid of the Sisterhood to help in his cause. The sisterhood was a mysterious cult of sorceresses that resided in the Temple of Gajiina, far above the northern cloud-line. Their temple was carved directly into the black mountains. The high priestess was a powerful witch in her own right. Once she had been a student at Meridia, but had been cast out for dabbling in the dark arts. Her expulsion resulted from a failed attempt to summon a terror wraith. King Celebus, a thousand years earlier, had vanquished the wraiths. Capturing their essence, he had imprisoned them in a schism outside of time and space. Chaniya had stolen the journals of Celebus and had used them to create a small rift in the schism. A terror wraith had reached through the rift and had begun to unravel the spell of binding. When Archmage Kalon arrived in the library he was confronted with not just one wraith, but a whole army of terror wraiths shrieking angrily as they attempted to loose themselves from their prison. It had taken the combined might of Kalon and the entire Mage Council to drive back the evil creatures and re-seal the rift. Chaniya was stripped of all honorable rank and suffered immediate expulsion from the island. So angered was Kalon by the student's betrayal that he had taken his staff and placed it to her head. The staff had burned in her forehead the mark of djah, a mark reserved only for traitors to the crown. Chaniya had never forgotten the humiliation suffered at the hands of the Archmage. For years she traveled across Terrus, facing ostracism at every turn. Finally, she had found an eager acceptance with the sisterhood at Gajiina. Over the course of the century Chaniya, had risen quickly through the sisterhood's ranks until finally she realized the power and station of High Priestess. Her heart embraced evil and with Lord Rune she shared a dark alliance whose goal it was to eliminate the sentinels of light and destroy all that the Archmage held dear.

For years Rune had delighted in the company and confidence of the Lady Chaniya. Indeed, the high priestess had become a willing and exciting bed partner for the dark-lord. Now she informed her lover that she had made progress on a unique and powerful spell that might ultimately destroy Meridia. Of course Rune had not shared this important tidbit of information with Brack, but then again why should he? He would bring Terrus to its knees, and then take care of his bastard brother.

* * *

Lord Vilus continued to feel the ill effects of the wakening-induced madness. In rare moments of lucidity he poured over maps and scrolls that depicted Meridia and the surrounding countryside. Since losing the services of the night demons, he had attempted to win over new allies. Finally, he formed a tenuous arrangement with the barbarians of the Black mountains, poaching them from Rune's territories. The barbarians were a fierce mountain people, preferring the rugged terrain of the hills to the gentle tundra of the plains. Only at times of famine or severe winter did the tribes surrender their high peaked homes for lesser elevations. Largely cannibalistic, barbarians lived off the meat of mountain goats, horned sheep, or occasionally the sick or ill of their own tribe. In a land where food was a precious commodity, the tribesmen saw little point in wasting meat, even if it was human. This indiscriminant culinary taste translated into a blood-thirsty and savage fighting force. Vilus, no stranger to savagery himself, enjoyed the company of the inarticulate clansmen. Baticus commanded an eagle's view of the Western reaches from its location in the Pyels. Though not as lofty an environ as the Black mountains, several thousand barbarians had made the pilgrimage to set up home around the bat-infested castle. Vilus had no desire to take on Meridia. His carnal pleasures centered on committing the greatest degree of torment, bloodshed, and terror his station would allow.

* * *

The remaining dark-lord, Damal, lay back in the hot-spring bathing pool enjoying the soothing warmth that flowed through his body. Naked servant girls ran tirelessly around him seeing to his every need. Since the news had arrived of the decimation of his legion of dragons he had been in a foul humor. Many servants and women from his harem had experienced pain, torture, and death to satisfy his anger and sadistic pleasures. Of the dark-lord's, Damal was Queen Sara's nearest neighbor. For the last eight hundred years he had invited her regularly to his extravagant parties but she had always declined his invitation. Now he found that he was in the unique mindset of forcing hospitality upon his erstwhile cousin. He had underestimated one of his brothers. Never in his wildest imagination did he think Vilus would have the guts or gall to attempt a kidnap of the ninth son. Now the spineless weasel had cost him his most useful servants. He knew that Rune and Brack would be plotting some damnable scheme to take on Meridia, and he also knew that neither one would include him in their plans. Certainly, there was no love lost between the children of Jesobi. However, now more than ever, they needed each other. Immortality seemed a high price to pay for not destroying his brothers. Still, he would bide his time and ride the shirt-tails of his more ambitious brethren. Then, when they had exposed themselves, or the enemy, he would make someone pay for ignoring him.

Chapter Twenty-Six

Celebus

Storm found himself drawn into the story. 'It was a fierce and violent era in the history of Terrus. Mighty dragons stalked the earth and man fought bloody battles of survival versus creatures of the dark. In spite of hardships, the formative world was undergoing a startling transformation as technology, intelligence, civilization, and commerce promoted man to a position of power. This position was solidified with the courageous efforts of a certain young tribal leader by the name of Celebus. Dark powers on Terrus had unwittingly unleashed a dreadful malevolence. From beyond the sphere of known space came the terror wraiths. Vaporous, ethereal, and untouchable, the wraiths swarmed across Terrus like angry locusts sucking the very life blood from the earth. There was nowhere to hide from the deadly touch of their ghostly appendages. Like thieves in the night the terror wraiths stole upon unsuspecting victims, suffocating them in their impenetrable cloaks of nothingness. No defense could resist their callous pillage, and the earth seemed to surrender to the inevitability of conquest and death.

One man stood as a beacon of light against the threat. Celebus rallied the barbarians of the north, the lesser dragons of the east, and the citizens and wizards of the out-world colonies. On an island in the heart of Terrus the leaders of the known world made a stand against the terror wraiths. It seemed as if the wraiths had an extreme disaffection to water. Consequently, the enemy dared not cross the Adearan Sea. Instead the wraiths wrought havoc, death, and devastation throughout the continental shelf. Celebus and his allies worked exhaustively to advance a solution to the parasitic menace. A device was engineered and placed in the hands of the tribesman. The device was untried and untested and no man was willing to sacrifice their life for something so indefinite. So it was that Celebus sailed out alone from the island aboard a tiny skiff. He alone stood upon the Bala Sands, to endure the fear of the terror wraiths.

The waning sun vanished completely as the blanket of writhing dark approached with unconscionable speed. Celebus stood firm repulsing the need to vomit and the overwhelming urge to run. At the very last possible instant, Celebus activated the device. Blood curdling screams of hatred intermingled with disconcerting bewilderment. Helplessly, the terror wraiths were drawn to the device by a definitive compulsion. Waves of indefinable blackness swept over and around Celebus. His body visibly quaked with fearful dread, yet still he held firm his ground. The putrid stench of evil pervaded every inch of his being, yet even then he refused to relinquish this last bulwark of defense. The torrid frenzy ended with exuberant finality as the last vestige of terror wraith disappeared from Terrus, imprisoned outside of time and space.'

Storm grew frustrated as he continued to read the story of Celebus. The description of the events and the nature of the terror wraiths read disappointingly vague. Little mention was made of the specifics concerning the device that had been engineered to trap the wraiths. The diluted history left Storm with more questions than answers and he made a mental note to pursue this story with the Archmage at a later date. Reading on, he learned more about the evolution of the royal family.

'Celebus returned to the island as a hero. The survivors of the shadow plague were eternally grateful to their savior. Word spread swiftly of the courage and heroism of the tribesman. In no time at all he had been crowned the first King of Terrus and so began the genesis of the Meridian monarchy.'

The remaining pages of the book afforded a sequence of events and successions leading to the birth of Elam and Jesobi. 'Celebus was the great-great grandfather of the crown princes and the grandsire of their father. King Celebus ruled for fifty years and was much loved by his people. His son, Corundun and his grandson, Tamrin were respected rulers. His great grandson, King Laburnum, also inherited the love of the people and was remembered as a kind and charitable monarch. In Laburnum's waning years, Elam and Jesobi became mortal enemies and brought the kingdom to civil war. The night the brothers disappeared from the field of battle, the beloved King Laburnum passed away. By now the crown was in disarray and the people, dissatisfied with broken promises and conflict, rebelled against the monarchy. The children of the crown princes scattered; all except for one. Sara remained on Meridia and through her determined altruistic efforts and kindnesses, attempted to recapture the people's faith in the royal family. The tiny island kingdom, called Meridia, remained the seat of power within Terrus and before long drew to it the finest intellects and minds the world had to offer.'

Storm finished reading just as the bells began to ring and the illusion of the windowed hall began to dissipate. This was only his third day studying in the hall and he wondered if he would ever truly become accustomed to the wonders of the Academy. He waited beside the arch as everyone crossed through. For two days he had not seen his friend Anyal and he found himself missing her company. Then, as if by magic, she was there beside him smiling and looking particularly excited.

"Hello Storm. How is Zira today? Has he forgiven me for calling him a dog yet? I had no idea he was a snow wolf. In my book today I read about them and there was a drawing that resembled almost exactly your Latsu."

"Zira forgives you," said Storm, "although I am not so sure he is as quick to forgive me these days. The long hours of class cut into our exploration time. For a week he has skulked around in the gardens and now is threatening to go adventuring without me."

Anyal laughed as she saw the sad expression that flitted across Storm's face. "We better get going before the arch decides to send us to our rooms for being tardy. Are you coming?"

Caelin Paul

The two of them stepped through the arch and for the first time they emerged together on the other side. Waiting for them, was Mage Dulkin. Standing at his side was a young man of about sixteen years.

Dulkin's voice sounded stony and harsh. "Ah so very nice of the young catchers to consider joining us. Now let me have the pleasure of introducing you to a third, this is Yurmin."

Chapter Twenty-Seven

Yurmin

Storm extended his hand in greeting to the olive-skinned boy. Yurmin looked at the proffered hand with disdain. Offended, Storm detracted his hand. Dulkin viewed the indifferent exchange with a sly grin on his face. Anyal, sensing the uncomfortable situation, attempted to diffuse it quickly by introducing herself to the stranger.

"My name is Anyal, and this is Storm, we are both students at the Academy just like you. We would be glad to be your friend and show you around."

"You are nothing like me and I do not need anyone to show me around," replied Yurmin.

"Now, now, Yurmin, you must be respectful to all your fellow students even if they are much less skilled," said Mage Dulkin. "Now, if the formality of introductions is concluded, let us begin today's lesson."

The teacher and his three students sat in a spacious square room. The centerpiece to the room was a stone fountain that sent streams of crystal water spouting toward the roof. Sparkling water splayed musically upon the hard quartzite surround as it fell from above. On every side of the fountain jutted smooth benches of grey granite laced with flakes of mica that flickered in the soft torch light. Flaming sconces provided illumination, sending strange shadows dancing into the darksome corners. The three youth took a seat on the bench and waited expectantly for the mage to begin speaking. A nervous anticipation prickled the air. Dulkin, seemed particularly in tune to the heavy atmosphere and allowed the discomforting silence to continue to pervade the queer surroundings. Intermittently, Storm stole his attention from the cold steely eyes of their instructor in order to take in more of the room. He noted that there was no visible door to the room and no windows. Some fifty feet above, a padlocked trapdoor extended across the hard-wood ceiling.

At length, Dulkin broke his silence. The Mage's voice grated on Storm's nerves. With an inflection of distinct disinterest Dulkin addressed his oration at the children rather than to them. "No doubt you think yourselves special. Archmage Kalon has suggested that the three of you might possess the aptitudes of a catcher. It is fallen to my responsibility to help you develop, hone, and harness these respective abilities. Of the three of you, Yurmin is by far the most advanced in the magical arts. He has skills which make him a master of the elements. Perhaps you would like to demonstrate this gift my boy."

Yurmin stood quickly, a pretentious glint in his eye. "It would be my delight and pleasure Master Dulkin." Long, flaccid limbs began to weave in gesticulating motions. Unintelligible words muttered from narrow, pasty lips. The flames in the wall torches burned effervescently surging into mighty columns extending upwards toward the ceiling. Yurmin controlled the creeping flames with one hand, even as he extended the other toward the fountain. With synchronicity, a funnel of water rose in concert with his hand motion. Soon the tower of water reached the height of the flames. Yurmin, all of a sudden, clapped his hands together and water met fire high above their heads. A loud crackling and fizzling occurred as cold merged with heat. Resultant steam hissed and clouds of grey vapor burst into being. Yurmin extended his fingers forcibly and the trapdoor above their heads burst open, revealing an azure blue heaven. Relishing its opportunity for freedom, water vapor poured out into the sunshine. Then, with appreciative finality, Yurmin uttered a single word. Obediently, the trapdoor slammed shut restoring an eerie darkness to the room.

In a blink of an eye, the water fountain and wall torches trickled and burned as if nothing untoward had occurred.

Dulkin clapped his hands together in a rare exhibition of positive emotion. "Congratulations my dear boy, what a wonderful display of elemental control," stated the Mage. "Now perhaps Anyal might show us a little of her talent." Anyal blushed, never one to flaunt her ability, the idea of performing in front of Dulkin was not something she relished. However, obediently she closed her eyes and forced herself to concentrate focus to a single thought. Slowly, she lifted off the ground, rising with graceful efficiency. Thirty feet from the floor she paused, and with the careful precision of a gymnast, performed a variety of unsupported somersaults, twists, and pirouettes. Storm felt his heart uplifted by the aerial presentation. The impromptu recital drew to a close and Anyal began to descend slowly. Suddenly, a spurt of water from the fountain leapt into the air hitting Anyal squarely on the cheek. The shock of the cold water jarred her focus and she began to fall. Storm watched in horror as the screaming girl plunged toward the stone tiled floor. Without thinking he leapt across the marble bench pushing Yurmin heavily to the ground as he went. Anyal fell like a rock. Storm braced himself against the wall, bent his knees, extended his arms, and prepared for impact. He saw the girl's body rush to greet him but the collision never occurred. At the last possible moment, Anyal recaptured her focus and instantaneously froze her fall. She hovered prone in the air, scant inches above Storm's arms. Anyal was livid, her face was red and contorted with rage. After righting herself, she stepped past Storm and confronted Yurmin. The taller boy was just getting to his feet when Anyal cocked her fist and clobbered him full in the face. He went down hard on the seat of his pants for the second time.

"Don't you ever try anything like that again," yelled the irate girl. "Who do you think you are anyway, marching in here acting all high and mighty, showing off and then trying to injure a fellow student?" Yurmin sat flabbergasted and stammered an apology that had an even more maddening effect on the hot-tempered Anyal.

Mage Dulkin had not said a word throughout the entire event. Storm noted the sardonic amusement that occupied the man's features. When at last the Mage decided to speak, Storm was not surprised to hear the condescending tone.

"Well, well, well. Our talented children have a lot to learn about manners. First, Yurmin you deserved that punch. You need to be a little more careful about when to assert your talent. As for you, Anyal, no matter what the distraction, you should be able to maintain your level of concentration. One day, it might well cost you your life." Next the Mage turned to confront Storm.

Pointing a gnarly finger at the boy, Dulkin positively spat the rebuke. "You should not be so quick to interfere in the affairs of others. Anyal made a mistake in letting Yurmin distract her. If she falls, it is not your place to catch her. Everyone needs to be accountable for their mistakes, even if it results in a bruise or two. Now all of you take a seat at the fountain. There are valuable lessons to be learned from every action. The first is an inner awareness of contingency action as opposed to angry reaction. Every task, and every element of magic, is predisposed to action. However, there is always a compelling force determined to unravel and destroy what we choose to manifest. Therefore, instead of reacting to the inevitable, one must be erstwhile prepared to fall upon an alternative path, a contingency choice if you will. This contingency must always exist before the act. Think well upon these words for one day they might be the difference between progression and obliteration. Now, Storm it is your turn to impress us."

Storm stood and walked to the center of the room. "What am I supposed to do?" asked the confused boy.

"Whatever your capacity or competence will allow," returned the mage.

Storm sighed and shut his eyes. Focusing concentration on the image of Anyal lifting from the ground, he attempted to mimic the levitation skill. No matter how hard he tried to focus on the skill, nothing happened. After several minutes he looked up to see Anyal's concerned expression and the smug expression on the face of Dulkin. Chancing a glance at Yurmin, his heart beat angrily as he watched the older boy unsuccessfully suppress laughter.

Child of Night

The sneering facade of the narrow-eyed mage, combined with the intermittent giggles of Yurmin, was almost more than he could bear. Storm felt rage surge through him. His blood raced frantically through veins and his mind swirled with pent-up emotions and unrecognizable images. Wind abruptly swept through the room buffeting the four figures with an impetuous fury. Suddenly, Dulkin's expression transformed from derision to fear. Not a moment too soon, he conjured a dome of protection over himself, Anyal, and Yurmin. Storm, outside of the barrier, lifted his arms to the sky. Conscious control surrendered to rage. The loss of Nicholas, the forced departure from his childhood home, the shadow of an unknown past and impossible future, compounded with the mocking sneer of Dulkin and Yurmin, became a single uncontrollable release of energy. The trapdoor above ripped from its hinges. Blue sky drew dark in front of their very eyes. Thunder clapped and lightning illuminated the heavens. The room shook and shuddered violently as masonry and bricks dislodged from their foundation. Marble flagstones ruptured beneath their feet and the benches around the fountain cracked and crumbled. A blazing fork of lightning slashed from the firmament and tore convulsively through the crystalline rock. The water sizzled and spewed molten hot as the fountain exploded in a dazzling eruption of silicate pieces. Walls around them caved inward and rubble rained down upon Dulkin's protective encasement. Still angry emotions raged within the young boy's frame. There seemed no respite to this frightening display of power. At the height of Storm's cathartic exchange, a figure materialized beside him. Kalon calmly strode to stand in front of the entranced child and touched him softly upon the shoulder. Instantly, Storm opened his eyes and the raging wind ceased. Tears sprang forth from red-rimmed eyes and the boy gave way to an unrelenting grief. Kalon held him close and soothed his hair with aged hands. Dulkin released the protective shield and stood amidst the rubble with an expression betwixt bewilderment and exasperation. Yurmin no longer smiled, but cowered against the decimated fountain. Anyal buried her head in her hands and cried.

Kalon spoke softly while at the same time sending disapproving glances in the direction of Dulkin. "I think that is enough excitement for today children. You are all three relieved of your studies for the next two days. I want you to take the time to relax and play. No reading or talk of magic, just enjoy the bountiful beauty of the island. In a few days we will meet again and I shall take it upon myself to teach the next lesson." Kalon shot Dulkin one final dark glance then clapped his hands, returning everyone to their quarters.

Storm succumbed to an uneasy sleep long before the kindly Archmage conferred him into the protective care of his guardian. Wolfy lay Storm down upon his cot of straw and crept quietly out to talk to Kalon. Zira had howled and cried throughout the duration of his master's elemental outburst. The wolf had tried to force his stream of conscious to join Storms, but found it closed to him. No amount of telepathic imagery could restore a link. Now Zira lay at his master's side licking tear-stained cheeks and cleaning the dust and grime that lay embedded in his hair. Wolfy looked at Kalon and sighed. The farmer had known immediately the cause of the fireworks above Meridia. Fearfully, he knew that Storm would be found at its core.

The Archmage shook masonry dust from the front of his robe. "You know he is an extremely special young boy," said Kalon. "Never in all my years have I been privy to such an abundance of energy and power. My meager ability pales in comparison to the force that lays latent within Storm. I do not know how to teach him, and I do not know how to help him control such a power. But try I must. Should the Academy fail in this undertaking, we will find his soul forever lost to the light."

Wolfy listened intently to what the Archmage had to say wringing his hands nervously together. "I love the boy Kalon, but how may I offer one such as him protection?"

Kalon paused reflectively before answering him, "Wolfy, he is untrained and vulnerable. Recently, he has had to accept much of dark feelings and little of pure light emotion. His past is a mystery and his future unreadable. It is for you, and any others that would befriend him, to teach him love, joy and happiness in the present."

Wolfy nodded. "Storm is all I have left Sir. I love him as a father loves his son. I will never desert him and while there is breath left within me I will do all I can to protect him."

The Archmage smiled gratefully, "as will I, my friend, as will I."

Chapter Twenty-Eight

Anyal

Anyal spent a sleepless night tossing and turning in her bed. The night was unusually warm and no breeze blew off the ocean. Her bed was soft and provided a welcome escape from the rigors of academia. However, the events of the day had left an alarming impression upon the girl. Finally, she relinquished the idea of peaceable slumber and arose to put on her clothes. Anyal worried for her friend. She knew what it was to be alone in the world and his spirit called to her. The moon was high in the sky as she slipped out of the bed chamber and down the hall to the stairs. Placing her stealthy foot on the first step, her attention was diverted by whispering voices. On the landing below she saw two shadowy figures engaged in conversation. Curiosity won her over and she failed miserably to resist the temptation of eavesdropping upon the two speakers. She recognized straightaway one speaker as being Yurmin. His timorous vocalizations had a pronounced capacity to set every nerve on edge. The second figure she did not recognize. Hooded, the man kept to the shadows and spoke in an accent with little inflection. Anyal floated noiselessly across the landing to a point secluded by a braided tapestry.

"He is a threat to the island and must be eliminated or exiled. The boy is a loose cannon and not to be trusted. His talents are not creative and useful like yours. Everything he touches turns to ashes. I am not even sure he is a true catcher. Catchers have control of their talents. Even that bratty orphan Anyal shows skill and control in her manipulation of air."

"What would you have me do Sir," returned the unmistakable voice of Yurmin.

"You must discover a way to get the boy discredited. Today's events did little to ingratiate him to the mage council. Unfortunately, he has the ear and sanctuary of Kalon and Queen Sara. However, if he were to break the law of the island, not even their help could prevent the arch from spitting him out onto the Bala sands. Indeed, you will experience great reward should your efforts prove fruitful. Now go. We must not be seen together. Remember your guardian has asked this of you and he would be desperately disappointed should you let him down."

Anyal shrunk into the shadowed recess of the tapestry folds as Yurmin scuttled back towards the bedroom complex. The unidentified stranger vanished from view before Anyal could get a look at his face. Realization hit her with the force of a freight wagon. All was not what it seemed on Meridia. The students had been informed that no evil could survive on the island without incurring the collective wrath of the mage council. Clearly, there was a flaw in the assumed impenetrable defenses of Meridia. Anyal wondered if the Archmage had any suspicions about Yurmin. She also wondered if the hooded conspirator was in fact himself a member of the council. Mage Dulkin had appeared pretty chummy with Yurmin at the lesson earlier.

Stealthily, Anyal continued on her original purpose. The ground floor was deserted. Slipping out one of the side-kitchen doors, she crossed the main courtyard to the stables. A deep rumbling came from within the stalls and Anyal froze in her steps to try and locate the source of the noise. Poking her head in at the stable door, she sighed with relief when she realized that the rumbling came from a certain snoring farmer. Wolfy slept in a small room on the lower level beside the tack room. Storm had commandeered the hayloft, much to the chagrin of Zira who was not overly fond of climbing ladders. Anyal lifted from the ground and drifted up to the second level. Storm breathed hard and twitched restlessly. Zira opened her eyes and gave a guttural growl of warning.

"The one who walks on air comes to visit," sent the snow wolf.

Storm sat up abruptly. Zira had sent a vibrant image of Anyal walking on a cushion of air just above his head. Anyal knelt down beside her friend.

"Are you alright?" she asked. "I could not sleep tonight. All I could think about was this afternoon's lesson and the mess you made of the north parapet."

"The north parapet?" asked Storm.

"Yes, the north parapet is one of the teaching structures attached to the academy. We were taking class in one small area of it but your little outburst caused the whole tower to be evacuated. It will take days for the royal guildsmen to repair the damage, even with the council's help."

A look of horror clouded his face. "I did not mean to cause so much damage." Tears welled up in the boy's eyes.

The black-haired girl reached across taking his hand in hers. "Do not be sad, no one was hurt, and Kalon himself said that the tower was much in need of renovation anyway. In fact, you will probably be thanked by the guildsmen for getting the chance to show off their artisan skills to the academy." Storm smiled. He knew Anyal was just trying to cheer him up, but he also knew the truth in what she was saying. The artisans loved nothing more than to demonstrate their skills, especially to the magicians who they felt looked down upon their craft.

"Can I stay and talk to you for a while?" asked Anyal.

"Sure, I could really do with some friendly company right now." Zira rolled his eyes and then sent an abrupt retort, *"oh, so my company is not friendly enough for you?"* Storm let out a chuckle.

"What's so funny?" inquired Anyal as she snuggled down beside Zira.

"Oh nothing, Zira just reminded me that I should not forget about him every time a pretty girl comes along."

Anyal blushed. "You mean you can talk to the wolf?"

Storm nodded, "it is not so much conversing as it is exchanging images, ideas and feelings. For a long time I could not understand what he was trying to say to me. Nowadays, I am able to fill in the missing pieces and comprehend almost everything he wants me to understand."

"I wish the same could be said for me," sent back Zira.

For the next several hours, the two friends shared stories from their past. Anyal talked of the wild forests of the southwest and the strange creatures that called the trees home. Storm was particularly intrigued by her stories of a creature called a wallah. The wallah lived in the Yiladan and was about the size of a small child. They were reported to be one of the oldest inhabitants of Terrus and many stories existed of their legendary colonies. Legend purported that these tree-climbing intelligents lived in breath-taking citadels high among the tree-tops. Stories suggested that only the elves were permitted access to the Wallah's lofty citadels, and few men were able to penetrate deep enough into the Yiladan to even attempt access to the mythical creature's domain. Anyal was one of the few villagers to have had contact with a Wallah. Anyal told Storm the story of her encounter with one of the forest creatures.

"On a trip berry hunting in the Yiladan, I became terribly lost. I tried desperately to retrace my steps but the path became ever more treacherous. Nightfall descended quickly, so I prepared myself for a night beneath the forest canopy. No sooner had I lain down to sleep than I heard a distressful moaning coming from nearby. I followed the sound of the crying and less than six trees distant I came upon a dreadful sight. There pinned in the steely jaws of a bear trap lay a youthful Wallah. Clearly, he had lost much blood and was dreadfully scared and hungry. Stalking him in a circle that grew smaller by the second was a large forest cat. The Wallah had used a tree branch clenched within his furry fingers to keep the big cat away. Now exhaustion threatened to overcome him and his eyes began to close. I shall never forget the despairing whispered moans of a creature preparing for an inevitable death. I raced into the clearing and delivered a hefty kick to the forest cat's hind quarters. That cat let out an angry yelp and bolted into the trees. The Wallah passed out unconscious and remained that way while I pried open the jaws of the bear trap. Next I bathed the wound in a nearby mossy spring, and wrapped the shivering

Wallah up in my warm shawl. The poor mite shivered with hunger so I fed him berries from my little basket. By now it had gotten very late so I settled down to sleep. I curled up against a tall oak tree with the bundled Wallah snuggled tightly in my lap. When I awoke the next morning, I found, to my amazement, that I had returned to my village. Beside me, lay a basket filled to the brim with wood-berries."

"What a wonderful story," said Storm. "But how can you be so sure that you weren't just dreaming it all."

Anyal grinned. "That's what everyone in the village said. Not a single soul believed my story no matter how many times I told it. The other children made fun of me and called me 'Wally' all the time. But I know what I saw and I remember what a magical feeling filled me as I tended that young Wallah. There is one other thing that convinced me I wasn't dreaming," said Anyal.

"What was that?" asked Storm.

"Well, I have never told anyone this before, but when I awoke that morning I found this lying in my lap." Anyal took from around her neck a strange looking pendant. It was a wooden circle with a blazing depiction of a tree centered within the sun. "I think this was a gift from the Wallahs, a token for my having helped one of their tribe. I was only seven summers at the time but I have worn it ever since and find it a strange comfort."

Zira slept soundly, breathing heavily with giant paws spread haphazardly across the bed-sheet. Storm yawned and let his eyes close. Anyal followed suit. Just as sleep threatened to conquer her, she sat bolt upright.

"Storm, I almost forgot to tell you something very important."

Despite his fatigue, he reluctantly opened his eyes and sat up. "What is it?"

Anyal talked excitedly. "I overheard Yurmin speaking to someone in the palace on my way down to visit you. Well, the man in the shadows told Yurmin that if he could get you exiled from the island then he would be rewarded somehow. I wish I could tell you who the other man was but I never got the chance to see his face. Perhaps we could confront Yurmin and get him to tell us."

Storm chewed thoughtfully on his lower lip. "Somehow I don't think Yurmin likes either of us very much and he will only deny the conversation ever happened. I guess I am just going to have to watch my step and stay out of Yurmin's way. Do you think we should tell Kalon about any of this?"

Anyal rubbed her jaw as she contemplated talking to the Archmage. "Why don't we wait a while and see if we can uncover the identity of Yurmin's co-conspirator. It would be nice to have some proof before we go accusing people of things."

Storm nodded in agreement then yawned. "Well enough excitement for one day, I think it is time we both get some rest." And that is how Wolfy found the two young people the next morning, curled up in little balls, atop a mattress of hay, on either side of the sprawling snow wolf.

Chapter Twenty-Nine

Chaniya

The high priestess lounged seductively on the divan beside the window. Rune eyed her with emotionless desire. He knew that the woman before him offered only a momentary diversion to his more important political machinations. Chaniya, also, he knew, held private counsel to her own evil intentions. Though each plotted their own damnable schemes, they were united in their pronounced hate of the sentinels of light. The sisterhood was a powerful ally. The Temple of Gajiina was second only to Meridia in accumulation of knowledge. Deep in their dusty vaults, stood shelves, stacked high with every book ever written on the magic arts. The sixty-four sisters who called Gajiina home were students of the dark arts and spent each day studying, learning, and practicing their evil craft. Chaniya had risen to prominence at an unfathomable rate of speed. From a young age she discovered the ability to retain every word she read. Not only was she able to read and retain information, but she had the innate aptitude of translating text into process and words into powerful incantations. None at the Temple could rival her skill and thirst for power. The previous high priestess had discovered this at the cost of her mortal life. Sensing a rival for her office, the superior had sought to banish Chaniya to the sphere.

The sphere was a horrific internment wherein the soul separated from the body without being allowed to proceed to Tellus. The resulting nightmare left a spirit and body in a vegetative state of conscious torment. Chaniya's predecessor had unleashed the spell of banishment only to be met with a counter-spell of gross magnitude. The ultimate irony lay in the superior's own spell delivering a backlash committing her own body to soul death. The sphere inherited an unwilling guest that fateful day, and Chaniya installed herself as High Priestess without entertaining a vote from the other sisters. The potency of her power and her apparent ability to so easily dispatch one of the most powerful spell-casters on Terrus, made her a force to revere and honor. The previous superior continued to lay in a waking coma within the catacombs of Gajiina, her body kept alive only through the kindnesses of servant girls.

Chaniya, had lived a hundred years already, but a spell of metabolic slowing greatly reduced the speed of the aging process. With the aid of magic, her body enjoyed all the privileges and accoutrements of a girl in her twentieth winter. Curvaceous and thin with well proportioned features, the high priestess never failed to attract willing bed partners. Dark hair flowed over naked shoulders and eyes the shade of jasper hypnotically danced above a regally set nose. The only visible blemish to an otherwise perfect face was the disfiguring scar she bore upon her forehead. This badge of shame declared to the whole world that she was a traitor to the crown. In spite of Kalon's curse, her disposition bespoke a polished self-confidence. Not a woman used to disappointment, she took whatever she did not have. To her, Lord Rune was just another conquest, another step along her journey towards destroying the Archmage. While he proved useful, she would continue to bed him. He was energetic enough between the sheets, and certainly she had experienced far more inept lovers.

"So my Lord, are you desirous to hear of the progress I have made?" Chaniya shifted her weight allowing the silk robe to fall away revealing a sensuous depth to her inner thigh. Rune licked his lips in anticipation of some future amusement.

"I am always delighted to hear of progress, particularly if it has anything to do with destroying the accursed wizard isle."

"Well my Lord it seems as if the misty rock has a few weaknesses after all. I have been trying to uncover the mystery of the arch they call the 'seefar.' It seems the arch is composed of a rare mineral called gylantium. This rock conducts and harbors more life energy than any other object on this world. Kalon has found a way to infuse this structure into the very core of Terrus. He has also given it predictive qualities I have not been able to comprehend. However, he has overlooked one significant flaw. As you know it is a law that no man or woman may enter the boundaries of Meridia if he or she is found to be less than pure of heart." Chaniya spat on the floor as she said the words. "Well the seefar expels people off the island regularly when a student is deemed unworthy to continue their studies. This is all well and good for testing the mettle of the Meridia students but what about everyone else? What you might not know is there are other such arches strategically placed on the island but which are hidden from view; how else could a farmer, fisherman, or servant be judged regularly as to their worthiness. Well, I have engineered a device to isolate the locations of the sister arches of seefar. If we could get someone on to the island, they would be able to avoid the gates and perhaps even destroy them for us."

"Ah, but how do we get someone on to the damnable rock?" asked the impatient Rune.

"That is the beauty of my plan. The person we choose would have to be someone weak-minded who can be persuaded to help us in such a course. Once he is on the island, he can only be removed by passing through an arch. I am sure it would not be too hard to find a simple-headed fisherman who would undermine a few stone arches in exchange for ensuring we didn't kill a family member or two."

Rune walked over to his scheming ally and lifted her forcibly from the cushions. "I like how you think High Priestess. This is a plan with some merit, but we can wait until morning before we recruit ourselves a fisherman." With that he delivered the willing female to the confines of his luxurious sleeping quarters, and then proceeded to satiate his hitherto unrelenting sexual appetite.

Chapter Thirty

Ambush

Beran led his patrol along the ancient High Street. The main road ran north to south from Kelanon to Garthlet, and passed through every kingdom garrison with the exception of the newly formed barracks at Sard. One of the legacies left by King Celebus, the road provided a safe means of travel throughout the known continent. Mercenaries and bandits preferred the less policed back roads and rugged cross-country trails that threaded ubiquitously throughout Terrus. Beran had been asked to accompany two squads of soldiers to Sard. With the opening of a new kingdom garrison, each commanding officer had received a request from the crown for the transfer of two squads to the new barracks. Ryad had decided to send Beran as an escort, largely as an excuse to get him away from the continued pursuit of Brack's paid hunters. Beran rode at the head of an advance patrol which included Jakes, one of the younger squadleads. Self-admittedly not the most accomplished of riders, Beran constantly struggled to keep his horse's head away from the road-side vegetation. Jakes grinned broadly when, for the twentieth time in as many minutes, Beran yanked hard on the reins of his willful steed.

"Sir, may I give you some advice?"

Beran looked across at the laughing Jakes. "If it is advice to help me control this accursed nag, then I bid you speak at length and without censure."

"A temperamental horse is much like a spirited woman," began Jakes, "to make them behave you must be forceful and kind all at the same time. If you are too forceful, they will break and hate you. If you are too gentle, they will take advantage and not respect you. However, if you love them, feed them, caress them, bathe them, converse with them, and at the same time inspire a little fear in them, it is amazing what a woman, or a horse, will do for you."

"I appreciate the advice Jakes, now I know why I have no luck with women either," said Beran. The two of them shared a laugh as they continued onward down the High Street.

The road ran along the precipitous frontage of a cliff escarpment overlooking the Icealic Ocean. To the west as far as the eye could see stretched cold, green sea water. The sound of waves breaking upon wind-swept rocks echoed resonantly from a hundred feet below. It was spring, yet the riders wore heavy fur-lined cloaks to keep out the biting sting of a cold wind that billowed off the ocean. To the east swept undulating moors, an inhospitable tundra where even the most hardy of nomads spent few days journeying. Beyond the tundra, lay nothingness, an unexplored morass of lifeless rock. The High Street marked the south-easternmost boundary of the known kingdom and was an area infrequently traveled and sparsely populated. Beran did not mind the chill air. On the contrary, he found the wind and cold invigorating. Life in the northern reaches had prepared him well for the dynamic changes that characterized the Terrus climate.

Sixteen men rode with him in the advance party. Nearing the steep-walled Jarinska Pass, the road narrowed and the soldiers were forced to ride just two abreast. It was late in the day and the sun swept its last vestiges of light beneath the far-off horizon. The plan was to ride ahead and secure a defensible campsite for the two squads that followed behind. As they neared the bottleneck entrance to the pass, Beran started to feel uneasy. He reined in his horse, who had given up foraging in the vegetative-less trail. The hairs on the back of his neck prickled and he rubbed the nervous itch with a calloused hand. Jakes, who rode beside him, noted the concerned expression on his captain's face.

Child of Night

"There is nothing to fear from the pass Sir. There is nowhere to hide and the canyon walls are too steep to conceal bandits or archers."

"Something just doesn't feel right," answered Beran. "Call it a sixth sense if you will, but I feel that trouble awaits us just ahead. I suggest we proceed with caution and have a man ride flank fifty horse lengths back. If we experience trouble, I want him to ride like the wind and warn Captain Crill."

Jakes sent a message up the line and two soldiers wheeled their horses and trotted cautiously back the way they had come. Beran gave the order and the patrol moved into the furtive shadows of the Jarinska Pass.

The squadlead was not exaggerating the sheerness of the avenue of igneous rock that voraciously swallowed up the remaining light. There was indeed no place for a bandit to hide and very little room to maneuver. Beran ordered torches lit. The lighted brands gave birth to a macabre diorama of shadows that flittered skittishly on either side of them. The pass was only a short league in length and despite the captain's misgivings, the end of the canyon arrived swiftly to greet them. Jakes knew of a wayside at the far end of the pass and it was to there that he guided the patrol. The road began to widen as the ocean returned to view. The moon in its fullness, cast a yellow swath across the salty desert. To the right rose the empty hills of the eastern reaches. Still, feelings of unease hung heavily upon Beran. Sensing their captain's apprehension, the other members of the patrol rode silently with nervous vigilance. The wayside loomed ahead of them. All along the length of the High Street were strategically built resting houses. These simple structures offered shelter and basic provisions such as candles, flint, blankets, fresh water, and occasionally food.

The riders came upon the seemingly deserted wayside and several of the men jumped down from their horses to secure them to the tie post. Beran continued to look suspiciously around, but the area looked completely devoid of life and no footprints disturbed the grey dust. As he slid from the saddle his hand instinctively went to his sword hilt. An almost inaudible scuff of a leather boot came from the direction of the sea. Instantly, Beran bellowed out warning, "Ambush!" Even as his patrol turned to heed their captain's warning, from the shadows sang deathly crossbow bolts. Men ducked behind horses to take cover. A new threat emerged from behind the wayside. Silhouettes sprang from hiding places beneath the lip of the overhanging cliff-face. Beran, realizing that they were surrounded, screamed out orders.

"Circle up, keep the horses between you and the wayside, draw your swords and don't break the line. Jakes, send a runner back through the pass, we need help and we need it fast." The squad-lead, anticipating his captain's request, hurled a blazing torch brand into the air. The sound of horse hooves echoed against the hard rutted road fading away into the distance as sounds of battle filled the dusky night. Jakes had stationed a man at the edge of the pass for just such a contingency. Now he hoped in earnest that his attackers had not thought to block the canyon.

Beran and his men were forced to fight on both flanks. The arrows had ceased momentarily only to be replaced by a horde of black clad broadswords. Beran cursed himself for not paying greater heed to his dissonance, a fact that he promised to rectify in the future, that is if a future existed beyond the night. His men were hopelessly outnumbered and at a strategic disadvantage being pinned down in the center of the roadway. Beran had personally trained this patrol and they fought savagely with skill and determination. Yet still he felt the pang of loss as men clothed in the colors of the Shupan Garrison surrendered souls to Tellus and spirits to the ground.

Beran yelled the order for all the torches to be extinguished and the line to be tightened. Death blows, the sound of steel clashing on steel, and the breathless exertions of antagonist and defender filled the night. Beran entered the berserker's rage without warning. His eyes glazed white and he found his night vision naturally enhanced. Whirling sword in biting arcs above his head, he opened a gaping hole in the onslaught of attackers. For every one swing of his broadsword, two assailants fell to their deaths. Jakes fought like a caged animal determined to protect his captain's flank and stave off mortal wound.

Beran, in his unconscious zeal, had surged away from his company swinging a now heavily bloodied sword in every direction of the compass. Fear of engaging the blond-haired warrior caused many an attacker to hesitate briefly in their attack. This hesitation cost many a soldier life or limb. Like ants over honey, still the wave of black poured over Beran and his men. The captain chanced a look back over his shoulder and the berzerker's rage faltered momentarily as he saw that only three of his men remained standing. Suddenly, the world went dark and he slumped to the ground unconscious. In that moment of distraction a fiercely wielded sword had smashed into the back of Beran's head. Fortunately, the shadow that threw the blow had unwittingly turned the edge of the blade so that only the flat of the sword pummeled Beran's skull.

* * *

Less than an hour later, the two squads from Shupan rode ferociously through the Jarinska Pass. Each soldier rode with swords drawn preparing for a battle that no longer existed. The spirits of every Shupan soldier sunk. The road was littered with bodies, swords, and dead horses. Clearly, the kingdom men had given a more than auspicious account of themselves. Twelve Shupan uniforms lay bloodied in the dust amongst some thirty-six black mercenary outfits. The captain, a seasoned veteran named Crill, sprang from his saddle and searched through the faces of the dead. After a few minutes he shrugged his shoulders and looked around as if he had lost something.

"Twelve dead but Captain Beran and Squadlead Jakes are not among them. Quickly, first patrol, search the area and see if there are any survivors, friendly or otherwise, who might shed some light on this affair. Second and third patrol, unload shovels and let us commit our fallen comrades to the ground. We will bury them in the lot beside the wayside. Fourth and fifth patrol, stack this scum and burn them. Sixth and seventh patrol, ride out along the highway and see if you can pick up any trail, but do not follow until we are all together. I do not relish losing any more kingdom men this night." Crill grimaced. He had been a soldier for most of his adult life and had fought many battles in defense of the kingdom. But the dark was rising and he felt it with every ounce of his being. This attack on kingdom militia was too well planned to be the work of simple bandits or untrained mercenaries. Even more disturbing was the fact that Beran and Jakes were nowhere to be found.

Chapter Thirty-One

Damalan

Beran opened his eyes slowly. The world around him blurred and the backside of his head throbbed. Raising himself to his knees, a flash of nausea induced spasmodic vomiting and he slumped once more unconscious to the icy floor. Many hours later he awoke cold, stiff, and face down in his stomach's regurgitation. His head swam and vision transitioned with fluid abandon between lucidity and blackness. Try as he might, he could not move his hands that were cruelly bound in front of him. The lower extremities were also cinched tightly with rope and every limb experienced the tingling sensation that results only from forceful constriction of blood vessels.

Using the wall for support, he willed himself to a seated position. Beran swallowed back blood and bile and resisted the temptation to resume a state of blissful unconsciousness. Any sudden movement caused explosive pain in his head, back, and groin area. He tried to recall the events of the night, but all he could remember was Jakes bloodied face fighting beside him, and a flash of agony as his head exploded with pain.

Slowly, vision cleared and he began to take stock of the crude surroundings. A small windowless cell with a thick barred door greeted his returning senses. The room was icy cold and a shrill draught blew from beneath the cell door. In the far corner there lay two dark shapes. By the color and form of their riding boots he assumed them to be members of his ambushed patrol.

"At least two of my men survived," he mused somewhat wistfully. Not knowing the true nature of his attackers, he wondered whether a fatal sword wound in battle would be more preferable to whatever dark fate awaited them beyond the locked cell door. Beran stared at the two bodies for some time but neither moved position or showed any discerning evidence of life. After an hour or more, he summoned the fortitude to embark upon the journey to the far corner of the cell. The suspense of not knowing whether his men lived was almost more than the captain could bear. With painstaking slowness, he shuffled on his backside across the floor. It took several minutes, and many bouts of nausea, to accomplish the trip. The first body was short in stature, a man Beran recognized as one of the more recently enlisted soldiers. He recalled that the man's given name was Chop. An odd name yet it somehow fit the stumpy soldier. Beran leant over the comatose man and discovered, to his relief that he still breathed, albeit shallow and irregular. Beside him lay the second body. Jakes had survived the skirmish on the road, but at what cost? The young squadlead lay badly beaten and blood soaked his tunic from stab wounds in the right forearm and chest. Still, fortunately most of the wounds appeared to be fairly superficial. The most visible damage exposed a grotesque distortion of the squadlead's left eye. Dried blood covered the forehead and cheeks of the young soldier, and the soft tissue had swollen to the size of a plum. Beran nudged Jakes with his foot; promptly engendering a groan. The squadlead opened his eyes and proceeded to suffer through a similar waking ritual to that of his captain. Beran, still a little fragile himself, waited patiently for Jakes to recover.

"So my brave squadlead, any ideas where it is we have been brought, or what the dragon's hell happened to us back there?" asked Beran.

Jakes shifted positions by dragging his head along the mildewed cell wall. "Well, I could be mistaken but I think we got our butts royally whooped." Jakes attempted to smile through the deep bruising of his face. "It seems like you were taking pretty good care of yourself until you decided to turn around and check on us. For a moment I thought you would beat the whole damn horde on your own." Jakes started to laugh, but a heaving coughing fit soon curbed such youthful exuberance.

"So, what happened after that sword smashed into my head?" asked Beran.

Jakes composed himself and then pursued a short explanation of the events that followed Beran's bludgeoning.

"After you went down, the odds were too great. Me and Chop were the only ones left standing against fifty. We thought we were gonners for sure. Although it went against every instinct I had, I threw down my sword and surrendered. I figured I was no good to you and Chop dead. They bound us pretty good and man-handled us down the road quite a ways. There were horses waiting and they tossed us around like onion sacks. During the whole ordeal no one said a word to us. You were out cold and Chop suffered the ill-effects of a concussion. I have never known anyone who could sleep the way he can. Oh, except for you that is." Again Jakes began to laugh, but thought better of it when the stabbing pain reconvened in his chest.

"We rode for several hours across some backcountry going away from the ocean as far as I could tell. I remember arriving at some massive gates and a courtyard that stank to high hell of manure. We were taken off the horses and a few of the guards were made to watch us. It seems they didn't get enough action at the wayside because they proceeded to give us all another royal beating. When they saw that I was awake they kindly helped me back to sleep. I can tell you firsthand, dusty boots do not taste good with only blood to wash it down. The next thing I know I wake up in this lavish bedroom with two ravishing beauties to keep me company."

This time it was Beran's turn to repress the urge to laugh. Jakes was certainly not a depressing cell-mate. While they had been talking, Chop began to stir. The soldier was in a bad way and could barely move without convulsing in agony. Beran felt along the man's rib cage. Not a single rib bone was left intact. For the next several hours, Chop coughed up blood. His breathing, for painful minutes, would become labored and heavy. The captain knew that the soldier would, in all probability, not survive the night.

A grating came from without the cell door. A small hatch opened in the bottom panel and a grubby hand thrust a dirty tray of stale bread and a flagon of brackish water into the room. Beran shifted his weight and sidled over to the door. Extending his feet, he caught the edge of the tray and slowly dragged it towards them. Together, Beran and Jakes sat Chop up against the wall and carefully tipped water into his cracked, dry mouth. Then, soaking the hard bread in the less than palatable fluid, Beran forced pieces into Chop's mouth and down his throat. The meager portion was not enough to fill one small child let alone three grown warriors. However, Beran knew all too well that at times such as this, even a mouthful, when proffered, was never to be refused.

The monotony of time passed slowly on. Occasionally, muffled voices could be heard in the passageway outside their door. Chop continued to lie unresponsively within a state bordering death. Beran and Jakes drifted unwillingly between uncomfortable sleep and a fractious waking state. Within the close dark walls, the men knew no comprehension of time. Whether the sun shone or the moon glowed they knew not. How many days had they spent in their prison? How long would they remain there? Thousands of questions pervaded the minds of the restless soldiers. Despite the soreness, fatigue, and bruised muscles, both Jakes and Beran harbored the desire to fight at least one more battle. Finally, the endless waiting abruptly ceased as the cell door screeched open. Six menacing soldiers advanced and dragged them to their feet with less than gentle affection. Even Chop, in the throes of delirium, was not exempted the gruff treatment. Men in black forced their prisoners through dimly lit passageways of slime-drenched rock. Both Beran and Jakes fell more than once as their legs attempted to shake off atrophying stiffness. Each time they fell they were rewarded with a harsh kick or a cuff to the head. Beran concentrated on remembering every detail of their transfer. In between punishments he counted steps and turns until they reached a wide stairway. The stairwell was worn and sunken depressions had been eroded into the center steps from a millennium of footfalls. Throughout their short journey underground, the captain had counted dozens of cells similar to the one they had been impris-

Child of Night

oned in. A simple calculation in his head informed him that the prison complex had room for several thousand more unfortunate persons.

A stout oaken door at the head of the steps was heaved open and dazzling sunshine cut blindingly into unready retinas. Even their escorts threw up hands to shield unprotected eyes from the staggering heat and brilliance of the Terrus sun. As his eyes readjusted, Beran noted that they had been led into an expansive courtyard. Other doors around the atrium had also opened and more prisoners were reluctantly led out. The wide variety of personages committed to chains held Beran in awe. Women, men, children, the infirm, black skinned, white skinned, mercenary, barbarian, and kingdom soldier all stood bound and helpless in the cobbled prisonyard. A single trumpet call rippled through the mid-morning air. Immediately, every black-garbed soldier stood at attention. From beneath the entrance arch, perpendicular to where Beran stood, a man entered. He was clad in a white tunic with gold trim and wore black leggings and spotlessly polished matching boots. At his side he wore a sword whose jewel-encrusted hilt sparkled vibrantly in the reflected sun. At least a head taller than anyone else in the courtyard, he cut a dashing figure as he walked masterfully to the center of the square. Beran swung an inquiring look at Jakes, but Jakes answered back with a barely imperceptible shrug. Neither soldier recognized the richly attired nobleman.

"Good morning prisoners." The voice was strangely metallic, yet overpoweringly seductive. "Many of you know who I am already, but let me introduce myself to those of you who have only recently become guests in Damalan. I am Damal, King of the Eastern Reaches and heir to the true crown of Meridia."

Behind him a kingdom soldier in the uniform of the Illian Garrison spat in the dirt and yelled across the silent square, "you are no king, and you are no heir to the throne of Meridia. Queen Sara is our true and rightful regent and she is the only monarch who is recognized as such within the Reaches."

Damal turned and his eyes flashed with anger. He strode purposively over to the dissenting soldier and looked him squarely in the eyes.

"Oh, let me assure you I am King of my domain, and as king I have the privilege of choosing which of my subjects lives or dies. As of this moment you are one of my subjects, and as of this moment I choose for you to die." In one fluid motion he slipped the ornate blade from his scabbard and drove it forcibly through the prisoner's abdomen. Withdrawing the sword, he thrust it expertly through the dying man's throat to prevent any last vocalizations. Instantly the soldier collapsed dead.

"Anyone else want to suggest I do not have the authority of kingship, here in my own house?" The silence that followed was undisturbed even as the dark-lord began a slow inspection of the prisoners. Beran approximated that over a hundred persons stood chained within the square. Periodically, Damal stopped to whisper words to the guards. Occasionally, a woman or girl would be closely scrutinized. The pretty ones were released, to begin a life of servitude to their new master. The less fortunate ones, usually the uglier women, were remanded back to the jail cells for the amusement of his renegade guardsmen.

By now, Damal had come upon the three Shupan Garrison soldiers. Chop was the first in line, supported on either side to stop from keeling over. Damal gripped the soldier's chin and snapped it up to look at him.

"So you are one of the Shupan vermin that gave my men so much trouble at Jarinska. Hmm, it doesn't look like you have much resistance left in you." Damal turned to face the rest of the prisoners and in a loud voice said, "let me show you how we treat traitors. Damal turned back to Chop and nodded to the guards that held him. The men drug the semi-conscious Chop into the center of the courtyard and forced him to his knees. Chop swung his head from side to side, delirious and completely unaware of the proceedings. Jakes, sensing what was to happen, instinctively lurched forward after his friend.

Beran extended a restraining forearm across Jakes chest and whispered, "for Chop it is better this way, do not bring attention to yourself, or you may earn a similar fate." Jakes tensed up and watched helplessly as Damal released the sword from his belt. Without any pomp, ceremony, or warning, he brought the heavy blade down upon Chop's head, cleaving it cleanly from his shoulders. The head bobbled across the cobbles landing wide-eyed at the feet of Jakes. Just as the execution concluded, a rider rode into the quad and approached directly the dark-lord. The messenger sprang from the saddle, saluted his master and handed him a message scroll. Damal read its contents, muttered a reply and then approached the young squadlead with sadistic amusement playing in his eyes. Chop's head lay in the dust at the feet of the Shupan men.

"Pick it up," ordered Damal. Jakes bent down and picked the severed head from the ground. Sinuous tendons and congealing veins dripped blood upon Jakes boots. "You have earned a day's reprieve. I have more pressing business to take care of. Take your friend's head back to your cell as a reminder of what happens when uninvited guests trespass on my land. Oh and do not fear, tomorrow you, and your blonde-haired friend, will meet a similar fate. Take them away."

Damal turned his back on the Shupan soldiers and moved away toward the courtyard arch. Every prisoner in the square seemed to breathe a collective sigh of relief. The shared realization was that they would at least live to sleep one more night.

The journey back to their cell block was swift and straight. The guards threw the two men gruffly through the narrow door and locked and barred the entrance. Jakes, who still held in his hands Chop's lifeless head, literally shook with anger. He shuffled to the corner and laid down his burden with tender carefulness, closing the eyes and saying a prayer to Sajan, the Warrior God, imploring the deity to accept Chop into his celestial home. Beran, not a superstitious or spiritual man, respectfully waited while Jakes conducted these last rites. As usual, his mind ran at a million thoughts per second as he weighed and weighted every conceivable plan for escape. He could tell that Damal was not a man of idle promises, if they didn't find a means to escape by dawn, their lives would be forfeit.

Throughout the day, Beran wandered the cell exploring every nook and cranny. He paid special attention to the door which seemed to offer the only egress, but his spirits fell as he was forced to accept that their jail cell was inescapable. Potential salvation came from a most unlikely source later that evening. A scrabbling at the door alerted the men that the mid-day meal was about to be issued. The tiny trapdoor opened and a small hand dropped a metal tray rudely on the floor. Unlike previous deliveries the trapdoor remained open. Beran dropped to his knees and lent his ear to the icy cold stone. Two beady eyes regarded him curiously from the shadowy corridor. Suddenly, the trap slammed shut. A few seconds later it opened again and the same youthful eyes stared inquisitively through.

"Hey mister, are you the giant they says killed fifty men with your bare hands up on the High Street? The guards are also saying that you are the same man that escaped from the pit in Mallicus."

Beran laughed, "so, my jailers spend time making up stories about their prisoners do they my young friend?"

"Lupick, he is not a story-monger. He says he was at the pit the day an Illian soldier beat up on Brack's legionaries and escaped over the wall. Lupick says you look just like him, and he also says he's gonna tell Damal all about you, so as to get himself a reward."

"What's your name son?" asked Beran.

"They call me Spit," came back the reply.

"So Spit, what are you doing working in the dungeons?"

"I was born in the dungeons, lived here all my life. Never have been outside, but I hears stories from the soldiers and other guards."

Beran suddenly felt sorry for the boy. "Have you never wanted to go outside and travel the world and see new things? There are towering mountains with snow capped peaks, and free-flowing glaciers that creep down their sides. The rivers flash over moss-covered rocks and giant trees, with broad branches, stretch their leafy boughs toward the heavens. Then there is the ocean in which swim creatures larger than buildings. Massive ships sail from port to port selling every kind of cargo you could imagine. There are silk traders, and exchangers of precious stones and metals. Fishermen ply the waters with nets as they catch lobster, sea salmon, and other fish too plenty to name. How old are you Spit?"

"They say I am eight summers, but I'm not sure. Hey, if I let you out will you take me on a ship? I have always wanted to see the ocean and I hate living in the dungeons."

Beran could barely believe his ears. He looked over at Jakes who flashed back the broadest of grins. "Spit if you get us out of here, I'll not only take you onboard a ship, I'll get you a job as a sailor if that is your desire."

There was a pause from the voice on the other side of the door. "I got to go. I'll come back at midnight when the guards are sleeping." The shutter slammed shut and padded footsteps faded away into the distance.

"Well Jakes, perhaps we might get an opportunity to fight our way out of this predicament yet."

Jakes just grinned, "well we'd better do it quickly otherwise I'm going to lose that cute figure I've been working on."

Beran grinned back, "hmm, to my eye it seems as if this forced diet comes rather timely."

The two continued to exchange friendly banter as their spirits rose with the anticipation of an unlikely pardon.

Chapter Thirty-Two

Escape

Time dragged on and minutes surrendered to hours. Just when Beran began to doubt the boy, the food hatch slid open and red eyes stared unblinkingly through the hole.

"The two guards on this corridor have passed out drunk so we might be able to sneak past them. I know a secret passageway that brings us out in the palace cellar, but from there I don't know where to go."

"I guess we'll have to make it up as we go along then," said Beran. "So how do we get out of this accursed room?"

A light jingling sound came from the other side of the hatch as Spit proudly produced a large ring of keys. A few moments later there was a click as the lock mechanism sprung free. Beran gently put his shoulder to the door and pushed. The sturdy wood screeched on rusted hinges as inch by halting inch the door swung outward. Each push sent a disturbing echo along the dark, narrow corridor. At the very first sound, Spit fled into the darkness. Beran and Jakes edged the door open enough to squeeze sideways through the gap, then, together they slowly closed it. Thankfully, the grinding of the aged aperture was less loud in the closing. As the door squealed shut the locking bolt engaged, leaving the two soldiers alone in the darkness.

A brief moment later, Spit reappeared with a grin as broad as the Southern Passage. "We thought you'd run off and deserted us," said Beran.

"Nah, just returned the cell keys before they were missed, oh and I found this."

Spit held out a grubby hand containing a tiny key. "I thought you might like to get out of your cuffs before we make a run for it."

Beran grinned, "good thinking, now if only we had our swords back."

Spit beamed knowingly and said, "I stole those back for you too, I hid them behind some barrels in the wine cellar."

Jakes issued a quiet laugh, "it seems as if we have made friends with the world's greatest thief. Well, Spit, my name is Jakes and this barbarian is Beran. We are more than happy to have made your acquaintance and look forward to your company. Now we are all acquainted, I suggest we remove ourselves before our little disappearing act is discovered."

Spit led the way stealthily through a maze of dimly lit passageways leading in the opposite direction to the courtyard trek they had made earlier that day. Every now and again grunts, groans, snores, or sobbing sounded from the cells they passed. Their guide, a runt of a lad barely tall enough to reach Beran's belt, walked barefoot. A tattered shirt clung tenuously to his skeletal frame. Torn knee-length pants supported by a fraying cord of string covered emaciated legs. Despite his size, the boy set a swift pace and Jakes and Beran were forced to breathe heavily in their pursuit. Spit moved without pause as he turned to the left and then the right, ran up steps and down narrow stairwells. Only once had they been forced to a standstill. A brightly illuminated guard-room came upon them suddenly and Spit turned hurriedly around indicating with a finger to his lips that they should all proceed quietly. On tiptoes the three stole across the passage out of darkness into shadow. Beran sneaked a glance into the room and noted that four men were seated on crates, drinking heavily and playing cards. So loud was their chatter that a herd of sheep could have passed without drawing attention. The endless maze of cells and passageways came to an abrupt halt at a seemingly impenetrable wall of rock.

Spit turned to the two men and whispered, "this is a secret passageway out into the palace cellars. I use it to go exploring and to snitch food from the kitchens." The boy fumbled amongst some innocuous debris off to the right side of the wall. Suddenly, a panel at the foot of the passage slid open. The oubliette was barely a child's length wide. Spit dropped to his stomach and quick as a rabbit scurried through the hole. Jakes took a deep breath and followed their diminutive guide. Beran, being a full head taller and wider than his companion, found the passage extremely tight. It took a good amount of scrunching, pulling, pushing, and wheezing to persuade his muscled form to shrink enough to engineer escape. With Jakes pulling hard on his arms and shoulders, and Spit yanking on his belt, Beran finally fell through the hole, landing on a hard floor covered with wooden caskets and barrels.

Spit hopped off to the left and engaged a hidden lever. Promptly the secret door dropped back into place. The boy then over-turned a nearby barrel revealing swords, scabbards, and a well-stocked cache of food together with a flagon of Lord Damal's best brandy. The three of them drank sparingly. As Beran advised, there was little point escaping from the dungeon only to lose their lives on account of alcohol-dulled senses. They ate greedily and quickly while making plans for their escape. According to Spit they were in the wine cellar one floor beneath the kitchens and two floors from the main palace. To gain access to the grounds, they would have to pass through the kitchens without notice. Fortunately, it was the dark hours of morning and most within the marble citadel slept. Spit led his companions past a century's supply of liquor caskets, beer barrels, and shelves of fermenting wines. A narrow ramp led to a widely aproned stairwell. At the top were two wooden doors that opened inwards to the kitchen area. Spit noiselessly cracked open the left side and beckoned for the two to follow him. The kitchen was vast. Row upon row of stove, cupboard, meat rack, and preparation table spread outwards in a fanning oval. Towards the far end of the room, three bakers were attending voracious ovens that swallowed bountiful trays of uncooked breads and pastries. Apart from the cooks, the kitchens were deserted. Jakes whispered a silent prayer to Nishu, the God of Good Fortune. The three ducked low under cover of some storage shelves and worked their way hesitantly down towards the oven area. Spit padded along with the silence of a cat. Beran and Jakes, on the other hand, stalked along with the careful subtlety of horses in heat. Again, fortune was on their side as the clamor of the oven billows and the clanking of metal bread-pans drowned out the obvious scuffling of boots and sword belts.

Spit turned and pointed to a door off to the left. Beran nodded in understanding and watched with wry amusement as the boy dove under a nearby table. He emerged on the other side just as one of the cooks was placing a dough tray in the oven. The sight of a boy materializing from beneath a table startled the man so greatly that his carefully kneaded load surrendered to gravity. Bread dough flew everywhere as the kitchen was thrown into uproar. Beran and Jakes took advantage of the commotion to slide from their hiding place, across the open floor, and through the door Spit had indicated. Meanwhile, Spit, who was well known to the kitchen staff, apologized profusely and helped the cooks clean up the mess. Minutes later the boy reappeared beside them munching on a sweet roll and grinning from ear to ear.

"I figured you two make too much noise to have made it out without cook seeing you. Anyways, I was hungry and figured on a roll or two for my efforts," said Spit.

The fugitives now found themselves within a servant's staircase leading up to one of the main floor dining halls. The steps were lit with wall torches that smelled lightly sulphurous and glowed with an eerie yellow hue. Beran took the lead and silently withdrew his sword. Spit trailed behind him and Jakes brought up the rear. The stairs veered sharply to the right and ended at a silk blue curtain. Tentatively, Beran drew it aside and sighed with relief. The dining hall was dark and deserted. In a silent whisper he asked Spit where they should proceed next, but his question drew only a shrug of the shoulders. In all his eight years, the boy had never dared venture any further into the palace than the kitchens. The punishment for trespassing in the royal palace was death, not a penalty he relished much.

Beran slipped through the curtain and slunk into the shadowy recesses of the tapestried walls. Spit and Jakes cautiously followed, each at a respectable distance behind. The dining hall was richly decorated with a long table and high-backed chairs. On every side, balconies on the two higher levels jutted out into the room. The floor was tiled with blocks of rainbow quartz that sparkled even in the depths of night-time gloom. Beran paused at the first archway and peeked out. His eyes feasted on an ostentatious display of luxury. To the right and left ran hallways of gold, and in front of him rippled the most extraordinary fountain he had ever set eyes upon. The top of the fountain was lost to the naked eye as water cascaded down its sides to splash in shallow pools of crystal. On every side of the sculpted water conduit, heads of every conceivable animal, bird, and water creature, extended from the trunk of a man. Water gushed from the mouths of the lifeless effigies that all seemed to rise fluidly from the sculpture's torso. Richly adorned with gold, silver, emeralds, rubies, diamonds, sapphires, pearls, and opals, the fountain fairly danced with color. Clearly, by the expressions on the faces of his companions, the lavishness of the artifice was not lost upon them. Although the face of the central fountain statue was lost in the darkness of the upper levels, Beran had little doubt that its features would be reminiscent of a certain resident dark-lord.

The captain snapped himself from the reverie and started down the right-side corridor. Not a sound was to be heard from any quarter and not a soul interrupted their passage. Clearly, fear was its own guard and caretaker within the walls of Damal's abode. Few, it seemed, dared to be seen walking the hallways at night and who would dare steal from the dark-lord, particularly if his earlier display of justice was commonplace. A window at the end of the corridor looked out onto the stables. Beran tripped the latch and quietly pushed it open. The drop to the ground was a short one. He held the window open for Jakes who hung briefly on the sill before dropping gently to the soft grass below. Beran held Spit's arms and lowered him down to Jakes before following. They crept to the first building and peered around the corner. A small wood fire burned in the east corner of the yard and four soldiers

Child of Night

sat huddled around it. From the shuffling and heavy breathing that was coming from inside the structure next to them, Beran guessed that horses were stabled there. He ducked back into the shadows and grinned at Jakes.

"Well Squadlead Jakes, it looks like we are going to have to fight our way out. I count at least four men guarding the main gate. The sky is already lighting and morning can't be more than a few hours away so I suggest we move swiftly. I will circle around the back of the stables and try to get close to the gate. You two find a way into this stable and saddle up horses. When you hear the first sound of steel come running and ride hard for the gate. Jakes, you ride with Spit in front of you and lead the second horse along for me. With any luck, we might be able to dispatch the sentries, ride out the gate, and break for the High Street before the alarm is raised."

"Good luck captain," said Jakes.

"Luck? Who needs luck when you have a good sword, and two strong men to watch your back?" Spit beamed as Beran playfully punched the young boy on the arm. Then he was gone vanishing into the shadows.

Jakes slunk to the rear of the stable and probed the boards looking for an easy way in. Spit followed in his wake, mesmerized by the excitement of being outside for the first time in his entire life. Closing his eyes, he let the cool breeze play upon his face. Stooping down, he rubbed his hand upon the grass and picked up loose soil which he let fall through his tiny fingers. Meanwhile, Jakes had found a few loose boards and carefully pried several off with his sword hilt. The squadlead sidled through the gap and beckoned for Spit to follow. Once inside, he let his eyes adjust to the murky gloom. They had entered directly into one of the stalls and the smell of manure and horse urine blasted the senses. Clearly, Damal's stable boys had a lot to learn about horse husbandry and how to look after animals. The horse within the stall whinnied uncomfortably at the intruders but calmed instantly as Jakes caressed his withers. Jakes unlatched the stall door and took inventory of his choices. There were twenty horses stabled within this one barn and tack hung outside every stall. Jakes had grown up around horses and had something of a talent for choosing strong mounts. Two black geldings, stabled next to one another, won his approving eye, and in minutes he had them saddled and ready to ride.

"Alright Spit, when I say now, I want you to fling open those doors as wide as you possibly can. I am going to ride out very fast and I'll pick you up and position you in front of me. All you need to do is hold on tight with your knees, I'll do the rest. Oh and Spit, whatever happens, I want you to know I think you are very brave. No matter the outcome, you gave us the opportunity to choose our own path. If Nishu is kind to us you will get to ride on that ship yet."

Jakes and Spit did not have to wait long for the agreed upon signal. Beran had moved swiftly to the outhouse nearest the gate. He let out a curse as he realized the lack of cover afforded in the last fifty steps. His plan for complete surprise would require something of a miracle. With a deep breath he strode out into the courtyard and walked authoritatively toward the group. The soldier on the far side of the fire saw him first and demanded to know what watch he was from. The question bought Beran just enough time to reach the gate and plunge his sword into the chest of the nearest guard before the alarm was raised. A night of staring into the fire was poor preparation for protecting oneself from Beran's ferocious blade. Three dead bodies littered the fireside before the horses arrived. Jakes had charged out into the yard, throwing Spit up in front of him as he rode. The fourth guard, seeing the quickness of the captain's sword, had sprinted away toward the sentry tower yelling alarm at the top of his lungs. Beran picked up a dead man's sword and hurled it with astounding force. The point of the sword dug deep into the fleeing man's shoulder blade as he fell screaming to the ground. Beran leapt into the saddle just as half-dressed soldiers started to fill the stable square. Lights flashed on as torches were lit and an angry murmur filled the morning grey.

Jakes didn't wait for an invitation to leave, but spurred his horse out through the gate and onto the cobbled road. Beran, a mere gallop behind swung low in the saddle as arrows began to pursue them. Moments later the storm of lethal arrow-points ceased as

Child of Night

they passed out of range of their antagonist's bows. Outside the gate, Beran mused over the lack of resistance they faced. Clearly, Damal feared little of invasion, and even less of a prisoner escape. The three rode as fast as their steeds would carry them. Jakes had chosen well and the horses ran with a graceful, lengthy gallop. The confusion in the palace stables had bought them a good head start and for the first hour of their flight there was no sound or sight of pursuit. The road they ran was well groomed and offered sure footing, and though the horses frothed at the mouth, they maintained a strong, steady canter. As dawn arrived, so too did the first signs of danger. Overhead a black tross swooped into view seemingly keeping apace with their flight. The tross was notoriously a bird of the dark and a large-winged cousin of the great eagles of the northern reaches. Spit, exhausted from the night's adventure, slept restlessly against Jakes who rode one handed, using the other to prevent the boy from falling out of the saddle.

After two hard hours of riding, Beran drew his horse to a halt beside a road-side pool. Clumsily, he jumped down and led the sweating beast to water. Jakes did likewise, leaving the boy asleep in the saddle as he walked. The horses lapped noisily to re-hydrate themselves after their unscheduled morning of exercise. The drink was prematurely ended when the ground began to shudder and quake beneath them. The two soldiers had ridden conservatively in the last hour to protect their horses. Clearly, their pursuers had little inclination to rest their mounts as even now the dust of the road and the ominous approach of a small army greeted their ears. Without any exchange of words, Beran and Jakes remounted and drove their horses from a walk to a gallop. Neither man dared to look over their shoulder and rode hard towards the west. Beran knew that if they could only reach the main road they might still have a chance of surviving the day.

The sound of the chase drew ever closer and their horses were beginning to falter. Breathing became labored and the mouths of their mounts foamed. Where once steps had been firm and strong, now the horse's gait was tired and unsteady. Spit, by now was wide awake and every few moments braved a look behind him with terror sparking in his eyes. The harsh reality of his treasonous act was something even an eight-year old boy could contemplate during a life and death chase. The road began to narrow as they rode up on a wash. Suddenly, Beran's horse missed its footing and collapsed its right foreleg into a pot-hole. Horse and rider went down hard upon the red clay. Jakes reined up and jumped from the saddle to render aid to his captain. The horse had fallen hard on Beran's ankle and caused him to twist it painfully. They were just short of the summit of a small hill looking down on the valley through which they had fled. Their pursuers were now so close that the black uniforms and silver steel of weapons were clearly discernible.

"Jakes get out of here now. Get that boy to safety. That's an order Squadlead."

"Sorry sir, can't do that. My allegiance is to my captain and if he is going to fight this ugly mob then I want to be here with him." With that Jakes swung around to Spit, who cowered in the saddle.

"Hold on tightly to the reins boy, and if the horse slows down kick him harder. Ride to the road and may the Gods speed you." Without another word, Jakes smacked the flat of his sword to the horse's rump and watched as it exploded up the last few steps of the hill and disappeared over the summit.

"Well captain, I guess we will get that one last fight after all," said Jakes.

"I should have you de-ranked for not obeying a direct order Jakes, but to be honest, if I am to die today, there is no man I'd rather journey to Tellus with. Stand ready; we have yet one more hopeless situation to face."

Beran beat the cloying road dust from his pants and leant heavily on the shoulder of his partner. The ankle was at worst broken, at best severely sprained. No hope of outrunning Damal's men on foot and a horse with a lame right front forelock presented a quite hopeless situation.

The two men stood alone in the dusty road to Damalan. Both men had swords drawn and burning resistance flooded their eyes. From their vantage point near the top of the hill it was easy to assess the numbers drawn against them. Beran gave up the count when it reached fifty and contented himself with the approximation that Damal had sent out at least seventy men to capture him. Beran smiled grimly. Their pursuers had ridden their horses like madmen. Certainly, the dark-lord's stables would be a little emptier by the time they returned. Not even the famed wild stallions of the Adearan Plains could have hoped to sustain such a frenzied pace, and live to ride another day.

The lead mercenaries rode up slowly, eying the soldiers warily. Beran was expecting a charge, or a sally of arrows, or maybe even ten men to approach with drawn swords. What he didn't expect is what followed. An avenue opened up between the pursuing cavalrymen and a massive black horse with flaring nostrils and red eyes stepped to the fore. Seated atop the majestic thoroughbred was none other than Lord Damal himself. He leant forward in his saddle and grinned evilly down at the two men.

"Ah yes, the Shupan soldiers from the courtyard. I should have disposed of you when I had the opportunity. You have certainly led us a merry chase. Many of my best horses will die today because of your failed attempt to escape. No matter, I will ensure that your death is a painful one to make up for it." Damal stared at Beran for a moment, then, pointed a black gloved finger at him.

"So you are the great Beran that everyone in the Southern Reaches is talking about. The legendary man that escaped my brother's infamous Pit. Hah, I expected a lot more from the fuss that everyone has made about you. They say you are unbeatable, undefeatable, unkillable, immortal, even. I think not! And moreover, for the entertainment of my soldiers, I think I shall enjoy the opportunity to show just how pale and insignificant you are. I am thankful that I did not know who you were yesterday when you stood before me at the palace, because then I wouldn't have had the opportunity to destroy you now. I am a fair man. Should you be able to best me with the sword, I will gladly let you go free and your friend here too."

Damal jumped down from his horse and unclipped one of the largest swords Beran had ever seen. A ripple of excitement went through the ranks of blackened mercenaries. Jakes backed away, hoping that the legend of Damal's sword was as exaggerated as the seemingly widespread story of Beran's. The two men circled slowly, weighing one another. Damal sneered, as a sadistic grin played vividly on his face. Beran was the first to act and drove his sword straight at his opponent's chest. Damal swatted it away with a lightning parry that left Beran's sword arm throbbing. Beran's movement was severely hampered by the injury to his ankle. He barely had enough time to readjust his defensive stance as Damal slammed his blade in a powerful scything action meant to sever his opponent's neck. The blow brought Beran to his knees, and again he was forced to resort to defensive maneuvers in order to prevent a killing strike. Damal was unconscionably fast, every movement was balanced and fluid with a strength and force he had never before encountered. It was only a matter of time until Beran received his first wound. A driving swing had rung directly through his resistance and Damal's blade sliced cavernously into the exposed shoulder. Blood poured from the wound as the sword wrenched free and, in the same movement, bit deeply into Beran's right thigh. Biting back pain, he retreated a few steps to steal some time and space. Damal advanced menacingly, demonstrating a flailing mesmeric performance of spins in the air as the blade twirled and fell in his hand. The dark-lord smashed the edge of his blade against Beran's sword and then pummeled the hilt into his face. Beran fell back in a concussed daze with blood pouring from a broken nose. Standing above him, Damal wielded an arcing blow straight down towards Beran's scalp. At the very last instant, the blonde-haired captain drove up his sword. Beran's hilt deflected the attack but his sword blade shattered, and the force of Damal's strike continued downward into Beran's exposed left side. Bleeding from three potentially mortal wounds, Beran closed his eyes and waited for the end.

    Blood clouded his vision as his hands went instinctively to the fine grained dust that comprised the road surface. Jakes watched helplessly as Damal rained down angry assault and injury upon his captain. The end was never in doubt and he bit back tears of anger. Now the giant dark-lord stood over Beran about to end his captain's life. Even as the fierce blade swung downward, Jakes screamed a single word, "left." Beran reacted instinctively to the command and rolled hard to the left while at the same time hurling road dust into Damal's eyes. Damal howled with fury as the silicate tore into exposed cornea. He rubbed his eyes furiously as the troops behind him started to murmur.

"You will most certainly die now," shouted Damal as he again advanced upon Beran, "and your friend will die an even more painful death."

"Ah, but not today I think cousin!" A ripple surged through the ranks of the black-clad mercenaries. By now, Damal's vision restored itself enough to view the ridge above. The crest of the hill filled quickly with royal garrison soldiers. Jakes looked over his shoulder and tears of anger became tears of joy. He noticed Spit sitting on a horse amongst the soldiers and winked at him.

Ryad strode down the hill and stood menacingly between Damal and Beran, his sword drawn and fire gleaming in his eyes.

"Now Lord Damal you have a choice. You can choose to continue your personal vendetta against my captain here, or you can take the more intelligent option and return home to your little cottage. Should you choose the former, I put you on notice that you will have to kill me first, then every member of the two squads that sit at my back. Your choice cousin, but please make it quickly I have still much to do today."

Damal glowered at Ryad and his muscular frame shook with rage. Although a rash man, he was not stupid, and he knew that the one man on Terrus who might be able to best him with the sword was Ryad. At this moment of mortality, he was not about to test the hypothesis that he was the stronger swordsman.

"I will let you and your two weak officers go," began Damal, "but the boy there belongs to me." Damal pointed a long finger at Spit who was seated on the same horse Jakes and he had ridden out of Damalan.

"No," shouted back Spit. "You can't let him take me back there. He will kill me for sure. Please, please, I beg of you don't let him take me." By now the boy's pleading bordered on the hysterical.

"By Queen Sara's own royal law, you cannot take from me a servant who is mine," sneered Damal.

Ryad shifted his feet uncomfortably. He looked at Jakes and Beran, "I am afraid he is right. The boy must be returned to him;

in this we have no choice." Ryad turned back to Damal who glowered back.

"However, Damal, it also says in royal law that all subjects must be treated humanely. I cannot prevent you from taking the boy back to Damalan. But, if you dare to hurt him, I will personally see to it that you are tried, convicted, and executed in a royal court of law. Do you understand me?"

"Perfectly cousin," replied Damal. Then to his nearest guard he gestured in the direction of Spit, "fetch the boy, we ride for home." Jakes and Beran watched helplessly as the sobbing boy was manhandled from his horse and carried back to the throng of black riders. As they rode off into the valley below, the last cries of Spit were heard wafting across the morning air, "you promised to show me the sea."

Chapter Thirty-Three

Nolina

The Archmage had done his utmost to shield Storm from the repercussions of his uncontrolled outburst in the academy's north tower. Many in the council had called for the boy's expulsion and no one more vociferously than Mage Dulkin. Kalon was immoveable on the subject and refused to be bullied by his lesser peers. Instead he had broken from protocol and taken upon himself the personal advising of the three young catchers. Since the lesson in the North parapet, Kalon exempted Yurmin, Anyal, and Storm from passing through the seefar arch. Instead, everyday Kalon met the students in the Hall of Windows and personally selected the classes for them. Sensing the apparent tension between the catchers, he saw to it that Yurmin was not sent to the same classes as Anyal and Storm unless he was the one instructing them. For their part, the two friends took great pains in avoiding Yurmin.

Most of the youth's lessons were ordinary and mundane. The academy instructors were eager teachers despite their student's occasional apathetic regard for class-work. Anyal and Storm captured information and knowledge at a staggering rate of comprehension. A mere three months into their residency, the two catchers had exhausted almost entirely the knowledge capacity of Mages Yurl, Leskel, and Bartrand. Control of the earth, air, and fire elements offered little challenge to Storm, and Anyal possessed an aptitude to rival her green-eyed friend. The high-order brethren enjoyed greatly teaching the two children their lessons and mutual respect abounded. The same was not true of Yurmin. His abilities were as sharp as those of his younger rivals but lack of respect for his elders was an abrasive personality quirk not lost on the mages. So rude was Yurmin to Mage Yurl that the latter refused adamantly to teach the boy further. The only members of the Mage Council who Yurmin showed anything akin to deference were Mages Kalon, Dulkin and Saltorini.

Several months had passed since Storm's arrival on Meridia. Only two teachers remained anonymous to the boy. Maegess Nolina, teacher of the healing arts and Maegess Mirren, mistress of water. This morning, after independent study, Kalon met the three catchers beside the seefar, and after sending Yurmin off to Mage Bartrand's workshop on sulphurous manipulations, he turned to Anyal and Storm.

Kalon's eyebrows knitted themselves together in unfeigned consternation. "Recently, I have felt a definite unease around our students. The stars are ill aligned and I cannot help but feel that Meridia is threatened. The powers of the dark are subtle and their evil creeps insidiously throughout the land of Terrus. The dark rises and grows ever more powerful. The passing of Abbot Nicholas has given them confidence as well as power."

Kalon paused, seeming to search for the right words. "Anyal, tell me how your independent reading assignment progresses?"

"I have been given a manuscript that talks about some ancient curse called the Aruk. The author states that at some point a prophecy will come to pass that might cause great death and destruction on Terrus."

The Archmage smiled with approval and then turned to Storm. "Do you think you can help us by recounting the ancient prophecy Anyal has been reading about?"

Storm shut his eyes and let his memory return to a dusty study at Three Towers, where his mentor, Nicholas, had once asked him to translate a passage from an ancient text. "If I recall Sir, it goes something like this:

'There is a power in the world which holds the balance of light and dark intact. This power is the Aruk. In all four corners of the world there are Sentinels; protectors and de-

fenders of all that is alive. Four belong to the dark, four to the light. The balance of power can survive only till such day as the ninth son is born and the Darkwitch is dead. Then at Cartis in the land of Bal, the one called Fleet of Foot will hold the fate of the world in hand.'"

The Arch-mage turned again to Anyal. "What do you think of this prophecy?"

Anyal was taken aback by the question. "I really do not know what to think about it Sir. There are many children's stories that talk about the Sentinels, but most of them all end with the defenders of light vanquishing the powers of dark. I thought the Aruk was just a fairy-tale."

Kalon smiled, "and you Storm, what do you think?"

Storm shifted his feet nervously. He remembered Abbot Nicholas had once charged him to find answers to questions regarding the Aruk. "Well Sir, I know that the Aruk is as real as you or I. Abbot Nicholas was a Sentinel of light and his sister Sara shares the same legacy. But if Nicholas was able to die then that must mean the person whom prophecy called 'darkwitch' must also have died."

Anyal listened intently to Storm's words. Suddenly, she blurted out, "Storm is the ninth son isn't he?"

Kalon smiled and Storm felt his cheeks glow crimson with embarrassment. He turned to regard his friend with an expression of bewilderment. "I am not the ninth son! I am just an orphan with a gift for the bizarre. Isn't that right Archmage?"

"We do not know who this Fleet of Foot, named in prophecy, is. Indeed we know very little about the future. However, we do know that a shadow of evil pervades the sanctity of our fair wizard isle. I have chosen to speak to you today in confidence because I feel strongly that the two of you will be called upon to play a significant role in the battle that will inevitably come. You must be ready for what trials will be yours to face."

Kalon paused and cocked his head to the side as if listening to a sound from a distance. "I know that something threatens the balance of the Aruk. Come with me children and you shall see for yourself." Kalon led the two children through the gardens pausing in front of an ivy-clad brick wall. The Archmage knocked three times upon the hard brick. Suddenly, the illusory brickwork transformed, and where once red brick stood, now an open garden beckoned to them.

No experience in their life-time could prepare them for the beautiful sights and smells that assailed their senses. This garden, within a garden, burgeoned with the most beautiful flora ever to be collected in one place. Storm recognized very few of the flowers and plants that grew there. His attention however, was drawn to the center of the rapturous display. Towering above them stood a tree beyond all mortal comprehension. Its smooth bark sparkled with a blue white veneer. Lofty branches swayed gently in the morning breeze, and from extended limbs hung golden fruits of many sizes and shapes. However, the most remarkable facet of the tree was the music that seemed to resonate directly from its wooded frame.

Kalon smiled appreciatively as he regarded the reactions of his young students. "This is the Life Tree. Its roots are very deep, reaching even unto the very core of Terrus. This one tree reaches out its subterranean appendages to every corner of our world. The vibrations of all good and evil are recorded by this wizened giant. This life-force you regard in front of you can feel every emotion, every fear, every action of hate, and every gift of love. Its song is a song of balance. Rarely, does the music resonate discordant or un-pure. I am informed by Maegess Nolina that the night Nicholas passed, the Life Tree momentarily stopped singing, and, once begun again, the song became the most melancholy ever heard upon our gentle world. It was also that night that the cinchona bark lost its fullest shade of blue. Storm, may we see your collusk for a moment?"

Storm withdrew from his tunic pocket the strange spherical object gifted to him by his once guardian, Brother John. Anyal watched with growing curiosity. As he cradled the glass ball in his palm, the colors deep within swirled in a maelstrom of whites and blues, tinged every few seconds with an infusion of deepest red. As if sensing the collusk's close proximity, the Life Tree began to sing faster and ever more morosely. Storm held the collusk up in

Child of Night

front of him and watched enraptured as tree and glass ball shared an unorchestrated synchronicity of light and color. Every shade of blue, white, yellow, gold, orange, and green, played upon the sheen of its bark and tree boughs.

"Perhaps you should return that strange ball to your pocket, young man." The voice came from directly in front of them, almost as if the very tree had spoken. An imperceptible shimmering occurred as a figure emerged from the body of the trunk.

"Welcome to my garden Anyal and Storm. Welcome too, Archmage Kalon." The strange woman nodded reverently to the latter. "Forgive the authoritative tone of my manner but that orb you held seemed to cause pain to my mother." Tenderly, the woman caressed the fine skin of the Life-Tree. Storm was lost for words and thrust the collusk back into the deep pocket of his tunic. Even the Hall of Windows could not compare to the illusion that stood before him. She was dressed in a long delicate gown of softest blue with long golden hair that crept surreptitiously toward the ground. Noiselessly she approached the small group stopping before Kalon and taking his hand in hers.

"Come let us all walk together so that we might become better acquainted. My name is Nolina and I am the keeper of the Life-Tree. My friend, the Archmage, also gives me the rare opportunity to teach worthy students the fine arts of healing. It has been a while since last you sent me students dear Kalon."

The Archmage smiled gently. "It gets harder all the time to find personages worthy to be in the presence of the true life-heart of our world. I am grateful to you for wishing to share your talents with my two young charges. I cannot read the future, but I feel that Storm and Anyal will benefit from your discipline before the darkness is turned." Kalon smiled knowingly at the maegess who acknowledged his meaning with a flicker of her long eyelashes and a squeeze of his hand. Storm could not help but notice that several of Kalon's wrinkles seemed to smooth away during the time he held contact with the young woman.

"I leave the two of you in good hands," said Kalon as he moved to take his leave. "Mark well the words and thoughts that you are taught. They may indeed save your own lives, the lives of those you love, and the lives of those whose names you will never know. Mark also well the crimson scars that came unto the Life-Tree during our introduction. It has been a thousand years since the gentle bark was infected by such spectral shades of the dark. It is of particular concern that the Matriarch sees fit to warn us of a possible attack by the dark here on Meridia. Thank you kind Nolina, well met." An abrupt shift in the sunlight and the Archmage was gone. Anyal and Storm were left all alone with the maegess.

Storm could contain himself no longer. "You live in the tree?" Anyal kicked him hard but Nolina simply threw back her head and laughed.

"The tree and I are one. Just as you are mind-linked to your wolf, I am spirit-melded to the Matriarch. I was a tiny child when the call came to me. My birth father died during the mercenary wars in the southern reaches. My birth mother sacrificed her life in giving birth to me. A kindly woman named Terel took me in when my grandmother passed. I was five summers in age. Shortly after that, the spirit of the Life-Tree called to me. So strong was the calling that I was brought to this very garden and into the very heart of the Matriarch by a magic as ancient as time itself. At first I was scared. Can you imagine a five-year old child suddenly imprisoned inside the trunk of a tree? However, the Matriarch could feel my distress and she cared for my every need and desire. A year passed before I realized that I was not a prisoner inside the tree but rather a willing daughter who could come and go as she pleased. One day I was playing in the garden and Kalon discovered me here. He seemed not at all surprised. It was almost as if he expected my arrival. I have been a part of the Mage Council for almost a century and I am honored to now be your teacher."

Storm's jaw almost hit the ground. "Did you say one-hundred years? But that must make you over one hundred and five summers in age. How can such a thing be? You barely look older than Anyal and me."

"The Tree of Life sustains me and chooses the manner in which I age. As you know, trees can live for many hundreds of years, the Matriarch and I share a symbiosis and now, one cannot live without the other. In respective terms of time, the Matriarch is relatively youthful, thus I am fortunate enough to retain a semblance of youth despite my chronology." Nolina smiled down at the children and swept her, now transformed, silver hair away from her eyes. "Now my sweet inquisitive children, it is time to begin our first lesson. You must not be frightened of anything you see or feel here in the garden. Some of our lessons might appear painful but do not ever forget it is only an illusion used to instruct the mind. I promise no harm will befall you here. Now relax your minds and close your eyes. I am about to bestow upon you a special gift."

Storm did as he was instructed, although he made no attempt to hide his apprehension. Anyal, on the other hand, obediently relaxed her body and prepared for the joining.

Nolina took her left hand and tenderly touched Anyal's forehead. With her right hand she gently applied a similar pressure to Storm's head. The moment the maegess made contact, both children felt themselves grow sleepy. Just as Storm prepared to embrace somnolence, a luminous energy exploded in his mindseye. Out of the dazzling brilliance emerged Nolina who beckoned to him. Storm excitedly ran to follow her. No matter how hard he ran, he could not close the distance between them. Suddenly, the maegess came to a halt and allowed the impatient boy to catch up. She crouched close to the floor as if studying something. Storm peered over her shoulder and noticed to his horror that Zira lay on the ground bleeding profusely from a fatal wound in his left shoulder. Storm felt, rather than heard, his scream of anguish. Nolina reached out and touched his hand. A reassurance washed over him like the incoming tide on a barren beach. Nolina guided her hand over his and then solicitously pressed Storm's hand over Zira's wound. Immediately he was aware of Zira's life force. Simple strands of energy infused with miniscule light particles flowed haphazardly throughout the wolf's large frame. Some lines were clean, powerfully regular and flowed throughout the body, ordered with purpose and meaning. The lines around the wound were broken, jagged, and fragmented. With Nolina's mental prompting, Storm began to make sense of the energy and carefully began sorting through the irregularities. He concentrated on capturing like energies and focused completely on cognitively fusing like colored lines of electrons, protons, and atoms together. Storm worked feverishly, periodically surrendering energy from his own life force when there was not enough within the body of the wolf to work with. As he worked, he felt life and warmth return to his faithful companion and his efforts were rewarded by an affectionate lick from Zira's stubbly tongue. Suddenly, Storm was aware that Nolina no longer rendered aid or encouragement. Rather, she stood over him regarding his work with an expression half-way torn between pride and amazement.

As swiftly as the illusion was created, it ended. Storm found himself lying in the rich grass of the garden with Anyal seated on the bench to his right, grinning like a mischievous infant who had just gotten away with stealing a cookie. Nolina stood beside her, smiling sweetly as the sunshine scattered colors about her person.

It was Anyal who spoke first. "Storm that was the most amazing sensation I have ever experienced. I actually was able to see life energy for the very first time. Nolina guided every move I made, and would you believe I actually helped you fix a broken arm."

"Your illusion was me? Cool, mine was Zira; she had an ugly gash in her shoulder. Nolina, did we really learn healing or was that just a pretend illusion?"

"Oh Storm the problem that was lain before you was very, very real. What you saw in your minds-eye was a portent of future and how you will be forced to use your new gift for the first time."

Storm shifted his position uncomfortably. He realized suddenly that he felt exhausted. "Do you mean to say my broken arm and Zira's shoulder wound are events that are actually going to happen?"

"Unfortunately, that is often the way. Although you will be glad to hear that you both now possess the skills necessary to handle just such a contingency." Nolina smiled down at Storm and then whispered quietly, "you have a natural talent for healing that I have never before seen in a mortal. However, you must not always be as generous in giving up your life-force. Just from today's lesson you will be tired for a day or two, give up too much and you might feel the effects for weeks or months."

Maegess Nolina suddenly paused to listen. Throughout the lesson the Life-Tree had continued to sing a mournful song but now its tone seemed more needful.

"The Matriarch has need for me children. I am so happy to have met you both and I look forward to continuing our classes together. But for now I must bid you farewell." Nolina walked gracefully across the verdant grass and stopped momentarily to wave goodbye to her pupils before surrendering her form to the contours of the Life Tree.

No sooner had she disappeared than they found themselves transported from the garden to the dining hall area. It was very late in the day and few students or servants still moved around the tables. Storm and Anyal spoke little as they ate. Almost subconsciously Storm reached inside his tunic and quickly withdrew his hand as the collusk burned red hot to the touch. From across the room, he noticed the lanky form of Yurmin walk past the open door, deep in conversation with Mage Dulkin.

Chapter Thirty-Four

Mirren

The next two weeks passed swiftly. Anyal and Storm spent their time in the Hall of Windows studying books of medicine and herbal lore that, as usual, miraculously appeared and disappeared before them. In the afternoons, the two children enjoyed the company and unique learning opportunities afforded by Maegess Nolina, keeper of the Life-Tree. Nolina's knowledge of the healing properties of Terrus flora was a marvel. From Abelia to the Zygopetalum orchid, she knew the new and old names for each flower and plant on their world. Storm did not realize the vastness of the Matriarch's garden until he and Anyal began to pursue their studies with Nolina. In the northwest corner grew every conceivable annual and perennial, bordered by countless rows of bulbs, corms and tubers. In the warmer northeast corner grew the cacti and other succulents, blanketed on each side by walls of variant climbers and creepers. Along the southwest brick-work, and deep into the far south-reaching gardens, grew a plethora of ferns, palms, cycads, and grasses. The fruit trees, nut trees, and dazzling orchids resplendently claimed the southeast section. The remainder of the garden space was blanketed with a broad diversity of vegetables, herbs, and shrubs. Nolina made no attempt to contain her preference for the scented shrubs. All along the respective walkways were positioned boronias, rosemary, gardenias, lilacs, myrtles, roses, oleanders, lavenders, and even the night-scented Cestrum nocturnum.

Child of Night

The days passed peacefully within the secret garden. No one ever intruded upon their studies save for an occasional visit from the Archmage. Even the sonorous melancholy of the Life-Tree had a soothing effect on Storm's unsettled spirit. Increasingly, his dreams had taken on a macabre life of their own. Night-time dreams were plagued with black-hooded figures, evil spellcasters, dragons, and mythical creatures of the dark that, until now had only been the creations of village story-tellers. On Meridia, he was beginning to accept that even fairy tales contained some semblance of truth. The only respite from the nightmares was afforded by the ubiquitous visions of a beautiful light-skinned woman, a companion to his dreams almost from the day he had first learned about the Aruk. Storm did not know whether she was real or merely a figment of his over-active imagination. Yet if she were real, he was no closer to uncovering her true identity. One day Storm told Kalon about the woman from his dreams. The Archmage had listened intently to the description Storm unfolded. His only comment was, "with time and patience even dreams sometimes make sense." Storm was never a fan of riddles and evasive answers only frustrated him more. However, the Archmage's all-knowing smile suggested he knew more than he disclosed.

Storm especially enjoyed the sojourns into Nolina's domain because she permitted Zira to accompany them. In fact, Storm had initially experienced a sensation of jealousy when first Zira made the acquaintance of Nolina. The Latsu had followed the maegess around the garden like a love-sick child. Few men or women, in Storm's experience, won the wolf's affection so readily.

The carefree days in the gardens came to a sudden conclusion. One day Kalon met them beside the Seefar Arch and instructed them that their lessons with Maegess Nolina were concluded. Storm felt a deep-set sense of sadness and loss. He had not even had the opportunity to say goodbye or to thank the maegess for her attentions.

"Kalon, would you pass on our sincerest gratitude to the Maegess for spending so much time with us?"

Kalon smiled, "she already knows. She told me just today that she has never known two students so quick to learn and who so naturally acquired the healing arts. It takes a lot to impress the keeper of the trees. Oh and Storm, she also asked me to pass on some advice. She felt impressed to tell you that your fate in life is inextricably connected to that of Zira. Her advice is to keep the wolf close to you at all times." Storm found these words puzzling. Indeed, he could not begin to entertain a possible scenario that would force them to be apart.

Kalon continued; "now my children, there still remains one special lesson to attend, with a very extraordinary teacher. No doubt you are filled with youthful curiosity as to the identity of a certain water mage. Maegess Mirren, like Maegess Nolina, does not often frequent the palace walls, and is rarely seen by students. She chooses very carefully from those selected to the bench. I am never able to force her to take on students, so I have waited patiently, just as you have, for her to call for you. Anyal, Maegess Mirren wants very much to meet you, but requests that on this first day she have private audience with only Storm. I thought that you and I might take the opportunity to work on harnessing that marvelous levitation talent of yours. Now Storm, tread carefully in Maegess Mirren's presence. You might be somewhat surprised at her appearance, try not to offend."

Kalon and Anyal disappeared and Storm found himself transposed to a tiny grotto. The cave walls glistened incandescently with all manner of precious minerals. An appreciable light was afforded by the glazed white reflection of the mercurial pool that placidly swum below his feet. Storm could perceive no exit or entrance to the grotto and found himself overcome with a feeling of severe claustrophobia. So real was the fear that the mental link between boy and wolf sent Zira into a discomfiting serenade of howls.

Zira's concern surged into focus. *What manner of box imprisons you? How might I come to you?*

Storm took a deep breath and tried to calm himself and relay images of reassurance; attempting to focus upon the beauty of the cave as opposed to the dread he truly felt.

Zira's imagery became ever more desperate. Storm viewed the world momentarily, through the Latsu's eyes. The wolf prowled

Child of Night

outside the wall that led to Nolina's retreat. Clearly, Zira thought Storm was within the walled garden. Scrabbling his paws against the aging masonry, the wolf started to howl. The vision transformed as the garden wall faded and Nolina appeared, beckoning the Latsu forward. Obediently, Zira stepped through the opening and raised his head to be petted. At Nolina's touch, Storm felt the presence of the maegess. In ideas rather than words she tenderly informed the boy that Zira would be well taken care of until he returned to the palace. As the mental link was broken, a wave of pure love and reassurance enveloped him.

Storm shifted uncomfortably and sat down upon the hard rock. Time seemed to have little relevance in this queer place. Hours must have passed since his arrival and yet still there was no sign of Maegess Mirren. Despite the apparent lack of a visible personage, he could not shake the feeling that he was somehow being watched and appraised. Finally, the silence undermined what semblance of patience Storm retained under his control. He stood up and finding a rock at his feet, hurled it into the middle of the pool.

"Is anybody out there? I am not fond of small, dark places. I would appreciate it if you would allow me to leave now." Storm's powerful voice echoed vibrantly around the curvature of the gem-studded edifice. No sooner had he spoken the last word, than the room underwent a startling transformation. In seconds, all that remained was the glassy whiteness of the pool and the rock on which he continued to stand. Surrounding him were tall trees enshrouded in rich green foliage with lofty branches that extended tall pinions toward a canopy several hundred feet distant. From between narrow gaps in the leafy thatch, Storm could perceive a blue cloudless sky. The trees grew rooted to the water's edge and, so dense were their trunks, no egress to the pool existed amongst them.

Sarcastically Storm shouted, "thank you this is much better." He then slumped disconsolately down on his behind and rested his head upon his knees. He was just deciding whether or not to take his chances in the trees, when the pool waters began to shift.

The movement began as a simple ripple that started in the middle and radiated outward. Imperceptibly, the ripples grew in tempo and rhythm. Storm noticed that once the waves reached the pool's edge, they disappeared into the earthy walls with no visible or audible splash. Storm watched the ripples grow, fascinated by their uniformity and patterned synchronicity. He was learning that the whole earth moved with a similar natural energy. This realization had a settling effect on him and he relaxed fully for the first time in many months. The ripples had a mesmerizing, almost hypnotic quality. Unbidden, he felt his body begin to sway in rhythm with the radiating waters. Taking their lead from the boy-conductor, a breeze picked up causing the lofty tree-tops to keep time with the natural rhythm of water, wind, earth, and man. The music-less concert crescendoed and Storm felt himself drawn at once to his feet. As he stood, a body mirrored his movement from within the heart of the pool. By the time he had reached his full stature, he found himself face-to-face with the woman of his dreams.

You are welcome here ninth son, he who is called Storm and he who is the rightful heir to the power of the Aruk.

Storm was stunned. First it was Anyal and now this mysterious woman. Why was everyone so ready to confer this title upon him? Despite the discomfiture he felt, he knew that the words she spoke were true. A part of him had always known. Now beside a strange lake, confronted by a strange Maegess, he accepted with finality the burden that was his to bear.

Storm heard her lilting words sing to him from across the water but noted with curiosity that the woman did not move her lips when she spoke.

My name is Maegess Mirren, mistress of water and grateful member of the Meridian Mage Academy. As she spoke the woman moved toward him.

The maegess was extraordinarily beautiful. She walked barefoot upon the glassy lake surface clothed from head to toe in a simple translucent gown of running water. Her dress was beyond all manner of description. Clear, sensual water flowed continuously with timeless fluidity over and around her frame. Her eyes were a piercing green, not unlike those of the boy that regarded her in awestruck disbelief. Maegess Mirren's hair was silver-white and her limbs extended regally with an unappreciable strength.

By the time she reached the rock on which Storm sat glued, fear dissolved into curiosity. Could his eyes be deceiving him? This beautiful maegess who he regarded before him was the selfsame woman who haunted his dreams. He vividly recollected the face that had guided him as he traveled the power matrix to rescue Zira's soul. Could this water mage be the same woman? As if in answer to his question, the emerald-eyed figure smiled and extended her hand, beckoning the young boy to join her.

Storm unconsciously took the proffered hand, stood, and stepped out on to the still water. Such was his faith in the illusion, that his feet barely contacted the watery carpet. Mirren led him out to the middle of the pool where two spouts had congealed themselves into ethereal chairs. She bid him be seated, never relinquishing her delicate grip.

Storm, I have watched you grow from a boy to almost a man. In less than nine moons you will reach your age-coming. I watched you play, as a boy, within my waters in the Northwood. I laughed while watching you and Zira play amongst the leafy low-peak lakes and the frosty fast-flowing waters of the Tame. I shared your sadness as you drifted down the river after leaving Sard. I laughed again when you came to Meridia and once more frolicked in my eastern river valleys and the ocean waves of the Adearan. Now I feel sadness once more as I perceive with just certainty that the days of your childhood on Meridia are drawing to a close.

Storm felt the underpinnings of fear rise in his breast when he considered the inevitability of leaving the wizard isle. "Maegess Mirren, why is it that you visit me in my dreams?"

A single tear fell from the water wizard's eye. Its unrestrained fall sent shivering ripples outward from the pool's center.

Oh Storm, so many stories to tell, so many adventures yet to be joined, so much uncertainty left to be unraveled. You have strength, energy, and abilities beyond mortal imagination. Are you surprised that a simple water mage cares deeply about what futures may befall you? I am drawn to those that share my love of the natural world. Since you were a small boy, you have been attracted to my domain. Should it then be so strange that I would not watch over your dreams and attempt to assuage the loathsome fears that others would choose to subject you to? In time, much knowledge still closed to you shall be opened. Until then, remember that I love you.

Suddenly, Storm experienced the sensation of falling. Mirren had let go of his hand and he found himself tumbling into a swirling whirlpool that had risen from beneath the docile surface. As water poured into his surprised lungs, he closed his eyes and gave himself up to the painless exhilaration of drowning. He opened his eyes and discovered around him, spectral phantoms of living energy. He could clearly distinguish the energy lines of one fish to another. Their light signatures became impressed deeply upon his mind. He noted for the first time in his life that each water-droplet operated separately, yet with oneness, to comprise the body of water. With his finger, he reached out and pushed against a yellow atomic line. The displaced line was enveloped by a strand of darker green and thus continued its flow. Suddenly, Storm understood the fluidity of the element. Clearly he distinguished between oxygen and hydrogen and the minerals that floated within the periodic matrix that was water. Laughing gleefully, he opened wide his lungs and expelled the remaining oxygen and carbon dioxide that resided there. In his next breath he dissected the molecular structure of oxygen ingesting the yellow strands of the earth's most abundant element. Breathing below the surface of the water was a mere selection process. Selectively choosing oxygen energy and disregarding all others, allowed him to breathe.

From out of the dark ahead of him, swam the maegess surrounded by seven dolphins. Tears of happiness flooded aqueous sight, and Storm surrendered himself to play. Time knew no boundaries within the sanctuary of the deep. Storm had never before experienced such joy and contentment as he swam playfully with the maegess and her cetaceous entourage. He watched incredulously as Mirren shifted her fluid form between that of a porpoise, dolphin, and mermaid. He noted that as each shift was fully completed, her signature energies remained the same. However, the clever manipulations of energies had the metamorphic effect of transforming the physical body into whatever marine form she chose. To Storm's utmost disappointment he found that his talent did not allow him the same structural-altering ability.

After hours of exploring the subterranean pool, one-by-one, the dolphins swum by and took their leave. As they did, Storm was amazed to realize that they blessed him with each of their birth names. The last to leave was a young dolphin, who swam affectionately through the boys legs, leaving the name "Bacal" riding the light-fused current of the water. When at last the graying dorsals were lost to the darkness of the deep, Mirren swam to Storm. Upon his head she brushed her lips in a fragile kiss and then was gone.

Storm awoke to find himself returned to his sleeping pallet in the hayloft of the palace stable. He lay awake, disoriented and confused. Clearly, he still had much to learn of the ways of wizards and magic. From below, came the guttural snores of Wolfy and beside him he noted the rising and falling of the chest of his beloved snow-wolf. Before long Storm felt his eyes succumb to sleep. That night there were no visions of darkness, rather his dreams were filled with the vivid, perfect form of a certain water maegess.

Chapter Thirty-Five

Olondo

The Olondo Garrison was a veritable hive of activity. A week had passed since Ryad had ridden into the courtyard bearing with him a captain close to death together with a badly beaten squad-lead. Captain Beran had lost a great deal of blood during his duel with Lord Damal. Ryad knew that most mortal men would have died instantly from one of Damal's severe strikes, yet the fair-haired warrior still breathed after three such wounds. Moreover, he recovered from his injuries at a startling pace. In no time at all, Beran was hobbling around demanding his sword. Jakes was not so quick to recuperate and had little desire to return to active duty while he could continue to enjoy the flirtations of the infirmary nurses.

Ryad had marveled at the resiliency of the two men, particularly Beran. Now his captain had faced off against two dark-lords and lived to tell the tale on both occasions. It was either dumb luck or something more. Ryad's intuition led him to believe that Beran still had much to contribute in the unfolding conflict with the dark. Perhaps even more a part than even the sword-master might appreciate.

"Hey Captain! Did I, or did I not order you to remain within the infirmary for the rest of the week," growled Ryad.

"Sorry Sir, I thought that more a suggestion than a direct order." Beran grinned a mischievous greeting. "I was going nuts lying there listening to Jakes spouting all that romantic poetry. Does he really think that mushy stuff works?"

Ryad laughed, "who knows, but I have it on good authority that he does get some very preferential treatment at bath time."

Beran grinned broadly, "well I guess he deserves all the tender loving care he can get after that last adventure." The captain grew somber. "You know Ryad I really felt like we deserted that kid. If it had not been for Spit, Jakes and I would not be here today. You would not believe the cold-hearted manner in which the bastard dispatched Chop right in front of our eyes."

Ryad grimaced and then clasped his hand upon Beran's shoulder. "You would be surprised to know what I believe. Although I am not proud to admit this, Damal is my cousin. We share the same grandparents alas my father's brother was a nasty piece of work. Damal, it seems, has inherited much of his more, how shall I say it, undesirable traits. He crossed the line when he ambushed your patrol. He claims that he mistook you for robbers and bandits, which of course is ludicrous. Damal walks a dangerous road at present. As for Spit, I know he still lives. There is no love lost between Damal and I, but he would not dare tempt my wrath or that of Queen Sara. He knows that we will be returning to check on the boy.

***

A mere two hundred miles distant in Damalan, Damal had taken special efforts to install Spit as a member of his household. The boy had demonstrated resourcefulness beyond his years and with mentorship, Damal was convinced that he might find a willing tool in the willful child. Besides, the boy was impressionable. Deserted by those who promised him much was all the ammunition Damal needed to move Spit to his cause. So it was that Spit began a new life as Lord Damal's squire, privy to the best foods, drinks, clothing, and other fashionable accoutrements that money could buy. Immortality had its disadvantages, and one such disadvantage of the Darkwitch's curse was that the son's of Elam and Jesobi could not bear children. Consequently, Damal had no heir. In light of this, he made a conscious decision to groom Spit to rule at his side as his son. It was not long before Spit forgot all about the promises made by Beran and Jakes. In a short period of time, Lord Damal had successfully brain-washed the child and begun the indoctrination towards a schooling in the dark arts.

Meanwhile at the Olondo Garrison, Beran had persuaded Ryad to allow him to resume his duties as Captain. The first order of business was to train the newly enlisted garrison soldiers. Eventually, Jakes declared that he was fit enough to resume active duty, and promptly received a promotion to the rank of Captain-in-Training.

"Captain-in-Training? What the hell is that? There isn't even a uniform patch for that rank," exclaimed Jakes.

Beran laughed. Clearly his former squadlead was feeling much better. "Ryad wants you to hang out with me and learn how to be a captain before he turns you loose in a situation that is going to get you and your men killed."

Jakes grunted, "well I might as well go commit suicide right now if I am going to have to hang out with you. Everywhere you go, unfriendly swords follow." Jakes grinned mischievously. "Hey what if I apply for a stint in the infirmary, you know, to make sure the nurses are doing their job correctly?"

Beran turned and cuffed the younger man's ear. "There will be no more time spent following Nurse Janella around. Oh, and if you offer to show her your private battle wound again, I'll cut it off for you."

Jakes crossed his legs and feigned a look of dire pain. "I guess I should go down and start training the new recruits then?"

"A wonderful idea, that is, if you can still remember which way up to hold your sword." Jakes headed down towards the training yard waving good-naturedly as he went. Beran smiled to himself. In his experience, he knew few close relationships. But here in the Olondo Garrison he already had found two men that he was proud to call friend. The sword-master had now saved his life twice, and the young squadlead had helped him survive Damal's blade. He only hoped that he lived long enough to one day return the favor.

Chapter Thirty-Six

Saltorini

Storm awoke to the sound of horse hooves outside the stable. It was unusual enough to hear horses ridden in the palace grounds of Meridia, but it was stranger still to hear the clip-clop of hooves before dawn. Clearly, the noise had been enough to wake even the deepest of sleepers, for Wolfy was already up and gawking at the spectacle that drew up to the royal stables. Storm lowered himself down the ladder and rubbed sleep from his eyes. Zira, followed closely behind sending a barrage of angry images that suggested a certain level of disgust at being forced to arise so early. Four beautiful white horses flowed into the stable courtyard. On their backs rode four young warriors. Their leader was a woman dressed in brown leggings and a soft green tunic. A matching hood and cape swept down her back, and at her side she wore a short sword. Attached to the saddle-bags, in like fashion to her traveling comrades, was a cross-bow and a quiver of carefully fletched arrows.

It was almost as strange a scene for the elves as it was for the stable's residents. Riding up to the stable doors they were greeted by the sight of a giant, a wolf, and a green-eyed boy who exuded more than the typical human's share of earth power. Elves, sensitive to the energies infusing all natural things, could not help but feel the strength of Storm's aura. The young woman reined in her horse beside them.

"Well met friends of Meridia. My name is Acrina, and these are my brothers, Welk, Fameran, and Jalin. We come to seek counsel with Queen Sara and the wise one. Forgive our seemingly rude interruption. We are not used to finding people in the stables when we come to visit."

"May I tend to your horses Lady Acrina?" Storm could not conjure the words of a greeting so stammered out an offer of assistance instead.

"I would be most grateful for such kindness young man. May I know the identity of such a polite and gracious host?"

Storm felt his cheeks burn at the complement and stuttered an almost incoherent reply, "this is Farmer Barley, my name is Storm, and the snow wolf is Zira."

One of the elves let out an audible exclamation of surprise as Zira emerged from the shadows of the hayloft. The three brothers exchanged knowing glances. If the Lady Acrina was surprised to see a Latsu on Meridia she chose not to show it. Instead she stared hard at the boy before her.

"So it is true there returns a human mind-meld to our beloved wolf kin?" Storm was caught off guard by the frankness of the statement. Or perhaps it was a question, which of the two he could not ascertain on account of the elf's inflectionless intonation.

"It is true, Zira and I are soul-melded," stated Storm.

"Then indeed our journey to the Wizard's Isle is well-timed. Prophecy finds purchase in these troubled times. There will be time to talk again before we leave Storm. I hope that I might find the time to become better acquainted with you and Zira." Acrina smiled and all the tension Storm had endured throughout their exchange dissipated.

Storm and Wolfy took charge of the horses and tied them to the stalls. Storm began filling the feed troughs with hay and oats while Wolfy removed the harnessed saddle-bags which were surprisingly light for such a heavy appearance. Curiously, there were no saddles to remove.

"These elves must be accomplished riders indeed. See there are no saddles, stirrups or other riding tack," stated Wolfy. "What do you make of them?" the farmer gestured in the direction of the palace.

Storm found the question funny and giggled. "Well I could be mistaken but I think they are elves."

"Really, I would never have guessed, you great nitwit. What I mean is what do you think they are doing here? I have never seen an elf before. I have heard they are very loath to leave the refuge of the Elghorian Forest. It must be a matter of great emergency that they seek the aid of Meridia. Mark my words, young Storm, no good can come of such a visit."

"You are such a portender of doom and gloom Wolfy. Perhaps the pretty lady is just out looking for a big brave farmer to sweep her off her feet?"

Storm ducked just in time as a horse brush whistled cleanly over his head and clanged into the loft ladder.

Wolfy and Storm decided to take an early breakfast and were surprised to see the dining hall bustling with activity. The arrival of the elves seemed a noteworthy event and a large number of people had turned out to stare at the visitors. Storm recognized many of his fellow students who continuously threw curious gazes toward the elven party seated at the head table. Acrina and Fameran were engaged in conversation with Mage Saltorini.

Storm took a seat at one of the minor tables and tucked into a loaf of bread buttered with fresh honey still warm from the Meridian hives. "Why do you think they are talking to Saltorini and not Sara or Kalon?" Storm had asked the question to Wolfy, but the answer came from across the table.

Seated opposite was a short squatty character of about thirty summers. Storm had only seen him once before, in a class conducted by Mage Corrin the head librarian.

The generously-weighted student talked between mouthfuls. "Mage Saltorini grew up with the elves in the Elghorian. He was orphaned and Acrina found him lying helpless one day while out riding the low road. There he was lying in a blanket, caked in dust, starving hungry, emaciated, and close to death. He was barely a month old, so they say. Well Acrina took pity on the child and chose to raise him as her very own. At the time, it caused quite the stir in the Elghorian. King Koradin was not happy at the prospect of a human growing up within his domain. His daughter must have won him over though. Saltorini is now forty summers in years and she is almost four times that. It is hard to believe, but the elf princess looks more like his daughter than his foster mother."

Storm was about to ask more questions when he heard his name called. "Storm, Queen Sara and Archmage Kalon request the pleasure of Farmer Barley and yourself at the head table." Storm looked up and noted the kindly, bespectacled face of Horatius, the Queen's First Advisor. The boy excused himself from the current company and followed the hunched figure of Horatius up to the Queen's table. He had not noticed Sara or Kalon enter, but there they were seated on either side of the Lady Acrina. Once Storm and Wolfy had joined them, Kalon cast his staff into the air and the room dissolved eerily around them. When order was once more restored, Storm found that he was seated at a conference table with nine other people. At the head of the table sat Queen Sara. In the place of honor to her right sat the Lady Acrina and to her right sat her three brothers. At Sara's left sat the Archmage, and next to him, Mage Saltorini and Wolfy. Storm found himself seated at the far end of the table directly opposite the Queen. She smiled at him across the paneled space.

"You will notice there is a chair still unfilled, we must wait a few minutes more before beginning our meeting."

Storm noted that one seat lay empty between Wolfy and himself. The wait was not lengthy as moments later a body materialized in the chair beside him.

"Well met brother." Sara smiled sweetly at the new arrival who grinned happily back. "For those of you who do not know Ryad, this fine man is Terrus's very own Sword-master, and more importantly my one remaining younger brother."

"A regular family reunion you have got going here today," said Ryad. "Saltorini, that mother of yours looks younger every-time I see her. Clearly you are not sharing the same diet."

Saltorini gave a raucous laugh and said "I think there must be magic water in that little wood she lives in."

The friendly banter terminated abruptly as the elf-princess stood to speak.

Child of Night

"Friends, I thank you for gathering here in Meridia. I realize that it is unwise for two sentinels to meet in one place so we will try and keep this brief. We could not risk transmitting messages over land or sea. The dark rises swiftly and the elves feel its presence throughout the Elghorian. Our patrols on the low and high road are frequently forced to engage Brack and Damal's mercenaries. Thousands of men are flocking to their cause, yet we do not know what that cause is. We do, however, surmise that it is inextricably connected to the fate of the boy."

Suddenly, everyone turned to face Storm. For the second time that day he felt color race across his cheeks as he underwent the close scrutiny of a people that knew far more about him than he knew of they.

It was Ryad who broke the awkward silence. He slapped Storm hard on the back and said, "what this little guy? You mean the fuss that is being made up and down the known world is over this little fellow?" Ryad winked at Storm out of the corner of his eye. "Surely, the dark would not have us believe that the balance comes down to a child not yet thirteen summers?"

"Ah, but there lies the problem sword-master. This child will be a man in some eight or nine moons if the calculations of the Abbot are correct." It was Jalin that had spoken. He continued, "when the ninth child becomes a man he will come completely into the fullness of his powers. There is no known precedent. The Lore-Master of the Elghorian says that we have a lot to fear from this 'little fellow'."

Storm felt uncomfortable. Was he invisible? Could they not see him sitting there? Everyone was talking in third person about things he had little understanding of. Now the elves, too, were convinced that he was the prophecy's ninth son. Surely at some point someone would clue him into just exactly what was going on.

Mage Saltorini cut in next. "Prophecy is clear that the final reckoning will take place in Cartis in the Land of Bal. We cannot protect Storm forever and if the portents of the Life-Tree are correct, we are about to undergo a true testing of the defenses of Meridia."

Sara listened patiently to the discussion on how best to proceed with Storm's protection. Finally, she cleared her throat and all attention swung toward her.

"I swore faithfully to my departed brother Nicholas that Storm would enjoy all the protections afforded by Meridia until such time as he is able to choose his own path." She gazed across the table and caught Storm's eyes in hers. "He is free to come and go as he pleases, as is the right of all students within the Academy. He is bound to the island by all of the indomitable laws and rules shared by others. Outside of Meridia's boundaries, I cannot protect him."

Wolfy's patience was running low. Not used to such formal affairs, he stood up and glared at those there gathered.

"You speak about the boy as if he isn't even here. Every night I listen to him toss and turn as his dreams are plagued by nameless terrors. He has done everything that you have asked of him, yet he is constantly kept in the dark. I have heard discussion of prophecies, of reckonings, of last battles, of various political intrigues, and of plots to destroy Meridia. Yet no one has had the forthrightness to tell the lad what the Gods name is going on. I suggest someone start talking and stop treating the boy like a puppet in some sick game."

The silence that followed Wolfy's outburst was indefatigable. Kalon spoke first, "Farmer Barley is of course absolutely correct. We have been so enveloped in weighing the probabilities and potential permutations of action, we have neglected to help Storm understand the dire situation that will soon present itself. This I intend to remedy soon after this meeting concludes." Kalon smiled at both Wolfy and Storm and was rewarded by a nod from the farmer and a grin from Storm.

"Ryad can we rely on you to have reliable escort positioned at Kurigan in the event that we need passage to Bal?"

"Kalon, you know me better than most. I will handle such an eventuality personally. In fact one of my captains is presently preparing an elite squad at the Olondo Garrison. They will be ready to start for Kurigan shortly."

Kalon nodded approvingly, "we hope still not to have to use their services but we must be prepared for every contingency." Kalon looked in the direction of Acrina. "What aid can the forest-folk afford in this quest?"

"Lord Koradin is loathe to commit the elves to this undertaking. However, my brothers and I are in agreement. We will make for the Yiladan in preparation for what is to come. We hope to secure alliances long forgotten from our friends in the Land of Bal."

Storm remembered Anyal's story of the wallahs, the tree-people of the Yiladan. Could it be they that the elves were preparing to seek out? The more he listened, the more he became confused. He hoped earnestly that Kalon would be true to his word and clear up some of his confusion.

Queen Sara concluded the meeting, and just like that Ryad disappeared and the remaining group returned to the main dining hall. From the reactions of the students and palace courtiers gathered for breakfast, Kalon had insured that their brief meeting went unnoticed and their presence unmissed.

Chapter Thirty-Seven

Acrina

Once back at the stables, Wolfy and Storm talked excitedly about the discussions of the morning. Suddenly, Zira sent a powerful image that startled Storm.

The tall nasty boy lurks outside. He smells of perfumed bedsheets. Storm smiled as he rose to his feet. He motioned to Wolfy with a finger on his lip as he proceeded to intercept the would-be eavesdropper. However, just as he was walking out the stable side-door a garbled scream, clearly Yurmin, sounded from the water trough on the side of the barn. Wolfy and Storm scrambled around the corner.

There was Yurmin being held underwater in the brimming rain barrel. Acrina had a tight grip upon the boy's ear and was not relinquishing her hold long enough for him to finish the various protagonist incantations that he sought to hurl her way. After several more good dunkings, she let him up and pushed him away from the barrel.

"Now young man, know that it is rude to eavesdrop on your friends. Oh, and know also it is rude to try and throw curses at another even if they are holding you under water." Yurmin glared at Acrina, yet thought better about retaliating when he realized that his persecutor was none other than the crown princess of the Elghorian. As he scuttled away, his proverbial tail set firmly between his legs, Wolfy and Storm burst into fits of riotous laughter.

Child of Night

When at last the mirth began to subside, Acrina pointed in the direction of the departing catcher and stated emphatically, "you need to watch out for him, his life-energy already grows dark. It will not be long before Meridia is forced to reject him." Acrina dried her hands then turned to Storm.

"Now, if you are not too busy I would be honored to take a stroll with you and Zira. I have asked permission of the Archmage, and he has agreed to give you the morning off from your lessons so that we might become better acquainted. Where would you have us walk?"

"How about the beaches? They are beautiful in the morning, especially when the breeze is blowing," suggested Storm.

Acrina smiled sweetly, "I would like that very much. Lead on my fine stable hand."

Storm found himself blushing once more as he led Acrina down towards the easternmost corner of the palace. He opened a loosely latched gate and immediately Zira burst into the open space pursuing the lazy gulls that were ill-prepared to play chase with the Latsu.

"You will never catch the feathered ones Zira," sent Storm.

Ah but yet they still move swiftly at my running. One of these days the bigger birds will not be so quick to rise and that will be a fine breakfast for me.

Storm frowned as Zira sent him the lustful images of a wolf tearing apart its feathered prey. During this soundless interaction, Acrina had watched Storm intently.

Finally, she spoke. "How is it to be mind-melded to a Latsu?"

The question caught Storm a little off guard. He had never been asked such a question. His relationship with Zira had become such a part of him, that he now found it hard to imagine life without their connection.

"It is hard sometimes," started Storm. "When we were first melded I thought my head would explode every-time Zira sent me a message. At first, the images were just a flash of colors, noises, and smells. Over time, I have been able to establish an order to the images he sends. Now it is no different than having a conversation in a language that is not your native tongue. You know some of the words but not all of them, thus you translate the words you know and fill in the pieces where there are words you do not understand. So it is with our mind-meld."

"Storm, I am truly jealous of your gift." A deep sorrowfulness had come upon the elf's countenance. "There was a time when all elves enjoyed the gift of mind-meld both with one another and with the animals and bird of the forest. It was a happier time before there were battles between the light and dark. The forest-people lived throughout Terrus. The woods and forests were our homes and we had little to fear. We are a peaceful people who live harmoniously in union within the natural energies and bio-rhythms of nature. Somewhere in the generations we were goaded into conflict with the barbarians of the north, with man, and even within our own people. Our woodland homes began to die. Men tore down our trees to build houses and merchants used the hearts of our forests in the construction of their might merchant ships. All too quickly, at least in the relative life of my people, we became disconnected with the natural world. Now we are a dying people, subjected to live our lives within the boundaries of the Elghorian, forced to watch while evil grows ever stronger in the south and on throughout Terrus."

Acrina sighed wistfully then continued. "Storm you have a gift. Never take such a thing for granted. Perhaps one day after the dark powers are vanquished you might teach me how to become restored with the woodland creatures I love so completely."

Storm felt the emotion of humility. Here he was on a deserted beach on Meridia with the second most powerful elf on Terrus, being asked for help and assistance in a task that he did not, even for a moment, understand. They stopped briefly on the sand to watch Zira's relentless quest to catch another gull. Storm stole a look at Acrina mesmerized by the forested coloration of her eyes. As he regarded her profile, he found himself lost amongst the trees, vines, ferns, and rolling valleys of her woodland home. Within the elf's eyes there shone the vibrant life of all that her race held dear. As he looked away to the ocean and regarded the waves breaking softly on the sandy beach he wondered what part he would ultimately play in destroying or protecting Acrina's natural world.

Chapter Thirty-Eight

Training

Beran wiped the sweat from his forehead. The sun beat down vehemently with fierce abandon upon the hard, clay, training ground. Twenty yards from where he stood, another soldier keeled over with heat cramps and was immediately attended to by one of the garrison water-boys. This was the eleventh man to succumb to heat exhaustion in the last two days. Beran was beginning to question his training regime. Was he pushing the men too hard? Ryad had made it clear that he was to weed out the weak and keep only the strong. It was unusual to have a garrison squad of twenty-five soldiers, but the sword-master had told Beran that this unit might be required for a very dangerous mission. The captain had not questioned Ryad further. If he said it was important, then Beran would not doubt him. Moreover, he would ensure that the twenty-five soldiers chosen would be the twenty-five best soldiers Beran could find.

Initially, the captain had been exasperated. The request had gone out to all squadleads from Shupan to Kelanon, to send at least two of their best soldiers to Olondo. Over 400 soldiers had converged upon Olondo to start the rigorous training program. By week's end only sixty-three remained. Beran had been, on the whole, disappointed with the skills and character of these so-called "kingdom's best." In his opinion there was a serious need to change the current structure of militia training programs. Some of the recruits had been eliminated on the basis of poor physical fitness. Others were removed from contention due to inferior sword or horsemanship skills. Then there were the soldiers who simply did not have the intelligence and smarts to earn a spot on the elite squad.

"Jakes?" The captain's voice boomed across the yard. A tall, muscular figure detached himself from a group of trainees and hustled over to join Beran. As usual, the indispensable grin of mischief played across the former squadlead's face.

"So are these men ready to see some real action? There is some trouble in Tumi, the fishing village just south of here. It seems some pirates have chosen to set camp off the peninsula and our sources tell us they are terrorizing the villagers. There is no better way to assess a soldier's mettle than real field training."

Jakes grinned knowingly. He knew his captain all too well. A field trip to Tumi was as much an opportunity for Beran to wield his broadsword as it was to determine if the trainees could hack a real-life battle situation.

"I think most of them will do alright, that is if they survive cramps, heat stroke, heat exhaustion, and your vicious tongue lashings." As if on cue, the twelfth casualty of the Meridian sun fainted directly in front of them.

"Well let's call it a day then shall we," said Beran. "Make sure everyone is ready to go an hour after midnight. This little visit to Tumi would best be conducted in the dark."

Sixty-three men, dressed in Meridian black, left the Olondo Garrison under cover of darkness. The only light afforded to them was provided by the sporadic comings and goings of the moon as it dodged in and out of cloud cover. The road to Tumi was little more than a rutted track. The Olondo Garrison traded with Keppell, a larger port town on the Icealic. Tumi, a much smaller community thus had little interaction with garrison soldiers. A messenger from the town had arrived a day earlier to inform Beran of the pirate's arrival at the peninsula. Needless to say, Beran salivated at the chance of exacting some revenge on these minions of the dark. He had not forgotten the pirate crew that had torched his ship and sent him, and six of his friends, to Brack's accursed pit.

Tumi was only ten leagues distant, and at a steady marching rate they came in sight of the peninsula after just two hours. They could have brought horses and cut the travel time in half, but Beran was still intent on using this sojourn as a training exercise. From their vantage point on a high cliff escarpment they commanded a birds-eye view of the land below. The dark hours of morning were nearly half passed, yet a great commotion could be heard in the village. Small fires burned on the shore-line, and loud drunken singing wafted up to them on the salty wind currents. Two shadowy vessels were moored at the small dock. A third giant ship was anchored several hundred yards off-shore. The latter, a massive schooner, cast an eerie silhouette with its large battering ram projecting from the prow. Beran swallowed back the adrenalin that churned within him. He was sure the larger ship was the very same vessel that had sunk his boat less than a year earlier. The brawny swordsmen prayed that the same slimy bastard still served as captain of the pirateer. Perhaps he might even get a chance to settle a score or two.

Beran turned back to his soldiers and issued quick orders. "Jakes I want you to take half the men and head for the village. Position a third of your men here, another third here, and the last third here." Beran drew the plan carefully in the dust.

"The remaining soldiers are to come with me. We will start with the two ships in dock. If we can commandeer the vessels quickly, we might be able to sail out and nab the third, but for now the large ship is not the priority. We came here to protect the kingdom people and to eradicate this pirate scum." Beran paused briefly for effect, making sure to establish eye contact with every one of his men. "The odds are not favorable. Each ship will contain at least fifty mercenaries. That is why it is important to observe stealth and to attack swiftly. The element of surprise can only carry a soldier so far. Get into position quickly and await the signal. When you hear my whistle, attack hard and attack fast. Do not hesitate and do not take second guesses. He who pauses will fall, and I would like to return to Olondo with most of you intact."

In small groups, Beran sent the small squad down to their positions. Getting to the docks unseen was a little tricky because of the open stretches of sand. A circuitous route around the far side of the hamlet and through the dock-side warehouses provided at least some cover. Clearly, the pirates expected little resistance from the village, for even the night-watches were more inclined to play cards and drink ale rather than keep watch for possible attack. Beran and his men, with stealthy feet, reached the docks unnoticed. Two long gang-planks extended down to the pier. The captain took a small whistle from inside his jerkin pocket and gave it one quick blast. A high-pitched note sailed out into the night. Moments later it was answered with the sound of steel meeting steel.

Jakes' men had burst forth from their hiding places and plowed head-long into the pirate horde that infested the village. Meanwhile, Beran had split his men and simultaneously they had rushed aboard the docked vessels. The battle on the pirate ships was joined with heated ferocity. The captain had underestimated the numbers of mercenaries aboard the boats, and he had also underestimated their apparent levels of intoxication. For drunken sailors, they wielded powerful broad-swords and sober daggers with remarkable competence. Jakes and his men had made short work of the unwelcome guests down in the village and quickly regrouped in the direction of the docks.

Beran ducked as a sword scythed through the darkness. Reactively he accelerated his knee into the groin of his opponent and satisfied himself with the knowledge that this brigand would not be procreating future generations of pirates. The deck was narrow, and Beran found himself forced to fight in close-quarters. At times he was even forced to resort to using plain old fists, hardy legs, bony knees, and his proverbial thick head. A weasel of a man jabbed to and fro with an angry looking dagger. In another time and place, Beran might have laughed at such a pathetic looking figure. However, at this moment he was pitted against an opponent who clearly knew how to use his weapon. The weasel snarled and bared a toothless smile. Suddenly, he rushed the brawny captain who felt the tip of the dagger graze his forearm. Angrily, Beran swung his shoulder to the left and grabbed hold of the pirate's hair with his right hand. Beran picked the little man up off the ground and hurled him violently into the main mast. So hard was the man thrown that the impact caused the main mast to crack all the way along its base.

Beran turned to review the progress of his men. Dispassionately, he regarded the motionless bodies of the cut-throats that were sporadically interspersed with those of the dead Olondo soldiers. For his men, he sent silent prayers to Sajan, God of Warriors, and for the pirates, well he hoped they would rot in hell. All of a sudden, the air was filled with the smell of sulphur. The ship was afire. Beran jumped to the lower rigging in time to see the anchored pirate ship release flaming arrows.

"Men of Olondo, jump ship," shouted Beran. "They are burning this vessel. Get off now." Beran's warning did not come a moment too soon, for within seconds the two docked ships were ablaze with spiteful flames. Those that had not heeded his warning were swept screaming into the conflagration. The remaining pirates had finally conceded defeat and laid down their swords. Meanwhile, offshore, the larger ship had raised anchor and steadily moved out into the Icealic current, cutting a long and onerous wake in the outgoing tide. A short time later it disappeared from view around the heady peninsula. Beran was not happy about losing his prey but at least the mission had been successful. Of his sixty-three men, forty-four of them would live to welcome the new morning.

Dawn arrived punctually, and with daylight came the honorifics of the Tumi villagers. Women of the village took it upon themselves to prepare a victor's breakfast, and the men set about repairing the gross damage that had been inflicted on their humble hamlet. While his soldiers ate, Beran went among the prisoners to question them. All-in-all, nineteen had survived the night. The punishment for piracy was hanging and during the morning hours this consequence would be exacted. Jakes' men were already rigging the scaffolds that would send the rogue's souls to Tellus. One prisoner did excite some interest in Beran. A seven-foot, ebony-skinned man seemed out of place amongst the shackled pirates. Every attempt to get the man to speak had proved fruitless. Then one of the prisoners informed the Captain that the Black giant was in fact a mute with no tongue. He had joined the ship only a week earlier when they had put in to Manti, a small fishing village below the Jarinska Pass. The dark stranger evidently had taken no part in the night-time struggle. During the battle, he had stood in the crow's nest and watched the proceedings from above. When the ship went up in flames he would have certainly died, but the main mast, already cracked from Beran's angry contribution, splintered and sent the top sail and crows-nest barreling into the icy ocean. The silent giant had spluttered his way to shore before being arrested by one of Beran's men.

Kingdom justice was handled swiftly and with little pageantry. The pirates were hanged from ropes rescued from off their own burning ships. Boxes were kicked away, and one-by-one the pirates were sent to their deaths, kicking and convulsing until no more air was left to swallow. The seven-foot giant was the last to be led to the scaffold. Beran watched from the side-lines as two of his men coaxed him up on to a box and draped a wiry noose around his broad neck. Something just didn't sit well with the captain. Silently, the giant locked his gaze upon Beran and two tear-drops fell to the dusty earth. When the box was kicked out from underneath him, he did not struggle, but rather hung limply preparing himself for the inevitable. Without knowing why, Beran strode to the scaffold, and in one clean motion severed the hangman's knot. The huge man fell to the ground gasping for air and clutching at his throat.

"We are taking him with us. Something doesn't feel right about killing this one. He did not fight us and he is certainly no pirate." Beran watched as two men lifted the prisoner to his feet and escorted him back to the village.

Jakes came to stand by his captain and said, "well you certainly know how to make a hanging exciting."

Beran grinned at his junior captain. "I just can't put my finger on it Jakes. I cannot help but feel that this man is innocent. Whenever I was around him, I felt a strange humility. It was almost as if he wanted desperately to confide in me a secret, yet voiceless he knew not how to do so. I must speak to Ryad when we return to Olondo.

Chapter Thirty-Nine

Sabotage

The surprise of the elves' visit was soon replaced with the monotony and routine of daily study. Storm had been one of the fortunate ones. For the three days that the elves had been in residence at Meridia, he enjoyed the fellowship and teaching of the forest-clad company. Acrina had accompanied he and Zira on many hikes around the island. Anyal had joined them on a trip to the Great Falls, but excused herself from future invitations. During the elves' visit, Anyal had felt like a third wheel. Storm, so caught up in the excitement of the moment, had quite forgotten the sensitive emotions of his erstwhile friend. Anyal, for her part, found a new emotion to confront, jealousy. What competition could she afford to a princess?

Acrina's brothers had also been avid teachers. Welk was a horse-master and loved nothing more than demonstrating his talents to a willing audience. Storm had ingratiated himself to the elf through the manner in which the boy cared for their mounts. Elven horses were exceedingly particular as to whom they would allow touch them. Only from pure and kindly spirits would they accept contact. Consequently, Welk was more than impressed that his horse not only allowed Storm to tend to him, but also allowed the boy to ride him.

Fameran was the friendliest of the three brothers and taught Storm how to shoot the long-bow. The first lesson was quite comical as the boy pulled back the elf's draw-string with all of his strength, yet could not even come close to pulling the notch to his ear. Fameran was not a large man, but Storm quickly came to revere the quiet strength exuded by the older elf. For their second lesson, Fameran cut and whittled a bow from an alder tree. Exquisitely carved, the weight of the draw was perfect for Storm's size and frame. On the inner-most side of the bow, Fameran had etched a unique symbol called a Kyeh. The mark was a thin, deeply grooved crescent enclosed within a circle of five stars. Fameran explained that each star represented one of the five ancient races, and the crescent characterized the earth. The elf informed Storm that the Kyeh, an elven charm, lent aid to an archer's aim. It helped very little that first day, for try as he could, Storm couldn't hit the stable door from ten paces. By afternoon and with bleeding calluses on torn fingers, Storm found he could at last hit a target from twenty paces.

The next day he practiced more with Fameran. The elf presented to him a finger protector to prevent calluses from opening every time he let go the drawstring. By the time his forest-teachers left, Storm could hit a horseshoe from a hundred paces. There were no goodbyes. Indeed, Storm did not even see or hear them leave. One night the white elf-horses were stabled below him, the following morning they were gone. In their place all that remained was a beautiful deer-hide quiver filled with thirty masterfully carved and fletched arrows. There was no note, but Storm knew within his heart that their paths would cross again before too long.

* * *

Storm had not noticed the elven party leaving but the northern dark-lord knew of their every movement. Spies from the sisterhood had their eyes firmly trained on the Elghorian and the High Priestess's servants were quick to inform Lord Rune of Acrina's movements.

"The elf-princess would do well to heed her father's warnings," said Rune. "Koradin knows that this is a fight he should not participate in. Why won't the meddlesome forest bitch listen to his advice?"

Chaniya's rejoinder was seductively wistful. "What possible challenge can the pointy-eared girl represent to us? The elves only have power within the Elghorian. Outside the elf-wood she is like a fish out of water. And as you know my lover, fish happens to be my favorite meal." Chaniya sat down beside the distracted dark-lord and began to wind her fingers aggressively towards his swiftly swelling manhood.

Suddenly, he caught her hands and violently threw them away from him. He stood quickly and strode to the table, lifting to his lips a goblet of wine. "So tell me Priestess, how does our plan to break Meridia progress?"

If Chaniya was offended by Rune's rejection she showed no evidence of it. "Just as we planned, I have bewitched the boatman. The simpleton will not even be aware of his betrayal until he is on the island. Then, I will remove the mind-block, and he will know that if he does not follow through with the task we have asked of him, his fat wife and six grubby children will all die a very painful death. Of course, he has no idea that I have already taken care of killing the family. He should be grateful. It must cost him a pretty penny to feed seven mouths, and some of them had very big mouths, or at least you would think they did by the sounds of their screaming." Chaniya's sardonic laughter rang throughout Rune's throne-room.

Rune allowed his co-conspirator a moment to exhaust her mirth. "So tell me how this device of yours works?"

Chaniya smiled demurely as she rose from the divan. Seductively, she let her gown fall away from her right shoulder, revealing a naked breast slightly perked from the chill breeze that blew through the throne-room window. "It is simple really. The whole far-seer arch scheme is nothing more than an elaborate network of gylantium. This mineral infuses the rock-core beneath the island. My device, when positioned directly over one of these gylantium networks, will begin a chain-reaction that should alter the structure of the volatile mineral. Not only will the rock lose its predictive qualities, but with luck, the reaction itself should cause a significant explosion on the little island. Seeing as the core see-far arch is located within the palace walls, it would not surprise me to see the crystal homestead blown to pieces. If we are fortunate, perhaps we could get rid of queen, Archmage, council, and ninth child all in one foul swoop."

Rune pensively tugged on his short beard. "Do not underestimate the Archmage. How do you know that he has not prepared for such an eventuality?"

"Kalon is too proud to believe that anything can touch his precious island. He will be expecting an attack, but he will not expect the attack to come in the manner in which it will be delivered." Chaniya, by now had reached Rune. While she still talked, she took his hands and positioned them around her swelling breasts. Soon the doers of evil were lost in their own selfish physical gratification.

***

Meanwhile, Jonarus, one of the royal boatmen, had just cast off from the Bala Sands. His head was filled with the happy images of a family he cherished beyond all else. He smiled as he remembered the eager faces of Jenna and Sorrell as he told them once more their favorite story before they fell fast asleep cradled in his arms. The passage to Meridia was swift and true. The white mists of the island willingly retracted as the prow of the boat touched the outermost layer of cloud. It had been a fairly eventful week. He had ferried the elves from Cormant to Meridia, and three days later given them passage to the Bala Sands. It had been a week since he had last seen his family and he longed for a return home to his fishing village. First he would ask permission of Horatius, and then return home to Purnell for a few days. Sometimes he wondered why he did not have the family come live on Meridia. Certainly, it would make life easier. Unfortunately, his wife could not be persuaded to leave the village of her birth. Her mother and extended family still fished the Adearan waters and plowed the Adearan plains.

Jonarus brought the boat to a resting place beside a simple jetty. Carefully he tied the barge to a bollard and then set out across the sand. He had only walked a few paces before he fell to his knees clutching his head in agony. The boat-man writhed in pain upon the sand, screaming as loud as his lungs would permit. The wind blowing off the water all but swallowed his petitions for help. As

Child of Night

the pain began to subside, his mind took on a new order. He no longer acted as Jonarus, son of Baff, he now operated as an unwitting pawn of the Lady Chaniya, High Priestess of the sisterhood, and willing ally to Lord Rune.

From his pocket, the once loyal subject of Meridia drew a queerly-shaped object that glistened in the late-afternoon sun. The boatman's eyes gilded opaque, as body and mind succumbed to the evil enchantment. Sightless, his eyes darted forwards and backwards in sunken sockets. Carrying the strange metallic object in out-stretched hands, he shuffled hesitantly through the deep sand. After a few steps, he dropped to his knees and began to dig feverishly with his fingers. Deeper and deeper the possessed man dug. When the hole was deemed deep enough, he placed the orb into the sand and activated a hidden switch. No sooner had this been done, than the man that had once been Jonarus the kind and humble boatman, was thrown backwards several hundred feet through the air. He was dead before his lifeless body touched the sand. The device had blown itself deeper into the earth and from its undercarriage extended two claw-like appendages. These appendages cut deeply into the mineral-fused bedrock.

High within the walls of the library, Archmage Kalon heard a man scream. Without a word he discharged himself from his students and ran into the hall-way. His path was intercepted by Mages Dulkin, Saltorini, and Corrin. Saltorini spoke first, "we felt it too Archmage. The island is under attack."

"But from where does this attack come? I heard a man scream and then I felt the ground beneath me convulse in panic." Suddenly the dawn of understanding burst forth across his face.

"They attack from below. Quickly, protect the far-seer, do not let them change the life-force of the rock below the palace. If their sabotage reaches the palace we all shall die."

Immediately, Corrin and Dulkin sprinted away toward the Hall of Windows and the far-seer. "Saltorini, take my hand, we must view the extent to which the damage is done." The two mages re-materialized atop the terrace. The terrace was a high platform above the palace that commanded a rich perspective of the island.

"Master, this bodes ill, the gylantium network is destroyed throughout the beaches and forests."

"It is the same in the fields," stated Kalon. "Look, the cancer creeps toward the outermost gardens. My friend we must sheer gaps within the networks. We cannot allow the metamorphosis to take over the palace. If it reaches the far-seer we might not survive to see the morrow."

Mage Saltorini understood straightaway the Archmage's plan and cast forth his arms to capture what life energy he could command as his own. Beside him, the Archmage was doing likewise. The once sun-splashed afternoon transformed into a blazing lightning-ridden tempest. Those watching from below stared in horror and bewilderment as two of the mage council drew energy from the very center of the artificially created storm. Electricity, captured and harnessed, was unleashed with violent precision. Lightning bolts surged into the hard rocky grounds that surrounded the palace. Moments later, two others of the mage council, Mage Leskel and Mage Bartrand, joined their elemental gifts to the task of permeating the far-seer network outside the palace walls. The fury of the unleashed power shook the walls and foundations of the crystal palace. Field-workers huddled together in frightened masses. Students and servants alike took cover within the palace cellars. Storm and Anyal, who were preparing for a walk with Zira along the beach, stood transfixed outside the stables as the four mages wielded a controlled power and fury down upon the heaving ground. This fearsome display lasted for only minutes in the true cycle of time. The powerful casting sent stones, rocks, roof slates, and trees raining chaotically down. Throughout the maelstrom the ground rose and fell with disconcerting irregularity.

As swift as it began, it ended. The rain clouds cleared and the radiance of lightning was replaced by the dazzling aura of the Meridian sun. Atop the tower, Archmage Kalon and Mage Saltorini fell exhausted where they stood. Severely fatigued, Bartrand and Leskel used the last of their energies to transport their colleagues to the infirmary. Dulkin and Corrin had dug in beside the far-seer and had enveloped it with every spell of protection that they could muster. Unbeknownst to them, Maegess Mirren had contributed to the safety of the arch by sending water out through the soil to congeal around the footings of the arch. Maegess Nolina had also coaxed the Matriarch into action by requesting that her roots displace temporarily the gylantum matrix beneath the arch.

So fierce was the elemental exchange, that a crater some eight feet deep had been created surrounding the palace and its gardens. The end product was a palace isolated upon a shelf of rock, surrounded by a waterless moat. The castle, though deep in foundation, had sustained great structural damage. As Storm and Anyal surveyed the aftermath, and the ensuing wreckage, Anyal could not contain her grief, and burst into tears. Storm tenderly took the smaller girl in his strong arms and whispered words of comfort. In his heart of hearts he knew the onslaught of darkness had begun. He also knew that before the week ended his part in that onslaught might ultimately be joined.

Chapter Forty

Expulsion

The days following the attack on Meridia were difficult for Storm and Anyal. Classes had been canceled indefinitely and the rumors in the hallways were that the Academy was going to be temporarily disbanded. Archmage Kalon and Mage Saltorini remained in the infirmary recovering from exhaustion. Meanwhile, the remaining members of the mage council spent long hours working with the guildsmen in restoring the structural integrity of the palace and surrounding buildings. Maegess Mirren, at the request of Queen Sara, had flooded the trench that surrounded the palace. Several bridges had been built to allow access to the surrounding countryside. Mage Yurl had returned one day from the beaches bearing the dead body of the boatman and a strange circular device that he had recovered from a deep hole in the sand.

One morning, almost a week after the attack, a messenger arrived in the stable announcing that Queen Sara had called the island's residents to an audience in the meeting hall just before noon. Wolfy, Storm, and Anyal were some of the last to arrive for the meeting. Zira trotted along nonchalantly at Storm's heels. Protocol and decorum had pretty much flown out the window in the last week, and Storm wasn't going to leave Zira alone for a second if he didn't have to. The four of them stood towards the back of the hall and waited for the clarions to herald the arrival of the queen. Little pomp and circumstance infused the meeting other than the horns. Sara strode to the dais steps and regarded her people with a soft emotion. Courtier, servant, shepherd, field-worker, fisherman, mage, student, and child, all gathered in front of their queen. A hush washed over the crowd as Sara prepared to speak.

"My dear friends, these are indeed troubling times. As you are no doubt aware, the Island's perimeter defenses have been compromised. The palace itself continues to be protected, thanks to the diligence and personal sacrifice of our wondrous mage council. However, the lands beyond the palace walls are no longer as safe as they once were. There will be an attempt to re-engage our outer protection, but until such time we live at a precarious disadvantage. I offer, to those who would choose to stay on Meridia, the protection of my home. Others of you are welcome to leave the island and return at a later date. It is with a heavy heart that we temporarily must disband the Academy." Murmurings and whispers flooded the room.

The queen raised her hand for silence, and once more all attention returned to the monarch. "We believe this will only be a temporary arrangement. Those of you that have earned your bench, I promise faithfully, you will be the first persons invited to return. Archmage Kalon continues to recuperate and asks me to pass on his sympathies to all. If you have any further questions, I would ask you to direct them to my counselor, Horatius." The queen left the dais and in her place stepped the bespectacled first advisor. While the island population attempted to seek further answers and clarification, Storm, Anyal, Zira, and Wolfy returned to the stables.

Still early, they continued through the gardens and out across one of the recently constructed draw-bridges.

"Where shall we take our walk today?" asked Storm. Zira sent back vibrant images of trees and squirrels asking to be chased. "Zira votes for the forest."

"Why not?" said Anyal. "I haven't been through there in a while. Perhaps we could follow that trail down to the river, providing of course the trail still exists."

"Have some faith my girl," began Wolfy. "Things aren't as bleak as all that. The castle gets to have some much needed window dressing, and now it seems you two get more time to be kids and play. I dunno, all those lessons would have me addled in the head if I had to study as much as you two do. I have half a mind to…"

Wolfy never finished his sentence. Storm let out an anguished cry of pain and immediately took off running. As if in answer, a mournful howl rose through the trees, from a clearing a few hundred yards ahead. Zira had not needed to send an image. Storm felt the cross-bow bolt hit Zira even before the bloody image arrived in his head. As he emerged from the trees, he watched horrified as Yurmin, standing over the palpitating body of the Latsu, prepared to notch another bolt onto his cross-bow. Storm flew at the older boy before Yurmin had time to react. The cross-bow fell to the ground and Storm pounced on top of him pummeling blows upon the boy's pocked face. In his rage, Storm had failed to notice Yurmin's accomplice creep up behind him and knew no warning as a heavy club slammed across his shoulder blade. Storm was thrown to the side and as he rolled he felt the bones in his upper and lower arm break. Yurmin quickly sprang to his feet. Blood gushed from a broken nose as he stooped to pick up the cross-bow.

Panic took over and Storm cast a spell of illusion on the bow. The weapon transformed into a powerful sea-snake. The distraction caused Yurmin to drop the bow, and Storm, now on his knees, sent a ball of manipulated air hurtling across the glade. It hit Yurmin squarely in the stomach and threw him thirty feet across the clearing. Wolfy and Anyal arrived just as the tall boy landed in an unconscious pile of contorted bones at the foot of a chestnut tree. There was no sign of Yurmin's partner. He had fled the moment magic became a part of the struggle.

Storm hauled himself to Zira and through salty tears he called the wolf by name. Although there was no conscious reaction, the mind-link remained strong. Telepathically, Storm caressed his friend's head and offered images of reassurance. At that moment, he remembered his very first lesson with Maegess Nolina. Clearing his mind, he placed his uninjured hand upon the wolf's shoulder.

"Wolfy! Help me. Can you pull out the shaft, I cannot help Zira unless I can see the whole wound."

Wolfy nervously gripped a tight hold of the barbarous arrow and slowly pulled it from the Latsu's body. Blood followed the retracted path of the arrow-head. Zira had lost a great deal of blood and faded fast. Storm sent a generous portion of his own life energy into his friend, and then, remembering the teachings of the maegess, set about fusing tendon to tendon, bone to bone, and nerve ending to nerve ending. The boy worked for hours while Wolfy watched over him. Anyal had run hard back to the main road where she found a boy headed toward the palace. She sent him with an urgent message to find a mage, and instructed him of their location in the forest. By the time she got back to her friends, Mage Leskel was already in the glade tending to the still unconscious Yurmin. Meanwhile, Storm had successfully completed the healing process. When he at last raised his hands, the only evidence of a wound was the blood-flecked fur that surrounded the bolt's entry point. Storm collapsed exhausted in the grass. Remembering her part in Nolina's lesson, Anyal took her hand and placed it upon Storm's arm. Closing her eyes she projected her senses into the wound site. Sure enough, as she had seen during the earlier lesson, Storm had suffered two complete breaks, one in the humerus of the upper arm and the other in the radius of the lower arm. Carefully, she captured like energies and wound them into a healing web. Ensuring that like lines of energy were aligned she deftly forced the bone fragments together. There was a brief burst of brilliant light as one side met the other then it was done. Healing the break of the smaller bone in the lower arm was much easier to accomplish, less lines to align and less space through which to move the broken pieces.

Mage Leskel appeared beside her and after checking the arm nodded approvingly. "You have talents beyond manipulation of air it seems," stated the mage. Leskel was Anyal's favorite elemental wizard and she was glad that it had been he and not another that heeded her call for help.

"Will he be alright Sir?" asked Anyal in a tired voice.

"He will now, thanks to you. He gave up a little too much of his own energy to help Zira, but nothing a few days in bed won't fix. I wish the same could be said for our other young catcher. I have already sent him to the infirmary. Whatever happened here, will certainly have to be accounted for in front of the mage council. A week ago, the verdict would have already been rendered. He who cast the first stone would now find himself expelled from the island. Alas the seefar does not now extend outside of the palace walls. These are dark days indeed. Come let us return to the palace and get you all some rest. I fear that rest is something that will be a luxury in the days to come."

Wolfy picked up Zira, and with Storm supported on one side by Anyal and on the other by Leskel, they were all transposed back to the palace.

Two days later Storm, Anyal, and Yurmin stood before the mage council within the south tower. Storm noticed that Yurmin now walked with a very definite limp. He could not understand what he had ever done to inspire such hatred in the boy. At first he had been deeply sorry and apologetic for his actions in the forest. Yet the memory of Yurmin standing over the dying body of his beloved Zira was enough to quash any further thoughts of sentimental regret. The wait was nerve-wracking. The audience before them was comprised of Kalon, Saltorini, Dulkin, Leskel, Yurl, Corrin, and Bartrand. Storm was disappointed that Mirren and Nolina were not included in the proceedings. Somehow he expected their allegiance would be with him rather than Yurmin.

Kalon looked much improved after his part in the elemental power display. He was the first to speak. "We have come here today for an accounting of action. What has occurred in the last few days is deeply regretful and cannot go unpunished. As each of you know, the laws of the wizard isle are immutable. Sadly, we do not have the objectivity of the far-seer to help us in this matter. Thus we must take credence in the evidence at hand and in the stories we have been told. Each of you has had the opportunity to be interviewed by Mage Corrin. During that discourse, he was able to ascertain the truthfulness, or deceit, of your telling. First, Anyal, you acted with integrity and compassion. You proved yourself adept in the healing arts and your genuine concern for your fellow students perhaps saved their lives. We can find no guilt in your actions and you are invited to remain with us on the island."

Anyal breathed a visible sigh of relief. The next to speak was Mage Dulkin. "The events of the last week have placed an undue burden of stress and emotional duress on all of us. We have determined that Yurmin's explanation of the events of three days ago also is credible. He has stated on official record that the cross-bolt wound inflicted upon Zira was nothing more than an accident. Furthermore, he states that his actions toward Storm were conducted in self-defense."

Storm could barely control his anger. "You are kidding right? That evil dung-pile attempted to kill Zira, not once, but twice. Then his bat-wielding friend broke my arm into little pieces. Now, I admit to perhaps being a little overly forceful in protecting Zira and myself, but Yurmin is as innocent as a dark-lord."

"You will control your outbursts in front of this august body my boy," sneered Dulkin. Storm scowled back as the mage continued his verdict on Yurmin's behavior. "It is the almost unanimous decision of the council to grant Yurmin the opportunity to remain on Meridia and to be able to continue his studies once the Academy is resumed. Storm stole a look in Yurmin's direction and watched a sly grin creep to the edges of the boy's mouth. All that Storm could think about was how much he wanted to beat the smile off his face. Indignation and unbridled fury radiated inside his breast. He did not even hear Mage Leskel begin his oration concerning Storm's fate.

"I was there and tended to the severity of master Yurmin's wounds. In my opinion such an attack goes beyond the realm of permissiveness. We have not been able to uncover whether there was another antagonist involved in this affair, thus we have only Yurmin's word against that of Storm. It is the unanimous verdict of the mage council that Storm should be stripped of all privileges on Meridia, and be expelled immediately. Already, word has been sent to Three Towers that you will be joining them before the end of the week. You may pack your things, say your goodbyes and be ready to depart by royal barge at mid-day tomorrow."

Kalon stood suddenly and declared, "this meeting of the council is adjourned." One by one the mages disappeared and soon only Anyal and Storm remained in the meeting chamber. Tears rolled unabatedly down Anyal's cheeks. Storm stood in complete disbelief. He could not believe that the council was taking Yurmin's word over his. All he had done was to try and protect Zira and now they were being expelled and sent back to live at the monastery. Well if that's what the stupid council wanted that's what they would get. Let them believe Yurmin. He would prove his true colors in due course and then the mages would be sorry.

Chapter Forty-One

Shipbound

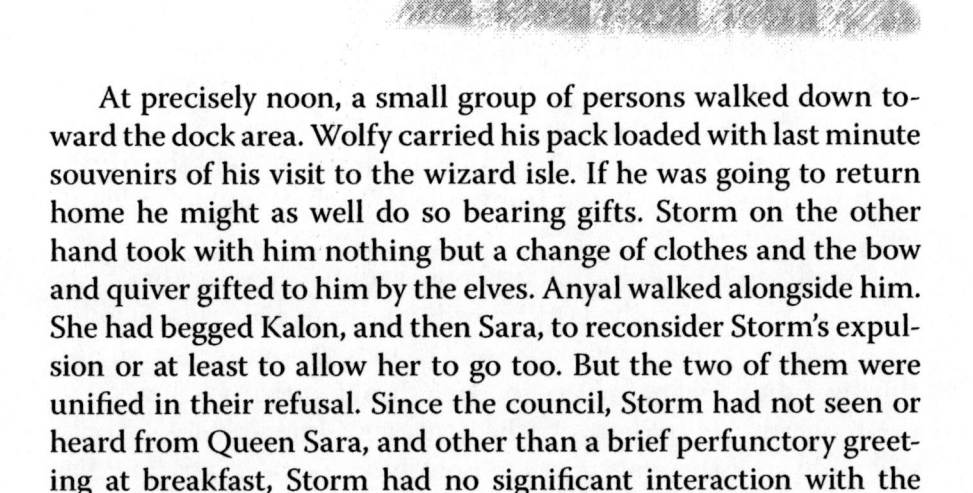

At precisely noon, a small group of persons walked down toward the dock area. Wolfy carried his pack loaded with last minute souvenirs of his visit to the wizard isle. If he was going to return home he might as well do so bearing gifts. Storm on the other hand took with him nothing but a change of clothes and the bow and quiver gifted to him by the elves. Anyal walked alongside him. She had begged Kalon, and then Sara, to reconsider Storm's expulsion or at least to allow her to go too. But the two of them were unified in their refusal. Since the council, Storm had not seen or heard from Queen Sara, and other than a brief perfunctory greeting at breakfast, Storm had no significant interaction with the Archmage.

They had arrived at the dock and there awaiting them was a royal yacht.

"Well at least they are sending us home in style," grunted Wolfy. Storm had to admit, for someone suffering the humiliation of expulsion this was a little surprising. He could only rationalize that Queen Sara felt bad about forcing him to leave and thus had chosen to at least make him comfortable on the short voyage across the Adearan Sea.

Zira jumped down onto the deck with Wolfy close behind. Anyal reached and grabbed Storm's arm before he climbed aboard. Tenderly she thrust an object into his hand. Before the tears came she kissed him quickly on the lips and fled back up the trail toward the palace. Storm stood alone, watching after the raven-haired girl that he now knew he loved. The sensation of her kiss lingered deep into the day. As the household guard cast off the ropes and the yacht pulled out of port, he opened his hand to regard Anyal's gift. There in his palm lay her most prided possession. The pendant which once had been a gift from the Wallahs was now his to keep safe until they were reunited. Storm studied the necklace. It was indeed a curious piece of workmanship. Finely carved, the tree was embossed upon a radiant sun fully encircled within a strange pattern. Storm clasped the charm around his neck and stood alone watching the island he had come to love, fade into the distance.

During the night he was woken by an image from Zira. *The wise one comes. He looks for you.* Storm snapped into wakefulness and looked around him. Sure enough there standing in the doorway was Kalon.

"Archmage! Why are you here?" Storm stammered the words, confused and disorientated from only being half-way to wakefulness.

"Well my boy, first and foremost I didn't have a chance to say good-bye. Secondly, I still owed you an explanation which I promised to render back when our friends the elves visited, and thirdly, I didn't want you to go away thinking that I believed everything Yurmin told us. On the contrary, I know that you spoke truthfully and the mage council does too. You see the island has magical properties that even I have yet to comprehend fully. One interesting quirk of nature is the pure energies that flow into our woodlands. As you might have noticed, Yurmin still walks with a pronounced limp. We have had our very best healers take a look at him and even Nolina attempted to correct his injury. Alas, life requires energy that is light, and Yurmin carries little, at least not enough to fuse that ankle back together again."

"Now where should I begin? Ah yes, first let me assure you that you have not really been expelled, rather been extended an indefinite leave of absence. By the time you return, the Academy will be working and functioning as well as before. The reason for granting you leave is, that we have decided, Yurmin requires our watchful eye and you do not. It is time for you to join your quest

Child of Night

my boy. We cannot protect you from fate's inevitability forever. I would like to remind you of the prophecy Abbot Nicholas once shared with you:

> *There is a power in the world which holds the balance of light and dark intact. This power is the Aruk. In all four corners of the world there are Sentinels; protectors and defenders of all that is alive. Four belong to the dark, four to the light. The balance of power can survive only till such day as the ninth son is born and the Darkwitch is dead. Then at Cartis in the land of Bal, the one called Fleet of Foot will hold the fate of the world in hand.*

Storm, these are important words indeed. You are the child of prophecy, and your feet must now take you to Cartis to pursue your destiny."

The Archmage paused before continuing. "As you know already there are forces of light and dark which balance, precariously, all life upon Terrus. For years one side has not been able to survive without the other. There are four sentinels of the dark and there were four sentinels of the light. With the death of Abbot Nicholas, the dark has the light at something of a disadvantage. You have met Sara and her brother Ryad, and in time you shall also meet Terel. These three individuals stand as the last bastions of hope to the civilized world. If the dark-lords win the upcoming battle, then life as we know it will cease to exist. This is why the elves are so fearful. They have lost much through the generations, but a conquest for the dark will end the lives of elves and transform the Elghorian into a lifeless desolation. The prophecy predicts that the balance can only be preserved until the ninth son is born and the darkwitch is dead. The Matriarch assures us that the darkwitch is indeed dead. The tree felt the evil pass on. We also are quite certain that you were born the ninth son. Your powers, abilities, your natural drawing towards the Aruk, all make claim to this. There is also the question of your birth-right. I alone know of your past and who your mother and father are. Please forgive me for not being able to tell you at this time. If I were to tell you now, your life and perhaps theres might be ended prematurely. I can tell you however, that they both still live. There is a time for the telling, but that time is not now. Storm, you must journey to Cartis, one of the oldest temples in the known world. It is a place where, despite its ruined appearance, the powers of creation can still be found stirring. I do not fully understand your path or what you must do when you arrive. But I do know this. You must travel there and you must be strong, for the entire future of the known world might well come down to the choices that you make there. One more important piece of information that you must not forget, the Lords of Light and the Lords of Dark, while very powerful, are at this time mortal just like you and I. We have lost Nicholas, and I daresay before the quest is done we might lose more. Now I must go. Remember those that love you. Sara, in particular sends her truest blessings. You will have guides to help you along the way. I have arranged for you to be met in Kurigan by Ryad and a hand-picked escort. Forgive the subterfuge. If any agents of the dark have infiltrated Meridia, we would want them to believe you have headed west not south. Good luck and may the Gods guard and protect you until we meet again."

With a flash of light, Kalon disappeared leaving in his wake a perturbed young boy. What could he, a boy of thirteen winters, possibly do against the combined might of the powers of the dark? He had already tasted a semblance of their strength one horrific night in Sard. Now the Archmage asked him to go willingly to a land he had never entered, to face a power he could not even imagine, and fight a battle he did not understand. Great, he thought, just what the average adolescent wants to do on his thirteenth birthday.

Chapter Forty-Two

Kurigan

Little in his life experience prepared Storm for Kurigan. The port city was the largest civilized conurbation on Terrus situated at the mouth of the Southern Passage. The colors, sounds, sights, and smells that engulfed the young boy's senses, as they tacked along the sea-front to the portage, were enumerable. The boy had never seen so many people gathered in one place. Wolfy, stood beside him on the top-deck regarding the looming city with apprehension. The farmer had never enjoyed the rare visits he was forced to make to the kingdom cities. The life he loved was the simple life of the farmer. Noting the fear that flitted within Storm's eyes, Wolfy reached his broad arm around the boy and squeezed a quiet reassurance. Storm looked up at his friend and smiled. If he was to face the unknown he was glad that Wolfy was there to face it with him.

The captain of the yacht artfully guided the vessel to a resting place at one of the empty docks. Storm noticed that empty docks were at a premium along the wharf. Every manner of ship, yacht, barge, war-man, skiff, and schooner were moored within the harbor. Each vessel flew different colors. Like his vessel, many of them flew the insignia of Meridia. He was brought out of his reverie by the first-mate who came bustling along the deck towards him armed with a parchment scroll.

"Master Storm, I was told to present you with this the moment that we arrived in Kurigan."

Storm took the scroll and broke the seal. The unmistakeable hand-writing of the Archmage fairly leapt from the page. Simply written the message stated:

'Proceed with caution and watch your back. Trust no one, not even someone bearing the uniform of a Meridian soldier. Follow the cobbled street at the end of the pier until you see the Shipwreck Inn on your right. The Inn is easily identified by the sign that depicts a ship running aground on a rocky shoal. Enter the black doors and go directly to the bar. Inform the inn-keeper that you would like a room for the night. He will show you to an upstairs room. Remain there and under no circumstances leave, or open the door. A man will come to the door and knock seven times, after which he will pass a note beneath the door. The note will read, 'I am Beran, First Captain of the Olondo Garrison, and by order of Queen Sara, your guide and escort to Cartis.' Only then should you let him enter. Take care and may Nishu watch over your journey.'

As he finished reading the last sentence the words began to fade and seconds later Storm was left holding an empty piece of parchment.

Wolfy thanked the captain for safe passage and proffered a single gold coin as was the custom. The captain smiled and wished them luck on their journey. Though he didn't say it out loud, the farmer thought to himself, 'we need more than bloody luck, we need a God's own miracle.' Kalon had visited Wolfy on board the royal yacht after speaking with Storm. In their brief meeting the Archmage had asked that the farmer consider traveling to Cartis with Storm. So much for a simple trip home Wolfy had thought. But he was not prepared to desert the boy he had sworn to protect, the boy that he now looked upon as a son.

It was a strange company that left the city wharf. Wolfy's broad frame and significant height made it difficult for him to pass unnoticed in a crowd. Combined with a green-eyed boy, and a large wolf, they might as well have been a carnival side-show for all the stares and attention they drew. Fortunately, the Shipwreck Inn was only a short walk. Wolfy pushed the door open and they stepped inside leaving the bright sunshine of conspicuousness for the musty dreariness of concealment. Few bodies frequented the tap-room at this early hour. The inn-keeper gave them a knowing look before installing them in an upstairs room. The room's furnishings were sparse. There were two straw-lined mattresses, a three-legged stool, a small table, and a basin that smelled distinctly of urine. There was no window and the only light came from a stubby candle that sat in a jar on the rickety old table. The floor comprised an uneven mismatch of splintered boards, and the low-cut ceiling bowed disturbingly. Wolfy had to stoop uncomfortably as he moved around the room. Even Storm, who had experienced something of a growth spurt during his stay on Meridia, found that he was forced to duck his head in places. The room placed their nerves on edge. Only Zira seemed to be comfortable, for he fell promptly asleep on one of the mattresses. He had not cared for the three-day ocean voyage sleeping only sporadically. Now he took the opportunity to make up for lost sleep.

With no window or time-piece to guide them, they lost all sense of time. Sometime around mid-day the monotony of inactivity was gratefully interrupted by the kindly inn-keeper. A tray of food slipped through a concealed hatch in a panel at the base of their door. Bowls of piping hot soup, a platter of bread and cheese, and a well-meated bone for Zira constituted lunch. It was not the finest fare and Storm decided he would rather not know the animal identity of the chunks of meat floating around in the brothy concoction. Still, it filled their stomachs, and at this stage of their journey he would take whatever he could get. After the meal, man and boy fell asleep on the makeshift beds oblivious to the stirrings of the dark.

***

News of the far-seer devastation had spread rapidly. Lord Rune sat alone in his throne-room plotting his next move. The High Priestess had certainly not disappointed him. If his sources could be trusted, the outer defenses of Meridia had been crushed and the ninth son flushed out. Now the boy, he was told, returned to Sard. No one was more aware of the prophecy than Rune. For the moment he would continue to bide his time and watch while his brothers fought amongst themselves. His immediate goal was to insure that the child never reached Cartis. No prophecy could be fulfilled if the boy was prevented from traveling south.

* * *

Lord Vilus continued to experience the inexorable throes of madness. He no longer cared for political intrigue, conquest, or damnable schemes plotted against the light. His only passion now centered on the satiation of an over-whelming blood-lust. The barbarians had proven to be a worthwhile ally and the wild-men from the North continued to flock to his lands. Vilus did not know if his brother had noticed this mutiny, then again he cared little about Rune's opinion on anything. The barbarians were a feral race and were obsessive in their vengeful pillages. They had all but exhausted their immediate food resources. Few peasant families or farmers remained west of the Northwood. Most had fled for the protection of the Sardik Plains. Now Vilus looked southward, to a new hunting ground for his carnivorous pets. As he poured over his maps, an evil glint came unto his eye. The least defended of all Sara's precious garrisons was Illian and with it a town full of peasants. Vilus licked his lips as he began to scheme expansion for his hunt.

* * *

Meanwhile, Lord Damal was so wrapped up in preserving his personal domain that he had not noticed the damage inflicted upon his neighbor's home. Archmage Kalon and the council had created a spectacular illusion that to the cursory observance showed Meridia to be intact and unblemished. Damal had no reason to doubt this outward appearance and contented himself with matters of attention within his own household. The training of Squire Spit proceeded splendidly. Damal, himself, had undertaken the training of the boy when it came to weaponry. On the first day of instruction, Damal had taken a perverse pleasure in slashing a wound upon the boy from groin to knee. His healers had sewed Spit up and sent him right back to the training yard. Spit learned a valuable lesson and worked almost desperately to attain a proficient level of competency with the sword. The boy did not love his new master but held a begrudging respect and earnest fear of him. Spit knew no illusions.of grandeur. The dark-lord was as fickle as a courting adolescent and would as soon end Spit's life as he would remove a stone from his riding boot.

***

One dark-lord not to be taken in by Kalon's mis-direction was Brack. Everything was going according to plan. His two infiltrators upon the wizard isle had yet to be discovered. Admittedly, Yurmin was sitting on dangerous ground, and Brack had no doubts that the wily Archmage was on to the boy. Still, Yurmin had played his part beautifully. Not only had he caused pain and harm to the ninth child but he had managed to get the boy expelled. Better yet, he had gotten himself absolved of all guilt in their confrontation. Brack allowed himself a rare laugh at the irony of the situation. However, as soon as he had learned of Storm's departure aboard a royal yacht, he had become suspicious. These suspicions were well founded. Earlier that morning, he had learned from his spy network that Storm had arrived in Kurigan.

***

Zira awoke long before the others and turned his attention toward the door. Boots scuffed on the stairs and he could differentiate clearly the scents of three men standing on the other side. He let out a low guttural snarl. Immediately, Storm was awake, rousing Wolfy, and indicating the door. A loud knocking preceded a voice that called Storm by name. Zira sent sharp images of warning infused with shades of red.

Master, these men do not smell clean. I think they are not friends to us. Do not open the door.

Storm returned a quiet reassurance. "The wise one warned us to only open the door for a man named Beran. Be silent, perhaps they will go away."

Again the door was beaten upon, this time more impatiently. "We know you are in there. It is alright, we are friends. We have been sent to take you to meet the Captain. He is waiting for us at the south gate. Open the door." The voice was gruff and devoid of emotion. "Fine, I guess we will just have to come in and get you then," stated the speaker.

The next moment an axe blade sliced through the oak paneling. Storm drew his bow and notched an arrow. Zira took up a defensive position in front of his master. Wolfy drew from his belt a simple hunting knife and crossed to stand against the wall to the left of the door. There the three of them stood watching while their door was obliterated by an enemy axeblade. As the first man stepped through the opening, Storm let loose an arrow. The shot rang true, impaling its deadly barb between the eyes of the approaching mercenary. With a glazed expression of complete surprise, the man dropped instantly dead. Suddenly, a new commotion filled the hallway. The remaining two mercenaries were forced to turn and fight a battle on two fronts. This skirmish on the stairs ended swiftly. Statuesque, Storm knelt in the far corner, a new arrow notched upon his long bow. A hand curled around the doorframe and threw a ball of parchment into the room.

"Fetch please Zira," Storm sent silently. Obediently, the Latsu snatched up the paper and returned it to his master. With one hand still holding tension to his bow, he uncrumpled the wadded message and read its contents, 'I am Beran, First Captain of the Olondo Garrison, and by order of Queen Sara, your guide and escort to Cartis.'

Storm let out an audible sigh of relief. "Please enter Captain Beran and be welcome." The blond tanned head of Beran cautiously ducked through the door's gaping hole. A sandy-haired man with a contagious grin followed on his heels.

Beran spoke first. "My name is Beran, first captain and friend of Ryad, Swordmaster of Terrus. I believe you have already met him. This is Jakes, my lieutenant captain."

"Hey is that a promotion from captain-in-training? If so I like it," smiled Jakes. Beran shot him a stern glance.

The blond-haired captain stooped to the floor and studied the arrow that protruded from out of the mercenary's skull. Carefully, he pulled the barbarous head cleanly from the dead-man and, while he cleaned the point on the mercenary's jerkin, he ran his fingers along the artfully crafted shaft.

"I have seen such arrows before. Arrows such as these once saved my life. The elves must indeed prize your friendship greatly to issue such a gift." Beran silently appraised these new allies. He knew already that keeping everyone alive was going to be an expedition as much of luck as ability.

"We would have come sooner, but we noticed you were followed from the docks. We only saw these three," Beran gestured outward to the unseen bodies in the hall-way, "but we could not be sure that there were not more. Your flight from Meridia is already common knowledge and thus our quest becomes ever more perilous. We must leave now while darkness still offers some cover of protection."

Wolfy, who had been silent throughout the introductions, stood to the fore with a look of mild exasperation playing on his face. "Look here Bernie!"

"Actually, my name is Beran Sir," interrupted the captain.

"Alright Beran, hows about you clue us in to just what the God's giblets is going on. Who are these men that followed us and where in the blazes are we going now?"

"All your questions will be answered in due course, Farmer Barley. But for now we must take leave of this place before Brack's men come looking for their dead friends."

The captain led them through the shattered door and down the narrow stairwell. Storm avoided looking down at the dead bodies. He felt adrenalin pumping through his veins. Tonight he had taken his very first life and it was an experience he found no joy in. At the foot of the stairs they turned left and threaded their way through a dimly lit corridor. Music and good-natured banter came from the direction of the tap-room, but Beran led the group away down an opposite corridor. He stopped before four wooden wine barrels. Together, Jakes and Beran moved them out of the way exposing a trapdoor beneath. With a flurry of settled dust, Beran pulled open the heavy door. After lighting a torch, he led them down the heavily worn steps motioning the others to follow. Storm went first, followed by Zira and finally Wolfy. Above, Jakes closed the hatch. A scraping sound indicated that the young captain replaced the wine caskets. A myriad of thoughts assailed the boy as he walked. Ahead, he focused upon Beran's flaming torchlight and found himself lost in the memories of a carefree youth that seemed now so very far removed.

Chapter Forty-Three

Travelers

The underground traveling party was periodically joined by other soldiers. No one spoke a word and Beran continued to lead the group through a never-ending array of tunnels and channels. Storm surmised, from the putrid stench of the water, that they walked through a lattice of sewage ducts. For long stretches the going was easy with wide dry ledges extending along their path. At other times they were forced to wade through waist-deep water that reeked of urine and excrement.

Zira especially resisted these impromptu swims. *Do humans really feel the need to store their waste?* Zira sent.

Storm chortled as Zira sent images of men and women relieving themselves. *Well my fine white-haired friend what would you suggest we do with it?*

Perhaps man could catch it and bury it in the ground far away from where they live.' The image of a man burying his feces in the woods came quickly to Storm's mind.

Again he found he had to suppress a giggle. Still, Zira did have a point. The water within the sewer system was particularly gross and it flowed, only a few feet, below the floor-boards of the houses above. After several hours of walking and wading, the light of Beran's torch halted. Ahead, there loomed a metal grill. Beran sent out a low-pitched whistle that was swiftly answered by a like tone. Hands reached from the other side of the opening and lifted the grill from rusting hinges. The night still slept deeply as they emerged from the sewer. Few stars penetrated the cloudy heaven. Storm quickly took stock of his surroundings. They had emerged from the side of a small hill overlooking the docks. Their exit appeared to be toward the far end of the harbor.

With the stealth and speed befitting mountain cats, rather than soldiers, the men in Beran's company stole down the slope bearing Wolfy, Zira and Storm in their midst. One-by-one the men jumped into a waiting barge and disappeared from view. Storm followed and found he stood in a steeply over-hung compartment staring at twenty or more serious looking warriors. Occasionally, one or two of them caught his eye and nodded a greeting, but for the most part, his strange companions remained silent. One soldier in particular drew his notice, a tall Black man, larger in stature than even Wolfy dwarfed the other soldiers. All were clad in black leathers with no discerning marks of membership or rank. Moments later the familiar form of Beran and the cheeky grin of Jakes appeared below the main deck-level. Beran indicated with a finger to his lips that all should continue to remain quiet.

There was a brief sensation of motion and the barge drifted from its moorings and headed for the harbor mouth. They were stopped only once by the harbor watch-man as he hailed them through the gates. Since leaving the tavern, Storm's heart had pounded so loudly that he was convinced all around him could hear it. Now, as the barge headed into the southern passage current, it beat a little faster. The barge rode a swift wake, and the helmsman tilled expertly a south-westerly course. There was little need for oar or sail in the passage, providing one was traveling north to south. Periodically, Beran would disappear to the deck, returning every few minutes to give his men the 'clear' sign. The barge followed a western tack. The marshed steppes spread ominously into purest blackness. The lights of Kurigan soon were swallowed by the obscure night. Despite their apparent solitariness, Beran maintained the order of silence. This seemingly over-cautious request was apparently warranted when he returned from one of his scoutings on deck holding up three fingers, pointing one in the direction of Kurigan and two in the direction of Nurendoc. The latter port city lay at the southernmost tip of the well-travelled canal. While not as large as its northern-most counterpart, it was in every way as mercurial and unlawful.

Jakes followed Beran up top. The boat from Kurigan was a barge of similar descript, while the two vessels that headed toward them were large oared yachts that flew no herald or insignia. The helmsman skirted as close to the western wall as the depth of the water would permit. In the darkness, they were able to move invisibly by the two larger vessels. Beran and Jakes held their breath in unison. The two men watched as a light shone from the barge that followed. Instantly, the two yachts beaded their way towards it.

Beran disappeared below deck. Storm could tell from the captain's eyes that trouble loomed on the horizon. In hushed tones that were barely audible Beran whispered, "listen all of you. Do not question what I ask of you; just do as you are told. We have been followed out of Kurigan. I was naieve to think that they would not be watching closely the comings and goings of vessels within the passage. Jakes is going to lead you over-board. Swim silently for the western shore. We are coming up on some sandy shoals and the bend in the passage will hide us from our pursuers, but not for very long. While we can out-run the barge, the two mercenary ships that have rendezvoused with him are another matter completely. Be ready for my signal."

The helmsman steered the barge into the curvature of the shoals and held the boat steady against an eddying current. One by one, Beran's men clambered over the side and started swimming towards shore, bearing swords and bows above their head. There were twenty-five soldiers, including Beran and Jakes. Every man in this special corps had fought beside him at Tumi with the exception of the giant Basq. The ebony-skinned mute had proven to be unappreciably strong, and, with a few short weeks of training had proved more than competent with a sword and staff. Contrary to the misgivings of some of the older soldiers, Beran had enlisted Basq in the roster submitted to the sword-master. In the Captain's mind, there was no question of the loyalty of his chosen patrol, and in that he included the speechless giant.

Beran waved a thankful farewell in the direction of the bargeman, then followed Storm and Zira over the side. Wolfy was not a good swimmer. If the soldiers swam with the grace of a porpoise, Wolfy moved with the semblance of an angry wildebeest, and made almost as much noise. Fortunately, the swim was short and before long soldier, boy, farmer, and Latsu were safely across and hidden in the bull rushes that avenued the passage. Their barge had once more pushed off into deeper water and continued southward. The hidden group did not have to wait very long before the first of the large yachts raced around the headland using the stiff current to gain purchase on the now empty barge. Its sister ship followed closely behind, and together they encircled the little transport vessel. Lights and torches flared as phantom figures jumped aboard the barge. An angry exchange transpired between the mercenary sailors and the trusted kingdom man. The barge captain took great pleasure in expounding upon the violation of shipping courtesy and the legal laws broken through illegal search and boarding. Storm prayed to Nishu, that the kindly helmsman would not be hurt. So much innocent blood had been spilled on his account already, and he did not want to have another on his conscience. Fortunately, the mercenary sailors were more interested in chasing down a different prey and hurried back aboard their larger ships before pursuing their invisible quarry further down the southern passage.

Beran waited several minutes, to ensure that the cutters were not going to return. Then, slowly, he crouched down on hands and knees and crawled through the river-side flora bidding his men to follow. Storm found Jakes inching along beside him and returned a matching grin.

For two days, Beran led the group through the lower steppes. The dangers were no less here than anywhere else. Quicksand continuously harassed them. Several men had to be rescued from an imminent deathsome fate. Wolfy and Basq earned a genuine respect during such encounters. Few of Beran's men could rival the humble farmer and the muscular mute in pound-for-pound brute strength. By the end of the second day in the steppes, four men had already sworn life-debt to Wolfy and several more to Basq. Storm found some humor in this and took whatever opportunity he could to rib Wolfy.

"Well you certainly found one way to endear yourself to the soldiers. If you want, I could have Zira lead a few more into the sinking sand and then perhaps we could recruit a regular discipleship." Wolfy threw a lump of mud at the boy's face which landed squarely on his nose.

"Oh that's mature. I suppose you feel much better now," blurted Storm.

"Much, thank you," retorted the grinning farmer.

Finally, on the third day they came in sight of the High Street. Their journey through the steppes had brought them just a few miles east of the Illian Garrison. When the party reached the garrison gates, Storm allowed himself the luxury of a single breath of relief. In truth, all he really wanted to do was return to Meridia. He missed Anyal, and he even missed his studies and the mage teachers. Storm found himself also thinking of maegess Mirren. Her presence, in his dreams, was a warm and settling one. However, he realized after the events of the last week, he would require far more than a water-mage's settling influence to keep him alive.

Chapter Forty-Four

Illian

Storm had never been inside a kingdom garrison before. The structure itself stood high on a hill over-looking the Icealic. At the foot of the hill a small industrious hamlet co-existed with the kingdom barracks. Illian was also situated at the western-most point of the ancient High Street. The old road wound its way northward through the western steppes from Illian to Bala. Wolfy had been to Illian before. It was a short journey to Sard, and he remembered that his father had traveled there with him on more than one occasion to trade. The clarity of his recollection was a little dim but he was sure the town of Illian had grown significantly larger since the days of his child-hood visits. The harbor pulsed with merchant ships and southern traders. A bustling metropolis full of interesting colors, sights, and sounds, the town of Illian certainly could not be termed dull. Unfortunately, Storm was not permitted to leave the garrison. In the days that followed their arrival life became decidedly routine.

Storm and Zira, spent most of their time walking the battlements and open courtyards One benefit to the forced confinement, was the time available to spend practicing archery skills. He spent long hours in the training yard shooting at apples, hay bales, posts, or whatever else he could dream into a target. Jakes noticed the boy's passion with the bow and permitted him to join the archer's squad in their daily training sessions. Storm preferred this greatly, for now he could shoot at real archery targets. He also enjoyed the competition. Invariably, practice culminated in some expedition of skill. Of course the vast majority of garrison archers utilized the powerful cross-bow. Storm's long-bow was a novelty, but no less deadly. The boy frequently held his own in competitions. The older and more experienced archers never succumbed to defeat, but in the few days he had been at Illian he closed the distance quickly.

The garrison's architectural structure fascinated Storm. The outer walls were constructed with brick and stone packed almost four-feet wide. The inner walls were timbered and coated in a black tar-like substance. Storm later learned that this tar prevented the wood from catching fire in times of siege. The garrison, significantly larger than Three Towers, covered the entire expanse of the mesa. Foundations had been secured to the granite bed-rock, which made most of the fortified structure nigh on immoveable. There were six open courtyards, five of which were assigned as training grounds for the stationed militia. Not a day passed when the yards were not teeming with the sounds of clashing swords, whirring arrows, impatient horses, or groaning wooden staves. On the periphery of each courtyard were the kitchens, soldier quarters and mess halls. Storm mused at the discipline and tidiness of the soldiers. For an area that housed almost four thousand soldiers, the garrison was kept pristinely clean and uncluttered.

The stables were manned by a host of boys, some not much younger than Storm. Their entire vocation in life was to feed, water, and exercise the horses. Sometimes, Storm watched them perform their duties and he thought wistfully how simple their lives must be.

The barracks had only two gates, one on the southernmost side, which overlooked the ocean and the High Street, and the other on the north-east corner, which commanded a strategic view of the steppes and the western tundra. The Illian garrison was second only to the Kelanon garrison in longevity of service. However, few garrisons had seen such a large number of attacks and battles. Before the recent eradication of Lord Vilus' evil demon brood, Illian and the surrounding fishing villages found themselves undergoing a continuous conflict. Then there were Lord Brack's insurgents who were a constant menace and nuisance throughout the north Icealic shore-line.

Three days after their arrival in Illian, a cadre of riders came galloping hard to the front gate. The gates were swung open and in rode Lord Ryad. Beran was the first to greet the sword-master and together they retired to the private war-room to discuss the events of the week. Hours later, Wolfy and Storm were called to an audience with the queen's younger brother. Ryad was pouring over maps when they entered. Zira, Storm's ever-present shadow, padded along silently at the boy's heel.

Ryad looked up at their arrival, and walked around the table to greet them with hearty shakes of the hand.

"It is so good to see you again my friends. I hear that you had a little trouble getting away from Kurigan. We had hoped to steal some time and get you here unnoticed. Alas the width and breadth of the dark-lords' reach is a length greater than we had anticipated."

"Sir, if I might be so bold as to ask. How long are we to be in Illian?" Storm was impatient to get the rest of the journey out of the way, and for better or worse, have life return to some sense of normalcy.

"Well my boy, if all goes to plan, we will be leaving the garrison tomorrow evening. I hope your love for sailing is not lost." Ryad chuckled lightly. He had heard that Wolfy had been able to keep very little down during the placid crossing from Meridia to Kurigan.

"Oh just great," began Wolfy. "Yet another adventure on the high seas. How favorable is the season for such a crossing?"

Ryad laughed heartily as he observed Wolfy's despairing look.

"Unfortunately, the rainy season is preparing to begin. We might find a few storms to speed us on our way. At first we considered taking the low road, but Lord Brack has far too many men in his employ to make that a worthwhile option. I think we are better off taking our chances on the Icealic. The kingdom's strongest and fastest war-ship will support us in our cause. On the morrow we should see the Catlina make port. She will be our flag-ship on the next stage of our journey. Do not look so glum Wolfy. Perhaps we will make it to Bal without even seeing a rain cloud."

"Yeah and my mother is the Queen of the bloody Elghorian," retorted Wolfy. Storm thought that funny.

"You mean to say your mother was an elf? Was she a tall elf?" Storm ducked the cuff that he knew was coming. Ryad roared with laughter, and that's how Beran found them when he arrived with dinner.

"I am sorry I missed the joke," exclaimed Beran. "I thought we all might need a good hot dinner." Beran cleaned a place at the table and spread out five platters of steaming hot food. Storm's eyes bulged when he saw the array of meats, cheeses, breads, and sweet rolls. Zira's nose sniffed rabidly.

Meat, I am hungry. Images of live chickens and cows drove into Storm's mind. The instinctual cravings of the wolf were still difficult to assimilate.

Sorry Zira everything is dead already. Storm grabbed a handful of the different meats on display and threw them on the floor. The wolf attacked them with fervor and seconds later looked up expectantly for more.

"You will just have to wait until we have eaten you big lout," said Wolfy, as he barged by the Latsu on his way to filling his plate. The night passed peacefully as Ryad outlined the plans he had prepared; plans he hoped would take them safely to Bal, and unimpeded, on to Cartis.

Chapter Forty-Five

Barbarians

Alarm bells clanged in the watch towers. Their onerous peal stirred a rude awakening. Storm dashed to the door pulling on a leather tunic as he moved. Zira pawed impatiently at the door. Before Storm could reach the handle, Wolfy threw it wide open.

"Barbarians! They are all over the place, like ants on a sweet roll. The village and harbor are under attack. Some of them are even attacking the garrison walls. Come see for yourself, but stay out of sight, and if it is at all possible, stay out of harm's way."

Storm grinned, "we are talking about me here aren't we? Then you know as well as I that you have absolutely everything to worry about."

Wolfy sighed and followed the impetuous boy into the dark courtyard. The garrison was in an uproar. Soldiers charged about armoring themselves and buckling on sword belts. Archers, already positioned throughout the battlement platforms plied arrows into the blackness. In the midst of the chaos, Storm watched Ryad and Beran dispatch orders. Wanting a closer look at what transpired below, he shinned up a nearby ladder. A macabre sight greeted his eyes. The slopes around the garrison were swarming with bodies. Torch-light threw grisly shadows that only served to increase the perceived number of barbarians steadily surging over the westward steppes. Sounds of screaming witnessed that the barbarian horde had already entered the city. Storm unstrapped his bow and notched an arrow. With rugged abandon some of the

Child of Night

barbarians had started to climb the garrison walls. Storm took careful aim and unleashed an arrow towards the south-east turret. His aim was true and he knew the satisfaction of contributing at least one enemy corpse to the garrison resistance.

While Storm offered his arm to the siege, Ryad and Beran prepared several garrison squads for a sortie outside the gates. Ryad shouted the command for the gate to be raised. It was not half-open when the swordmaster spurred his horse toward the aperture. Behind him in tight rank rode five full squads. As the gate parted the more foolhardy of the enemy rushed toward it. Their mistake was never realized. Wave upon wave of war-horse galloped over them. Skulls were crushed by powerful hooves as the kingdom militia unhesitantly drove toward the port town. In the wake of Ryad's cavalry, Beran led out five squads of infantryman. The third wave, a squad of cavalry under the command of Jakes, surged out into the surrounding villages. Finally, Captain Crill emerged with ground fighters to engage and destroy the barbarians assaulting the walls.

Ryad rode with a furious energy toward the village. Several of the enemy felt the full force of his wielded broad sword. The sword-master was disturbed. This unannounced attack was unprecedented in his experience. He recognized the adversary as the barbarians of the Black Mountains, but he found it difficult to believe that Lord Rune would act in such a desperate, chaotic fashion. Rune was calculating, cautious, and carefully pragmatic. This uncoordinated nightmare was more typical of the actions he had come to expect from his more insane cousin, Vilus. Ryad's misgivings proved painfully accurate when he reined his horse in at the city gates. Sitting atop the town's central watch-tower, laughing hysterically and casting fire-balls down upon the frightened masses, was none other than Lord Vilus himself. In a children's book, the sight of a toad-like figure sitting cross-legged atop of the highest building in Illian could very well have been viewed as comical. However, the harsh reality of the bloody nightmare that unfolded within the kingdom city was completely devoid of humor. Ryad made straight for the watchtower, barraging through every barbarian that dared stand in his path.

"Vilus! I demand that you have your animals remove themselves from my city." Despite the carnage and sounds of battle that raged around him, Ryad's voice boomed with the force of a thunder clap.

The dark-lord turned his attention to the sword-master and burst into riotous cackles and hollow laughs. "Your city? I didn't happen to see Ryad, Lord of Light on the city name plaque when I rode through the gates."

"Vilus, you will stop this madness and leave immediately or I will be forced to remove you myself." Ryad summoned from deep within all the life energy he could muster. His sword arm began to pulse with light.

Vilus flinched nervously. "You are such a killjoy Ryad, I was just having a little bit of fun. After all, these mortals, you are so quick to protect, aren't worth my spittle."

Ryad could contain his anger no longer. The full power of his summoning unleashed itself. A jet of pure white light shot from his hand and careened into the watchtower. The steel bells and slated roof dissolved instantaneously. When the dazzling brilliance of the casting evaporated, there was no evidence of the dark-lord, save for a maniacal echoed laughter. With the disappearance of Vilus, Ryad turned his attention back to the battle. By now, Beran and the foot soldiers had reached the city and now proceeded to dispatch the enemy with staggering efficiency. The barbarian mass out-numbered the Illian soldiers by more than ten to one, but were no match for the trained swords of a kingdom army.

Beran heard a woman scream from a nearby cottage. He charged through the entrance way to find three carnal creatures preparing to dismember a terrified girl. Shaking visibly with fear she had retreated under a table in the corner. The captain did not give the monsters an opportunity to turn. He dispatched the first with a dagger thrown through the neck and the second with a powerful sword thrust that shattered the sternum. The third beast whirled around swinging a chain filled with spikes. Beran jumped back in time to watch the menacing weapon bounce harmlessly off the cottage wall. Before the barbarian could prepare a second attack, Beran smashed a fist into his face, and impaled him forcibly with his sword. The little girl sobbed loudly beneath the table, rocking backwards and forwards on her knees. Cautiously, he pulled her out and into his arms. Retreating from the house, he noticed the gored carcasses of two nameless forms that he surmised had once been the girl's mother and father.

The battle raged deep into the early hours and on through to dawn. Storm had worked his way through several hundred arrows. He lamented the loss of the elven shafts but knew full well that each arrow had contributed worthily to the struggle. He had not seen head nor tail of Wolfy or Zira. Throughout the night Zira had sent back images of battle. Evidently, Wolfy and the Latsu had participated in the charge to the oceanfront.

When the fighting started, Wolfy found himself once more reliving all the pain and anguish he experienced the night the demons came to Sard. Again he saw the faces of his beloved wife and children as the evil dragon-brood butchered them in front of his very own eyes. He was tired of running from the dark. Instinctively, the incensed man had grabbed a sword and, with Zira at his back, waded into the melee. The farmer was more accustomed to a pitchfork than a broadsword, but strength and instinct overcame him as he relentlessly worked to even a personal score that yet remained unsettled. Zira, also, shared little love for the minions of the dark. He too had not forgotten Sard and, taking Wolfy's lead, sent many barbarians to violent deaths. Years later, Illian soldiers would still recount the tale of the Farmer and the White Wolf. No ten soldiers could match the combined deadly passion of the crazed giant and the ferocious Latsu. For a time, Storm found himself forced to mentally block the rampant blood-lust images Zira sent to him. Such images made it difficult enough to shoot straight let alone hit a moving target.

With the sunlight the barbarians retreated back into the steppes. Ryad had relayed orders back to the garrison, and Jakes prepared three freshly mounted squads to go after the fleeing enemy. Daylight also brought a devastating death toll. The population of Illian had stood at a stable ten thousand people for three generations. When the dead were finally commited to the ground, the town's population had been reduced by four thousand. The butchery and devastation extended even to the outlying farm districts. The garrison too had sustained severe losses. Several hundred infantryman and many more horses and mounted soldiers had met their deaths through the course of the night's fighting. Thanks in part to the talented and courageous archers, at no time were the garrison walls ever breached. Many of the bowsmen and women, including Storm, bled profusely from fingers cut to shreds by the constant pulling and releasing of drawstrings. Ryad ordered every barbarian body to be stacked and burned. When the bonfire was lit, the barbarian body count reached over eight thousand. Storm watched the bodies begin to burn and thought bitterly that the spirit journey to Tellus would not be a lonely one this day.

Chapter Forty-Six

Sisterhood

Rune was incensed. How could his brother be so void of commonsense? Not only did he have the nerve to poach barbarians away from the Black Mountains, but the feeble-minded fool now wasted three-quarters of their population in a senseless attack, on a no-name port town. The dark-lord had spent the day attempting to summon his sibling, but Vilus, as if expecting the summons, had instated an impenetrable block. Thus, Rune stalked the corridors of Rillic. The few servants who unwittingly came upon his path suffered severely. Not only had he been slighted by Vilus, but he also had lost contact with the ninth child. He had been led to believe that the boy and the simple-minded farmer that accompanied him were returning to Sard. A royal barge had alighted upon the Bala sands but no boy, wolf, or farmer had stepped off. Clearly, the Archmage was playing a game with him. If not to Three Towers, then there could only be one logical destination for the child – he was on his way to Cartis.

***

While Rune threw tantrums and waited for Vilus to accept a summons, the dark-lord's bed partner was busy with her own machinations. Chaniya cared little for the petty squabbles between the light and the dark. The only thing the High Priestess cared about was power and the ultimate destruction of Kalon and his precious wizard isle. Her little device had almost worked to perfection. Despite, the Archmage's transparent illusions to the contrary, Meridia was as unprotected as a rat in a viper pit. Without the see-far, almost anyone could now get on to the island. The palace and its grounds were still a problem, but Chaniya enjoyed a good conundrum and she would find a way to solve that puzzle before too long. When news of the absolution of the Academy arrived at the Temple, Chaniya was ecstatic. The Temple at Gajiina was in the process of recruiting its own students and with luck she hoped that many of the displaced Meridian academics would choose to continue their studies with the sisterhood.

Her alliance with the dark-lord Rune was proving quite fruitful. However, the time was coming when their partnership must ultimately be severed. True, Rune had power, power even greater than hers. Still, she remained convinced that there had begun a subtle shifting in the balance. This ninth child had turned everything on its head and she was intrigued to see how the prophecy played out.

Rune did not know, and thus could not appreciate, the words of a second prophecy contained within the ancient writings of the Book of Gajiina. When the sisterhood first convened, the world was young and the women were wise. One woman in particular commanded admiration for the gift of second sight. A simple woman, she lived inauspiciously in an ocean village on the shores of the Icealic. Fishermen journeyed from miles around to seek advice on fishing grounds. Fisherman's wives visited the old woman for guidance in petty matters of daily life. Even young men and women would waste her time with questions on romance and love. A maegess discovered the true power of this blind fisherwoman and persuaded her to leave the village and travel north into the Black Mountains. Together they founded the sisterhood and the Temple order was named for the blind oracle. Before her death, Gajiina had recorded many words of prophecy. Many such prophecies had already come to pass. She had predicted the coming of the terror wraiths and their subsequent vanquishing. She had also forseen the forming of the Aruk and the emergence of the light-dark balance. But the prophecy Chaniya cared most about was what Gajiina recorded would follow the destruction of the Aruk.

The High Priestess lovingly caressed the pages of the old book. Countless spells of preservation had been committed to safeguard the integrity of the aged pages. Whenever she perused the old journal she was always drawn to the same page. She knew the words imprinted there by heart:

The time of the balance shall pass the call. One by one the immortals fall. The undead princes return unknown. Only one assumes the throne.
A true line of kingship thus restored. Power to the sisterhood thus assured.
Yet rise there will a new found force. A new generation runs its course.
Twins are born and thus aligned. A mighty mage shall then unbind.
New light then shall gender birth. Yet still dark powers shall walk the earth.

Chaniya must have read those words a hundred thousand times. She cared not for any interpretation of meaning. Already, with the death of Abbot Nicholas and the instability of the Aruk, prophecy was being fulfilled. The words could not lie. It stated explicitly that the power of the sisterhood would be assured and she was certain that she, Chaniya, High Priestess of Gajiina, would be the one to receive such power. Now if she could just hurry along the bit about 'one by one the immortals fall.'

Chapter Forty-Seven

Discovery

Lord Brack was impatient. His insane brother's assault on Illian was a distraction he could do with out. The ninth child was well protected; it would take far more than a score thousand unintelligible barbarians to undermine a kingdom garrison. He was infuriated that the boy had eluded his capture in the flight from Kurigan. The child was getting too close to Cartis. Well soon, Ryad would have to make a decision to take the low road or risk the ocean. Knowing the wily swordmaster, he would choose the latter and rely on the speed of the Meridian cutters. Either way, Brack was more than prepared to intercept them.

For the moment, he forced his attention back to Meridia. Yurmin was being kept under constant surveillance. The Archmage was a perceptive man and, by now, would have realized that a traitor worked within the palace. It was only a matter of time until the discovery would be made. If he was to have any chance of destroying the wizard isle he would have to act quickly. Rune's little trick had been quite impressive, but even he lacked the knowledge of his older brother. In order to destroy the larger body, one had to concentrate on ripping out the heart and its accompanying arteries. The heart of Meridia was the Matriarch, the Life Tree.

* * *

Far outside the palace walls, two shadowy figures converged upon the boathouse. One hunched figure placed personal belongings aboard one of the royal barges.

Child of Night

The second figure, a tall, wiry boy of almost thirteen winters came to stand beside the dock-worker. "Are you leaving?" he asked.

"I have requested time away from the island yes," replied the man in shadows. "But first we have an errand to run for the master. Yurmin, you must not disappoint your guardian. He has been well pleased with the progress you have made, but this last task is dangerous and will require every bit of your skill, craft, and cunning."

Yurmin shrugged his shoulders. "Have I yet to disappoint?"

The older man spoke in conspiratorial hushed tones. "Meet me in the palace gardens beside the southwest corner in exactly five hours. Oh and Yurmin, make sure you are not followed. The mage council watches you closely. It would not do for you to be seen leaving the residence wing in the middle of the night. Now go and do not be late."

Yurmin cringed. Not a boy that liked taking orders, he certainly did not enjoy being ordered around by a puny old man. Still, he was not ready, or willing, to test the patience of his guardian, even if that guardian lived many thousands of leagues south of Meridia.

***

The world slept peacefully as Yurmin rose from his bed that night. He spent the next several minutes perfecting his illusion. The exertion brought beaded perspiration to his brow. With a pious pride he admired his handiwork. The illusion of a youth sleeping peacefully beneath the satin sheets of the four-poster bed was flawless. He went to the window and muttered a spell of invisibility. Instantly, his body transformed to nothingness. He was about to leave through the window when he paused. Yurmin had already tested his door and the hall-way, discovering that both were webbed with an intricate spell of warning. Clearly, the council wanted to know when Yurmin left his quarters. He cast his senses around the narrow window portal and grinned. There were the imperceptible blue and green webbed lines of energy that fused another spell of warning. The boy projected his senses into the masonry of the outer wall and was relieved to discover that the damnable wizards hadn't seen fit to encapsulate his entire room in enchantment. Carefully, Yurmin began to manipulate the energies of the wall. Mortar and brick dust fell to the velvet carpet as the elemental student mentally rearranged the stonework to form a window of his own design. Once the opening was wide enough, he stepped out and calling upon the air currents, he levitated to the ground beneath.

Yurmin met the old man in the agreed upon place. Standing in the shadows of an ivy-swamped red-brick wall, he carried a bucket filled with a dark liquid that spluttered and frothed willfully against the metallic sides of the container.

The old man spoke first. "I need you to engineer me an entrance to the garden beyond this wall." He gesticulated with a long finger to the ivy-wall behind him. "Then I require that you cast an illusion of normalcy around this site. Look well and ensure that every detail remains unchanged. Whatever noise comes from the garden it must be contained fully within your magical net. Do you understand me?"

Yurmin did not entirely understand his accomplice's purpose but he would play the part asked of him.

"Whatever you say old man, but you had better make this snappy, I cannot be sure how long my bed-room illusion will last." Yurmin threw his arms toward the wall, and in like manner to his earlier manipulation, reconfigured the brick-work to form a narrow entrance. The hunched figure did not wait for the spell to be finished. Guiding his volatile load carefully through the opening, he squeezed his tiny frame through the gap and disappeared from sight.

Once in the garden, the saboteur moved with conviction and a single-minded purpose. The Tree regarded his coming and her song grew discordant. The outer skin pulsed with amberous red. Louder and louder she sang out her warning. The old man was only twenty steps away from the tree when Nolina unfolded her form from the body of the Matriarch. When she saw the identity of the night-time visitor, she smiled and extended her hands in greeting. From between the folds of his cloak, the shadowy intruder produced a serated dagger that he plunged deep into the heart of the maegess. Instantly, the robes of the maegess flashed crimson red, the blood of her wound became intertwined with the manifestation of the colors of the dark. As Nolina slumped unconsciously to the ground, the murderer reached the tree and unhesitantly threw the contents of his pail onto the smooth skin of the Life Tree. In the next instant, flint and steel were married producing a spark that leapt to meet the incendary liquid that had already begun to permeate the tree's roots.

The mighty Life Tree burst into flames. The screams of the dying Matriarch shattered Yurmin's illusion and throughout the entire continent of Terrus there rose an agonizing shriek that grew to a mighty crescendo as the Tree fought for survival. The perpetrator of the crime stood silently with tears staining his face and his body sagged with exhaustion. Nolina screamed in writhing pain as she shared the anguish and horror of her protectress. In a final act of courage she crawled on her belly to the base of the tree.

Kalon materialized in the garden moments before other members of the council. Together they watched helplessly as Maegess Nolina rose torturously to her feet. Spreading wide her arms she embraced her mistress and drew to her the evil cancer that burned upon her conflagrated skin. Nolina was thrown forcibly into the air. The maegess hung weightlessly in the air with her head pulled back and her mouth silently mouthing unheard screams. Agonizingly she reached again for the tree and was rewarded a firey appendage that sprung to meet her extended hand. Slowly, the burning thread became a tenuous rope and a beam of burning light that painstakingly transformed into a chaotic inferno. Imperceptibly, the burning energy enveloped the dying maegess.

The mage council watched awestruck as Nolina drew to her the fire, the pain, and all the agony of her beloved Matriarch. All the while the tree resisted her sacrifice and sang a song desperate and sagacious. The drawing complete, Nolina radiated the captured conflagration. Before the end, she looked down on her friend, the Archmage, and sent a single emotive farewell. Finally, with aching passivity, Nolina levitated herself into the heavens before releasing the pent-up light energy in an implosion of color. So bright was the release, that all those viewing the night-time sky on Meridia were blinded participants in Nolina's selfless sacrifice.

When darkness again returned to the island, the brutal reality of what had just occurred settled in. One of the mage council was now dead. The Tree of Life stood significantly scarred, and the powers of dark had finally infiltrated the purest sanctity of the crystal palace. But who could have wielded such power. Who had access to Meridia's most protected inner sanctum? Mage Leskel returned from the outer garden dragging beside him the embittered but utterly defeated body of Yurmin. Kalon bit down hard on his lower lip. Why had he not expelled the boy when he had the opportunity? Now the Matriarch's symbiont was forever gone. And who was the blubbering white-haired fool who had set the Tree of Life ablaze. Kalon strode across the garden preparing inside to unleash his personal fury upon the perpetrator. Reaching down his staff, he turned the face toward him. Even in the darkness, there could be no mistake, the murderer was none other than Horatius, First Advisor and trusted servant of the Queen.

Chapter Forty-Eight

Banishment

Horatius stood before the Queen and mage council in the spacious audience chamber. The sun's rays were just beginning to pierce the stained glass windows that braced between soft white marbled walls. The Queen sat in the seat of judgment on a raised dais at the north end of the room. The mage council sat rigidly on the platform immediately below her. The events of the previous night were still a subject of disbelief for Sara. The queen had known Horatius for fifty years and never once had the man suggested that he was capable of such a crime. Yet today they were gathered to cast judgment on the man. Not an intelligible word had passed the first advisor's cracked lips since the attack. His demeanor moved fluidly from depressive sobbing to illucid muttering. His eyes flitted backwards and forwards in sunken sockets. The spectacles, that had been such a part of his character, had fallen in the garden and no one had thought to pick them up. Attempts at interrogation had proved fruitless. Even the mind probe attempted by Mage Dulkin had rendered little in the way of motive for the atrocity, although it revealed much of the man's madness.

"You leave us no alternative Horatius, Son of Zilth." Queen Sara chose her words carefully. Her emotions bordered on despair, yet she, more than most, was aware of what her station required. We sentence you to an eternity within the sphere." If Horatius knew what such a fate meant he never showed by outward emotion. Sara continued, "Your soul will be separated from your body, and your spirit and body will continue living with the knowledge of your crimes until such time as your body dies. You have forfeited the right to succeed to the next stage of soul-life. You are now the property of the soulless, and may the Gods show the same mercy unto you that you chose to show Maegess Nolina." Sara nodded to two of her household guards and they promptly stepped forward to lead the old man away.

"Kalon, what do you make of that?" asked the queen.

"I do not understand your highness. There is no motive for this crime, and no explanation for the behavior. I can only believe that he has fallen under an evil influence and the dark has laid claim to him. But who controls him is only the realm of supposition."

The queen nodded her head pensively, then lifted her eyes and gave the order for the next prisoner to be brought into the royal chamber.

Accompanied by Mages Leskel and Yurl, Yurmin was led, fettered into the audience hall. The council was taking extra precautions to ensure the cunning boy did not suddenly disappear. Kalon scowled. Yurmin was still several moons from manhood and technically still a child. The punishment for the defiant catcher had been a debate that had lasted several hours at mage council. The Archmage wanted the boy sent to join Horatius in the sphere. In his opinion, no good could possibly come from releasing Yurmin to the world. But, as Dulkin reminded the council, technically Yurmin's only offense was escaping undetected from his room and agreeing to perform an illusion in the palace garden. Yes, a maegess had been murdered, but there was no evidence to suggest that Yurmin played any kind of significant role in the crime, or that he even knew such a crime was to take place. A mind probe had confirmed the latter, yet the boy seemed to show no remorse for his part in the dark plot.

Kalon procured a deep breath and rendered judgment upon Yurmin. "You have been found guilty of treasonous acts and thus will be banished forever from Meridia and the known kingdom." For only the second time ever in his long life, Kalon extended his staff in a mighty arc that crashed down upon the frightened boy's forhead. Yurmin cringed and fought to escape his captor's hold. As the tip of Kalon's staff contacted flesh, Yurmin screamed. A smoldering three-inch scar in the form of a circle with four thin lines crossing through it revealed itself. This brand upon his forehead was the mark of djah, the badge of shame reserved for only those who were mage-born traitors, enemies of the Meridian monarchy.

"You will not be quickly forgotten or quickly forgiven. Your actions are irreprehensible and contradict all the teachings of the Academy. Should you ever return here, or be found in any kingdom city, your life will become forfeit. Now be gone."

A clap of silver light caught Yurmin and threw him roughly into time and space. Moments later he awoke to find himself facedown on the smooth white beach that was the Bala Sands. Blood trickled from his nose and pain pulsed from the imprinted wound at his temple. Slowly, he gathered himself and rose to his feet. Without so much as a look at the wizard isle behind him, he set his feet south and started immediately the tenure of his banishment.

Chapter Forty-Nine

Reesa

Reesa awoke drenched in perspiration. Silently, she dropped to the floor and searched for her leather sandals. Stealthily she shuffled to the bedroom door and sidled out on to the landing. The farm-house slept on, oblivious to the strange occurrences of the outside world. There were still many hours until dawn and a new day of chores, yet something called to the girl. Outside the stars were vibrant and the wind was chill. Winter came early to the mountains and the girl regretted not taking the time to put on her warm sheep-skin coat. In the moonlight, Reesa could distinguish clearly the familiar form of her foster-mother standing alone beside the milking sheds gazing south across the plains. Reesa stole up behind Terel and wrapped her little arms around the larger woman's waist. Terel smiled down at the child and lifted the little girl into her arms.

"You felt it too, didn't you little one?" Terel smoothed the willful locks away from the little girl's eyes. "Tonight the world loses a powerful mage." Waxing prophetic, the distant horizon burst into a momentary dioptric cacophony of orange light. Even across the many thousands of miles, Nolina's death-rite was powerfully staged.

"Mother, why did she have to die?"

"Oh Reesa, these are troubled times and even good people die sometimes."

Tears welled in the little girl's eyes. "I think the wizard who just died has a mother who is very sad. While I slept, I saw her weeping. She is very lonely and in my dream she asked if I would come be her daughter."

Terel studied the little girl carefully. How could she have been so blind? Reesa was an empath. Many of the other children often made fun of the dark-haired girl. If one of the animals were hurt, Reesa felt their pain and if one of the children was sick or hurt, she would mirror their emotions. In fact, Terel had experienced first-hand the girl's empathic power the night her brother Nicholas died. Foolishly, she had ignored the gift hoping that the girl might grow out of it. Nolina had arrived on her doorstep with a similar gift and lived for two years with Terel before mysteriously vanishing. Many years later, Terel discovered that the sweet foster child had become the symbiont of the Life Tree. Now Reesa stood there in the moonlight informing Terel, matter-of-factedly, that the Matriarch was calling her to service.

"Tell me child, what does the mother say to you?"

At first Reesa knotted her brow in consternation, as if trying to understand the question before giving answer. "She says that she is old, tired, and sick. Moma, someone tried to hurt her but they killed her daughter instead. She asks for you moma to bring me to her." Reesa reached her tiny hand to Terel's cheek and placed her spindly fingers upon her foster mother's forehead.

A distortion of space rushed around her and Terel found she walked in the Matriarch's garden. She realized that this was not a physical teleportation but rather an astral projection of herself to another place. The tree swayed limply as the charred boughs deflected all manner of reds, yellows and oranges. First-hand through Reesa's empathetic connection, she was able to view the considerable damage and injury suffered by the Life Tree. Terel permitted her consciousness to merge with that of the Matriarch. In the same manner a mother soothes a child, Terel tenderly whispered, "I will bring Reesa to you." Then suddenly, the sentinel found herself returned to Marindoc along with a child that slept peacefully within her arms. Terel kissed the little girl's cheek and deposited her safely back within her tiny cot. The old woman pulled the sheets around Reesa and sat beside her singing tender lullabies until the cockerel crowed to herald a new day.

That morning Terel packed a travel bag and called her many foster children together. The oldest boy was Lamkey, a strong youth of fifteen summers. Terel conferred upon him the leadership and responsibility of the Farm. One-by-one she said her goodbyes, and with them the promise of a swift return. Then the old woman and her innocent foster-child walked to the front gate and hand-in-hand down the track that led toward the High Street. At the last bend, Terel stopped, turned and waved a cheery farewell. All morning she had smiled and kept a positive energy in front of her young family, but now her heart ached to have to leave the serene familiarity of her farm and children. As the two of them walked together, Reesa broke the silence. "I know you are sad mother, even if you smile lots."

Terel squeezed the little girl's hand. "You are right Reesa, I am sad. It has been many many years since I left Marindoc, and I am not fond of traveling.

"Do not fear moma, I will take care of you."

Terel stopped and dropped to one knee enveloping the little girl in a warm hug. "I know you will my sweet girl, I know you will."

Chapter Fifty

Catlina

Late in the morning, the Meridian navy's flag-ship sailed into port, flying the royal insignia at half-mast in respect and deference to the Illian dead. Ryad stood alone on the pier awaiting the cutter to be secured. As soon as the gang-plank had been extended, Ryad shouted up to the first-mate. "Permission to come aboard Sir?"

The first-mate looked over his right shoulder as if seeking a higher affirmation, then turned back to the sword-master.

"You are welcome aboard the Catlina Lord Ryad." Ryad nodded his thanks and strode aboard the largest and fastest ship within the known reaches. He was greeted by a mountain of a man who, by disposition rather than uniform, commanded the position of Admiral.

"Admiral Dax, it is good to see you." The two friends embraced warmly. "I am glad to see that you dressed up for our meeting this day." Ryad grinned slyly. The Admiral was bare-foot and dressed only in cut-off pants and a tattered undershirt.

"These are troubling times my Lord Ryad. I cannot have enemy archers mistaking me for the captain of this vessel." Ryad smiled knowingly. Dax was a sailor and a warrior first, and an admiral second. He had taken the leadership position grudgingly on Ryad's recommendation some fifteen years earlier and had yet to don the Admiral's cap and jacket.

"Well my friend, no doubt you have heard of our recent run in with the damnable dark. Vilus was behind the attack. I am still unsure of the motive, but if I were a wagering man, I would stake a year's pay that he attacked for his own personal amusement rather any attempt to gain a strategic advantage." Ryad gazed toward the city where the grey smoke of suppressed fires still filled the sky. "Dax, you would not have believed the butchery. Women were raped and gored in front of their precious children's eyes. Old men were snapped in two and babies in the cradle were plucked and gnawed upon." Tears came unbidden to the sword-master's eyes as he recollected the carnage.

"There was no warning. Of course we reacted quickly and our men gave an admirable account of themselves, but the infidels from the North killed many before we could engage them."

Dax placed a calloused hand upon Ryad's shoulder. "Before all is said and done, dark deeds will be accounted for."

Ryad smiled at the Admiral and nodded, "I hope that is so my friend, I truly do."

***

Earlier that day in the twilight of morning, Jakes had led several squads from the garrison to pursue the barbarian's westward flight. A great many of the dark-ones were hewed down and executed, but the greater majority reached the marsh-lands before they could be over-taken. Jakes was impetuous but not stupid. Too many good men had lost their lives already for him to risk their horses in the boggy mire. Reluctantly, he turned the men back for Illian and contented himself that the pursuit had sent many of the enemy to a confrontation with Reamog, the God of Retribution.

Back at Illian, the citizens attempted to restore order and normalcy to their lives. The garrison soldiers worked tirelessly alongside the people, re-building homes and assisting with the burial of the dead. The Catlina had brought some relief in the form of timbers, food, and willing hands. Dax and Ryad left the harbor and turned toward the city. The occasional townsperson raised a head to acknowledge the sword-master but most of the citizenry hung their heads in despair.

Storm stood surveying the scene that played out below him with emotional reservation. He was beginning to feel restless. It was difficult to not see much of the recent chaos as somehow his fault. The closer he came to fulfilling his quest, the greater the death toll that surrounded him. Whereever he traveled, people died and seemingly there was not a damn thing he could do about it. Storm had watched the Meridian vessel glide into port and butterflies went to war within his stomach. He had studied the maps in Ryad's war room at length. Bal lay a few hundred miles south, and the Catlina was the unfortunate ship to earn the right to bear him there.

Later that afternoon, Ryad called Storm and Wolfy to his study. The sword-master looked up cheerily as they walked in. Beran, Jakes, and the Admiral were also there.

"Ah Storm. My archers tell me that you have quite a bow-arm." Ryad grabbed a quiver from the table and thrust it into the boy's hand. "It seems as if you have garnered yourself some friends. Several of those that stood beside you last night went out at dawn and recovered twenty or more of your elfin arrows. They even took the liberty of cleaning and re-fletching them for you."

Storm felt moved to tears by the kindness of the Illian archers. He stammered a semblance of a thank you and slipped the quiver across his shoulder. The long-bow had become a part of him and he felt almost undressed without it.

Ryad looked away and exchanged small talk with Wolfy while the boy composed himself.

"Wolfy, I have instructed Beran to take the time, during our ocean passage, to give you some personal instruction in how to use the broadsword. Many soldiers have found that it is easier and far more effective to use the cutting edge of the blade rather than the flat side. Although clubbing the enemy to death serves the same purpose, a carefully aimed killing blow that utilizes the point will ensure that the blade lasts longer and that the fighter expends less energy." Wolfy grinned sheepishly. His excursion into the city during the night, although now a story of legend, had not been the most graceful of endeavors.

"Now let me introduce Admiral Dax, the captain of the Catlina. We have spared no expense in making sure that you have the very best company on the next stage of your voyage." Ryad certainly had a gift for levity and the ability to make light of even the most dangerous of situations.

"Tonight we leave for our vacation in the southlands. I hear the weather is just lovely this time of year so pack light and do not forget your soap. If I am going to have to endure a week-long boat journey with you lot, I want, at least, my sensitive nose-buds not to be offended. Oh and that means you too fur ball." Ryad looked straight at Zira, who cocked his head and chose that moment to sneeze. Instantly, the room erupted into laughter.

∗ ∗ ∗

Few were awake to see the Catlina leave port. Throughout the day, Ryad had sent small groups of men from Beran's special squad down to the docks. He hoped that such a ploy would throw off any unfriendly eyes that might be watching the harbor. The last group to board the flagship had been Ryad, Wolfy, Storm and Zira. Now the four stood at the stern watching silently as the Illian lights diminished in their brightness.

Storm had never been on a war-ship before. From hull to crow's nest it was sixty man-lengths tall, from bow to stern a further forty. Seventy-three men, including the Admiral, comprised its crew. The Catlina was the pride and joy of the Meridian fleet. She was strong, fast, and well-crewed. Mercenary ships avoided her and in five years sailing the Terrus waters she had never yet been bested or boarded. Towering sails were supported by sturdy masts. Ropes as thick as trees threaded their way throughout the rigging. Below deck, three cavernous levels contained the sleeping quarters, the oar galley, and the cargo compartments. Occasionally, the Catlina was called upon to transport all manner of weapons, food, soldiers, building supplies, and trading goods. Today the only cargo was the extra twenty-five soldiers that made up Beran's elite corps.

Tonight the moon shone full upon the empty waters that stretched endlessly beyond them. There was little wind and Storm found it curious how the huge vessel was able to sustain such good speed out across the water. Though there was a galley and oarlocks for the powerful oars, no sailors manned the galley benches. The mystery was absolved when Dax introduced him the next morning to a short man with ghost-white eyes. The man's name was Kell, and he was an Academy trained weather mage. Storm, had always wondered what students did when they graduated from the Meridian Academy. Kell had been a part of the Catlina crew for its entire commissioned life. Indeed, Dax and Kell were the only two sailors that remained from the original crew. Despite, the man's rather odd eyes, Storm found himself liking Kell. Kell was fascinated by Zira and his uneven gaze followed the snow wolf everywhere he went. The two became fast friends from the moment they were introduced. Since leaving the wizard isle, Storm had been particularly conscious of how different he was to everyone else. But here was another man who understood elemental power and who had shared similar experiences within the famed Hall of Windows.

Chapter Fifty-One

Twins

Lord Damal stalked the grounds of Damalan. He had just received an urgent missive from Lord Rune informing him that the ninth child was on his way to Cartis. Rune had extended the call for all his siblings to meet him in Mallicus. Damal, not an aficionado of traveling, only did so when absolutely necessary. Although he was loath to admit it, this situation reeked of necessity.

The letter had exacerbated an already foul mood. Earlier that same day he had learned that his household had been diminished by two persons. A eunuch by the name of Basq, and a whore from his harem, Milaw had vanished. Not only were they unaccounted for, but the two of them had not been seen for a number of weeks. Damal enjoyed the service of literally hundreds of men and women; they were his possessions, his playthings, and now two were missing. He had spent a large part of the last two days interrogating and torturing servants and concubines. Despite the sadistic gratification of watching others suffer, Damal had attained little information as to the whereabouts of his missing property.

***

Meanwhile, many leagues distant from Damalan, a frightened woman hid in the cellar of a kindly net-maker in the fishing hamlet of Manti. For almost a month she had hidden within the closeted walls. The cellar was clean and dry and a mattress of straw and coarse blankets had been stretched out across the floor. Adjacent to the crude bedstead was a lidless trunk. Even as she rested upon the bed her attention was drawn to the makeshift crib. Tiredly, she stood and crouchingly walked toward the chest. The woman smiled as her eyes fell upon two beautiful infants, no more than a few weeks old. The two girls were identical twins. From the azure-depths of their eyes to the snowy whiteness of their hair and skin, the two children were indistinguishable, and to all except their mother, impossible to tell apart.

Milaw picked them both up and returned to her bed. The twins squirmed unrelentingly as they engineered themselves positions of comfort for their morning feed. After the initial discomfort of breast-feeding, Milaw had now come to enjoy this connection with her children. As she nestled back into the pillows she reflected on the events of the last few weeks.

Her escape from Damalan had been daring. It had become impossible to hide the rounding of her belly toward the end of the pregnancy. The manner in which she wore her robes and her ability to stay out of the way of the other women had become an intrigue in itself. She had found a surprising ally in the subterfuge. A giant of a man she knew as Basq had protected her. He was a mute Eunuch, a servant in Damal's home. Damal would not allow anything less than unabating loyalty in those that served him. All man servants were castrated to discourage them from entertaining amorous relations with his harem possessions. The majority of servants also had their tongues removed. Damal had little use for the senseless prattle of these mortals. Milaw and he had become close friends and Basq had taken care of her every need, even going as far as ensuring his friend had the best foods afforded from the kitchens. Friendships within Damalan were strictly forbidden and many of the other women she shared quarters with were becoming increasingly hostile to this special attention. Finally, the need for escape had exceeded the fear of the consequences of remaining. Milaw had communicated this desire to Basq, who, though clearly frightened, had acted as a willing accomplice.

A disturbance in the early hours of the morning, a few weeks earlier had sent the palace into an uproarious commotion. Two prisoners had escaped from the dungeons and, from the upper apartment windows, Milaw had seen Lord Damal ride out of the estate in hot pursuit. Basq arrived moments later ushering her clandestinely from her quarters. No one noticed the two servants slip out a side gate and begin their flight across the barren countryside. The journey began on foot and Milaw felt like her lungs and heart would explode, so swift was their departure. At some stage, Basq had tenderly lifted her into his arms and continued his unhesitating run, nervously glancing over his shoulder looking for a chase that never came. A few miles outside of Damalan, Basq stopped beside a stand of conifers. Beyond the tree-line was a small croft with several horses grazing in the pasture. Basq left Milaw and stealthily stole into the field. He returned moments later leading a chestnut carthorse of good disposition and advanced years. He lifted Milaw effortlessly into the saddle before guiding her horse onward. The fugitives had ridden all day without rest or pause. Morning, afternoon, and evening drifted into night. Milaw, exhausted and terrified, had almost fallen from the saddle many times. The strong arms of Basq had caught her more than once. Finally, she had succumbed to exhaustion and experienced a fitful sleep where she dwelled upon the retributions that would be fanatically delivered should they be captured by Damal.

Milaw had awoken to the sound of waves beating against rocks. Their flight had taken them almost directly south and then a little west toward the High Street. Basq had silently led them across the main road and down a narrow trail that dropped hundreds of feet to the ocean. In near pitch blackness he navigated a faultless path over rocks and other obstacles. In the distance, scattered lights rose into view. Suddenly, Milaw experienced the surgence of labor pain. She bit violently down on her lower lip repressing the excruciating throb that distended her swollen belly. Waves of nausea swept over and through her. Basq, realizing the urgency of the situation, stirred his fatigued mount to a quicker step and headed directly for the nearest light.

One cottage sat back from the rest and because of its location allowed the travelers to arrive at the door without passing any other. Basq had peered in at a window and noted an elderly couple sitting in stiff-backed chairs mending nets by candle-light. The Eunuch had lifted Milaw down from the saddle and knocked loudly at the door. Just at that moment, the pregnant woman could contain her pained cries no longer. Basq deftly led his horse away from the house and disappeared into the dark. When the door swung open, an old bespectacled man and his portly wife were greeted with the sight of a woman enduring the latter stages of painful labor. The man was frozen and stood there open-mouthed. It was his wife that saved Milaw's life and the lives of her two, yet unborn, babies. Immediately, the old woman had begun yelling orders at her befuddled husband. Milaw was taken into the house, the door slammed shut, and the task of birthing twins begun. Less than an hour after her arrival in Manti, Milaw was the proud mother of two beautiful twin girls. The old net-maker transformed the cellar into a nursery and his wife had willingly become the nurse-maid in helping Milaw cope with the two infants. Milaw discovered that her savior's names were Misho and Birin, and thus decided on the names Misha and Brina in order to honor them.

Milaw was deeply aggrieved to lose her erstwhile friend and support, Basq. A couple of days later she had heard Birin talking about a strange, tall, Black man who had been taken aboard a mercenary ship as a hired hand. Milaw knew then that this act was Basq's last loving attempt to protect her. He had known that his stay in Manti would have been a beacon of light to Damal and his men should they choose to pursue them. As the twins nursed, Milaw shed tears for her tall, brave, protector. Under her breath she uttered prayers to Nishu, willing the God to watch over Basq and afford him the blessings of long life.

Milaw was indebted to the net-makers who had saved her life. These were perilous times indeed and no one appreciated more than Milaw, what a terrible risk the older couple were taking in hiding her. She resolved that once she had regained her strength, she would secure passage out of Manti and try to make it to a kingdom port or perhaps even a kingdom garrison. She had no friends or family, but she was resourceful and determined. One thing she did know, she would kill herself and her children before returning to Damal's palace.

Chapter Fifty-Two

Premonition

The Catlina's course, combined with fair winds, helped the ship make decent progress for the two days out of Illian. The winds accommodated Mage Kell's efforts, but the ocean currents were stiff and repellent. The north to south crossing of the Icealic was always arduous due to powerful under-tows, water spouts, and fickle currents.

Storm found Admiral Dax to be one of the most interesting men he had ever met. His smile was infectious and his eyes held a distinctive twinkle that suggested a mischeviousness more akin to a boy of ten summers rather than the most revered sailor on the face of Terrus. Storm experienced a deep humility as he regarded the talented men that surrounded him. He knew the men were duty bound to follow orders of their crown monarch the Queen of Meridia. However, he found it disconcerting that so many soldiers, sailors, and friends were being forced into perilous dangers on his behalf.

Wolfy appeared starboard beside him, grimacing in pain. Storm smiled inwardly. He had watched the burly farmer take a brutal punishment at the hands of Captain Beran during the many hours of weapons training he was being forced to endure.

"So Wolfy," Storm began, "I was under the impression that the purpose of sword fighting was to cause the other man the most pain. If I didn't know you better, I would say that you are letting Beran win."

Wolfy threw a cuff at the boy's ear which tasted only empty air as Storm ducked artfully out of reach. "I will have you know that I managed to land two pretty decent blows on Captain Unbeatable." Storm laughed. "The man is inhuman. I have never seen anyone move so fast, perhaps with the exception of Lord Ryad. Just when you think you have the upperhand, he unarms you or sends you flying through the air on bruised butt cheeks."

"So how did you land your two blows if Beran is so invincible?"

Wolfy's eyes glinted as he whispered conspiratorily, "the first hit I gave him when he unarmed me and then turned away. I hit him over the head with a mop that was lying on the deck rail." Storm laughed until his sides ached. "The second time, I pretended that he had broken my wrist with one of his godforsaken parry ripostes. He stopped to inspect my wrist and I bopped him on the noggin with my sword hilt."

Tears ran in rivulets down Storm's face as he imagined the surprised expression on Beran's face. He laughed so hard that he was smitten with a wave of hiccups. The attack of merriment only grew more tempestuous when, who should walk around the corner but, Captain Beran nursing a sizeable purple bruise atop his head.

"Farmer Barley, you are a cheat and a cad. That little stunt is something I would expect from one of Brack's mercenaries, not an honorary member of the Queen's militia." Despite the harshness of the words, Beran grinned widely. "However, you have taught me a worthy two lessons today. One, don't turn your back on a mop-wielding farmer, and the second, don't believe another word that comes out of a farmer's mouth."

The three of them enjoyed a rare mirthful exchange, a communication altogether uncommon over the course of recent days.

Storm and Wolfy shared a bunk in the lower deck captain's quarters. Beran, Ryad, Dax, and Jakes also shared the same space. Storm slept in the bottom bunk which allowed Zira to curl up beside him. Zira was not comfortable aboard the Catlina. Frequently, he sent images to Storm that left little doubt as to his opinions about ocean travel. During the day, the Latsu had taken to sleeping in an obscure corner of the ship's kitchen much to the chagrin of the cook. But it wasn't long before the wolf had ingratiated himself to the cook, a concession that ensured an endless supply of table scraps.

＊＊

    The ship fought constantly to hold its course for Mingoran. Nights were restless and Storm spent a great deal of time tossing and turning in unison with the rise and fall of the ship's prow. Zira, for his part stretched languidly across the narrow bunk snoring loudly. In this fitful state of semi-consciousness, Storm's head continued to be filled with visions of battle. Fleeting images of faceless enemies attacked him and his friends on all sides. One dream in particular recurred with unwelcome regularity. It always began with a fight on board the Catlina. Storm and Zira would be fighting alongside Wolfy and Beran when all of a sudden the image would transform into a blank nothingness. Desolately alone he found himself surrounded by a nameless evil. Dark-hooded creatures with no faces whispered words of an ancient tongue. In his dream he was vividly aware of gross manipulations of life energy. They were conspiring to entrap him and force his soul away from his body. He mouthed the words that would conjure a defense. Even as he did so, he experienced the prickly sensation of the evil spell-cast. Invisible tendrils of darkness wormed their way sensuously into the intricate map-work of Storm's defense. The boy watched helplessly as powerful energies converged upon his person. Filaments of dark green light permeated his last shield and, like a lethal arrow point, began to penetrate his epithelial tissue. Storm convulsed in an attempt to get away, but there was nowhere to run. He began to scream as first contact with the evil was made. Suddenly, the world around him changed. Figures emerged from the shadows and he was momentarily aware of a silver ghost standing over him.

    Storm chose that moment, to sit bolt upright in his bunk crunching his head on Zira's jawbone. Sweat gushed like a river down his arms, side and back. Looking around he regarded a multitude of worried faces. Tonight his little nightmare had just about woken the entire crew. Zira stood statuesque over him snarling

Child of Night

and staring into the darkness. Wolfy reached a reassuring hand to the boy's sweaty brow.

"It's only a dream Storm. Too much sun and fish food if you ask me," stated the farmer. Wolfy's attempt at levity did little to ease the tension experienced within the cabin. "Do you want to talk about it?"

Storm smiled up at the concerned faces, "no I think you are right, just a bad dream. The closer we get to Cartis the more jittery I become. I am sorry for waking everyone."

Ryad knelt down beside him and ruffled his hair. "No man aboard the Catlina could hope to imagine the burden you bear Storm. But know this -- every man aboard this vessel will die willingly before they allow anything bad to happen to you. Now let's get you back to sleep. The currents are being unusually favorable and we might sight land tomorrow." The others began to move away as the swordmaster bent over to tuck the boy in. As he reached over him, Ryad whispered silently, "mind well your dreams young one, at times of peril, the fates may see fit to heed you warnings of what it is you are to face." Ryad kissed Storm's forehead tenderly and returned to his own bunk.

Storm lay awake for many hours until finally, his eyes grew heavy and his head sunk into the comforting warmth of Zira's silver coat. Again, the boy found his head filled with images of an unfathomable clarity. Fortunately, this time the images were in a form that brought reassurance and joy. Maegess Mirren came to him in sleep. She held him close while she sang a lullaby. The lullaby was a simple poem, yet the words seemed to hold a strange and powerful import. He listened intently, hoarding every syllable, word, and sentence:

> *The time of the balance shall pass the call. One by one the immortals fall. The undead princes return unknown. Only one assumes the throne.*
>
> *A true line of kingship thus restored. Power to the sisterhood thus assured.*
>
> *Yet rise there will a new found force. A new generation runs its course.*

Twins are born and thus aligned. A mighty mage shall then unbind.
New light then will gender birth. Yet still dark powers shall walk the earth.

He did not know, or at the moment care, what the words meant. So enraptured was he with the warming embrace of Mirren's voice and the tender touch of her loving arms. The water mage sung the same verse several times and then the vision transformed. Storm found himself beneath the ocean surface. He regarded his form and noted the smooth curvature of his dorsal and white-tipped flukes. The unmistakeable presence of Mirren swam at his side. She playfully nipped at his right flipper and sped upwards toward the surface. Storm followed gleefully and broke the surface to a fearful sight. The Catlina was beset by six mercenary vessels. Through aquaeous vision he viewed the ensuing battle and watched as the mercenary fleet attempted to surround the Meridian flag-ship. The dolphin-form of Mirren pushed him back beneath the surface and sent him a telepathic communication that was both urgent and kind.

Storm you must take the next step in your journey alone. Not even Zira can journey with you if you want to save the lives of your friends and the people of this world. Seek out the Wallahs, they will be your guide to Cartis. Do not fear for your friends on the Catlina, they are courageous and mighty warriors and will fight valiantly. Remember all that you have learned, tomorrow you will be one with the ocean but swim fast and swim true. My friends, the dolphins, will arrive to guide you before the sun reaches its zenith. Then, Mirren was gone swimming into the darkness of the ocean deep. Several hours later he awoke to sunshine pouring through the deck hatch.

Chapter Fifty-Three

Sea-Battle

Zira prowled the mess deck in anticipation of an early breakfast. Storm climbed up the wooden galley steps and took a deep breath. The salt-air stung his face as the sun climbed swiftly above the distant horizon. A brisk breeze billowed through the sails and a contagion of excitement infused the Catlina. Throughout the previous day numerous sightings of birds and flotsam suggested the proximity of land. One man who did not share the convivial humor of his colleagues was Admiral Dax. Years of experience, triumph, and error invented a man that was cautious to the extreme. Many who served with the Admiral described him as a perpetual pessimist. Those that truly knew him called this quality calculated reservation. Now, Storm watched the ship's captain survey the open sea with eye to spyglass. By his body language, Storm could tell that the man was uneasy about something. Ryad, also noticing this apparent sense of unease, sought out his friend.

"Is their something wrong Admiral? "You look nervous."

"Aye, Ryad my friend, things have been far too easy on this passage and we are deep into that pit viper's godforsaken territory. I have felt uneasy since daybreak. I feel as if we are being followed although I cannot see anything off port or starboard side. We know that nothing tailed us out of Illian. It is most strange, when I look out on the eastern water I think I detect a shimmering but when I look through the eyeglass I see nothing."

Ryad knew better than to ignore a seasoned captain's suspicious nature and called for the weather mage. Kell scurried along the main deck to the helm's platform.

"Kell, can you send a cast out on the port side ranging ten leagues distant?"

"What am I looking for swordmaster?" asked the curious magician.

"Oh, I don't know anything that might seem a little out of the ordinary."

Kell shut his eyes and let his senses leap out across the briny ocean waters. Suddenly, panicked, his eyes shot wide open.

"Captain, there are six mercenary cutters off the port and bow. They are cloaked with a spell of invisibility and they are closing fast. Indeed two of the vessels have already moved ahead to cut us off."

Dax swore curses as he began bellowing orders.

"Battle stations men! It seems as if we are about to have company. Unfurl the main sail. Let's see if we can outrun the buggers. Kell give me all the wind you can muster. Ryad, get your men armed and ready, this could get a little unpleasant before the day is done."

The Catlina whirled with body and motion. Storm opened a link to Zira. In moments the snow wolf was beside him, licking his chops from an early scrounged breakfast.

Zira, we are about to be attacked by mercenary ships. I have to go on ahead of you. Maegess Mirren came to me in a dream and told me to ride with the dolphins.

As if in confirmation, four spinner dolphins leapt out of the water and set in at the boat's prow, occasionally disappearing to play amongst the Catlina's wake.

Zira was clearly unimpressed and resistant to the notion of Storm journeying on to Cartis without him.

Why cannot I swim with you? asked the stubborn wolf.

If I had the power to transform my best friend into a porpoise I would. Storm sent an image of a smooth fish-like entity with Zira's head attached to it.

Zira snorted, *You go smell of fish and I will stay and fight with the two-legged ones.*

Storm dropped to his knees and buried his head in the wolf's coat.

I love you with all my heart Zira. When this is all done I promise we will once more adventure in the Northwood. We will swim in the rivers, climb the mountains, and chase the fleet-footed deer.

Zira returned images of appreciation and licked the young boy's tear-spackled cheek.

I will hold you to that promise green-eyes, now go before it is too late.

Storm tied a tiny message coil to Zira's neck. Then, after securing bow and quiver to the weapons harness on his back, he swung his feet overboard and dropped silently into the icy waters below. Submerged beneath the waves, he experienced fear as salt water entered his unprepared lungs stilting the words of transformation. Water streamed into his mouth and he started to panic. Suddenly, he felt his body lifted back toward the surface. Beneath him four beautiful spinner dolphins pushed him upward. Coughing and spluttering his head broke the water's skin and he gratefully gulped a gallon-measure of air. The Catlina was already a quarter mile away. As he completed the words of transformation, his last human vision of the Meridian ship was obscured by the materialization of a mercenary vessel off its stern.

***

Storm dove deep and searched the obscure depths for his guides. The familiar form of Bacal appeared beside him. Good naturedly, the small dolphin prodded him into position beside a large female and off the right fluke of an even larger male. Bacal led the way with the fourth dolphin swimming a few body lengths behind him. Cognizant of Mirren's teachings, Storm focused on retaining his tenuous connection to humanity and the corresponding purpose of his transformation. Legends abounded of shape-shifters that had become eternally trapped in their metamorphic shape after assuming the very conscious of the animal they had sought to become. Zira's thought process remained connected to his even as he swam a league beneath the icy ocean currents. The constant reminder of who he was and what he had to do was reinforced continually by the raw emotions of his beloved symbiote. Storm remembered also the words of Nolina. The Maegess had warned him to never be apart from Zira. He realized, at that moment, that she referred to not only their physical presence, but also the mental connection that now comprised a significant part of their respective identities.

* * *

While Storm headed swiftly toward Mingoran, the Catlina was forced to take evasive maneuvers. Six mid-sized mercenary cutters materialized out of nowhere and converged upon the flag-ship at great speed. The Meridian navy-men were a well-drilled crew and as soon as the enemy was in range, the first volley of flaming arrows and sling-shot were efficiently dispatched. Before the pirates could react, three of the six ships were ablaze with flames searing sails. Kell stood at the prow using his elemental powers to stoke the flames with billowing winds centered directly upon the enemy vessels. The Catlina crew fought on all four fronts. The cutters had surrounded the Meridian ship. Even as three of the mercenary ships burned, the remaining three plowed straight toward them.

Beran's elite archers picked off as many enemies as they sent arrows. Dangerous shafts zinged from lethal long bows. However, for every mercenary that fell, several more stood to take his place. Admiral Dax viewed the battle from atop the helm's tower, screaming orders while attempting to steer his ship away from danger. Finally, he threw his hands up in the air and conceded the inevitable. The Meridian flag-ship was going to be boarded and there was little he could do about it. As he shouted the words, "prepare to repel all boarders," he found himself itching for a fight.

The mercenary vessels were smaller than the Catlina which still afforded a significant advantage. Beran's archers continued picking off those that were brave enough to extend boarding planks and grappling hooks. Dax had seventy men on board, and Captain Beran had his elite corps of twenty-five. Unfortunately, the force they faced was almost four times greater than that number. Eventually, sheer force of numbers saw mercenary crews spilling over the railings onto the Catlina deck. Ryad and Dax fought savagely on the starboard front, while Wolfy and Beran held down the port side with ferocious gusto. Jakes and Zira, swung sword and teeth with reckless abandon at the rear of the vessel.

Blood flowed freely, as bodies were brutally dismembered. Beran, almost instantaneously, assumed the berserker's rage. The possessed blond swordsmen together with the towering farmer fought back-to-back against the surging bandits. A weasely-looking man jumped on to the deck and threw a small device at Beran's feet. The device exploded and sent the powerful captain backwards into some empty barrels. Smoke filled the deck making it difficult to discern friend from enemy. Beran lay stunned, but was rudely reengaged to the harsh reality of the battle at hand. He felt the thud of a fist as it landed on his jaw. Looking up through hazy vision he watched helplessly as his assailant prepared to throw a cruel-looking dagger. The man's sneer quickly transformed to a look of surprise as the unthrown knife fell from his hand. Looking down he regarded dispassionately the sword point that had been thrust through his lower abdomen. The ivory-teeth of Basq positively gleamed from the heart of a smiling face. Blood dripped wetly from the mute's sword. He nodded to Beran, then turned and waded unhesitantly into a band of three mercenaries who had made the mistake to breach the Catlina's side at the side that Basq's angry sword played. Wolfy reached down a massive hand and yanked the Captain to his feet.

"Are you going to sit there and rest or are you going to give Basq and me a hand with this rabble?"

Beran grinned up at his friend. "From where I am sitting it looks like neither one of you needs much help."

There was no more time for small-talk as a new wave of mercenaries leapt into the fray. Before too long it became difficult to move around the deck. Bodies littered the floor, and kingdom soldiers were forced to defend themselves while standing atop the dead and dying. The day was far advanced when Admiral Dax and Ryad appeared beside Beran.

"The bastards have torched the lower decks, and their accursed grappling hooks have destroyed the hull. She's taking on water in a bad way. If we are to survive this little skirmish I suggest we consider securing alternative travel arrangements." Dax certainly had a way with words. Ryad knew better than most just how hard the Admiral would take the loss of his flag-ship.

"Beran, Wolfy, come with me, let's see if we can persuade our friends to loan us a boat." Ryad set off across the quarter deck moving between combatants like a trained performance dancer. Without pause, he vaulted over the side of the Catlina landing ten feet below on the deck of one of the enemy cutters. Beran and Wolfy followed his lead and found themselves facing ten angry looking pirates. Ryad turned to his friends and let out an audible sigh. He then unsheathed his mighty broad-sword. Its sharp metallic edges glistened in the light of the day's dying sun. The swordmaster effortlessly wielded the heavy blade as if it bore no more weight than a spoon. In three mesmerizing arcs of the sword, four brigands fell lifeless on the deck. So swift was the strike that two decapitated heads still bore expressions of horrific surprise imprinted upon their faces.

"Leave some for us you great big bully," shouted Beran as he drove a deliberate parry into the gullet of another man. Wolfy found himself backed up by two cloth-headed rogues who ran at him at the same time. Wolfy's extraordinary long arms reached out and grabbed the men by their oily hair, and in a single motion, hurled them off their feet and into the Icealic.

"They are not the smartest pirates in the world are they," grunted Beran as he dispatched the last of the sailors. "It looks as if the entire ship's party has chosen to fight on board the Catlina. That certainly makes it a little easier for us to steal their ship." Beran and Wolfy began releasing the grappling hooks that secured the mercenary vessel to the Catlina. Ryad was already in the helm throwing his weight to the wheel in an attempt to steer the ship away from its temporary mooring.

The battle had raged throughout the entire day. Night closed fast, and the Catlina was sinking quickly. Four of the mercenary fleet now decorated the ocean floor, and of the remaining two vessels, only one was seaworthy enough to have any chance of making landfall. Word had swung quickly through the Catlina that

Ryad and Captain Beran had taken a ship hostage. One-by-one the surviving members of the Catlina crew and Beran's elite jumped ship. Zira sailed majestically through the air landing in a heap of fur and legs amid the torn rigging. The Meridian ship continued to fill with seawater as the remaining mercenaries fled to their last remaining vessel limping around on the far side of the Catalina. A reluctant Admiral Dax was the very last to leave the flag-ship. He jumped aboard Ryad's recent acquisition with his ever-present grin and a sparkle in his eye. An explosion and ear-splitting screams from the direction of the other mercenary boat provided a backdrop for his sadistic humor.

"Figured now was as good a time as any to unload that cargo of Kelanon oil we were carrying. However, if you ask me it is an almighty waste of perfectly good kingdom fuel." Dax watched emotionless as the Catlina began its final fateful voyage. Beran was about to throw off the last grappling iron when the Admiral staid his hand.

"How about we wait a few more minutes to see if the bastards really were able to sink the old girl?" Beran grinned back at the wily Admiral and locked the grappling iron back into place.

Meanwhile, Jakes conducted a thorough inventory of the human casualties. Only seven of the Catlina crew survived, yet an inexplicable twenty of Beran's elite still breathed, including a blood-soaked Basq, whose ebony skin glistened with a crimson hue. Unfortunately, a few of Beran's men promised a night-time addition to the death toll. The weather mage was accounted for, which left only Storm.

Wolfy noticed the absence of the boy first. "Storm, where is Storm?" Wolfy's voice grew panicked as he cast his eyes first across the captured vessel and then back across the waters separating them from the sinking Catlina.

Ryad gently laid a reassuring arm on the beleagured farmer. "He is long gone my friend. He jumped overboard before the battle began. He has chosen to go on ahead of us, guided by the pure spirits of the ocean."

Tears rose in the farmer's eyes. "You mean we let him go off alone?"

Ryad smiled gently. "Have faith my friend, our paths will cross again more quickly than you know. The boy is more a man than we give him credit for, and I am sure he felt that his presence onboard the Catlina during the struggle might have been a distraction that would have claimed ever more lives."

Zira, sensing Wolfy's discomfort jumped up and placed his front paws on the man's chest. Looking down, his attention was drawn to the message coil secured with a bow string around the wolf's neck. Opening the container, he unraveled a note written hurriedly in Storm's lazy scrawl. Out loud he read:

"Do not worry. I go on ahead and will meet you in Cartis. I love you all, protect Zira and keep Wolfy out of trouble, I need someone to keep me smiling when all is said and done."

Tears streamed from the bearded giant's eyes. "Well that's that then. Let's get going, if the boy says to meet him in Cartis, then off to bloody Cartis we shall go."

Chapter Fifty-Four

Melding

The boatman steered the barge toward the blanketing mist. Terel felt water vapor attach itself to her hair and coalesce upon her outer garments. The tiny girl beside her, shivered within the folds of her warm shawl. Slowly, the invisibility of the fog gave way to the majesty of color that was Meridia. Awaiting the travelers at the royal dock stood two solitary figures. Terel let forth an uncharacteristic yelp of emotion and impatiently willed the barge to dock faster. The ropes were not yet secure when Terel nimbly leapt on to the jetty and raced into the outstretched arms of her older sister.

"Sara, how are you? You look younger everytime I see you. It fills my heart with such joy to be with you once more. I cannot believe how long it has been since I last enjoyed the beauty and hospitality of your wonderful island."

"Indeed it has been far too long sweet Terel." The queen regarded her younger sister with a softness that bespoke a true affection and sibling love. "Of course you remember Archmage Kalon."

The old man behind Sara shuffled forward, leaning heavily on his gnarled staff.

"Terel, I am so blest to see you again. The years have not been as kind to me I fear. I thought perhaps my years might prevent me from again visiting with one of the kindest souls to walk this tired world of ours." Kalon smiled affectionately as he hugged the woman. "So, Sara informs me that you continue to mother a multitude of children up there in Marindoc?"

Terel grinned expressively and beckoned for Reesa to come join them. "Indeed I do, and I am blessed to have one of my special children accompany me on this journey." Terel exchanged knowing glances with Queen and Archmage. "I feel that perhaps the Academy might be a fitting learning environment for Reesa." The little girl hid between the folds of her mother's traveling cape, peeking shyly up at the two strangers.

Sara smiled and knelt down on the dock. "Do not be afraid my child. Your mother and I are sisters, which makes me your Aunt Sara. Some people call me Queen Sara, but I would be honored if you would just call me Aunty."

Reesa giggled. Suddenly she wasn't so scared anymore. With a happy skip, she ran into Sara's arms and allowed herself to be swung into the air. Together the group turned and walked up towards the crystal palace, home to the once fabled Meridian Academy.

After a brief meal in the main dining hall, Sara suggested a tour of the palace and its gardens. Terel was surprised at how smitten Reesa was with her newest family member. At home, Reesa rarely spoke to anyone, preferring to isolate herself. Indeed, many of the other children believed the girl to be slow in the head. Of course, Terel knew differently.

The Archmage had chosen to accompany them on the walk around the gardens. Terel had no doubt that he was privy to the life-aura that exuded from the raven-haired child. Kalon had asked few questions content to hold his peace and allow the sisters to become reacquainted. Sara and Terel, for their part, conversed like little school-girls returning from vacation. Much of the exchange centered on mundane subjects like fashion, politics, plants, and family. Reesa busied herself by exploring the polished walk-ways and playing in the marble fountains.

Passing into the southwest section of the gardens, a strange singing filled the air. Immediately, Reesa took off at a run and headed directly for an ivy-strewn wall. The three adults watched bemusedly as the little girl pulled up short of the wall. With eyes closed she began to sway in concert with the symphony that emanated from the Life Tree. Kalon and Sara again exchanged surprised glances. Non-mage born, were not privy to the ability of hearing the song of the Life Tree. Yet, here in front of them, the Matriarch herself called and beckoned to the child. The song was a joyous, wordless cacophony of hope and serenity. For the first time since Nolina's passing, the Life Tree issued a semblance of positive emotion. Reesa listened contentedly to the rising and falling of the Life Tree's modulations. Her whole body quivered in time and rhythm. The little girl felt her heart race and an overwhelming yearning come over her. Silently, Terel picked up her daughter and followed Sara and the Archmage back to the castle.

That night the council was convened. In attendance were Dulkin, Saltorini, Corrin, Yurl, Leskel, Bartrand, Queen Sara, and Terel. The only notable absentee was Maegess Mirren. The Archmage took the floor of the council chamber and delivered a hasty speech.

"Thank you, for gathering here tonight. Our honored guest is Mistress Terel, Guardian of Light, heir to the crown of Meridia, and true birth sister to Queen Sara, Daughter of the Crown Prince of Terrus." A murmuring reverberated around the council chamber as the introduction concluded.

"As you know the Mage Council recently lost a most beloved daughter in Maegess Nolina. The Life Tree barely escaped destruction. Had it not been for the last selfless act of sacrifice on the part of Nolina, the very heart and foundation of this world would have been destroyed. We have done all that we can to repair the damage and soothe the pain of the Matriarch. Unfortunately, without the emotional energy of her symbiont, the Matriarch continues to die." The Archmage paused to choose his next words carefully. "These are perilous times my friends. If all goes well in the southlands we will yet have the opportunity to play a part in protecting the Aruk and see the balance restored. The ninth child continues his journey toward Cartis along with Lord Ryad. However, here quite unexpectedly we have been blessed by the visit of, not only the queen's sister, but also her foster-daughter Reesa. We have good reason to believe that Reesa is the Matriarch's chosen. Earlier today we witnessed the Life Tree call to the child. The connection was quite irrefutable. I stand before you today, to request the immediate reinstature of the Meridian Academy, and the permission to accept Reesa as a student. If there is a consensus amongst the council, and if mother and child consent, then tomorrow I desire to allow the Matriarch and child to meet."

Questions and debate raged into the late evening hours. Many of the council were uncomfortable with a child so young becoming a symbiote for the Matriarch. However, Kalon quashed such objections when he reminded the council that Nolina had been only four summers at her choosing. Others argued of the impact of re-instating the Academy at a time that was so unsettled. Yet, at the conclusion of the session, a vote was cast, and a unanimous decision reached on both questions. The council supported the re-instatement of the Academy with the caveat that screening of students would be modified and more strictly controlled. In the matter of Reesa's melding with the Life Tree, the council had been divided until Terel took the floor.

"Reesa is my daughter. She is an empath beyond your powers of understanding. I was there the night the Matriarch called to her. This frail, tiny girl, whose future you debate, experienced more pain the night Nolina died, than all the pain and torment any single person in this room has experienced in their entire life-time. Reesa desires to serve the Matriarch. Indeed she understands that this was the destiny she was born to. You do not have the right to dictate the girl's future. This future was pre-destined even before life began on Terrus." Terel returned to her seat, quivering with nervous tension. After her forceful speech, no council member dared vote against Reesa being allowed to experience the merging.

Early the next morning, Terel crept in to wake her sleeping daughter. She knelt at her bed-side and caressed the dark hair that fell in rivulets down the sleeping girl's neck. Softly, she sang her lullabies and nursery rhymes that she had sung tirelessly for many centuries. Sunlight flooded the room and slowly the sleeping girl stirred. Her eyes fluttered open and shut and tiny hands crept up to envelop Terel's neck. Together the two of them shared that innocent bond of love only known by a mother and her beloved child. When they did eventually arise, the morning was half-spent. Terel helped Reesa to dress in the fine white gown that Queen Sara had gifted to her. She tenderly brushed the girl's long hair and twined silver bows within her braids.

After dressing, Reesa turned to her foster mother and asked innocently, "do I look pretty today? I really want my new mother to like me."

Tears welled up in Terel's eyes. "You are the most beautiful little girl I have ever set eyes upon in my entire life. Today you look like a princess."

Reesa ran into Terel's arms and squeezed with all her little might.

After a late breakfast, the Archmage joined Reesa and the two sisters at the dining table. Together they re-traced their steps of the previous day through the expansive palace gardens. Today the singing was louder and more sybillant. At the Southwest wall, the party was joined by several other members of the mage council. Kalon gestured in front of the ivy-clad wall and a green gate appeared. Since the treachery of Horatius, the Archmage had taken it upon himself to secure the secret garden with several new protective spells. Now, only the Archmage knew the secrets of admittance to the garden. He laid a hand upon the gate and proffered a silent utterance. Immediately, the gate swung inward and the singing rose to an almost deafening crescendo. There was no doubting the intent of the sound. This was a song of welcome, a song of joy, and a song of happiness. Reesa broke away from the group and ran toward the tree.

The trunk of the Matriarch remained charred and pitted. Despite the charcoaled roots and crusted veneer, the upper limbs danced in a translucent shade of crystallized white. Reesa stopped short of the tree and turned suddenly. Her eyes sought those of her mother. Terel bravely swallowed the pit of emptiness that dwelt in her stomach. With tears brimming in her eyes she nodded a reassurance and waved her daughter on. Reesa smiled and playfully blew Terel a kiss. Then, she turned and skipped to the foot of the tree. Without hesitation, the tiny girl extended her hands as high as she could reach. To the casual observer it was nothing more than a little girl on tiptoes embracing a giant tree. But even the most casual of observers would never be prepared for what transpired in the next ten seconds. The tree began to pulse and glow with purest white light. So dazzling was the spectacle that many, of those gathered, threw hands up to guard their eyes. There within the center of the captured brilliance a tiny form shifted at the extreme of rationale vision. In moments, it became impossible to distinguish between the form of girl and tree. All the while, the Matriarch sang her song of celebration. Branches and whimsical leaves radiated soft yellows, sparkling whites, and porcelain blues. Then, with a final explosion of light and power, the dioramic exhibition concluded. No longer was the Life Tree's body scarred and soiled. The bark glistened silver and the polished smoothness of its skin sparkled softly.

Not a dry eye existed amongst the crowd. Even the stoic visage of Mage Corrin corrupted in tears of happiness. Throughout Terrus, the transformation of the Life Tree was felt. Tempests temporarily ceased, dying trees and flowers suddenly bloomed. Unparalleled harvests were drawn from the fields that day, and fishermen captured more fish than they would be able to eat and sell in a month. Barren, rocky, mountains bloomed with wild poppies and mountain irises. Even the hardest of mortal hearts suddenly learned the power of forgiveness, albeit for a transitory moment.

The melding had been swift. Terel leaned on her sister for support. She could not help but feel desperate at the loss of one of her most beloved foster daughters. Sara encircled Terel with a strong arm and supported her as they left the garden. As they left, Terel felt a tree limb brush her hair. She looked up and saw a silver leaf break away from its tenuous post. The oval leaf drifted noiselessly upon the morning breeze and alighted itself in the palm of Terel's hand. Turning the leaf over in her hand, she visibly started. There, clearly imprinted in the reverse side of the silver leaf, was the image of Reesa. Reesa's smiling face and deep-set eyes gazed adoringly back at her as if to say, "Mother do not worry for me, I have returned home."

Chapter Fifty-Five

Gathering

No pomp or pageantry heralded the arrival of the Dark-Lords in Mallicus. Brack's more than humble abode had been volunteered as the gathering place for the dark brothers. No love existed between the sons of Jesobi, and Brack certainly was not going to over-extend himself in the hospitality department.

Lord Rune arrived first. A servant sidled nervously into Brack's study to inform him of the arrival. Brack waved the boy away and continued reading over the manuscript that lay before him. He was nobody's lackey, and he sure as hell wasn't his brother's doorman. Rune would just have to wait. Unfortunately, patience was not one of the most endearing qualities of the dark, and Brack's study was again interrupted, but this time by Lord Rune himself.

"So dear brother, you are too busy to extend the courtesy of a welcome?" Rune's venomous voice curdled harsh and bitter. "Of course if this is a bad time, we could always put off the visit until we all are dead. Or had you forgotten the little problem we have to resolve?"

"If you are talking about the ninth son, I have not forgotten. Even as we speak, six of my best ships are enroute to intercept him."

Rune sneered derisively. "You think six little boats are going to be enough to take down a Meridian warship under Admiral Dax, with Lord Ryad running interference? I think not. Have you checked on the progress of your little raiding party?"

Brack could feel his temper rising. He repressed his anger by biting down hard on his lower lip. The metallic taste of blood filled the sensory receptors of his tongue.

"I was about to scree for them before you arrived. Perhaps you would like to join me?" The words spoken were hard and sharp, and the tone was not lost on Rune.

"Why not, I am in need of some entertainment. Let us see how your famed mercenary sailors account when pitted against the Meridian navy's finest flag-ship. I am sure that six-to-one odds is a sizeable advantage, perhaps you might have at least afflicted some damage on the opposing team."

Brack literally shook as he fought to hold on to composure. Turning his attention to a tall looking glass hanging on the corner wall, he uttered the words of a spell of far-sight. Instantly, a wispy fog began to curl around the edges of the glass fragmenting the reflection of the dark brothers. Slowly images coalesced within the mirror. The unmistakeable vision of the Catlina, half sunken and completely crippled appeared. The flag-ship was being towed haltingly by one of Brack's own mercenary cutters. No sign existed of any other vessels. Brack forced the screeing to leap out for many miles in every direction, but all that greeted the searching eye was league after inexorable league of cold, frigid, black sea-water. Reverting back to focus on the one ship that still floated, he noted that it was badly beaten and large gaping holes thrust ominously from its pitch-turned hull. A tattered name plaque read, "Warrior," a fitting name for this last surviving sea-worthy vessel. Brack's eyebrows knitted with consternation and he was violently aware of Rune's presence behind him. The dark-lord had sent his six finest ships together with a multitude of seasoned sailors and warriors, and yet here there only remained one cutter. Not only that, but why was the Catlina being towed? Why hadn't they simply sunk the ship and all that sailed on her?

Brack switched his vision to the Warrior's deck. At first the images were hazy, then, all of a sudden the tanned visage of Ryad conversing with a laughing Admiral Dax sprung into focus. Brack let out a guttural recrimination extending his arm towards the mirror. Blue balls of fire leapt from his fingers and obliterated the seer window. Pieces of glass scattered themselves throughout the room embedding sharp edges in chairs, carpet, and richly embroidered tapestries.

Rune threw back his head and howled with laughter. "You fool! Did you really think six little ships could take on a Lord of Light and the ninth child, disposing of them as if they were cheap street whores?"

Brack whirled around, driving a right hook directly into his brother's face. The sound of crushed cartilage was joined with an unabating blood flow from a broken nose. Brack had followed up his blow with a violent kick to the knees that sent Rune crashing to the floor. So swift came the attack, that Rune had no time to effect counter measures. Now his bastard brother approached him with the glint of murder fixed firmly in his eyes. Brack raised his dagger purposefully, when behind him the external doors flew open. In this momentary distraction, Rune rolled to his right and crunched a hefty kick into Brack's groin. The dagger fell harmlessly to the carpet. Brack summoned a cast and blue light formed around his body. Meanwhile Rune had recovered enough to call forth a protective shield of red light that flowed around him in a frenetic spiral of energy. No sooner had he stabilized the shield than a vortex of blinding blue smashed into it. Even with his shields up, Rune was thrown backwards across the room.

Damal, watched with wry amusement playing on his face. There was nothing like a good family squabble to keep life interesting. Beside him stood the drooling, babbling, mess that was, Lord Vilus.

"Well Vilus, what do you think? Should we let them play for a little while longer, or should we step in and stop them before they decide to obliterate this nice house?" Vilus stood nonresponsive, his hollow, lifeless eyes showing an emotionless insanity.

"Well you are not much help are you my bat-loving friend." Damal smiled at his older sibling then strode into the center of the room.

Brack and Rune were now facing off just yards apart. Both dark-lords had extended their life force toward the other, and rich battalions of color danced lividly around the other. Both held light shields of stunning power and both held a steady pulsating lance of furious energy designed to definitively destroy the other. Sweat beaded upon brows and muscles contracted to full capacity.

Damal stopped short of the warring brothers and performed an elaborate machination with his fingers. Another image sprung into existence hanging precariously in the electrical currents of the room. This image was a place they all knew well. The temple of Cartis stood dark and foreboding above them. Stone monoliths towered like granite vultures awaiting their first feed. Damal's voice was provocative:

"Gentlemen, I would like to propose a truce, at least until we can take care of this silly little prophecy. I can think of many other things I would like to be doing right now, and a family vacation to Cartis is not one of them. However, seeing as we currently have the advantage of four-to-three in the Balance of the Aruk, I suggest we refrain from killing one another until such time as we dispose of the child."

During Damal's speech, neither Rune nor Brack had taken their eyes off the other. They had heard every word, yet neither trusted the other enough to be the first to relinquish their guard. Vilus snickered hysterically beside the door and even Damal seemed to be enjoying the tense standoff. Rune balked first, and slowly reduced the power contained within his shield. Brack followed suit, and in seconds the colors of light and energy that had made the room a battlefield were nothing but a memory.

"Brother, I am sorry for hurting your feelings." Rune's words were carefully chosen and proffered in a manner that was neither, apologetic or congenial. "It was a good plan to try and take the ninth son while at sea. Although you didn't kill him and his band of babysitters, it does look like you slowed them down a little. We will now have ample time to get to Cartis and prepare our welcome. We shall leave first thing in the morning, if that is to the agreement of everyone. In the mean-time perhaps we could impose upon our host for some food and a place to rest for the night."

Brack wordlessly walked to his desk and pulled on a large cord that hung behind it. Bells rang deep within vaulted corridors answered punctually by a quorum of servant boys.

"Show my brothers to their quarters and find someone to clean up this mess." With that, Brack dismissively returned to perusing the maps that lay across his desk.

Damal and Vilus followed the servants out of the study. Rune was the last to leave. As the self-proclaimed leader of the family, he was not going to depart without having the last word.

"If you ever try to do anything like that again, I will destroy you and make that destruction a very slow and painful one." Rune then left the room abruptly. For all of his bravado, Lord Rune was disconcerted. During their exchange, he had felt the enormity of Brack's reserves of power. He had certainly underestimated his bastard brother, something that he would not do again. As he followed the page toward the guest quarters, he mulled over schemes designed to inflict the greatest amount of pain and harm on this new enemy.

Chapter Fifty-Six

Nemet

The soldiers and sailors aboard the Warrior were in high spirits. Despite almost insurmountable odds, they had lived to see another dawn, sunk five enemy ships, commandeered a vessel, and saved what was left of the imperial flag ship. Admiral Dax was in especially jovial humor. He had been adamant that the Catlina should not be left behind, and thus the skeleton remains of the once glorious war-ship were being hauled along in Warrior's wake. Dax spent many an hour telling those that would listen about his dream to re-build the Catlina and the modifications he would inform the shipwrights to include in her rehabilitative construction.

The next morning brought sight of land. The weather mage had worked tirelessly throughout the night to ensure that the Warrior held her course. Despite his efforts, the cutter was badly beaten and forced to make land-fall some fifty leagues east of Mingoran. Dax consulted a yellowing map of the coast-line.

"It looks as if the nearest kingdom port is Nemet. That is if you can call anything on the damnable southern coast kingdom anything. Perhaps we can commission the shipwright's guild to refit the Catlina."

Ryad laughed good naturedly. "I hope that hunk of junk we are towing knows how lucky she is to have a captain that loves her as much as you do. You realise that it will take months to make the Catlina sea-worthy again?"

"Oh well, I guess I'll have to just follow you around and make sure you don't get yourself killed. Then after the boy does his thing in Cartis, perhaps I could take a little holiday. Know any good houses of disrepute? Oh, and the more disreputable the better."

Ryad laughed, "Dax you are a rogue, but a rogue with a heart as big as the Icealic."

"Yeah, but hopefully with a heart not quite as cold as her waters. Did you know it is possible to frost-bite your bits and pieces even in summer down here?"

"Land ahoy!" The cry floated down from the lofty crows-nest, spurring the decks below into a pandemonium of organized commotion. The white shingled roofs of Nemet were soon to be seen bespeckling the low-land hills. Nemet was a port town and host to trading vessels from all points of the compass. As the Warrior neared the harbor mouth, the harbor-master's skiff drifted out to greet them. A rather pompous little man with an uneven beard asked permission to come aboard. The Admiral called down his assent and the harbor master climbed the rope ladder like a spindly capuchin.

"Bless me barnacles if it ain't me old pal Captin Dax." The visitor's face extended into a wide grin. "I ain't seen ead nor tail of thee in near on fifteen summas."

"Then Billum, you probably haven't heard that it is Admiral Dax now, First Officer of Her Majesty Queen Sara of Meridia's Maritime Navy and Admiral of the Meridian Flagship, the Catlina."

"Well shimmer me timbers and knock me flat as a haddock. I always knew you'd amount to summat. I tought it mite be more a pirite than an offica tho. So if ya don't mind mes askin, where is the royal flagship and why are ya cummin to Nemet board dis pot of sea-gull dung?"

"Ah yes," began Dax. "You see, we had a little trouble a few leagues back. A fleet of mercenaries took a liking to our fine Catlina. We had to fight off the twenty ships they sent against her, and then we had to steal one of theirs just to escape with our lives. The mighty Catlina would not go down though. No matter how many grappling hooks, balls of shot, or fires set upon her, she refused to be beaten. Take a look for yourself. Billum we are asking permission to bring her in to Nemet for some minor repairs."

Billum climbed up on to the helm platform and looked back towards the stern. Suddenly he creased into uproarious laughter. "Mina repairs? You'd be better off sellin her for scrap and startin aul over."

Dax opened up one of his contagious grins, "I think she is salvageable and the Queen's treasury will be more than happy to pay a worthy Nemet shipwright a significant price to take on the job. Do you have anyone in mind that might help us?"

Billum still sniggering as he regarded the dilapidated vessel following them. "There's one Wright dats nuts nough to take ya monee. Drebbits boat ouse is down at Pier tirty-tree. Yers best be careful tho, he bes a wee bit strange in da ead and don't takes well ta strangers, particuly tall dark uglee ones who cum visitin dare ole pals onlee once evry fifteen summas."

Ryad had listened with mild amusement etched upon his face during this exchange. However, he, more than anyone, knew of the importance of time in their quest to reach Cartis. "Harbormaster Billum do we have permission to come ashore at Nemet and can we be directed to lodgings for the night?"

"Of course sir. Let me jus stamp Captin's pass and we should be aul set."

Dax held out his small ledger so that the bearded Billum could punch an ugly smudge onto the clean open page.

As Dax guided Warrior into port, Ryad stood at the helm beside him. "So the story is twenty mercenary vessels that the brave Catlina vanquished now?"

Dax grinned, "hey by nightfall with a little bit of luck the Catlina will have defeated thirty enemy cutters and still outran the remaining ships on one sail and with no rudder."

Ryad laughed, "Dax, I thought making you an Admiral was going to make an honest man out of you. I was wrong the only way that will happen is if we find a woman blind enough to agree to marry you."

"Ah that's where you are wrong my dear friend swordmaster. I have already found my fair mistress, and her name is Catlina."

Child of Night

The Admiral masterfully guided Warrior into a berth at pier thirty-three. Drebbit's boat house was a veritable graveyard of vessels. Disconcertingly, Dax noticed that there appeared far more boats of the sinkable variety in dry dock. As soon as the gangplank was down, Dax disappeared to find the ship-wright, Drebbit. Ryad took Beran and proceeded to seek out a ship-house that might be willing to afford them passage to Mingoran. By low road they were easily fifty leagues away from their intended destination. Jakes busied himself with organizing the elite. Dax had agreed to join the squad along with four of his crew which returned Beran's elite to its capacity of a full twenty-five. The remaining soldiers, sailors and those injured were secured quarters in various establishments throughout the city. Those well enough to travel would be picked up and returned to Kurigan or Nurendoc on the next available Meridian vessel.

Wolfy was one of the first to disembark. He was no sailor and his land-lubber legs longed for the feel of solid earth. Zira almost bowled him over as he stepped off the gangplank. The wolf had stalked the Warrior impatiently waiting for it to dock. Wolfy called after him, but there was no stopping the Latsu. In a few brief moments, the wolf had disappeared into the low-lands beyond the dock area. Wolfy stared after him, and quietly to himself he muttered, "go get him boy, go find Storm and keep him safe."

* * *

Zira's link with Storm had been tenuous at best. The dolphins that accompanied his master swam at unimaginable speeds. Their sleek bodies cut through the murky ocean waters like a knife in melting butter. At first, Storm had sent back physical images related to his environment and body sensations. After a while those images transformed from cognitive thoughts to sensory impressions. Such images became increasingly difficult for the young wolf to decipher and track, yet still he hung to the thread of consciousness that would ultimately save Storm from assuming the dolphin form forever.

Storm lost all sense of time and distance. His one focus was to remain as close to his guides as possible. Bacal disappeared periodically but always returned to guide them. After a seeming eternity of swimming, the pace began to slow. Storm became aware of his partners emitting sonar-like articulations out ahead of them in the water. These echoes reverberated back to them in powerful sound waves that imprinted in his head images of strange forms nearby. Storm realized he was experiencing echolocation, and the images he perceived were the result of the innate sonar the dolphins used to detect objects along their path. Soon the pace of travel was reduced to slow passage through a world of subterranean coral and volcanic rock. At one point, Storm felt his shoulder graze against a coral protrusion. An agonizing wave of pain and nausea shot through him. Following that encounter with the strange coral formation, he swam more carefully and attentively. This underwater forest of corals stretched for a great many leagues, yet ended as quickly as it began. Bacal surfaced with a stunning celebratory leap and somersault. The others performed similarly. Storm thrust his head above the surface and marveled at their athleticism. In the near distance were lights. Storm sent to Zira impressions of shades of different hues, which was little more than his cetaceous vision would allow. The dolphins led him to a large oval opening beneath the water's surface. A rusting grate fell eerily from disintegrating hinges and Storm knew little difficulty in engineering an entrance. Though the dolphins prodded him onwards they didn't follow him into the strange tunnel. Each in its own way, and with its own signature voice, echoed the briefest of farewells. In a surprisingly human-like gesture, Storm found himself raising his flipper and waving good-bye. Reaching out for a mind-link, he patterned words of thanks. This projective attempt at communication was rewarded by the vaguest of mental touches by Bacal, who for the second time in recent experience blessed him with his name.

    Storm continued alone up the tunnel. It was obviously a man-made structure, and by the stench and material that flowed around him he surmised he walked within the Mingoran sewer network. After swimming several hundred man lengths his head broke the surface of the water. Confused, still in dolphin form, and alone in the sewer tunnels, he began to lose grip on why he was there. At that moment, his fate rested completely in the strength of his beloved wolf. Sensing the urgency of the situation, Zira had forcefully driven his entire will into the boy's waning conscience. In that most precarious of moments, he recaptured an awareness of who he was, and why he was there. Like flint on flint, a spark ignited that, fueled by Zira's constant promptings, became a mighty conflagration driving its way from fluke to nose. Storm suffered, almost unwillingly, the transformation from dolphin to man. The pain of the metamorphosis lasted only momentarily, yet in that second he knew the death of one and the ensuing birth of another. His eyes struggled to open and he found himself crying salt tears of sadness for the loss of his dolphin form and the crystal tears of elation at the regeneration of his one true human form.

    Pitch blackness enveloped him. He felt around his body and sighed with relief. Tunic, jerkin, pants, boots, bow, and quiver, all still attached to his body. Least he was not going to have to endure the next leg of his journey naked. The water was freezing now that he did not have the dolphin's blubber to insulate him. Storm shivered as he began to edge his way along the slimy walls of the tunnel. The water crept above his waist and every few steps he lost his footing disappearing briefly beneath the river of excrement. It was an interesting irony when he reflected that in two visits to kingdom cities he spent more time exploring the sewer system than the roads above ground. Beginning to lose sensation in his feet, his teeth chattered louder than a room full of schoolgirls. If he didn't get out of the water soon, Storm knew hypothermia would kill him. Ahead a light peeped through a crack in the roof. A drain cover, a half man-length wide stretched out above his head. Taking his long-bow tube, he beat on the hinges that supported the grate. Gradually, the bolts squirted loose and the drain cover swung open. Nimbly, Storm scrambled up out of the sewer, jamming his legs against the tunnel side as he went.

    He emerged in the garden courtyard of a very sizeable building. Soaked from head to foot, he found that his stomach demanded sustenance. With no idea where he was, or where to go next, he crept stealthily up to the rear door of the house. The residence was vast. Massive bay windows extended between buttressed beams that supported a structure that was at least four levels tall. A stiff brass handle beckoned from the door and Storm took the invitation and nervously turned it. Well-oiled hinges offered little resistance as the door swung inward. The boy could not believe his good fortune. This outermost door led directly into the kitchen. Massive bread kilns, pantries, meat cellars, and vegetable larders stretched around the room. In one of the pantries, Storm helped himself to a large loaf of oat bread and several apples. A tin jug packed in icy well-water contained rich, creamy milk. Storm ate and drank noiselessly. He was famished and feeling guilty about trespassing and stealing food. Inside his tunic pocket he produced several small coins and tossed them into a dish in the corner. At least his conscience could be clean about reimbursing his mystery host for food and lodging. However, there was little he could do about the guilt he carried regarding his desertion of the Catlina. How long had it been since he left the ship? What time of the day was it? How were his friends faring against the mercenary ships? For the first time in his life he had run from a fight. For all he knew, his friends could be dead or worse still fatally wounded. A fine courageous warrior he turned out to be.

Having eaten well, his eyelids grew heavy. In minutes he had fallen fast asleep on a heap of old potato sacks. A commotion outside the pantry door stirred him to wakefulness. The door swung open and a lantern blinded him. The next thing he knew, a fist the size of a watermelon smashed into his face. The consequence of the blow was an immediate return to unpleasant slumber.

Chapter Fifty-Seven

Koradin

Beran and Ryad had convinced a former Meridian navy man to afford them passage to Mingoran the next morning. Skirting the southern coast was not the most profitable venture for most captains. It had taken the promise of a fairly large sum of gold, together with several appeals to the man's sense of patriotism. The latter finally won through, and the Captain agreed to take them aboard the Stork at first light for half the agreed upon fee.

On returning to the dock-land inn, Ryad excused himself with the promise of a swift return after taking care of an important errand. Leaving the eastern city gate, he walked into the low-land hills surrounding the town. Once out of sight of the city he took from within his robes a small nondescript device. Setting it on the ground, he engaged a hidden switch on the outer casing. The air shimmered around him and he felt his spirit depart from his body. In moments the ghost-like apparition, that was the essence of Ryad, came to a binding standstill within the depths of a thickly-treed forest. Alone within an empty glade, the Lord of Light shouted loudly in the Elven tongue.

"I Lord Ryad seek audience with his austere greatness, the mighty Lord of Elghorian, King Koradin, Ruler of the Elven Kingdoms." The illusion of an empty glade transformed itself into a veritable hum of activity. Ryad marveled at the sights that were before him. In the years that he had become elf-friend he assumed that he would, at some point in time, become accustomed to the beauty of the Elghorian Forest. Hidden deep within the southern woodlands stood the last bastion stronghold of the elven race. Many centuries earlier, when Ryad had assumed the mantle of swordmaster at the Shupan Garrison, he had befriended Fameran and Jalin, King Koradin's two sons. Ryad had saved Jalin's life from a squad of mercenaries bent on torture and death. This kindness had never been forgotten by the Elven ruler, and Ryad had become one of only two humans afforded the rights of travel within the forest.

The elves were a dying race. No one knew how the elves had come to live on Terrus. Even the wisest of their kind, those much older than the sentinels of light and dark, had lost the knowledge of their shared history.

Elven society was hierarchial on Terrus. Three tiers of society still comprised their race. This class system was not artificial, but rather organismic and synergistic. The lowest level was the "el-terr-iankaa" loosely translated, elves of the earth, or those that chose to live in harmony with the earth. These elves were the keepers of the creatures that called the forest home. From the lowliest squirrel to the mythical unicorn, the "el-terr-iankaa" protected life. The "el-vert-iankaa," were the keepers of the trees. Whereas all fauna were the domain of the earth elves, all flora fell within the guardianship of the tree elves. The latter made their homes in the lofty branches of the Elghorian, while their lowlier brothers and sisters were more comfortable with living accommodation on the forest floor. The last tier of elven society was the "el-hava-iankaa." These elves of the sky were the protectors of all that flew in the heavens and all that chose to call the tree-tops home. These brother and sister elves also made home in the network of villages and cities that interlaced themselves throughout the Elghorian's thick branches. The royal family was predominantly of the "el-hava-iankaa" tier of elven society. The lore-masters instructed that the "el-hava-ankaa" once bred symbionts for the dragons and mighty eagles of the Northern Reaches. However, this was not a hierarchy of family tradition and hereditary claim. Indeed, the king's own daughter, Princess Acrina, was not "el-hava-inkaa," she was in fact "el-terr-inakaa" and thus lived among the earth elves and helped guard and protect Elghorian's forest animals. Elves were set apart at birth through the patriarchal blessing of a lore master. These elven seers studied the stars, path of birthright, and the life aura of the newborn before casting judgment. Though many elves born to the same family were tiered in like society, it was not unusual for children in the same family to be blessed into all three hierarchies. So it was that elven society flourished and prospered even as Lord Brack continued to decimate their lands and force them to live ever deeper within the heart of the diminishing Elghorian.

Ryad was admitted immediately to the council chambers of His Majesty, King Koradin. Koradin was not alone. Surrounding his throne patiently waited his four children, Prince's Welk, Fameran, Jalin, and the Princess Acrina. In the elven tongue, Ryad bestowed upon the royal family blessings of happiness, love, and protection of their earth, trees and children.

"You are very kind Lord Ryad, and your command of the elven tongue is exceptional for an outlander." Koradin's voice was deep and authoritative. The king wore a gown of shimmering silver braided with filigree leaves of gold and green. A simple silver circlet upon his head was the only indication of station. However, in these sacred halls, there could be little doubt as to who held the title of King of the Elves.

"I see that you seek audience with us at a time of great peril to both yourself and those of your kind. It takes a man of exceptional skill and courage to separate his spirit from his body. I pray that you speak swift and true so that you might return your astral form to its host."

"King Koradin, I thank you for your insight and your appreciation of the seriousness of my coming. The prophecy moves swiftly on to Cartis. Your children have sought audience in the council chambers of Meridia and are well aware of the dangers that threaten our earth. I promised them then that I would seek your halls at a time when the need was greatest. That time has now come sire. Even as we speak, the boy called 'Fleet of Foot' journeys alone to Cartis. We do not know what dangers he will experience on the way, but I believe his courage will see him to his destination. What I do not know is whether we have the strength in number and the power in hand, to defeat the dark powers at Cartis. My brother Nicholas is lost to us and the dark have much power beyond that which we understand. The mage council from Meridia will fight for us but the Sisterhood of Gajiina are now willing tools of the enemy. Sire we plead for your help and alliance in the battle to restore the Aruk."

Ryad paused and bowed his head in deference and respect to the king as he waited with bated anticipation for the words the King would speak.

"Lord Ryad, the sentinels of Light have long been our friends and allies. Over the generations we have chosen to avoid meddling in the affairs of men. However, you have seemingly earned the willing support and faith of my fair children." Koradin tenderly reached out and squeezed the hand of Acrina. "So it shall be that in this battle against the Lords of the Dark we stand united. King Koradin, Lord of the Elghorian pledges his support to Swordmaster Ryad of the family of Elam. Fameran, Jalin, Welk, Acrina, and five hundred of our best warriors will ready themselves immediately for the ride to Cartis. We will take the secret ways through the southern reaches and camp in the Yiladan until you join us. I thank you friend Ryad for your warnings. May the Elven kings of the lost generations watch and protect you."

Ryad bowed a humble farewell and willed himself back to his body. As his spirit once more fused with his core, he knelt and proceeded to regurgitate his stomach contents. This form of drastic astral projection was perilous and akin to turning the internal organs inside out. It was a long hour before Ryad was strong enough to regain his feet and return to Nemet. In that hour he reflected deeply on the impossible future that lay before a green-eyed boy not yet thirteen summers in age.

Chapter Fifty-Eight

Waif

Storm woke to explosive pain. Reflexively he reached for his face and cautiously pressed against the swollen tissue around his nose. His cheek throbbed and the left eye would not open. Ignoring the angry pounding between the temples, Storm made a quick appraisal of his situation. Tunic and pants still clung damply after the midnight swim through the sewers. Rough iron bars forming the door suggested a less than hospitable accommodation. The flagstones were smooth and cold and the walls dark and confined. Beside the door lay a small stale piece of bread covered in dirt and a filthy tankard half-filled with a grey fluid that Storm hoped was water. His beloved bow and quiver were gone and his boots had been removed. Nibbling on the soiled loaf, and bravely attempting to swallow small mouthfuls of the brackish fluid, he remembered the advice of Captain Beran. The swordsman had told him once to never forsake offered food, especially if you were unsure whether it might be your last. In light of this meal, he wondered whether even Beran would be brave enough to taste such a fare.

Reaching for his throbbing temple, he placed a hand over his eye. Whispering healing words in the old tongue he let threads of self-conscious penetrate the trauma. He sighed with audible relief when he realized the damage extended only to the superficial soft tissue. The internal structure of the eye itself was intact. For the next several minutes, Storm set about re-fusing broken blood vessels and manipulating the energies of his body to redirect blood flow to and away from the injured tissues. The end result was a partial restoration of full vision, and a marginal amelioration of the pain between his ears.

Other body parts showed evidence of discoloration and bruising suggesting a less than gentle journey to the prison. Attempts at self-healing exhausted him to the point of sleep. Reluctantly, his head slumped downward upon his chest. Finding a way to escape could wait, what harm could there be in sleeping for a few more hours?

A rustling of keys woke him. Time knew little familiarity within the stone walls. Disconcertingly, he realized that his link with Zira was strangely silent. In itself this was not altogether unusual, maintaining their telepathic connection required energy and intense concentration at both ends of the link. It was also fatiguing and difficult to maintain if one or the other endured strenuous exertion. Earlier, Storm had captured images of trees and vegetation passing by at great speeds. Zira was evidently on the move, and he hoped that this movement took him toward Mingoran.

The keeper of the keys passed by Storm's door and opened the adjacent cell. A dull thud echoed through the corridors as some unfortunate soul slammed into a stone wall.

"That'll teach you to steal from the market. I guess we'll be hangin two brats tonight instead of just the one." The jailer laughed scornfully as heavy boots pounded away down the hallway. Storm could feel a rage well up inside him, but remembering his teachings at the Academy, he willed it still and sucked in a deep breath. He knew that the cell could not hold him for very long. At his choosing he could disassemble the room brick by brick and stone by stone. However, he was not of a mind to draw undue attention unless it was absolutely necessary.

Storm sidled over to the heavy metal door and studied the hinges. They were corroded and flaky to the touch, yet the iron remained strong enough to afford an obstacle to his departure. Next, his attention was drawn to the locking mechanism. Crude and out-dated, the configuration operated on the premise of a double latch. Storm closed his eyes and drew upon the air within the prison building. A window casement several stories above, blew open, allowing air currents from outside to enjoin the stale, stagnant air of the gaol. Storm summoned these currents, finely sculpting them into the semblance of a narrow key. Manipulating the air particles, he invited the intangible construction toward the lock. Once inside the locking mechanism, Storm gently applied pressure to the phantom key, altering the molecular configuration of the water vapor contained therein. Through a process of mental sublimation and freezing, the misty apparition hardened into ice. Freezing water vapor poured willfully into the apertures of the locking mechanism molding a perfect fit. With a mental twisting of the elemental key, the latches disengaged themselves and the door swung outward. Storm staggered against the door-frame and took long gasping breaths. His studies at the Academy were cut short far too quickly and he was still not able to ration his exertions when it came to elemental control.

The corridor stretched empty. A single torch light illuminated the passageway. An endless avenue of cell doors extended deep into the musty darkness. Remembering the guard's words, Storm peered into the cell next to his. A small figure cowered in the far corner. The ragged mass visibly shook but from fear or cold, Storm could not tell. Commonsense told him that he should escape now while he had the opportunity. Instinct and conscience contradicted such sentiment. In the darkness he weighed his options. So many people were relying on him, and if Kalon was to be believed, a whole world depended on him. There was no time for distractions and using his magical ability only weakened him further. Yet, he knew that he could not leave this mysterious stranger to a fate that, for lack of his gift, he would be forced to share.

Again, the boy called upon the air currents and infused within them the sculpting words of the old tongue. He watched, enthralled in his own workmanship, as a second key of water vapor formed in the cell door's lock. Subconsciously he turned the latches and was gratified to hear the mechanism click open. Storm pulled the door open a crack and called softly into the darkness. "Hey is any one there? I am a friend that is here to help you escape."

Yellow eyes peered up at him and the mass in the corner scuttled toward him. It was a boy, no more than seven summers.

Storm bit back his anger as he regarded the beaten face of the youth crouched before him.

"Hello, my name is Storm. I heard them bring you in. I was in the next cell and I managed to get out. I don't want to be hung tonight and I am sure you don't either." Storm smiled in a weak attempt to comfort the obviously terrified boy. "What is your name?"

The boy just smiled and looked up at him with orbs of luminescent yellow. Storm shrank back against the door as he regarded the open mouth of the small child. The boy had no tongue. Where there should have been a tongue, there gaped a dark void of nothingness. Storm knelt down beside him and placed his hands upon the tiny shoulders. "I will make sure nothing happens to you."

Suddenly, the youth reached both his hands to Storm's cheeks. A flash of light and Storm felt his eyes roll back in his head. His mind was assaulted by fantastic images, colors, and a myriad of collective experience. In an attempt to throw up mental barriers, he succumbed to horror as they shriveled like paper in a fire. The boy held fast to Storm's face and the mental assault began to slow. Words started to form within Storm's mind.

They call me Waif. I am the youngest son of the Guilder, Lord of the Guildsmen and Leader of the Mingoran Underlife. You are friend. Thank you for saving my life. I am blood-debted to you.

Storm thrust the boy away and staggered backwards against the wall. Immediately the images and words halted.

"What in blazes was that?" started Storm. "I have never felt such power in a mind-link. Waif, it is a pleasure to meet you but next time let me prepare myself when you choose to have a conversation."

The boy just smiled at Storm, tenderly took him by the hand and slipped out the door. Storm allowed himself to be led. He had not the faintest idea which way to go, but his tiny guide seemed quite sure stepped. Moments after leaving the cell, they arrived at the foot of a steep stairwell. Waif slowed and pressed a small forefinger to his lips. Storm noted with awe that Waif made as much noise in movement as he did in speech. Storm had always prided himself on his ability for stealth, but compared to Waif, he was an infantry bugle boy heralding the arrival of an army.

Nearing the top of the stairwell, voices drifted into earshot. One man argued with another.

"Are we going to hang every kid in the city? That last little urchin was just trying to feed himself, and the older kid looked like he had just been fished out of the ocean. How he ended up in the Governor's larder is beyond me."

"Orders are orders Bilk, and if the Governor says hang my own mother, that is just what I am going to do."

"Well I don't like it. The men who brought him in say that the little one is an underlife. If the Guilder gets word that we are hanging another one of his people there's going to be hell to pay in the morning."

The second man cleared his throat and spat on the floor. "The Guilder is nothing more than a low-life cheating crook. The sooner we find him and snap his head the sooner life will get back to normal around here. Did you hear? The Governor has placed a reward of a thousand gold pieces on his head. If I didn't have to hang around here babysitting prisoners I'd be out looking for the old codger myself."

Storm peeked in at the door. Waif quietly crouched behind his legs. In the brief second Storm had looked into the room he captured every important detail. Two men sat on stiff-backed chairs playing cards at a rickety table. The room was illuminated by a single lamp that swung from the ceiling. A heavy door in the far wall looked to be the only exit. Beside the door spread a pile of miscellaneous items. Amongst the boots and clothing, Storm noted excitedly that his long bow and quiver occupied a conspicuous space. He turned back to Waif and smiled what reassurance he could muster. The two guardsmen were almost twice his size, but at least they had the advantage of surprise. Storm motioned with his hands what he wanted Waif to do, punctuating his directions with a balled fist that he drove into his own palm. Waif grinned and nodded assent.

Storm took up an offensive position hugging the wall and prodded Waif to step into the lighted room. The tiny boy calmly strode into the room and waved cheerily at the guard that was sat facing his direction. Storm grinned to himself. Despite the boy's diminuitive size, he certainly didn't lack courage. The jailer bolted to his feet upsetting the table in the process.

"Hey, how did you get out of your cell you little bugger? His partner spun around and pulled a flashing dagger from his belt. The man who had first spotted Waif hurried across the room. Waif turned tail and fled back into the dark corridor. The massive guard followed only a step behind him. Storm struck out his leg allowing the momentum of the man to pummel the floor. In the wink of an eye, Storm jumped on top of his victim pinning his shoulders to the floor. Grabbing a handful of oily hair he pulled back the bigger man's head and drove the face, into the black flagstones of the passageway. Immediately, the man passed into an oblivious stupor. His partner burst into the corridor and aimed a cruel dagger for a place between Storm's shoulder blades. Waif, seeing the danger, jumped on to the guard's back and plunged little fingers into the man's eyes sockets. The gaoler reached his hands to his face and screamed with pain and rage. The dagger fell from his grasp and Storm rolled quickly over to where it had fallen. In one swift motion, the catcher sprung to his feet and plunged the dagger deep into the man's chest. There was a brief gurgling, then, the man fell dead on the floor with Waif still hanging from his neck.

Storm picked the boy up and hurried into the lighted room. In moments, he had retrieved his boots, bow and quiver. He noted Waif's bare feet. By the grime and dirt that caked them, he surmised that the boy never wore boots. Finding a short cape on top of the pile, he swung it over the boy's shoulders. Storm tried the door handle and was relieved to discover that it was not locked. The door opened up into another long passage with several branching corridors. Again Waif led the way and Storm, again, submitted himself to being guided.

"This is not the first time you have been down here is it Waif, my young friend?" The boy looked up at Storm and smiled. They had almost reached the far end of the corridor when voices echoed through the chamber. Waif pulled Storm into an alcove not a moment too soon. Out of a side tunnel stepped five figures dressed in black. He had seen such uniforms before. These were Brack's men.

As if confirming his assumption, one of the men whispered, "if the constabulary really did catch the kid last night, old Brack is going to be really happy. I bet he'll reward us good for bringing the kid in."

One of the other men in a surly tone answered, "yeah, the reward will probably be not getting sent to his wretched pit. The sick bastard prefers punishments to rewards any day of the week." The men laughed as they proceeded on towards the jail cells.

"Waif, we have to get out of here. They are going to discover our escape in a few moments." Waif with his ubiquitous tongueless grin pulled Storm back into the corridor and down the same branched tunnel that the mercenaries had exited. The two of them were now running. The unmistakeable sound of discovery reverberated through the heavily stoned catacombs. Waif abruptly stopped at a cobbled wall. The sound of the chase increased with every second. Calmly, Waif beat his little fists upon the wall. Storm noted the organized pattern of blows and watched stupefied as a whole section of the wall slide inward. Without hesitation Waif popped through the opening. Storm followed, crouching low in order to clear the top wall. No sooner had they crossed through than the wall slammed shut behind them. The sounds of chase all but disappeared and Storm found himself alone fumbling along in pitch blackness. As panic prepared to set in, he felt a tiny reassuring hand reach for him.

Chapter Fifty-Nine

Dwa-Aglon

In pitch blackness, Storm knew the vaguest impression of walking within a narrow series of tunnels. Waif led them on a topsy turvy undulation of turns and straightaways, yet always downward. Perhaps an hour or more passed before Waif stopped abruptly. The bigger boy bumped right into him almost sending them both crashing to the floor. Waif squirmed loose and hammered against a blind wall. Storm noted again the rhythmic cadence of blows. Clearly, Waif was beating a password repetitively. Panic rose inside of him. Storm had always known a significant fear of darkness and it had taken every reserve of strength to not unleash bolts of light into the corridor. He found a strange comfort in the little hand of his guide, but what did he really know about this unlikely savior? Storm was musing about this fact when light suddenly filtered through cracks in the wall. The walls dissolved and the two boys found themselves standing in a stunning grotto surrounded by men, women, and children of all ages. Standing in the center of the stone basilica was a tall olive skinned man of middle years. Storm found the scene breath-taking. The domed cave was enormous and its walls were studded with every conceivable jewel and gemstone. At the foot of the walls ran countless networks of tunnels, all seemingly converging upon this jewel-encrusted nexus.

Storm's eyes quickly adjusted to the new found light. He realized that the figures he thought were children, in actuality, were not children at all. In his studies at the Academy, he had read about the "first-beings." The first beings were the founding civilizations of Terrus. Among these first beings were the Wallahs, the Elves, and the Dwarves. Anyal had introduced him to the knowledge of the true existence of Wallahs, and he himself had met elves in the flesh when they had visited Meridia. But here, standing before him were dwarves, real, blood-flowing, air-breathing, little people. He had figured dwarves to be like dragons, a figment of legend and an extinct people. Indeed, not one of the old books even suggested that dwarves still remained on Terrus.

The olive-skinned man approached and opened his arms to Waif. The boy let go of Storm's hands and happily launched himself at the large man.

It seems we owe you a debt of gratitude outlander. Storm looked around him. Everyone stared at him, some with smiles, others with curiosity, and others with expressions of distrust and fear.

You have returned to us the thought-child who we feared was lost. He disappeared a few nights ago while traveling above ground. Storm looked around him confusedly. He assumed that it was the olive-skinned man before him who spoke, yet the man's lips did not move.

Ah, I see you are confused. Let me introduce myself. I am Jaloran, Leader of the Guildsmen and Ruler of the Underlife. Your ears cannot hear my words because I speak with my mind. You are standing in Dwa-Aglon, a sacred site of the Dwarven race and a structure that allows men, women, and dwarves to communicate without the spoken word. Every word spoken here is shared by all that are in attendance. Here there can be no deceit, lies or deception. Jaloran extended his arms in an encompassing sweep of the cave.

Here dwarves and men live in harmony, beneath the ground, away from the evils that consume Terrus. We are humble men and women. The surface dwellers call us the underlife and have no love for us. Many of my people are outcasts. We have been called criminals by those above, yet we steal nothing that we do not pay for, and we hurt no man who does not first seek us harm. Now who are you?

Storm felt the consciousness of all those gathered as they awaited his reply. He considered throwing up shields but thought better of it. Before speaking he cast out for his link with Zira. It was tenuous, but he wrapped a thought around it and cast a net of Zira's conscious in a protective layer atop his own.

"My name is Storm and I travel from Meridia to seek out Cartis in the Land of Bal. All I seek is safe passage through your lands."

A murmuring reverberated around the light-encrusted walls of Dwa-Aglon. There was a lot of pointing and confused conversation.

Jaloran smiled, *so you are Storm, child of Three Towers and ninth-born son of the Aruk.* As he spoke, Jaloran placated the gathering by raising his open hands. *Now it becomes clear why Waif disappeared from our midst. My son sought you out. Waif is something of a prodigy. He was born without tongue or vocal cords. Indeed, many of the underlife wanted us to destroy him before he reached his first winter. Many, and some still do today, believe he is cursed to be a minion of the dark. What do you think of him Storm of the Aruk?*

Not used to the mind talk, Storm continued to talk aloud in his own voice.

"I believe Waif is a gifted telepath blessed with exceptional power. This place is filled with a power that I do not understand. However, the energy that resides dormant in your son might rival that of this Dwa-Aglon. If I were you, I would consider allowing him to leave this place for study at the Academy on Meridia."

The Wizard's Isle? Why should I send the heir of the Guilder to a school run by meddling warlocks?

Storm noted the hostility in the man's words. Clearly, Meridia held little regard in the esteem of this ruler of the underlife. Choosing his words again carefully, Storm began, "Waif is a child much like I. As such his abilities are young and immature. Without training or understanding, he might pose a significant threat to himself, those he loves, and even those he is forced to hate. Without the knowledge of how to control his talents he may even one day destroy your home." Storm had not meant to say these last words, but the impression had come to him with a harsh reality that would have been difficult to suppress in these surroundings, especially with such a perceptive audience.

Again mental murmurings assaulted his senses. Jaloran hushed the people. *We will grant you safe passage through the under-world of Mingoran. My people will guide you to the outer-most boundary of the Yiladan. From there you must travel alone for even we cannot enter deep within the Yiladan and would not do so without leave of the guardians of the wood. As for Waif, the decision to stay or depart is within him. No dwarf or man is forced to remain a Guildsman. However, should they leave, they will be banished forever and the memories of Dwa-Aglon wiped from their mind. You too, Storm of the Aruk, will be forced to undergo the erasure, although I fear we take a risk in setting you free. I am aware of the symbiosis you share with your wolf. We cannot guarantee that the wolf will not retain impressions of Dwa-Aglon even as we erase yours. However, the old ones see the strength and power you have to fight the dark, thus your life will not be forfeited today. Now let us find you sustenance before you embark upon your journey.*

Jaloran clapped his hands, and the grandeur of Dwa-Aglon transformed into a spacious dining hall.

The tables were packed with people and boys and girls ran to and fro carrying serving platters laden with steaming hot dishes and bowls filled of every conceivable fruit, vegetable, and pastry. Storm felt his mouth began to water as he took a place at one of the benches. Waif sat beside him dressed in his ever-present smile. Storm smiled back and ruffled the boy's hair with his hand.

"Well we are a right pair aren't we? You don't talk at all and I have a habit of talking too much." Storm laughed out aloud, then, took on the pleasurable task of satiating his growling belly.

Chapter Sixty

Convergence

The world moved and with it the most powerful forces on the face of the planet. On Meridia, Kalon debated with the mage council. Gathered beside the Life Tree, the most powerful spell-weavers on Terrus discussed their participation in the upcoming battle. Kalon knew war to be an inevitability, one that would likely result in a significant loss of life.

"Friends and fellow teachers, we have little recourse in this matter. The balance will be restored, or forever lost in Cartis. If the dark-lords triumph there will be anarchy and chaos. Countless lives will be lost and one-by-one the Lords of Light will fall. The Sisterhood ally with Lord Rune and we must be there to counter-act their challenge. In like manner, Sara, Terel, and Ryad must be prepared to confront the sons of Jesobi. The elves are martialling their forces to lend aid to the kingdom offensive. Our scouts report that the dark-lords army numbers several thousand mercenaries and barbarians. Lord Ryad cannot afford to leave the kingdom garrisons wholly unprotected, and even with the aid of the elves, we will find ourselves significantly outmanned. As for Storm, there has been no sight or correspondence in a good many days." Silence held the garden in thrall while Kalon spoke.

"Maegess Mirren saw to it that the boy made landfall safely in Mingoran. What has befallen the boy since his arrival there is not known to us and all attempts at contact have failed. We can only pray that the boy's courage and strength will prevail and that he will indeed reach Cartis."

Sara sat on a grassy bank next to her sister. In her arms, Terel held a small girl with silver hair and a complexion of starlight. Reesa had grown considerably in the short weeks since the melding. Despite her outward physical transformation, she still retained her shy spirit and tender disposition. Each of the mage council had begun their various levels of instruction, and all were astounded at the latent ability of the child. Reesa loved learning and embraced each and every opportunity. The Matriarch's wounds miraculously were now fully healed. The bark was porcelain smooth and her trunk unblemished. Sinewy limbs pulsed in soft energies of white and blue. Suddenly, the girl sat bolt upright and cocked her head to listen.

In a voice that was sweetly chime-like she stated simply, "Storm is alive and guided by the dwarves. He is accompanied by a boy that must not perish in the upcoming struggle. They are almost to the Yiladan. Mother feels their footsteps upon the roots of her ancestors."

Kalon smiled knowingly. Not even he understood the power, range, and nature of the Matriarch, but he guessed that her roots were a vital connection to the natural world.

"Well dear friends, it seems that the time has come for our departure. We will join the Elf-camp south of the Yiladan Forest. If you would now all encircle the Matriarch, we will impress upon the Life Tree for aid in our travel.

So it was that Archmage Kalon, Queen Sara, Princess Terel, Mage's Dulkin, Saltorini, Corrin, Yurl, Leskel, and Bartrand came to arrive in the Yiladan. The transposition lasted little more than seconds. The defenders of light re-materialized in an encircled link around one of the Matriarch's sister trees. Awaiting their arrival was the Princess Acrina and Prince Fameran who bowed deferently to Queen Sara. Members of the elf party guided the travelers to their quarters while Sara, Terel, and the Archmage joined the Elven leaders in conference.

* * *

Some twenty leagues south, a quite different encampment had sprung up overnight. A massive temporary fortress had been built on the backs of many hundreds of mercenary soldiers. Prowling the structure alongside the dark army was the Sisterhood. Chaniya, with thirteen of her most powerful brethren, had arrived a day after the dark-lords. The High Priestess had an invested interest in this particular prophecy. She certainly wasn't going to miss the opportunity to play a part in its fruition. Outside the fortress, camped the remaining barbarian force fresh from their bloodthirsty assault on Illian. Vilus had tempted the savages to Cartis with promises of rich meat to satiate their cannibalistic appetites. Of course, he intended that meat to be of the human variety.

***

Lord Ryad, Captain Beran and the 'elite,' including Admiral Dax and the weather mage Kell, had sailed westward along the coast-line to Mingoran. An uneventful march along the ancient Yiladan road had brought them to the elf camp a day after the mage council's arrival. Cartis lay a morning's march down the river valley. The site for their camp commanded a rich view of the surrounding countryside. To the north, the dark-lord's camp-fires could be clearly discerned against the grey wintering sky.

Chapter Sixty-One

Wallahs

Storm enjoyed greatly the hospitality of the Underlife. Few spoke to him directly, but their attitude toward him was not antagonistic. Jaloran sought him out only once before they left. They had been readying to leave when the Guilder approached. Waif followed Storm everywhere, watching his every move and refusing to be out of sight for more than a few moments. Jaloran watched bemusedly from the entrance way for several minutes before intruding upon them.

"It seems my son has become quite taken with you." Jaloran's speech was warm but guarded. "Waif is a special child loved by some scorned by many. He never knew his mother, and indeed I never really did either. If he is to leave Dwa-Aglon, can you vouch for his safety?"

Storm furrowed his brow. "Sir, these are perilous times, I cannot even vouch for my own safety. I will however pledge my life that while breath remains within me I shall seek to protect your son. That is, of course, until we are able to retain the safety and protection of Meridia."

Jaloran nodded, then knelt down and beckoned for his son. The Guilder took the boy's hands and placed them to his face. Father and son closed their eyes and shared a tender parting. Storm turned away respectfully as tears fell upon each one's cheeks. When their wordless farewells were concluded, Jaloran stood slowly and heaved Waif into his arms.

"Storm, I am not privy to future. All I understand is the now. What I do know is that you carry a burden of an unfathomable magnitude. My son worries about you. He tells me that he must go in order to protect you, despite the fact that I have secured your pledge to keep him safe. Follow your heart he who the prophecy calls 'Fleet of Foot.' If ever there is doubt in your mind, know that love is the one true emotion that even the dark cannot hope to vanquish. The dwarves will guide you as far as the Yiladan. From there you must proceed due south to Cartis. May Nishu favor the path you choose."

Storm thanked the Guilder for his blessing and kind words then hefted up his pack. Across his shoulders he strapped the long-bow and quiver. Before securing the quiver he reached inside the leather-lip pocket and pulled out the collusk. The strange orb glowed blue and white scattered with infusions of red. Jaloran raised his eyebrows when he saw the collusk but said nothing. When all was ready, the small group departed down a mine shaft heading southward.

Two dwarves led the way. One carried a torch, but Storm knew that it was more for the benefit of him than anyone else. During their escape underground, Storm surmised that Waif had inherited the perfect night vision of the dwarven race. Legend was rife with stories of the industrious first beings. Mighty cities had been chiseled underground by the hands of this fascinating race. Some writings had suggested them to be a fierce, war-like people, while others focused on their unparalleled ability for creation and artistry. The pictures he had seen in books depicted the dwarf as a ferocious looking, bearded, warrior. Storm noted with interest, that the vast majority of the dwarves he met in Dwa-Aglon were clean-shaven and kindly looking. The journey underground was flat and easy-going. The tunnels were widely spacious and Storm found he could walk uprightly most of the way. They stopped for a lunch of bread and cheese, washed down with a sweetly fermented fruit juice. Storm felt his energies return and his spirits rise. For a moment he completely put out of his mind the dangers that still lay ahead.

All too quickly the perils of the quest returned. In late afternoon they came once more into sunlight. Storm covered his eyes and blinked repeatedly to help his eyes acclimate to the sun's radiance. It had been days, perhaps as much as a week since he had last seen daylight. He reflected back on the days since leaving the Catlina. He had traveled beneath the murky waters of the Icealic, entered the sleeping city of Mingoran through the sewers, been beaten and thrown into a dark jail cell, and then experienced an escape underground through the pitch black passageways of a Dwarven city. It was no wonder that his eyes struggled to re-orient themselves to daylight. If Waif, or the two dwarves, suffered a similar discomfort they showed little indication of it. The small party hiked for another hour. The grassy plains soon became a lush, coniferous landscape. At the foot of a mighty fir tree the dwarves called a halt. One of the little men pulled a strange metallic object from his pack. Storm remembered what Jaloran had said about the need for erasure regarding the location and awareness of Dwa-Aglon. First the strange device was placed on the head of Waif. As the dwarf prepared to activate the erasure, he tumbled forward to the ground. An ugly feathered arrow protruded from his back. The air around them suddenly filled with lethal arrow-points. Storm grabbed Waif in one arm and half-dragged the remaining dwarf with the other. A score of arrows whistled into the very spot where, moments before, the three of them had stood. Storm sought refuge within the tall trunks of the trees. The arrows heralded from the direction they had traveled and their deadly flight left little doubt as to intent.

Breathless, Storm stole a glance over his shoulder. With fear rising in his chest he watched the woods fill with black-clad mercenaries. From the corner of his eye he picked up movement. The enemy, he realized, sought to flank him. The remaining dwarf now ran step for step with the taller boy. Storm still held Waif tightly under one arm, using the other to carve a path through the trees. A scream behind him and the second dwarf dropped, three arrows etched through his chest. Storm continued to run as the unrelenting flow of arrows dogged his every step. Waif began to squirm and Storm looked down to see blood gushing from a wound in the boy's calf. An arrow had perforated the muscle tissue. Storm's lungs burned from the forced exertion. All of a sudden, two dark figures stepped into his path. Cut off as he was, panic set in. Horrified, he found that he could not concentrate enough to draw a spell. One mercenary swung his broadsword in a dangerous arc that barely missed his head. A blood-curdling howl and a bolt of silver leapt across his line of vision. In one swift snap, the Latsu tore out the attacker's carotid artery. Blood splayed in all directions as the mercenary clutched at his throat. The second man suffered similarly as the enraged snow-wolf tore a bloody hole in his face.

About time you got here, Storm sent the image as he set out running. *You will never know just how happy I am to see you.*

Zira returned an affectionate greeting. *Would have found you swifter but I cannot smell your dirty skin when you crawl underground,* retorted Zira. *If I had been any later, I would be looking for a new master.*

Well my furry friend, you still might unless we can get away quickly. Any bright ideas?

Zira sent the image of a ledge a few hundred feet away. Storm saw the rise coming and spurred a last vestige of effort in an attempt to clear it. He jumped the ledge and lost his footing. With Waif still tightly wedged in his arms, and Zira scrambling down the slope at break-neck speed ahead of him, Storm flipped six or seven times, head over heels, down the mossy bank. His free-fall was concealed by the thick foliage and he traveled twice the speed of his regular running gait. The downward plummet ended at the foot of an oak tree. From their hiding place he could hear the angry voices of his pursuers as they beat the ground, thrusting deadly sword points into potential hiding places.

Waif had passed out unconscious. From fear, concussion, or loss of blood Storm could not tell. Voices closed in around them and his eyes scanned for possible places to hide. Again Zira's quick wittedness saved the day as he leapt toward the roots of an adjacent tree. Zira waited while Storm carried Waif. Crawling on his belly he pushed the insensible form of Waif ahead of him. Storm wriggled toward the tree and pushed the small boy crudely in under the gangly root section. Right behind them, Zira barreled into the makeshift hide. Storm was surprised at the space afforded there. Suddenly, to his surprise, a furry hand reached down and tore the pendant away from his neck. The hand had come from deep within the blackness of the trunk. Zira snarled and bared a full set of teeth. Storm quickly sent an image of what Anyal had described a Wallah to look like. Instantly, Zira quieted and cocked an ear to listen. A squeaking noise sounded above their heads and then six hands reached down and yanked all three of them up into the hollows of the tree. Storm experienced the sensation of being pulled upwards at an alarming rate by his pack straps. He was glad that he had not chosen to discard the pack during the chase. He could only imagine the body part that the tree creature would be using had he not had the pack on his back. Zira was not so fortunate and clearly did not enjoy being pulled into the air by his hind legs. He snapped his head backwards and forwards trying to get at the furry arms that held him.

Storm remembered Anyal's story of the Wallah's, the small furry first beings that called the Yiladan home. He hoped that whatever was yanking him through the boles of the tree was a friend of the Wallahs. It seemed like a very long sojourn up inside the tree. Storm had not taken the time to notice how tall the trees were, but he loosely remembered stories of trees that grew as tall as mountains, and tree-tops that were so tall, their lofty tops were forever hidden in the clouds. When the pulling and tugging halted, Storm hung upside down next to the squirming Zira and beside the unconscious Waif. An important sounding interrogation proceeded above him. The language was unlike anything he had ever heard before. Occasionally, there was a word that resembled the Old tongue, but on the whole, he could not make head nor tail of most of the words being expunged.

Finally, the two boys and the wolf were roughly hauled the last remaining feet to a wooden platform. Storm sat patiently while one of the three Wallahs subjected him to a careful inspection. Zira crouched beside his master watching their kidnappers carefully. Resistance in the form of a menacing throaty growl persuaded their hosts to maintain a healthy distance. Storm rested a hand atop Zira's head to reassure him. Next, one of the furry creatures stepped forward waving Anyal's pendant in front of Storm's face. With a lightning-like reflex Storm snatched the pendant out of the Wallah's grasp and pointed at his chest declaring forcibly, "MINE!" He then re-threaded the clasp and hung it back around his neck. The three Wallahs adjourned to a distant corner of the platform to no doubt discuss what to do with their catch. Storm took this opportunity to study Waif's injury. The arrow had sheered completely through muscle tissue barely missing bone and blood vessels. Storm snapped off the arrow head and eased the shaft from out of the exit wound. Immediately, blood began to flow freely. Shutting his eyes, he clasped hands directly over the wound site. Even as he began reciting the words of healing, he reflected on the promise made to Jaloran. The pledge to ensure his son's safety was clearly not off to the most auspicious of beginnings.

With the healing completed, Storm opened his eyes. The manifestation of his healing ability had drawn quite a crowd. When his eyes shot open, the Wallahs jumped a foot back. Waif slowly began to stir. Looking to the nearest creature, Storm pantomimed drinking from a cup while at the same time pointing to Waif. In the old tongue he shouted "Rattui!" meaning water. The Wallahs looked excitedly at one another. After a brief exchange, one of the smallest disappeared only to return moments later bearing a deer-skin filled with water. Storm took a swig to validate its contents then poured the crystal-clear fluid onto Waif's parched lips. The effect of the water was miraculous. Waif opened his eyes and gaped open-mouthed at the Wallahs surrounding him.

Storm looked up and, for the first time, regarded the network of ladders, bridges, and wooden platforms that intricately threaded their way throughout the lofty tree-tops. Well at least this journey could not be described as dull. He had traveled by boat, by dolphin, by foot, by land, and now it looked as if he would be forced to travel by tree-top. Now if he could just work out how to communicate with these seemingly friendly tree-folk.

The mutual staring session concluded with the arrival of a grey and wizened looking Wallah. Preparing himself for another pantomimed conversation, Storm started to gesticulate wildly. The old Wallah laughed.

"No need for that young man, I speak the old tongue." The Wallah's voice was as old as the tips of his fur. "I am Wodoc, Leader of the Wallahs. We have been expecting you. Our friends, the elves, warned us that you might be journeying through the Yiladan. We have never before seen mercenary warriors daring to enter so deep our forest domain. These indeed are perilous times. I have been asked to escort you, and those of your company, to the southern-most boundary of the Yiladan. There, I am to confer you into the hands of Lady Acrina, Elf-Princess and heiress to the Elghorian throne."

Storm sighed an audible expression of relief. "Thank you for your kindness King Wodoc."

The old Wallah laughed. "Oh no young man, it is not King Wodoc, a simple 'Wodoc' will suffice. Our race does not recognize kingship as do your people. I am the leader of the Wallahs because I am the oldest not, necessarily the wisest or most qualified. When I pass, the next senior Wallah will take my place." The Wallah sighed wistfully. "We attempt to teach our young the old tongue, but it takes many years to learn and there are few uses for such a language in our tree-top home."

"Well kind Wodoc, we owe you our lives and we will never forget this debt. My name is Storm, and this is Waif. The wolf is my symbiont and his name is Zira."

The old Wallah nodded and said, "you are very welcome here Storm, son of Terrus. There has been a prophecy of your coming, but how the prophecy ends no one knows. Come let us away, we are told that the forces of dark have already begun to gather south of Cartis."

Storm felt the familiar fear, knot within his stomach. The end of his quest approached, yet he found himself less sure of his ability to succeed with every passing step.

Wodoc led the small party across a nearby bridge then proceeded to take them on a winding journey through the woodland giants. A wispy cloud cover hid the far off ground that roamed beneath them. Above, the sky was cloudless and blue with a yellow sun that shone intermittently through the leafy canopy. Zira was the most uncomfortable of everyone. Not accustomed to heights, he padded along at Storm's heels sending images that left little to suggest this adventure was in the least bit exciting or enjoyable. During their passage, Wodoc talked without pause. Storm learned much of the tree-climbing Wallahs. Similar to the elves, the Wallahs shared a stewardship for their natural environment. The Wallahs also shared a collective conscious. If one Wallah was hurt, the entire populace felt something of the pain. When a Wallah died every member of the population experienced grief, and conversely when a new Wallah was born, the elation accompanying such an event was shared as a universal emotion. Wodoc also taught Storm that his people were not indigenous to Terrus but rather supplanted from another world. Storm did not know what to think of such a claim. Perhaps he might ask Kalon about the Wallahs, if he ever got the opportunity.

    Most of the conversation was an explanation of Wallah culture and their manner of living. The Wallahs were intelligent, sentient beings that had a shared language. They were also master craftsmen as exemplified by the workmanship of their floating highways. Periodically, the group would pass elongated platforms on which were situated intricately sculpted homes. Many times these residences were free-standing structures similar to those found in the local villages. Other times, Storm was amazed to see houses completely carved out of the upper boughs of the trees themselves. However, the extent of their creative expertise was not highlighted until they reached the center of the Yiladan. In the heart of the forest, set in multiple layers, was a full fledged city. The community was a bustle of life and productivity. There was a market, a meeting hall, banquet houses, shops, a school, even a building that was explained to be a library. The curious thing about having a library, in the fair city of Yaboria, was that not a single one of the Wallahs could read. Even old Wodoc was completely illiterate when it came to understanding the written word. The Wallah language was linguistic not literal, as such there was no equivalent written word.

That night, Storm, Waif and Zira were treated as guests of honor. The finest forest foods were set in front of them to eat, and by the time the friends went to their eider-down beds, they had completely forgotten that they were in a city staked several hundred feet above the ground. Storm curled up with his beloved Zira and looked upwards into the Terrus night sky. Both Spring and Winter moons could be clearly discerned through the leafy canopy. It was a clear night and despite the altitude, the air was calm, still, and warm. As he fell asleep, he found himself wondering what the Wallahs did when it rained.

Chapter Sixty-Two

Cartis

True to his word, the next morning, Wodoc escorted Storm, Waif and Zira through an open labyrinth of platforms and rope bridges weaving their way southward toward the edge of the Yiladan. The journey from Yaboria proved quite uneventful. Wodoc continued his incessant monologue regaling the beauties and histories of the arborial kingdom. Zira plodded silently along between Waif and Storm. A night sleeping upon the swaying platforms served little to ease his ill humor. Waif, in contrast, seemed to be enjoying the adventure immensely. The boy bore no visible scar from the arrow wound and bounded along the elastic skyways. By late afternoon the traveling party arrived at the place Wodoc called Terminus. The last platform hung precariously below the cloudy ceiling. The wizened Wallah hopped sprightly on to the uppermost wooden railing that put him at Storm's head height. Wodoc gestured toward the open valley that stretched into the far distant reaches.

"Down there is where your fate lies. At the head of the valley your allies await you. The fires rising toward the end of the first valley are those of the dark-lord's camp. Midway between the two camps you will find the ruins of Cartis. The abandoned temple is one of the oldest structures on Terrus. Some say the place is cursed. Few mortals live brave enough to walk within its walls. You have journeyed far my child. Even the Archmage was powerless to assist you in this journey. Yet, despite the odds stacked against you, here you are."

Storm looked into the graying eyes of the Wallah. "What do you mean Kalon was powerless to help me?"

Wodoc smiled. "Attached to the prophecy are a number of related passages, rules if you will. This is often the case with prophecy. No member of the mage council and no member of the family of Elam or Jesobi were allowed to use their magic arts to directly assist or impede your travel. This has been both a blessing and a boon. Have you not wondered why no dark-lord has appeared directly in your path? Such an act would be a forfeiture of life in the great game of the Aruk. Lord Ryad walked a dangerous road when he agreed to accompany the Catlina out of Illian. You have had the entire army of the dark chasing you since you left Meridia, yet somehow you have eluded them. By the new moon two day's hence you will have the opportunity to restore the Aruk to its former balance."

Storm was confused. "Then how was I able to gain aid from Maegess Mirren? If it wasn't for her I would never have escaped the Catlina."

Wodoc smiled knowingly. "That Archmage is a wily one, I will give him that. Officially, Maegess Mirren is not a true inducted member of the Academy. She calls Meridia home but is a free spirit much like the Matriarch's symbiot. The water mage and the tree spirit are powerful beyond imagination. They are above the petty laws and machinations of those mortal born."

Storm was baffled yet intrigued. "I was told that there has to always be nine members of the mage council, if Mirren is not a member of the Council who is the ninth mage?"

Wodoc smiled. "Can you keep a little secret Storm?" Storm nodded affirmation. In conspiratorial tone, Wodoc whispered, "the ninth mage is the oldest member of the Wallahs. I just don't like to travel. Every family of the 'first beings' is represented on the Mage Council. Have you not wondered at the short stature of Mage Yurl?" Wodoc winked at Storm.

Storm smiled and patted the older Wallah tenderly on the shoulder. He knew that Saltorini was an adopted son of the elves, and if Yurl was dwarven-born that meant the only 'first being' not represented on the mage council was the dragon. Then again the race of dragons had been exterminated almost a millennium ago.

Storm's musings were interrupted by the sonorous reverberation of a hunting horn below. Wodoc smiled down at the two boys that stood before him. "We had better get going, we certainly don't want to keep the elves waiting. The forest dwellers are not always the most patient of company."

"We?" exclaimed Storm in a surprised voice.

"Ah yes! I forgot to mention that the mage council actually invited themselves to this little party. I am old and inkling for one more adventure." Wodoc's eyes sparkled mischeviously. "I would not miss being with you at Cartis for all the leaves in the Yiladan."

Storm gaped open-mouthed as Wodoc stepped over the wooded rail into nothingness. Instead of falling, he hung statically to empty air. I'll meet you at the bottom. The pulleys system is a little too slow for my taste." With that, the little Wallah disappeared from sight."

The strange display was not lost on Zira or Waif who both stared transfixed to the spot the furry Wallah had occupied just a few moments before. Storm smiled and led them to the waiting roped conveyance. The platform that lowered them to the ground was rickety and held together with thick vines. It wasn't so much the contraption that worried Storm, but more the gleeful Wallahs at the top whose idea of controlling the descent was to allow the makeshift elevator to free-fall for unpredictable periods of time. Fortunately, the stop-and-start descent was swift and abrupt. Soon the party felt firm earth under foot. Storm smiled as Zira flashed an image colored with relief. Turning, he looked directly into the friendly eyes of Acrina and Fameran.

Fameran grinned broadly back at Storm. "I see that you still carry that old bow I whittled for you. I Hope you have got a little bit better using it?"

Storm smiled, "I think I can hold my own with it these days."

"Well if fortune be on our side, perhaps we will have an opportunity to see just how much you have improved. But for now we must ride quickly. We encountered some resistance on the way here and I do not doubt we shall suffer a similar inconvenience on our return trip."

Fameran's recalcitrant fears were answered when a mercenary squad crested a hill a short furlong away. Storm swung Waif into the saddle then hopped on behind him. Noting Acrina's puzzled expression, he mouthed, "I'll explain later." Wodoc had vanished so the three horses drove hard for the encampment. The mercenaries rode a hot pursuit. The heavy breathing of the chasing mounts suggested their pursuers were closing the distance all too quickly. Acrina rode next to Storm, and shouted across to him.

"Think you can jump a fence or two?"

Storm grinned. He was now an accomplished horseman and the hours of practice in the Meridian fields had prepared him well for a cross-country steeplechase. His horse was fearless and followed the elf's mount flawlessly over three tall hedgerows. Zira ran at his heels jumping through the bushes rather than over them. Zira sent Storm an impression of disgust:

How about you tell pointy-ears that I am a wolf, not a horse.

Storm leaned forward in the saddle pressing Waif forward into the horse's mane in preparation for the next jump. Execution was flawless. As he hit the ground he regarded with audible relief the approaching legion of kingdom soldiers. At their point, rode Captain Beran and Jakes. Both men threw him a grin as they powered their horses past the elves on a line to intercept the enemy. The mercenaries took one look at Beran's squad of elite riders and promptly peeled off toward their own camp, riding as if the very demons of hell gnashed at their heels. With the threat gone, Storm slowed his horse to a brisk canter allowing Zira to catch up. The wolf, clearly not enamored with the cross-country run graciously conceded images of gratitude for the slower pace.

Beran drew up alongside Storm. "About time you got here young man. We were starting to think that you would never show." Beran wore a mischevious grin on his face. "We had quite the skirmish out there on the Icealic. Lost the Catlina but stole one of their ships. The good news is that Wolfy finally learned how to use a sword."

Storm laughed as he remembered the beatings his guardian had taken at the hands of Captain Beran during practice sessions onboard the Meridian flagship.

"I would have loved to stay but who can resist the opportunity for a long swim in the Icealic, especially this time of the year."

It was Beran's turn to laugh. "Well, my young friend, it is indeed good to see you. I have been ordered to accompany you to the command tent as quickly as possible." Suddenly, the captain's attention was drawn to the boy huddled in Storm's lap. "So it looks like you made a new friend on your travels?"

"This is Waif. He saved my life back in Mingoran and I wanted to introduce him to the Archmage." Storm exchanged a significant glance with the tousle-haired captain.

"Well Waif welcome to the family. Things certainly are never dull around here, and if you hang around this one, you will be sure to have the most exciting life of any man, woman, or child this side of the Black Mountains."

The encampment loomed large in the near distance. Sitting atop a tall hill, it was a spectacular defensible location. The entrance to the stockade lay on the south-side of the camp. Around the perimeter rose tall pickets with dangerous looking pikes protruding from tall earthworks. The walls were a man-length thick with deep spaces between the outer and inner structures. As they rode through the front entrance, Storm noted the war machines and catapults that littered the compound. The command tent was situated toward the rear of the stockade, so the riders were forced to ride almost the entire length of the encampment. As they rode, a cheer rose up. Storm felt himself blush a deep shade of crimson. Here were hundreds of ordinary men, and some women, cheering for him as if he were a hero returned from battle. He was no hero, in fact he had done little more than run from conflict during his entire journey to Cartis. Now he was forced to endure the discomfiting treatment befitting a hero. Ashamed, he hung his head low and willed the horse to ride a little faster.

Storm passed Waif gently down to Beran then dismounted. Zira swept to his side lending strength and encouragement. Acrina and Fameran allowed their horses to be led away by pages

Child of Night

and together the group entered the tent. A massive table and a multitude of benches had been crudely constructed for the war council. As the party entered, everyone rose to their feet. At the head of the table conversing with Kalon was Wodoc. The aging Wallah talked in excited tones as the Archmage listened intently. Sara broke away from the party to welcome Storm. The queen was dressed in riding pants and a leather jerkin. At her side she wore a long sword and a plain-hilted dagger.

"Storm we have been so worried about you." She suffocated him with a powerful embrace and planted a tender kiss upon his forehead. "I always knew that you would make it to Cartis, but I worried that the burden upon your shoulders is a weight too unfair to bear alone."

Storm smiled, "I am never alone, I have Zira and many others helped me along the way."

In a booming voice, the Archmage adjourned the meeting and beckoned for Storm to join him. There were tears in the old man's eyes as he tenderly placed gnarled hands upon the boy's shoulders.

"You are a brave young man Storm of Three Towers. Do not be ashamed by the applause and recognition you received on your arrival. There is no man or woman amongst us that has sacrificed so much and received in return so little. I want you to know that you always have a choice. You can even now choose to return to Meridia and forget that the prophecy even exists. However, the unfortunate consequence will be a submission of the entire power of the Aruk. Currently, there are four Lords of the Dark and only three remaining Lords of Light. You hold within you the balance. I do not rightly know how or why. I have surmised that perhaps you are the man destined to assume the mantle held once by Nicholas. However, it could also be that you are the first of a new generation of sentinels. Perhaps, you possess a power that will render the Aruk extinct. We only have words of prophecy to guide us, and the words only instruct that you will hold the fate of the world in your hands. That fate will remain yours whether you choose to proceed to Cartis or walk away. As Wodoc informed you, we could not force or coerce you to travel here. You have arrived here by your own accord, and if you continue on this quest you must do so again by your own volition. However, in this final conflict we are here to stand at your side."

Kalon looked weary. The wrinkled folds of skin that scarred his face were convoluted in an expression mixed with pain and fatigue. Storm realized in that moment that the decision to go to Cartis was an easy one to make no matter if the decision cost him his life.

All at once, the tent flap burst open and a dark shadow stretched across the floor. Storm's face erupted into joy. "Wolfy!" The boy ran pell mell into the hearty embrace of his life-time friend. Tears streamed down the farmer's face as he held the boy close.

"Oh my dear child! You cannot imagine how good it is to see you. I almost jumped overboard to go looking for you." Storm grinned as the image of Farmer Barley splashing around the Icealic came to mind. Zira shared the image and howled with happiness. The wolf leapt up on to Wolfy's chest, extending his enormous paws to the giant's shoulders, licking a salty tongue across the spluttering farmer's face.

Kalon regarded the joyful reunion with impassivity. "How about the two of you go grab some food in the mess tent? We can talk more later."

"Thank you sir," stammered Storm. As he was about to leave, Storm broke away from Wolfy and turned back to the Archmage. "Sir, is this a bad time to ask for a favor?"

Kalon's face burst into smile. "No, Storm, on the contrary, I would say that this is perhaps the most opportune time in your life to trade in a favor."

"Well Sir, you see, I found a boy in Mingoran. His name is Waif and he is the son of a man named Jaloran. Jaloran is some important leader of dwarves and men that live underground." The Archmage raised his eyebrows on hearing the man's name. "Well, you see sir, I promised to take care of Waif and make sure that he had the opportunity to attend the Academy. I know I am not a mage, but we shared a telepathic link briefly that almost sheered my head in two. I have never felt such a power in my life. He is a mute and cannot talk, but I think he would benefit greatly from instruction at the Academy."

Storm quieted, waiting for the old mage to respond. "I have spoken to Wodoc about your new found friend. He has been able to sense the same power in Waif that you have discerned. I swear that when this business is done, he will be awarded a bench in the Academy." Storm smiled and turned to go. But before he left, the Archmage called after him, "Storm, I would hope that when this is all done, that you too would seek to return to Meridia to finish your studies. I can think of at least one young person who would be most aggrieved to not have you return."

Storm felt himself blush for the second time that day as he remembered the lingering kiss of a certain raven-haired resident of the wizard's isle. "I would be most honored to return to Meridia with you Sir, that is if there is a Meridia to return to."

Storm followed Wolfy out of the tent leaving the Archmage all alone. Storm's last words resonated loudly in his ears. "Yes indeed dear boy, if there is a Meridia to return to!"

Chapter Sixty-Three

Confrontation

"So, do we have a plan or not?" Damal grew more irritated by the moment.

"I travel half-way across this accursed world and now you tell me that there is no plan." Damal rose, unsheathed his sword and smashed the steely edge into the table. The heavy wood splintered, caving under the power of the blow. Maps, manuscripts and letters scattered everywhere.

"Sit down Damal!" Rune's voice was steady and collected but underneath the cool exterior he was fit to blow. "Unfortunately, this prophecy does not give us a whole lot of guidance. The ninth child has arrived in Cartis and will no doubt make for the temple tomorrow. Now that we are all gathered, the rules change somewhat. The boy is fair game for either side. He will be forced to choose sides and, when he does, we must ensure that it is ours that he chooses."

"And how do you plan on doing that, big brother? If you have been watching his life thus far you will be aware that his entire relationship and family comprises the other team." Damal, spat on the ground in visible disgust, "how do you expect to win his allegiance when the Light-Lords and Mage Council stand around cheering him on?"

"The boy is young and his mind is immature. If we can separate him from them, we might yet be able to swing him to our cause." Rune paused for effect. "Do you really believe a boy who has yet to reach manhood can compete with the combined mental might of all four dark-lords? The sisterhood have pledged to distract the mage council and Brack and Vilus's men should be more than enough to handle the damnable elves."

While Vilus sat in the corner oblivious to the proceedings, Lord Brack sat stoically listening to the two brothers quibbling about details. He had not forgotten his altercation with Lord Rune. On the contrary, he would not soon forget the offending insult of his older sibling. The few days since leaving Mallicus, Brack had been silent keeping a solitary company. They had traveled by horse on the low road. Damal had wanted to use a spell of transposition, but Rune knew the importance of caution and the harsh reality of their mortal state. Such a spell offered far too much risk when traveling to an unfamiliar territory. There had been little conversation on the road. Brack's mercenary force had traveled on ahead, so the foursome rode unaccompanied to Cartis.

Brack was a student of the game and believed that the Aruk would take care of itself no matter what manipulation the boy was submitted to. For now, he was content to follow along in the slipstream of his siblings, thinking much and committing little.

**

In marked contrast to the unplanned chaos of the dark-lord's camp, Lord Ryad saw to it that his camp was managed with extraordinary discipline. Every movement was planned with precision and eye to detail. The command tent table had been converted into a topographical model of the temple and the surrounding area. In strategic areas around the ruins, different colored pebbles were placed as markers indicating where each detatchment of troops would be deployed. It had been decided that the Light Lords would accompany Storm and Kalon to the temple itself. The mage council's responsibility was to neutralize the sisterhood and afford aid to Captain Beran's men. Beran, Jakes, Dax, and Crill were placed in charge of the kingdom armies and Acrina, Fameran, Welk, and Jalin divided up the elven warriors among the four detatchments. The plan was to deploy a layered offensive in four waves at each corner of the temple. Kalon had instructed the captains that they should under no circumstances allow enemy fighters entry into the ruins during the battle.

***

The day of prophecy started with a solemn gathering within the Light-Lord's camp. Ryad strode forward to speak to the men and women warriors.

"This day will go down in the lore of our world as a historic day. Today we fight for not only our own lives but the lives of mothers, fathers, sisters, brothers, family, friends, and our unborn children. Today we fight for freedom and the innocence of light." A cheer rolled across the gathering. Ryad continued. "History may not remember our individual names, but it will celebrate our collective efforts. We must overcome this evil or perish in the attempt. May the Gods protect you and may the fates keep your sword arm strong and your bow finger true." The gates of the compound opened and the march to battle began.

***

The specific detailing of troops and archers for one camp balked a marked contrast to the shambles of organization that characterized the other. As soon as a messenger rode in with news of the kingdom men marching on the temple, a horn of battle blared throughout the camp. Mercenaries grabbed shields and swords and randomly charged toward the ruins. The kingdom men were in place long before the first mercenary soldiers arrived. The orderly rows of Meridian infantrymen held their respective first lines with long extended pikes. Behind them stood the first line of bowman and, at their backs, a second line of archers. The final line of defense was held on each corner by the swordsmen and soldiers armed with cross-bows. Beran and Admiral Dax commanded the northern-most squads, Crill and Jakes the southern detatchments. Within the company of the latter, Storm and Zira walked. Beside the boy traveled Sara, Terel and Ryad. The three sentinels were armed with swords and wore leather halberds, thick pants and heavy boots. Kalon hobbled along beside them wearing his customary grey hooded robe and carrying his rune-scripted staff.

Storm looked over his shoulder nervously. Waif had vanished earlier that morning. Storm had told the boy that he would have to remain behind in the stockade. Waif had not taken this order well and promptly disappeared into hiding. Now, as the battle was about to be joined, Storm wondered where his young friend had gone.

Storm's quiver brimmed full. One neatly fletched arrow already slept in his bow. An endless swarm of butterflies buffeted his stomach and he found himself repressing a needful urge to urinate. Less than an hour after leaving the encampment they reached the outermost walls of the temple. In the distance, Storm heard the first clash of steel upon steel. However, the temple itself was eerily devoid of people or sound. It was late in the day and long shadows were beginning to form. Zira growled a guttural warning and the hackles rose along his back. The group edged their way toward the center of the edifice. Peering between the Sentinel's shoulders, he regarded the structure that lay before them. They stood overlooking an atrium. Eight steps led down to a stone dais. Within the strange amphitheater he noted eight sets of eight steps spaced at uniform intervals around the perimeter. Each set of steps led down to the stone dais. Tall obelisks of obsidian, four man-lengths high guarded the head of each stairwell. On the stone platform below was a nondescript crumbling stone altar.

The temple appeared to be empty. Dying sunlight left the ruins shrouded in an ashen twilight. Kalon ushered the group down the nearest steps toward the stone altar. The silence was eerily unsettling and every nerve snapped taut with anticipation. Storm knew that the mage council was evenly dispersed around the outer perimeter. Surely, if trouble loomed there would be some kind of warning.

Alas Storm's musing proved to be just wishful thinking. An explosion of light filled the amphitheater. Storm threw up an arm to guard against the dazzling play of electricity. Zira, not immune to the temporary blindness, howled with rage beside him. Then, all at once, the light subsided and the temple returned to darkness. As vision restored itself, Storm perceived movement. The sentinels and Kalon extended a protective circle around the boy. Above them, four figures stepped from behind the mysterious obelisks. In their wake followed women in long flowing gowns that seemed strangely out of place in these shady surroundings. Quickly the sisterhood encircled the top level. The women began to chant eerily in a tongue Storm did not recognize. The dark sisters were creating a barrier of energy. Thirty feet apart, tongues of black light sprung from their extended arms and in seconds the entire perimeter of the temple was enclosed.

One of the dark figures above moved into the moonlight. He was a handsome man, tall with striking features. His words were tantalizing and had a mesmeric effect on Storm.

"Dear cousins. How nice to see you all once more. How long has it been? Four, five, six hundred years since our last reunion? It is unfortunate that we have to meet under such unfortunate circumstances. We have the advantage and you know it. Even now our barbarian friends rip through your precious kingdom forces. As for your pathetic mage council, they are stuck outside and there is not a damn thing they can do about it. So, that leaves only the family."

Kalon began to raise his staff, but whatever spell he prepared to unleash remained unspoken as Lord Rune continued his oratory.

"I wouldn't be so quick to point that thing at me old one. You forget yourself. We are standing on holy ground. Right now, you are standing on top of the world's magnetic core. Ah, you don't believe me? Search beneath and see for yourself."

Without averting his eyes from the dark-lord, Kalon plunged his conscious into the ground. He realized his error too late. In the moment of his distraction a powerful rifle of dark energy careened into his mid-section throwing him, like a rag doll, fifty feet across the temple. A tall black-haired woman with silky white skin and penetrating eyes stepped out of the shadows behind Rune.

"Chaniya!" Sara veritably spat the name.

"Queen Sara, I wish I could say it is nice to see you again but that of course would defy truth. As for the meddling old fool you call an Archmage, he and I still have a score to settle. I have yet to thank him for the scar he gave me." Chaniya levitated toward the crumpled body of the Archmage unleashing another bolt of energy from her outstretched fingers. Kalon again lifted into the air and was thrown violently against the temple wall. The high priestess threw back her head and laughed scornfully. Ryad and Sara both drew energy from the ground and cast it toward the traitorous enchantress. Their attack never reached the target as hazy shields of green light shot up around her.

The temple ruins were suddenly transformed into a battlefield the like of which had never before been seen. So fierce and electrically charged was the contest that even the two sides battling outside the temple knew a momentary distraction.

Storm stood amid the electrical storm, confused and bewildered. Kalon had fallen, the mage council seemed unable to breach the sisterhood's perimeter, and the Lords of Light were outnumbered. Storm crouched beneath the stone altar and pulled Zira close to him. The dark-lord who had introduced himself as Rune was locked in a fierce struggle with Sara. Pulsations of energy and particles of light, reflecting every color of the spectrum, coalesced into powerful weapons and solid, protective shields. The two sentinels matched wills and neither seemed to gain an advantage. To Sara's left, Terel was enjoined in a similar struggle. Her combatant was still shrouded in the shadows of the ruins. The dark-lord she battled was relentless. There were no pauses or breaks in the cycle of his energy emissions. Light streamed in a constant flow of anger toward the frail woman. No offensive retaliation came from Terel. Completely out-matched she focused all of her concentration and energies on maintaining her light shield. Ryad fared little better versus the two remaining dark-lords, one a weasel-looking man with narrow eyes and a hooked nose, and the other a giant of a man with a fighter's body and a chiseled physique. The only saving grace for Ryad was the apparent lack of focus on the part of the smaller dark-lord. Vilus paused periodically in his offensive to admire his reflection in the obsidian surface of a nearby obelisk.

While the sentinels manifested their significant power, Storm searched the far corner for any sign of life from Kalon. The high priestess had momentarily stopped to view the spectacle of light that danced within the walls of the temple. Storm crept from his hiding place and ran swiftly to where the Archmage had fallen. He put his ear to the old man's chest. An uneven thready heart-beat echoed in his ear. Placing a hand upon Kalon's head, he sent out a thread of conscious to locate the wound. Two holes the size of watermelons had been seered into the Archmage's abdomen. The internal organs were completely destroyed or displaced. Even as he worked to psychically suture the external wounds he noted, with bewilderment, that the wizard's body attempted to repair itself. Storm was confused about the arrangement of the Archmage's internal organs. The heart was overly large for the chest cavity and strange extensions protruded from plates around the spinal cord. At the base of the spine, Storm noted fifteen sacral vertebrae unfused that extended downwards through the mage's leg. He tried to put such distractions out of his mind as he worked feverishly to infuse healing light and energy into the old man's traumatized frame.

Chaniya was enjoying herself immensely. Perhaps she would see all seven sentinels wipe each other out tonight. It would certainly make life more interesting for her. The high priestess thirsted for power and hungered for death. With death came opportunity. The Archmage was a fool. He had been called the most powerful wizard on the planet. Now he was dead and she his vanquisher. Casting her eyes to where his body lay, she viewed with fury Storm kneeling beside him, whispering words of healing. Chaniya screamed with anger and transposed her life energy so as to reappear beside the body. Re-materializing beside the crumpled body, she suddenly felt agony careen through her groin. Zira, seeing Chaniya appear out of thin air, unhesitantly hurled himself toward her. He found purchase in the pelvic bone of the high priestess and closed powerful jaws with the force of a thunderclap. The woman staggered backwards tearing at the wolf's head. Zira clamped down ever more forcefully, refusing to relinquish his hold. Blood pulsated through the dark fabric of the priestess's outer garments. Her screams quickly underwent a transformation from mere rage to excrutiating agony. Zira continued to apply increasing degrees of pressure to the woman's pelvis and groin. The pelvic bone finally shattered and the hip fractured into a multitude of pieces. Finally, Zira let go his quarry and bounded back to stand rigidly over his master. The High Priestess screamed hysterically as blood pooled

Child of Night

at her feet. The pain was so severe she could not focus on delivering the words of healing.

Exhausted, Storm staggered away from the Archmage's body. He had expended far too much life energy. Zira, sensing the boy's struggle, had pulled him from Kalon and perhaps not a moment too soon.

The old one will live. You did well, but if you surrender more of your life energy you will die. I do not relish the idea of being an orphan so young. Zira sent a flurry of images to the boy, and Storm conceded that his friend was right.

During the healing attempt, the battle had turned badly for the Lords of Light. Terel's shields were a patchwork of shattered light fragments and her body a convoluted quilt of burns and bruises. Sara continued to hold her own, but was now forced to withdraw some of her resources in order to help defend Terel. Lord Ryad retreated toward his sisters and looked haggard and exhausted. Storm moved towards the altar leaning heavily upon Zira. Lord Rune followed the boy's progress with shifty eyes. Sara, no longer threw bolts of light. He realized that it would only be a matter of time now. Closing his eyes, he directed Vilus to go after the boy. With a manical laugh, the mad dark-lord disengaged his attack on Ryad and transposed himself to the dais below. Storm saw the dark-lord coming and with all the strength remaining he extracted an arrow from his quiver. As he withdrew an arrow, he dislodged the collusk from the quiver's pocket. The strange metallic ball rolled away from him and lodged itself in the masonry at the foot of the stone table. Out of the corner of his eye, Storm noted that the ball burned a shade of blackened red. Notching an arrow he let it fly. The arrow flew true and the point lodged deep within the dark-lord's thigh. Vilus looked down in surprise, bent down and pulled the shaft demonstratively from the resistant muscle. The dark-lord advanced menacingly and Zira leapt for the sentinel's throat. Storm screamed, "NO!" but the warning arrived too late. With a casual flick of his wrist, the dark-lord caught the wolf in a harness of red light and whirled him spasmodically around his head. With a wild whoop he launched the paralyzed animal into the sky. Storm watched with tears flooding his vision as Zira traveled sixty feet into the night sky, before plummeting to the ground. The Latsu landed in a crumpled mass off to the side of the stone platform.

Chapter Sixty-Four

Collusk

The battle outside the temple raged bloody. The mage council realized swiftly their error when the sisterhood weaved their sinister shield around the temple perimeter. The seven wizards had worked tirelessly to dissolve the barrier, but to no avail. The enchantment comprised an evil beyond their understanding. Wodoc had drawn the council together and suggested they focus their entire life-energy on a single point in the macabre fence. At first, this strategy had provided some level of success, but every time a mage was able to penetrate the barrier, dark energies would rearrange the molecular integrity of the field and fill in the gaps.

* * *

The kingdom men fought bravely on all fronts. However, hopelessly outnumbered, the forces of light were reduced to fighting on just two fronts instead of four. Captain Crill succumbed to a stray arrow early in the skirmish and his command had been assumed by Jakes. The young warrior reassembled his troops at the top of a narrow gulley. The walls on both sides were severely steeped allowing Jakes to hold steady against the enemy pouring relentlessly out of the south.

Beran and Admiral Dax did not enjoy such positional advantage. However, with the welcome services of twenty elven archers they were holding their own. These marksmen expertly picked off the insurgents from over a furlong distant. Wolfy fought alongside Beran and together the two of them carved a mighty scythe through the never-ending barrage of enemy soldiers. A woman's voice shouting orders drew Beran's attention. The Princess Acrina, with blood splashed blade fought savagely in the thicket of battle. A bandage loosely held together a significant flesh wound to the thigh. No barbarian axe or mercenary blade could match her skill. Beran stood transfixed by the athleticsm of the elf. This momentary lapse in concentration almost cost him his life. Wolfy stepped across to parry the ill-meaned death blow.

"Hey how about we leave the elf-admiring for later in the day," bellowed Wolfy.

Beran grinned back at the farmer, "I told Ryad that having women soldiers would distract the men."

In between blows, Wolfy grunted back, "the only man I see distracted right now is you. How about you give me a hand with these?" A squad of ten mercenaries approached tentatively. Wolfy and Beran grinned at one another and then with a blood-curdling shriek waded into the melee. Beran felt the berserker's rage overwhelm him and for the next hour, feelings of passion translated into carnivorous slashes of his beloved sword edge.

* * *

While the battle outside remained undecided, the battle within the temple walls seemed a foregone conclusion. The Archmage lay unconscious and close to death. Sara, Terel, and Ryad now huddled together in a corner focused intently on self-preservation. Rune, Brack, and Damal stood above them pummeling wavering shields with light energy and scintillating emissions of electricity. Zira slumped comatose, his once proud skeleton a contorted jigsaw of fragments. Storm leaned defeated and exhausted against the altar table. High above, the sisterhood continued to stand entranced, committed to the dark spell they weaved. Their mistress lay amongst the rubble in a state of semi-consciousness bleeding profusely from the life-threatening wound inflicted by Zira.

Vilus approached the boy with a glint of madness emblazoned across his face. Storm looked desperately for anything that he might use for a weapon. His body riddled with fatigue, he realized ruefully that he had not the energy to conjure up a carnival trick, let alone a full blown defensive cast. Off to his right he saw the collusk. The orb now radiated a strange reddish-black hue. Storm remembered the words of Brother John the day he departed Sard, "If the ball should ever become black, then the whole of Terrus will have much to fear." Rolling to his right, he felt his fingers close around the sphere. The collusk was scaldingly hot to the touch.

Vilus bent down and grabbed the boy by the hair. Storm scrambled his legs trying to find some purchase on the smooth floor. The dark-lord hauled him violently away from the altar. Squirming evasively, Storm turned to face the dark-lord. With the blazing collusk in hand the boy smashed his fist into his adversary's face. Vilus collapsed to his knees screaming, holding hands over a shattered, bloody nose. Not knowing why, or what he was doing, Storm staggered toward his friends. The light-lords still lay cowering behind their makeshift electron shield. Fearfully, he could see that their strength failed. The collusk continued to cruelly imprint the flesh of his hand, pulsing fiercely, generating an unimaginable heat. The strange sphere grew ever darker as black mists swirled within its glass intermittingly pervaded by flashes of crimson. As if in concert with the strange ball, the air around the temple grew darker. Stars that once had shone so brightly above were sucked into a blanket devoid of color. The power of the dark-lord's assault caused every hair on his body to stand to attention. Stealing a glance upward his eyes locked briefly with those of Lord Rune. Rune's eyes went first to Storm's, then to his hand and back to his eyes. In that briefest of moment he suddenly understood the nature of what Storm held within his hand. Entities within the collusk screamed and writhed with anticipation. Rune realized too late his mistake in underestimating the child.

Storm thrust the hand containing the collusk into the flow of energies emanating from the dark-lord's attack. He screamed as he absorbed the life energies emitted by all six sentinels. Brack had seen the look in the child's eyes and knew what he planned to do with the collusk. However, even he was not able to withdraw his life energies swiftly enough. Immediately, Storm became a conduit of staggering proportions. Screaming, he felt himself lifted into the air and a vortex of light and electrical impulses leapt around him in a strangely sensual display of power. Sentinels stood open-mouthed as the green-eyed boy rose from the ground. The sisterhood's enchantment fluttered and splintered as the dark energies that sufficed their spell were sucked into the vortex. The mage council quickly withdrew their attack as each felt the inexorable pull of life energy. Soldiers, mercenaries, and barbarians stopped fighting to regard the impromptu light display conducted in the skies above them.

Storm knew a brutal awareness of the pain that seered throughout his youthful frame. His mouth still gaped wide in a scream that now had lost its sound. The boy's entire body rhythmically pulsed in concert to the dazzling luminescence that enshrined him. Every emotion he had ever known became a band of light emanating from his slender frame. Every hardship, every loss, every pain was a part of this new profound enlightenment. He looked passively down upon the earth that spread beneath him. What had this world ever given him? He knew no parents and no home. He faced danger at every turn and even those who called him friend had, in effect, used him for their own selfish design. What loyalty did he owe anyone? He was now a God. With a turn of his wrist he knew that he could obliterate every man, woman, and child that stared fearfully up at him. If he chose power, then none could stand against him. If he relinquished this power he would be a man just like everyone else. Did he want to be like those who manipulated him? Now he had the chance to choose his own path.

Storm struggled inwardly as two alien consciousnesses penetrated his mind. One, an evil beyond comprehension, while the other seemed innocent, pure and gentle reaching out and extending compassion. Briefly, he pondered these strange intrusions and became distantly aware of another. The latter was a part of him yet separate. Storm experienced only the now. Who was he, where was he from, what was he doing, and why was he being forced to make a decision that he did not understand? Like a horse flicking away an annoying fly, Storm continued to ignore the tendrils of a mind that he knew he must not ignore, yet was afraid to conjoin. The euphoria of flight and the energies that he continued to draw from the very core of Terrus filled him with an insatiable avarice. Spreading his arms he dove for the ground sweeping the stammering Lord Vilus off his feet. Supporting the frightened dark-lord tenuously by hands clasped to the face, Storm careened upward into the heavens enjoying the exhilaration of the life energies absorbed from his blubbering prey. The mind of the once mighty sentinel was as concrete as horse's excrement. Separating the spirit and soul from the body was effortless. Storm embraced the electrical charged convulsion that was the departing spirit. Desperately, Vilus cast out for escape, but Storm drew every protonic cell to him. The soul fled upward to the heavens, but even this was not beyond torment. Casting out a band of energy, Storm trapped the frightened soul subjecting it to a torturous manipulation within his energy-radiant vortex. After a time, Storm grew bored of such play and released the insane soul to Tellus.

Below, the world had grown dark and cold. The Archmage was being attended to by Saltorini and Dulkin. Kalon's eyes flittered open and he viewed for himself the horrific sight that held so many around him in thrall. The ball of energy that contained Storm was now many man-lengths long and wide. Within the heart of the ethereal celestial light a dark light throbbed and pulsed in stark contrast to the myriad of colors that enmeshed the boy. Kalon regained his feet leaning heavily against Saltorini. Wodoc shuffled up beside him, his eyes a decorum of fear and anguish.

"Storm lives no longer. I fear we have failed him Wodoc. Indeed, I fear we have failed this very world." In answer to this pessimistic appraisal, the vortex of light hurtled downward from the heavens seeking further sustenance for its insatiable appetite.

Chapter Sixty-Five

Balance

Like a peregrine falcon in the heat of the hunt, Storm swooped to the ground. He licked his lips expectantly. Certainly there existed no dearth of foods to choose from. Snatching up a member of the dark sisterhood, he prepared to launch himself into the sky when a voice tore viciously inside his head screaming, *"STOP!"* Confused and disorientated, he let the woman fall unceremoniously to the ground. Hovering scant inches off the stone floor, the entity cast sightless eyes around the temple. Again the voice intruded upon his conscious.

Storm you are not a murderer. Zira needs you, he is dying. You must go to him now!

Other voices drowned out the former. One voice spurred him on, insidiously flattering him with promises of omnipotent power and riches beyond consideration. Still another voice pleaded with him to spare the mortal's lives. The boy tore at his hair and beat the collusk about his head. Who was this Storm? Who was this Zira that he was meant to save? Why should he save anyone? In response, the small loud voice answered him.

If you don't save Zira millions of people will die and I, your friend, will be among them.

The mental link drew Storm's attention to the stone dais in the center of the ruins. There, a small boy gazed imploringly up at him.

Who are you boy? Why do you stand there telling me what to do? Do you not fear me?

With tears in his eyes, Waif held tight to the mind-link. *I once saved your life and today I want you to save the life of Zira in return. You are my friend and I love you like the brother I never had.*

Who is this Zira that you speak of?

Waif pointed to the limp, lifeless body of the Latsu.

The sentinels and mages watched with a strange fascination as the illuminated form drifted to the temple floor and hovered directly over the spot where Zira lay. Waif nervously stepped off the platform and approached the energy form. The tiny boy then bent down and took Zira's head in one hand and reached out tentatively to touch Storm with the other. If Waif experienced pain in the connection, no one of those gathered knew it. Immediately, Storm was aware of Zira and their connection. Tears of joy came unbidden to the boy's eyes as he stroked the tenuous lines of energy that afforded the snow wolf's connection to his own life source. Storm regained a semblance of memories. He saw Zira and Anyal, Wolfy and John, Beran and Jakes, Sara and Ryad, and then he saw in the flesh, Waif. At once he knew the one true emotion – the love of one man for another.

Storm's attention drew back to the collusk. Taking the orb in his right hand he hurled the object with all of his strength and will. The sphere smashed into the wall and instantly imploded into a million tiny fragments. No sooner had the collusk shattered, than the light energy infusing Storm's body petered out, leaving behind a scared, naked, and very confused boy of almost thirteen years. Attention suddenly averted away from the shivering boy. Those gathered within the temple walls were staring toward the site of the collusk implosion. As the dust began to settle, two figures emerged from the debris.

Ryad dashed past his siblings and knelt at one of the men's feet. With tears in his eyes he spoke words that reverberated around the temple ruins. Words he had spoken many times in dream.

"Father, welcome home."

Sara and Terel rushed to hug their own father, the crown Prince of Terrus, Prince Elam. A similar reunion occurred a few feet away as Brack, Rune, and Damal knelt in deference and homage to their returned patriarch, Prince Jesobi, son of King Labernum and descendent of the House of Celebus.

Storm remembered little more as the exertions of the day finally took their toll. He collapsed in an exhausted coma on top of Zira. Wolfy found him several minutes later and covered him in the coarse jerkin that he stripped from his own shoulders.

When he awoke, Storm found himself surrounded by friends and strangers. The Princess Acrina was administering cool rags to his forehead and Wolfy sat on a stool beside him holding his tiny hand. Zira slept peacefully at the foot of the bed and Waif stood staring at him, the ever present smile splayed upon his features. Storm sat up while Wolfy helped him orient the pillows.

"Hey Wolfy I had the wildest of dreams. You would never believe the adventures I had while I slept."

A tall, stately looking man who Storm did not recognize stepped forward.

"You will learn, young man, that dreams contain a true semblance of reality, more so than many will believe in the telling. The world of Terrus owes you a debt of gratitude. The balance of the Aruk is once more restored and I, Prince Elam, heir to the kingship of Terrus, am deeply indebted to you for securing my freedom. It is a brave and courageous man that resists the powers of the dark. Still, I am afraid that this is only one battle in a war that has yet to begin. However, at such a time I would be honored to serve with you as a general at my side. Now try and sleep we can talk again later." The prince patted the boy affectionately on the shoulder then turned and took his leave.

Storm watched Prince Elam leave the tent with a fascade that was both befuddled and awestruck.

"There you go again falling all over yourself for royalty," laughed the jovial farmer.

"Is that really the lost Prince? What of his brother Jesobi?"

Acrina answered him. "It is true indeed. The lost Princes have returned to Terrus. The mystery of where they have been and what will transpire now they have returned, are still stories to be unfolded. In the confusion following their appearance, the dark-lords spirited Jesobi away and the sisterhood vanished, taking with them the traitor Chaniya. The barbarians fled into the southern reaches and many of the mercenary force surrendered to the kingdom militia."

"What of the Archmage?" asked Storm.

"He said that he will talk with you shortly," answered Acrina. "Currently, he is still recuperating under the watchful eye of Wodoc of Yaboria. "He also told me to let you know that you and Waif are due to start classes at the Academy in one moon's time. In the meantime, he suggests you might have an interest in a vacation before returning to Meridia. Mage's Saltorini and Leskel have volunteered to accompany you to Three Towers. Farmer Barley and I will be going along just to keep an eye on you." Acrina smiled at her young patient and smoothed the dark hair away from his eyes.

"It was a very brave thing you did Storm. Your name will be forever legend amongst the lore-masters of the Elghorian. Oh yes, and the name of a certain young telepath will also accompany your name in legend." The elf princess turned and beckoned to Waif. The small boy ran into her arms and allowed himself to be lifted into the air and placed on the bed alongside Storm. Ignoring the stiffness and pain, Storm reached over and pulled the younger boy into a tender embrace. As he held him close he whispered a single silent thought, *Thank you!*

Chapter Sixty-Six

Reunion

It was a strange group that arrived at the newly constructed Sard Garrison. It had taken almost two weeks to travel from Cartis to Sard. The mage council had offered their aid to make the journey swifter but Storm had had his fill of magic for a while. The contingent that left Cartis was large. Many of the captured mercenary soldiers chose to swear allegiance and fealty to the new crown prince and thus were assimilated into the kingdom garrison forces. They had traveled by the western road to Illian to avoid another crossing of the Icealic. At the turn-off to Mingoran, they said their farewells to Admiral Dax and Mage Kell. Dax had spent the better part of the previous week enlisting a new crew for his beloved Catlina. Now, his only hope remained that the shipwright Drebbitt had been able to perform a miracle on his one true love. Jalin, Welk, Fameran and the remaining elves also turned off at Mingoran. They were going to travel to Nemet with Dax and then ride eastward to the Elghorian. Fameran kept his promise and the days out of Cartis were filled with daily archery competitions. The elf prince was most impressed with Storm's progress and even feigned defeat a couple of times.

At Illian, there were emotional farewells to many of those soldiers who returned to serve at the garrison. The remaining party traveled onward north via the High Street.

Captain Beran persuaded Lord Ryad to allow him leave to go inspect the new garrison at Sard. Of course, everyone knew that

Child of Night

the real motivation behind such a journey had more to do with a certain elf princess than any vocational responsibility. So it was that seven riders and a wolf reined in at the watch-tower of the Sardish garrison. A seven-year old mute, two wizards, a military captain, an elf princess, a man mountain of a farmer, and a green-eyed boy with wolf in tow asked for permission to enter. A familiar voice granted them entry and as the heavy gate opened, a lithe, raven-haired girl dashed out to meet them. Anyal jumped into Storm's arms and joyously allowed herself to be swung around. Zira leapt playfully around the two, nipping at Anyal's heels until she finally turned to give him some attention.

"As soon as they told me you were coming home I asked for permission to come to Sard. I needed to get off the island anyway. I was going crazy not hearing how you were. Then the mage council disappeared all of a sudden and I feared the worst. I am so excited to hear all your stories." Anyal took him by the hand and led him inside the garrison, all the time bombarding him with questions that she would not give him the time to answer.

Later that same afternoon Storm and Zira, accompanied by Wolfy and Anyal, started up the old familiar mountain trail. Beran and Acrina had chosen to go for a ride in the Northwood and the two mages were taking a well earned nap in the barracks. The sun beat down fiercely and the friends were sweating profusely by the time they reached the tall wooden gates.

"Anyone home," shouted Wolfy.

An unfamiliar face popped his head over the gate tower. "Hello can I help you?"

"Ah yes, could you let the good Abbot know that he has visitors?" asked Wolfy.

"Sorry, Abbot John is sequestered for his daily meditation session. He has told me that under no circumstances should he be disturbed, unless it is of course an emergency."

Wolfy and Storm looked at each other and promptly burst into laughter. Suddenly, another face popped up over the ledge.

"I'd know that laugh anywhere. It haunts me at night-time sometimes. I never knew anyone, in my entire life that could eat so much. Wolfy is that you? Bless my cabbage soup if it isn't

Brother Storm too. Well don't just stand there Brother Willard, open the gate. These are family." Brother Orm winked at Storm then disappeared. In no time the sonorous bells of the abbey were peeling a rapturous welcome. Into the courtyard flocked the residents of Three Towers. Brother Felix, Brother Robard, Brother Tomas, Brother Orm and many other familiar faces of Storm's youth swelled around him giving hugs and exchanging hearty handshakes. Suddenly, a door opened and a blustery Abbot John scuttled into the courtyard.

"What is this commotion? It is afternoon meditation and we should observe such in silence not with shouting, giggling, and the peeling of bells. Now let me…" John never finished his sentence as he noticed for the first time the boy he had raised. The Abbot startled everyone with an almighty whoop of happiness as he crushed the tall boy in a powerful embrace. Storm returned the fervor of the greeting. Shutting his eyes, he enjoyed the quiet emotions of being home at last.

About the Book

An ancient prophecy many centuries old is wakened upon the world of Terras. The sentinels of light and their four dark counterparts are stirred to action with the birth of the ninth son. The orphan child, Storm, is thrust into a world of magical adventure where he must use his wits, courage and cunning to avoid the clutches of the dark. Accompanied by his faithful snow wolf Zira, Storm travels to the island of Meridia where he is invited to join the acclaimed Academy. His training as a catcher ends prematurely with an attack upon the wizard's isle. The boy then embarks upon a quest to reach Cartis where the fruition of prophecy will come to pass. During his travels Storm befriends Lady Acrina of the Elghorian and unwittingly saves from certain death, Waif, the son of the Guilder, ruler of the underlife. Assisted by the elves, wallahs and other faithful friends he does indeed arrive at the ruined acropolis at Cartis. Facing impossible odds, Storm joins with the Lords of Light in a fearsome struggle against the dark.

About the Author

Child of Night is the debut book for Caelin Paul (Paul Wright). Originally from Reading, England, Caelin teaches at Southern Virginia University in Central Virginia. An avid coach, scholar, and athlete he still finds time to pursue his true passion for writing. Many of the characters within his books are based on true-life persons. Even his beautiful wife Layna and charismatic daughters Brianna and Misha make appearances within the pages of "Child."

Printed in the United States
39372LVS00003B/7-78